# BLOOD YELLOW

## DEMONSONGS BOOK 2

E J FROST

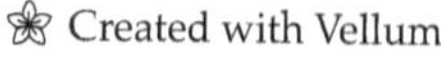 Created with Vellum

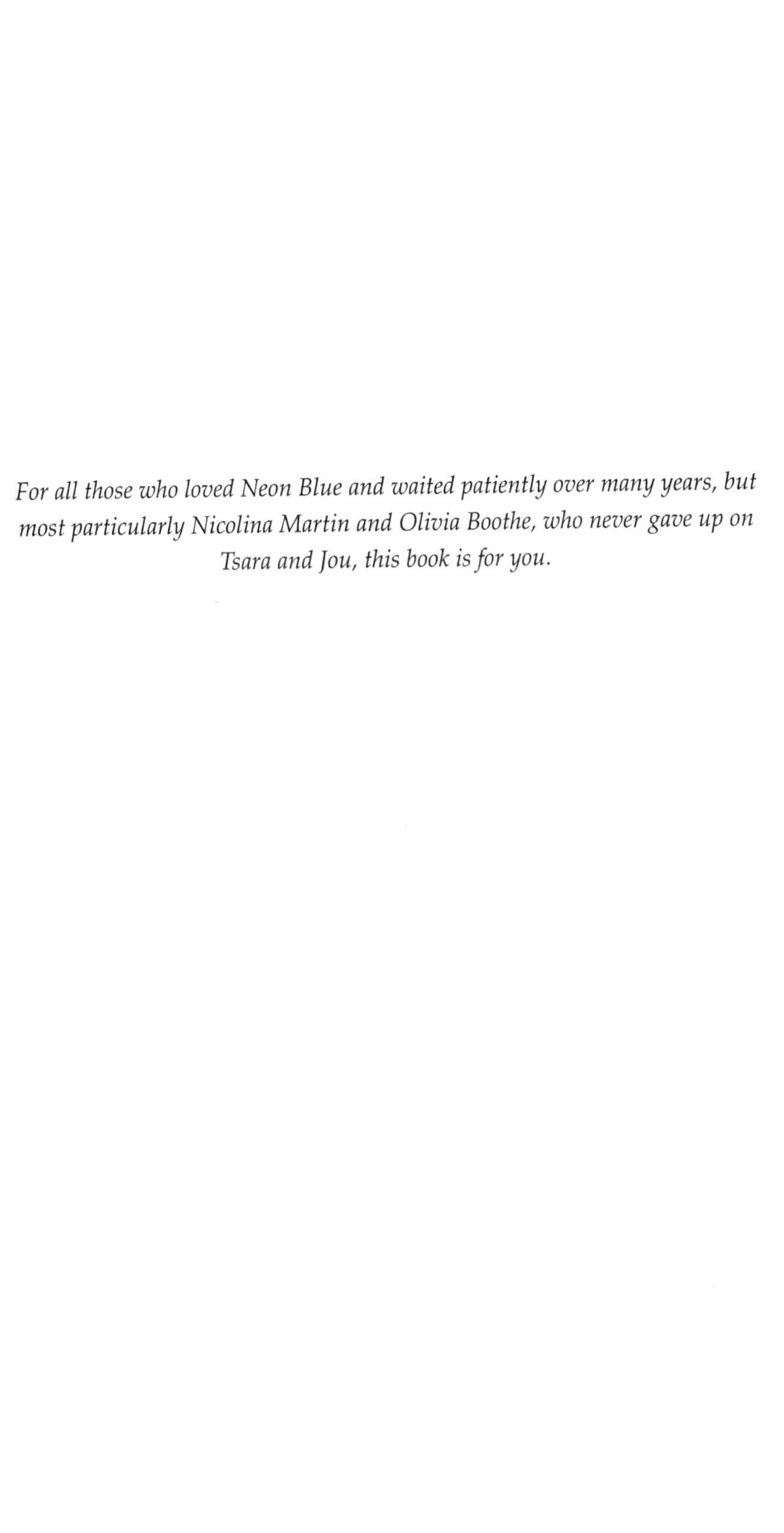

*For all those who loved Neon Blue and waited patiently over many years, but most particularly Nicolina Martin and Olivia Boothe, who never gave up on Tsara and Jou, this book is for you.*

# CHAPTER 1

Vampires suck.

I can't say from personal experience, although if my night gets much worse, I might find out. There's a pretty major disadvantage to being the only human in a room with several unhappy vampires.

"This was not one of us," the vampire's speaker, Hill, says again. I can feel the irritation roll off him in waves. It has a sour smell, like stale sweat.

I shift uncomfortably in my chair and wish I had a cup of coffee. Any flavor would do right now. Just something to warm me in this chilly, formal room. In the artic environment of anger and distrust between the four vampires and the handful of shifters who are staring at them.

But there's no coffee. Nothing to eat or drink, in fact. It's the first wake I've been to where there wasn't any food. But then, shifters do things differently.

I don't want to commit the *faux pas* of summoning a cup of coffee if there's a reason that there's nothing to eat or drink, but I'm in need of comfort. It's been a long day. Toby's wake has been hard. I rub my thumb over a strand of beads circling my left wrist. Sometimes touching them makes me feel better. But not tonight. I'm drained, and I want something to hug. Something more than a memory. I *reach*. A cream and gold-streaked lizard, no bigger than my cupped hands, appears in my lap with a puff of steam and the whiff of sulfur. Wizard, my familiar, turns three circles in my lap, his tiny claws prickling through my pants, and settles down with a grumble that sounds vaguely like a purr. I stroke the soft, scaly curve of his body. Touching him makes me feel better instantly. Warmer. More relaxed.

"Are you suggesting this was one of the clans?"

My calm only lasts a moment. Then Ana's question makes me tense again, because it's not really a question. It has the flatness of an accusation. Ana's usually more diplomatic. But since it's her foster-son, or what's left of him, who is lying in the casket at the far end of the room, I guess her lack of diplomacy is understandable.

Hill shakes his head and I look away. When the vampires move, they blur oddly. Their carefully cultured appearance shreds and I see the desiccated skin, the wisps of hair clinging to bare skulls, the burning eyes, the fangs that protrude from behind thin lips.

There are disadvantages to having Second Sight.

I glance at the woman, who stands quietly behind Hill and the master vampire, Leid. Hill introduced the woman as Rosaleen, but she gave me a slightly different name when she appeared on my doorstep two nights ago to ask for my help in averting a war between the shifters and the vampires. Róisín, she called herself, pronouncing it *Roe-sheen*. That name tastes true.

Róisín doesn't blur in my sight when she moves. Nor does she turn into an animated corpse. She's as beautiful in my inner vision as she is in my normal sight. Dark hair and perfect, pale skin and bone structure a model would kill for. But her eyes burn constantly, a dark flame lit with hints of blue.

I rub my hand over my eyes and try not to think of where I've seen eyes like hers before.

I scrub my hand over my eyes again and focus on the vampire's speaker. "I'm not really clear on what you *are* saying. If it wasn't vampire and it wasn't a *therian* . . ." I use the word the shifters call themselves to avoid offending any of them. Pissing off the heads of the shifter clans is a bad idea. "What are you suggesting?"

"You're supposed to be the expert on demons," Hill responds. "That's why our master requested that you attend this meeting."

I narrow my eyes at him, not caring that it blurs him into the animated corpse. He's just touched a very raw nerve. "I'm not an expert," I snap. "I've dealt with one demon. One."

That's not entirely true. Dealing with that one demon has made me a target for the infernal, and I've had to deter the unwanted attentions of several other, minor demons since I banished Jou. But those were imps, with barely any power. Easily bound, easily banished.

I barely survived the major demon I've dealt with. I may never get over him.

"Tsara, do you think this could be a demon?" Ana asks me. Her expression shifts from grief-stricken to horrified, and I understand why. Demons don't just eat flesh. They have a taste for souls, too.

I shake my head. "Toby was pure of heart. They don't go after the innocent." Something I know from personal experience. I stroke Wizard – a gift from my particular demon – with more concentration and wish that we were anywhere but, in this cold, hostility-filled room.

"Vampires don't take flesh," Róisín says softly from behind Leid.

"Revenants do," I respond, thinking back to my Supernatural Creatures tutorial in college. The undead are not really my thing, but I know the basics, and I know that a revenant will eat anything it can get its claws on.

"As do ghouls," Róisín says. Still softly. The way she's spoken to me from the beginning. Softly, gently, and with a hint of sadness. I have yet to see her smile.

"This wasn't a ghoul kill. They hunt in packs. And they have a very distinctive attack." Which I've seen first-hand. If it had been a ghoul kill, there wouldn't be anything but scraps to bury. "Whatever killed Toby, it wasn't ghouls."

I shift in my chair again, both because it's an uncomfortable straight-backed chair and because, deep-down, I don't believe it was a vampire. But Toby died of blood-loss, unheard-of for a shapeshifter.

And blood-loss is vampire territory. Or so the therians have decided. Which means war.

"It was not one of us," Hill says. He sounds like a broken record, and I frown at him. He's the vampires' voice, their public speaker. Can't he come up with something better?

"Your protestations are unconvincing," Ana says. I guess she feels the same way.

The other shifters have been quiet, letting Ana do most of the talking. Now Sheshdhar, head of Clan Hisaka and one of the three members of their ruling council, leans forward in his chair. "Your master says nothing. Why does he not speak?"

His precise enunciation comes from a more formal time and place —the British Raj if the rumors I've heard are true—but his 's'es have a little more sibilance than they should and betray his nature.

Leid lifts his gaze from where he's been contemplating his folded hands and meets the shifter's eyes. Even though I'm not on the receiving end of that gaze, I shiver and hug Wizard to my chest, a move the salamander protests with his growly little hiss. Leid's burning, black eyes are not somewhere I want to look. Not even obliquely.

"I am content to let my speaker speak for me," Leid says. His voice is quiet, low, but carries twice the weight of Hill's. He's been biding his time, I realize, waiting until he needs to inject that authority into the conversation. He must think it's going pretty well, then.

Which means I'm missing something.

"And the *horai* speaks for us. We will not lift the declaration of war. We will continue to hunt you until you give us the murderer and justice is done."

I squeeze Wizard tighter. I didn't know they'd already declared war.

"The truce between *vampirii* and *therian* has held for more than a century," Hill protests. "You break it as though it was of no consequence—"

"*You* broke it—" Ana cries, and it's just shy of a hawk's hunting cry. Which tells me how close she is to the edge.

"No vampire in the city did this," Leid says. "I would know."

I watch him for a moment while the shifters protest. His face is utterly still, his body relaxed in the hard-backed chair. But there's a flickering in my peripheral vision. His aura. And it's not nearly as peaceful as the rest of him.

"You control all of Boston's vampires," I say, beginning to reason my way around what he's *not* saying. "And none of them killed Toby. So, what if it's not one of Boston's vampires? What if it's someone new? Something not under your control?"

Which would kill my revenant theory. Revenants aren't capable of travelling on their own. Travelling requires thought. Or at least enough planning to avoid being caught out when the sun rises. My memory from college is that most revenants fry before they manage to graduate to full-fledged vampire, unless they have one of the greater undead looking after them.

Of course, it could be one of the greater undead, looking after a revenant, and using it to kill. Which puts me back at square one. I just really don't know enough. And I'm not a detective. Or a demon-expert, no matter what the vampires think.

Leid turns his dark, smooth head to look at me. I quickly look down. I *so* do not want to look the big, bad vampire in the eye. "The vampirii in my territory are all well-known to me. Their slow hearts are beacons in my evernight."

It's very poetic, particularly the way he says it, in rounded, private-school syllables, but none of the shifters look impressed. I'm not, either, but I'm less obvious about it, I hope. "What if this one's good at hiding from you?"

"There is no such creature," Hill says, scowling at me.

I blow my bangs out of my eyes. That's the thing about supernatural creatures. They're almost never willing to admit that there's something they don't know, or that they could be wrong. I should be used to it from dealing with the therians, and the fae, and my one, insufferable, greater demon, but it still gets on my nerves.

I glance at Ana and shrug. "I'm open to suggestions." I want Toby's killer caught, too. I had a soft spot for the furry teen, and Ana's my only real friend among the therians. The others come to me when they need something, but Ana's the only one who's ever made any effort to get to know me. To be a friend.

After the last few months, I'm a little short on friends.

"If we knew what did this, we would have brought you its head," Róisín says. Still softly. Still gently. And I've no doubt that she'd speak in that soft, gentle tone when presenting a decapitated head, too. The undead are like that.

Yet another reason they creep me out.

"You bring us no answers and expect us to believe your empty words while one of our young lies dead not ten feet away?" Sheshdhar shakes his head disbelievingly.

"We've brought you the truth," says Leid's bodyguard. He's leaning against the wall in the classic bodyguard position, except that his hands are crossed over the pommel of a sword that's almost as tall as I am. He speaks for maybe the second time in the half-hour the vampires have been here. Hill introduced him as Bone, which doesn't suit him. He's anything but bony. I haven't seen many vampires, but the ones I have seen have all been like Leid: tall and slender and elegant. Maybe they only recruit from a tall, slender, elegant set. Bone's tall enough to fit their mold, well over six feet, but he's not skinny. Anything but. He's muscular like he's in training for Mr. Universe.

I've only seen a better-developed body in all its glory once. And Jou had an unfair advantage, being a demon and all.

I shake my head. It's been nearly three months. Three months since I've dreamed of him. Three months since I've heard his voice in my head. He's forgotten about me. Moved on to easier prey.

I wish I could forget him as easily.

"I taste no truth in your master's words," Sheshdhar says dismissively.

I rub my hand over my face, wondering if I want to get in the middle of this. Sheshdhar and his clan are not my favorite people. They're usually the cause of shifters showing up wounded on my doorstep. Like their reptilian cousins, they're venomous and vengeful. I don't really want to cross the Naga. But unlike Sheshdhar, I do taste the truth in the vampires' words. More so Róisín and Bone's than Leid's. Leid is hiding something, possibly many somethings. But Róisín and Bone believe what they've said. Which probably makes it true.

"Whatever you think," I say, more to Róisín than the others. "I'm no expert on demons, but demons usually take souls, not flesh. Why would a demon do this to Toby?"

Róisín and Bone shake their heads, which makes Bone blur in my Sight. I glance away. I don't want to see all that hard muscle shrivel to whatever it becomes when he goes vampy.

"We hoped you would know," Róisín responds.

Great. Not only don't I, but with Ro and Justinian and Denys and Timmi dead at the hands of my last demon, I don't even know anyone I can ask.

I shrug and glance at the casket, and as I do, I catch Ana's eye again. The terror's left her face, but her eyes still hold that wild, keening grief that they've held since Toby's death four days ago. There's so much grief in her eyes that she should explode with it.

But you don't explode with grief. That's something else I've learned in the last few months. You don't explode with grief, or shrivel up and die from it, although you wish you could. You just trudge on from one empty moment to the next, through grey days that never seem to get any brighter.

I meet Ana's eyes and stare into grief that's fresher than mine, but no less painful. "I'll try to find out what did this," I say finally.

Hill sits back in his chair with a creak of his leather jacket. It's a self-satisfied creak, and it irritates me, because that creak tells me that I've been manipulated. The vampires want a cease-fire, and someone else to take the heat if the killer can't be caught. As Ana's friend and an ally of the city's shifters, I'm a convenient pawn.

A pawn who really doesn't like being used.

I drape Wizard around my neck. Pull on the connection with the sphere of Air that Wizard gives me and shape it into a shield around my mind. Sliding my feet out of my dress shoes, I put my soles flat on the floor and call on Earth to ground me. Shake the string of beads on my wrist to wake them. Protected by my Elements, filled with the demon's strength, I look directly into Leid's eyes. "Let me make it clear that I'm doing this for Toby's clan. They have a right to see his killer called to account."

Leid holds my eyes, and I see a thousand lifetimes of love and hate, kindness and cruelty, nobility and pettiness play through his eyes. Unbearable beauty and unendurable horror. And I know in that moment that he doesn't just take blood from his *donors*. He also sips from their souls.

"Surely," he says mildly.

"I won't hesitate to tell the therians if the killer turns out to be a vampire. I want that understood."

Hill starts to object, but Leid holds up a long-fingered hand. "I would expect nothing less."

"Fine."

Leid and I stare at each other for another moment. I look away first, and stroke Wizard to stop the chill I can feel spreading outward from my bones. Vampires really creep me out.

Leid rises and that seems to be an unspoken signal. The tightly packed group breaks apart. Two of the shifters drift toward the front of the room to pay their respects. The vampires move towards the door. Ana comes to stand beside my chair and when I rise, she takes my hands. Her skin feels hot and brittle against mine.

"How are you holding up?" I ask. It's the first chance I've had to speak to her today.

A tear spills, and she doesn't try to hide it or wipe it away. "I am lost," she says.

"I understand." And I do. When Jou stopped speaking into my mind, when I knew he was really gone, that was exactly how I felt. So lost that I didn't think I could face another empty day.

"I would never have asked you—" she begins, trails off when I shake my head. I know she wouldn't have asked me to help find Toby's killer. Ana's got very traditional ideas of debt and honor. Her family already owes me one for healing Toby when he was savaged by a Naga. She wouldn't ever ask me for anything until that debt is paid.

"I'm glad to be able to help." If Ana was human, I'd say more. About how Toby was a great kid and how he didn't deserve anything like this. But she's not and a lot of it has already been said. All that's left is for me to squeeze her overly warm hands.

"If you need anything—" she begins.

Gallien, Toby's titular father and head of the lycanthrope clan, approaches, nodding his bearded head vigorously. "Anything at all."

I smile at both of them. "I'll call. And that goes for you, too. If you need anything, call me."

Ana leans forward and brushes my cheek with hers. A kiss of wingtips. "I'll come to the house in a few days."

"You're welcome anytime. I'll see you soon." I give her hands another squeeze, smile at the other therians, and make my exit. Before anyone asks anything else of me.

————

There's a long black limo double-parked outside of Ana's brownstone. I ignore it. I don't need a car to travel anymore. Just a quiet place to slip into the Earth unobserved. The alleyway between Ana's place and the neighbor's is dark and quiet enough, once I get away from the Christmas lights the neighbor still hasn't taken down, but before I reach the darkness, the limo's door opens, and the vampire bodyguard Bone unfolds himself from the cream leather interior. He's still wearing his black shades despite the January darkness. But then, I wear shades, even at night. I'm guessing it's not for the same reason, though.

"Our master has instructed us to take you home."

I glance into the limo, half-expecting to meet Leid's horrific stare, but it's Róisín sitting in the back seat, her long dress neatly tucked under her. She doesn't smile, just pats the seat beside her.

"I'm okay," I say.

"He'll take it badly if you refuse," Bone persists.

Shit. I really don't want to offend Leid. Particularly not after standing up to him in the meeting and getting off so lightly. With a resigned sigh, I climb into the limo and settle Wizard on my lap.

Bone climbs in after me, twisting to get all that bulk through the door. He sits down opposite me and Róisín and raps on the smoked window dividing the back of the car from the driver's seat. Probably a vampire or two in the front. I'm surrounded. The thought makes the small hairs on the back of my neck rise.

With a whiskey purr, the car moves off down Marlborough Street.

Róisín knows where I live, so I don't bother to give directions. I just say, "I've got a sick salamander at home."

Róisín nods. "We won't delay you."

Bone leans forward in a creak of leather and clasps his hands between his knees. "Our master wants us to offer our assistance."

He makes it sound very distasteful, and I feel a flash of sympathy. Helping the demon-loving witch track down the critter that chewed up a shapeshifter is probably not as glamorous as wielding that massive sword in his master's defense.

But he's a vampire, and I don't appreciate the way his Master is playing me. "So sorry," I say, and it comes out nicely sarcastic.

Róisín gives Bone a glare. "Leid is quite sincere in his desire to find the killer and put a stop to this."

Of that I have no doubt. Boston's vampires are very circumspect. They keep to their own white-shoe and weekends-on-the-Vineyard crowd. Having the therians declare war on them is probably putting a major cramp in their style.

"I'll do my best, but like I told you, I'm really not any kind of expert on demons."

"We're here to see you do," Bone says. When I raise an eyebrow, he clarifies. "Do your best."

Now he's getting on my nerves.

Wizard reacts to my ratcheting tension, hissing at the vampire. His tiny claws prickle my thigh as he arches into a threat display.

"Look," I say. "You clearly don't like me. And the feeling's totally mutual. So why don't you tell your master that you made me your very nice offer and I very bitchily told you to fuck off, and you can let me out at the next corner?"

Bone sits back in his seat. I can tell he's glaring at me behind the designer shades.

"We can help," Róisín says. Her voice is still quiet, but there's an undertone to it now, a kind of reverberation that sets my teeth on edge.

And suddenly I know what she is.

"You're a *cyhraeth*. A *bean sidhe*." I turn and look at her. The pale, perfect skin. The dark, silken hair. The long, smooth line of her throat that can swell to emit a blast of infrasound that can liquefy human organs at fifty feet. "You're fae, not a vampire. What are you doing with these guys?"

Róisín shifts in what might be surprise, but quickly stills. "Leid and his people have been very kind to me."

Kind vampires. That's a new one. "Yeah, okay. Whatever. I appreciate the offer, but I pretty much do things on my own." So much so that I don't even have a coven. "I'll call you if I need anything."

Róisín and Bone exchange glances, and Bone shakes his head.

"Leid has . . . requested that we stay with you. To assist you," Róisín says.

To spy on me, and make sure I don't find out anything the vampires don't want me to.

I try to make light of it. "What, you're going to trail around after me until I figure it out?"

Bone shifts forward again, clasping his hands between his knees, but this time he hangs his head.

Oh, great. A vampire watch dog.

"No, uh-uh. Sorry—"

"We won't intrude," Róisín says.

I shake my head in disbelief. I'm *so* not having a banshee and a vampire shadowing me. I slip my feet out of my shoes. Shift Wizard to my shoulder. I've never Earth-Walked from a moving vehicle before, but the car's tires are touching the ground, so it should work. "I'll call if I need help. Thanks."

I *reach*, feel the warm, gritty embrace of my Element, and sink into the Earth. Darkness. A sense of perfect freedom, primal and sensuous. I could stay in the Earth forever. And there have been times recently when I've been tempted. But I really do have a sick lizard at home. And something of a life to go back to. So I focus on where I want to be. The smell of clean clothes, detergent, the faint acrid note of heating oil. And the warm nest I've made for a sick fire salamander under my hot water heater.

I blink and look down at Izzy's nest.

Wizard hisses a soft greeting to his sibling from my shoulder. Izzy doesn't respond and I drop to my knees next to the nest, shaking a cloud of dust out of my hair and clothes. Earth-Walking's a messy business.

Izzy lies curled in the nest I've made for him from pieces of pink, fireproof insulation. His scarlet and cream hide has dulled to a mauve color only a few shades darker than the insulation. Patches of raw tissue show through where the scales have flaked away. One of the patches is bleeding. Poor thing has been scratching again.

I rub Izzy's forehead with the tip of my finger. His head is the only place that hasn't been affected by the scale-rot, and it's the only place he can stand for me to touch him.

The salamander grumbles and stretches out his neck, trying to induce me to scratch the underside of his jaw. His movement splits a raw patch on his neck and a bead of blood runs into the insulation. He gives a small, piteous whine.

"Oh, Iz." I scratch very gently under his jaw. Scales flake off around my finger, even though I'm not using my nail and I'm barely applying any pressure. "It's spreading, isn't it, poor boy?"

Izzy doesn't reply. The salamanders don't talk, at least, not to me. Jou always seemed to know what they were thinking. Without him, I just muddle along on their body-language.

And Izzy's body language says in all capital letters that he's going downhill.

"It's time to try another potion, Iz. I'll be right back."

I set Wizard on the floor to keep his brother company and run upstairs into my herbarium. The feeling of cold linoleum underfoot as I cross the kitchen floor makes me realize that I left my good dress shoes in the limo. Damn.

The healing potion's not one I've used before. I brewed it this afternoon before the wake, while Izzy was sleeping off the last one. Brewed so hot I came out of my hearth room scorched and dripping and threw myself directly into a cold shower, even though heat doesn't affect me the way it used to. I made the potion up as I went along. Feeling my way. Using things that felt right. It smells right to me, but I don't know if it will work. Nothing else has.

I pick up the vial from its trivet with an oven glove. Even the bottle's hot. I carry it back downstairs gingerly, not wanting to spill any of the potion bubbling inside of the open flask.

Izzy drinks the potion obediently. He's been exceptionally good since I banished his master. The only command he won't obey is 'go home.' Every time I've tried to order Izzy back to Hell, he scrambles to the top of my refrigerator and perches there, hissing at me. So, I've stopped trying, and he's stopped hissing and we've gotten along fine. Until he began shedding scales all over the house and the first of the horrible raw patches appeared a few days ago.

Wizard encourages his brother, licking his snout until Izzy finally hisses in annoyance. I pick up Wizard and give him a scratch while I watch Izzy to see if there's any change. Izzy curls up and closes his eyes, but the raw patches don't improve, the way they should if the potion was working.

I sigh in frustration and head upstairs for some couch cushions so I can sit vigil with my salamander without getting bruises all over my butt from the cement floor.

# CHAPTER 2

A harsh ringing jolts me out of a broken doze. The edges of a dream knock around behind my eyes. Swirling red wings like a bloody murmuration of starlings. Laughter that seems to come up from deep underground. The crash and hiss of magma meeting the ocean in a spray of black rock. I start, spilling Wizard off my lap.

*Answer the phone, sweetness.*

I rub my eyes to chase away my dream, give the grumbling lizard a pat, and climb wearily up the stairs.

"Hey, *chica*," a familiar voice says when I answer the phone.

I carry the handset over to my kitchen table and prop my head on my elbow. "It's kind of late, Dead," I say, checking the clock above my stove. It is, too. Past midnight, and Dead knows that, unlike him, I have to work in the morning. "What's up?"

"Disturbance in the Force." I hear him chewing.

"Seriously. Did Yoda tell you that? And what are you eating?"

"*Costillitas,*" he mutters around a mouthful.

"Costillitas at midnight. You're going to get fat." Dead's on the very solid side already, so it's more a warning than a joke.

"I'm comfort-eating. Since neither of my favorite white people will give me any, I have to console myself with food."

I snicker, despite the lateness of the hour and my exhaustion. "Wen wouldn't appreciate being called *white*, and you're barking up the wrong tree with both of us."

"I'd bark up both your trees if you'd let me, chica."

"Gross." But I laugh. "So seriously, what's up?"

"I am serious. Something's very wrong up your way. You'd feel it if you'd crack open a shield."

I rub my hand through my hair and leave whatever shields I have firmly in place. Dead and some of the other *magi* I've met talk about their psychic shielding like it's something they can raise and lower at will. I can't. I'm not aware of mine; I've got no conscious control over it. My shields are just there, keeping me safe, keeping me sane.

"I've got a dead werewolf and a pretty serious case of post-holiday blues, but nothing else going on that I know of." And a sick salamander, but the less I tell Dead and anyone else of my involvement with the infernal, the better.

"A dead werewolf doesn't sound like a problem. Sounds like a solution." Dead sniffs. His prejudice against therians—a prejudice most of the magi I've met seem to share—is the only thing I don't like about Dead. Even his half-hearted attempts to get in my pants are more amusing than annoying.

"For me, it's a problem."

"Well, I know what you need."

"What's that? And if you say a good screw, I'm hanging up."

Dead chuckles, a nice tenor chuckle. Nothing like Jou's bass rumble. So it shouldn't remind me of him, dammit.

"You need a week in the sun, chica. You and my deadboy brother both. Forget packing. Bring an itty-bitty bikini and hop the next plane to Miami. I'll meet you at the airport with a bucket of Mojitos and two of my brothers and we'll show you what a good time really means."

I laugh. I wouldn't be caught dead in a bikini or caught by Dead in a bikini. "Dead, I love you."

"Oh, you tease! You say that when you're all the way up there and

I'm down here and you know how crazy it makes me when you talk dirty to me."

"Learn to Earth-Walk," I respond. That would be quite a trick, since Dead's a necromancer, not an Earth mage, but if anyone could learn to Earth-Walk, it's Dead.

"Oh God, dirtier and dirtier," he moans, setting me giggling. "I hope you freeze to death in that cold northern bed tonight."

"Not likely. It was sixty degrees today." So warm I didn't even wear a jacket to the wake.

"It was what?" All teasing disappears from Dead's voice.

"Sixty degrees. The forsythia bushes are flowering. Warmest January I can remember."

"And you don't think that's strange?"

"Global warming." I shrug. "I haven't been messing with the weather, and I'd think our friends in Atlanta would come down like a ton of bricks on anyone who has."

"Mmm." Dead sounds non-committal. Probably about both our 'friends' in Atlanta, the *Aedis Astrum*, whom we've both been invited to join and have some pretty serious reservations about, and about the weather. "They have their limitations. Look at that thing with your friend and the demon."

"Uh-huh." I give him non-committal back. Wen-Long told Dead about my misadventures with Rowena and the demon she summoned while they were drinking, and I really wish Wen had kept his mouth shut. The fewer people who know about what happened, the better. It's already brought me a considerable amount of unwanted attention.

"Nothing else going on, huh? 'Cause whatever is coming your way feels pissed-off. Large-style."

"Large-style? Who are you, DJ Necro?" I rub my hands over my face. "I'm going to bed. I'll give you a call over the weekend, okay?"

"I'll wait with bated breath. Kiss the deadboy for me."

He means Wen, who is also a necromancer, and whom I'm supposed to be helping move from Philly to Boston over the weekend. Which probably isn't going to make the vampires who want me to spend my weekend tracking down Toby's killer very happy.

I sigh. "I will. G'night."

I hang up and sit with the phone in my hand for a moment. I didn't want to tell Dead about Izzy's illness, but there is someone I can talk to about it.

I hit the speed-dial and wait while Bo's phone rings three times and the answering machine picks up. He and Merida always screen their calls. But they'll both be up, despite the hour. I've never met two more dedicated night owls.

He picks up half-way through my message about Izzy's affliction. "Greetings, my young apprentice."

I smile into the phone. Bo has a serious *Star Wars* fixation. Even more so than Dead, who came to the Temple's Yule ball dressed as Princess Leia, complete with breakfast-roll wig.

"Master," I return in a breathy rasp. I can't do much of a Darth Vader imitation at the best of times, and midnight is not my best time, but since I'm going to ask him for a favor, I can play along a little.

"A sick salamander, hum?" he says, referring to my unfinished message.

"It looks like the scale rot my goldfish used to get." When I had goldfish. I've never been particularly good with pets. "He began shedding scales a week ago, and now he has these awful raw patches all over him. Nothing I've tried is helping."

"You've tried the usual potions and spells, I assume."

"Everything I could think of. I even improvised today."

"Now I know it's bad, if you're improvising."

I smile wearily into the phone. Like me, Bo's a recipe guy. We both prefer to shape magic through the exacting process of brewing potions, and we both like working from instructions.

"Well, there's always Earth's Blood," he says. "It would be more effective on an Earth Elemental, but a salamander's probably tied closely enough to the Earth that it should work."

"I've never called Earth's Blood."

He *tsks* softly, and I *tsk* back. Bo's very traditional. He was trained in the apprentice tradition of European wizards, studying with a master Earth-mage for two decades before going out on his own. He doesn't approve of the patchwork training I've had from my family in their Romany traditions and the largely theoretical education I got at Wydlins Special School for Girls and Bevington College.

"Do you want me to talk you through it?"

"Um, no," I say slowly, because as soon as he offers, I know I can call Earth's Blood. The knowledge opens up in my mind when I put a name to it, the same way the knowledge of how to Earth-Walk opened up in my mind when I needed it. I know how to reach deep into the dark well of energy that is my Element and instead of sinking into it the way I do when I Earth-Walk, call it into myself, mix it with my own blood, and squeeze it out between my fingers onto the affliction. In my mind's eye, I see myself daubing it on Izzy's mottled hide like mud.

My fingers slip on the phone, and I switch hands, wiping my sweaty palm on my pants absently. Wet warmth soaks through to my skin. I stare down at the red-brown streaks I've just left on my best pants.

Shit.

"Er, I think I've just figured it out."

"Really? Yoda's beard, you're fast, m'girl."

"Yoda did not have a beard." I'm not the *Star Wars* aficionado that Bo and Dead are, but I remember that much. Bo, on the other hand, does have a beard. A very handsome salt-and-pepper goatee that he keeps trimmed close to his chin and that he likes to stroke when he's thinking. I bet he's stroking it now.

"He should have."

"Mmm, anyway, I'm going to give this a try. Thanks, Bo."

"You're welcome." He yawns. "Glad I could help. When are you coming to see us?"

I rub my hand over my face but stop abruptly when I feel the gooey wetness that I've just smeared up my cheek and into my hair. Damn, I'm going to have this stuff all over me by the end of the night. "I'm tied up tonight and tomorrow."

I don't mention that I'm helping Wen move because Bo and his partner, Merida, didn't seem to like either Wen or Dead when we all met in Atlanta at Christmas. Bo was polite to Wen, but I think that was only because the necromancer was my guest. Merida, who treated me like a long-lost sister, sniffed at Dead like he smelled bad and kept talking over the two necromancers like they weren't in the room. It didn't help that Wen and Dead had been in the hotel's hospitality suite for hours before we met up and were three sheets to the wind.

"Sunday then. Mer keeps asking, and you know how dangerous it is to keep a Water witch waiting."

I don't actually. Merida and the other Water witches I met in Atlanta were the first I've ever met. Elemental magi were rare at school, and the few there were Air or Fire mages. Like Rowena. I'd never even met another Earth wizard until I met Bo. But I chuckle, since the moment seems to call for it, and say, "Sorry, I'm going to have to take a rain check. How about next weekend?"

"Sunday dinner. Mer wants to feed you. She says you're too skinny."

"Thanks," I say drily. Bo and Merida have taken a parental interest in me, and while it was cute for a while, it's getting old quickly. I have plenty of parental figures in my life already, even if they're mostly dead. I don't feel the need for more. "I'll see you then. Give my love to Merida."

We say goodbye and I set the goo-covered phone down on my kitchen table. I'll wipe it off later, when I'm not still goo-ing. For now, I rush back downstairs, eager not to waste any of the goo.

Izzy and Wizard are asleep, curled up together in Izzy's nest. I nudge Wizard with my mind. He stirs, blinking black eyes up at me. I hold up my dripping hands and he obligingly crawls out of my way, out of the nest. I settle cross-legged on the concrete floor, the final indignity for my dress pants, and let Wizard climb into my lap. Even though he's an Air Elemental, doing any kind of magic is easier when I'm touching my familiar.

Goo drips from my hands, running warm and wet down the undersides of my arms and into the sleeves of my satin shirt. It's going to need to go to the dry cleaners, too. I sigh and touch my fingers very gently to the terrible raw patch on Izzy's neck.

A warm tingle spreads up through my hands as I work, spreading the red-brown sludge over Izzy's broken skin. He wakes and looks up at me but doesn't move until I've finished one side. Then he rolls carefully onto his back so I can do his tummy.

I haven't seen his belly in a day or two. It looks like he's been skinned. Red muscle and white tendon show through the peeling scales.

"Oh, Iz," I say, feeling the hot prickle of tears.

The salamander blinks up at me stoically. I hold my hands over him, letting the Earth's Blood drip onto his belly, not wanting to touch that terrible raw length. Not wanting to cause him any more pain.

The goo drips off my fingers slowly. One drop at a time. I can't tell if it's working. It feels right, but then, the potion smelled right, and it didn't help him. I want more, faster. I *reach* deep, down into the depths of the Earth. Into the warm, gritty embrace of my Element. I feel it flow up through me. Mix thickly with my blood. My heart thunders in my ears, laboring with the effort of pushing that thickness through my veins. And for the first time, I understand the danger of Deep healing. It requires something of the healer. My body has to give of itself to this magic, and if the toll is too great, I might have to choose between healing and surviving.

But not this time. This time, my heart pounds but beats on, my blood mixes with the Earth's. An intense sense of *rightness*, like the afterglow of really good sex, fills me. The goo pours out of my fingers, spattering onto Izzy's belly. He lifts his head, keeps it above the fall as it becomes a flood, drenching his nest and spreading in a pool around us, soaking through my pants.

I yank my hands away, hold them up in front of my face. It's an effort to pull myself away. To close the connection that might kill me but feels too good to stop. I clench my hands, goo squelching between my fingers. Breathing deeply, I concentrate on shutting down the flow to a trickle. Not too much or I'll shut myself off from my Element completely. Just enough. My hands stop dripping and I wipe them on my much-abused pants.

The salamanders hiss in unison a second before it hits. A temblor that rocks the house on its foundations. I grab Wizard and shelter him in the curl of my body. The cool basement becomes an oven, unbearably hot. Sweat bursts out all over me. I gasp for breath, retch dryly as incendiary air rushes down my throat and into my lungs. I pull on my other sphere, Air, to draw a cooling breeze to me. The temperature drops, leaving me shivering. The sweat on my skin dries to a sticky film. The breeze swirls around me, teasing my bangs. I can feel it trembling just on the edge of control. Shutting down my connection with the Earth has left a void and Air wants to fill it. I push it away, but the power isn't ready to go. It struggles, resists. Fingers of power ruffle through me, seeking another avenue.

Pain shoots sharp through my temples, down my spine. I've hurt myself pushing my magic before. This feels . . . different. It spreads through my body, hard, burning spikes of pain, impaling me in a dozen places. I force it out, straining and finally mastering the energies trying to fill me. I push it out of me and take a deep, relaxing breath.

I have a second to look down at Wizard, who blinks up at me.

Then agony rips up my back, so sharp it forces my mouth wide in a silent scream. It swells, a huge hand ripping out my spine, vertebrae by vertebrae. I scream so hard something in my throat tears.

And then the pain passes. As if it never was. It leaves me trembling and clutching at Wizard, but not hurting. Not even aching, except my butt, from sitting on the cold concrete floor, and my throat, from that scream.

"Wow," I gasp to the salamanders. "That sucked."

A distant subterranean rumble answers.

———

The morning news reports a minor earthquake, centered on Cambridge, Massachusetts.

"Somerville, you idiot," I say to the television, around a mouthful of nutty granola. It's not Jou's pancakes, but nothing is, so I shouldn't be thinking about them, dammit.

I watch the quake coverage, snorting when a bleary-looking expert from the U.S. Geological Survey appears to explain plate tectonics. Bet he was up all night. Boston's not known for its earthquakes. While I'm washing my cereal bowl, the three salamanders start a game of tag between my feet and the legs of the kitchen table. Wizard leads a charge into the living room, trailed by Iz and Gizzard. I smile even when I hear a crash of ceramic. Seeing Izzy up and around is a huge relief. Besides, Wizard will fix whatever they've broken. He's a very conscientious familiar.

I dress in old clothes, both because I'm brewing today and because my hands are still goo-ing a little. They goo-ed through the few hours of sleep I got, if the state of my sheets is anything to go by. My clothes will be covered by my work smock anyway, and since a certain demon is no longer around to comment on what I wear, I don't really care what people think about how I look.

"Your Dala says brown doesn't suit you, *káulochírilo.*"

"Does she?" I say, without looking around. I know from the direction of my uncle's voice—and the faint smell of cigarette smoke that always accompanies his manifestations—that his ghost is perched on the end of my bed.

"And she wants to know what happened to your hands."

I finish tying a silver and macramé belt I made at Wydlins around my waist. It's less a fashion statement than because I've lost weight over the past two months and my pants will fall down if I don't do something to cinch the waist. My palms are red brown. Great. It'll be all over my clothes. I check my clothes, which have miraculously escaped goo-ing, and walk into the bathroom to wash my hands. My uncle's ghost trails me.

"So, eh?" he prompts when I don't answer him immediately. He hasn't learned any more patience since he died.

"Earth's Blood," I respond. I glance at him over my shoulder, curious to see how he reacts. I come from a long line of Romany witches, some of whom must have been Earth-witches for me to be one, since, according to the parabiology course I took at Bevvy, the trait is genetic, but I don't remember any family stories about this particular talent.

He trails after me, his lower body blurring into ether as he moves, his face creased in puzzled lines. "What's that?"

Guess I'm not the only one who missed any family tales of healing brown goo. I flip on the faucet with the back of my hand to avoid getting crap all over the tap and begin to rinse my hands under the water. Nothing rinses off, and my hands feel smooth when I rub them together. Skin on skin. I shut off the tap and stare at my palms. "Shit."

"It's not coming off, is it?"

"No," I answer absently while I inspect my hands. The color only covers my palms. The backs of my hands look normal. I rub my thumbs over my palms. Nothing comes off and my skin feels cool and smooth, not slick or sticky.

Fuck. I suppose I can always say its henna.

"What *is* it, *chavi*?" my uncle asks a little more insistently.

"It's a healing spell I did last night." I pick up my toothbrush, gob on some toothpaste and begin brushing. In the mirror, I see my uncle's ghost roll up. I shiver. I hate it when my family ghosts do that. Normal ghosts flit away into nothingness or fade discretely. Mine roll up like a window shade. It's creepy.

I watch my reflection as I brush, waiting for my uncle to reappear after he's consulted my grandmother or whatever relative he's gone off to talk to. They used to talk in front of me. Not anymore. Not after I tore apart my grandmother's ghost during a screaming argument over Jou. Two months later, she still can't manifest fully, and the rest of the family is handling me with kid gloves. The way you handle someone irrational, or mentally ill.

I glare at my reflection in the mirror. It's the same face I've seen for years. Maybe a little gaunter, the brown eyes a little more shadowed, since sleep doesn't come easily to me anymore, even when I'm not dozing on a cold concrete floor. As I watch, a flicker of light stabs across my left pupil. Lightning. It strikes in my eyes constantly now, ever since I used magic to tear open a portal between the planes. It's the reason I wear sunglasses whenever I'm out in public, even after dark. My hair's darker—I dyed it black, to match my mood—and a lot shorter since I shaved myself almost bald in a crazed moment of defiance after a night of dreams in which Jou used my hair to tie me down before he fucked me to death.

I almost miss those dreams now.

I rinse my mouth and turn away from the mirror. The face may be the same, but I don't like the person who wears it as much as I used to.

———

Evonne's smile, a brilliant flash of white in her dark face, welcomes me to the clinic. She greets me with the same smile every morning. No matter how hectic it is, no matter how bad things have gone, she still smiles that same smile at me every day. During the last couple of months, there have been some days when the only thing that's gotten me out of bed has been knowing I'd see that smile.

"It's a brewing day, right?" she asks as she hands me two message slips.

I nod. "What do you feel like, cinnamon or amaretto?"

"Mmm." She ponders coffee flavors seriously for a moment while I read the slips. Mrs. Shaw calling to reschedule her appointment from eleven to eleven-thirty, and Peter Buscelli. I crumple the second message and throw it into the trash basket by Evonne's desk. Try not to think about it while I wait for Evonne to decide.

"Cinnamon," she says finally. "It covers the taste of that astro-what-ever better."

Astragalus. I've been spiking Evonne's coffee with a tincture of astragalus to help with her carpal-tunnel syndrome. She complains about the taste, but not about the effectiveness of the herb, which has helped where surgery hasn't. "You got it. Is Lin in?"

"Mmm-hum. She's got sessions all day."

I nod, a little curtly. It shouldn't sting as much as it does. Lin doubled up on her acupuncture appointments to keep the clinic going while I couldn't brew the fertility potion that's the secret behind our success. Because that's what partners do, she reminded me. Cover for each other.

But I've never needed anyone to cover for me before. Because I've never fallen apart before. And she's continued scheduling back-to-back sessions even after I pulled myself together. Even after my magic came back. I can't complain, because the clinic's still edging back into the black after two disastrous months. But I can't help but wonder if she's still covering, or if she's got something else in mind.

Like going it alone.

I carry that cheerful thought with me through my office and into the hearth room beyond. Witchlight flares as I enter my hearth room and Wizard greets me at the door. Commuting with him on the T, even glamored to look like a handbag or fur collar, was problematic. Hissing handbags are a little conspicuous. So now when I commute, he teleports and if people give me funny looks on the train, at least I know it's not because of the lightning salamander I'm carrying.

"Sorry, boy, coffee first." I tell him as he waddles hopefully toward my cauldron. He shouldn't be hungry after last night. The power I raised to heal Izzy flowed through Wizard; it should have replenished the magical reserves that fuel the little Elemental. But looking at him, I see the dullness of his scales. The slackness of the skin around his ribs. He's hungry; he shouldn't be, but he is.

"C'mere, boy." I hold out my hands and my salamander jumps into them. I give him a scratch under the chin. He immediately rolls over in my hands to present his belly for scratching. As I'm ruffling the loose skin of his neck, I close my eyes and *call*. A trickle of power. A breath of wind. A faint blue spark. I flatten my hand over the lizard's belly and push the energy I've summoned into him.

He responds with his purring hiss. I feel the belly under my hand round. When I open my eyes, I see that his scales are smooth and glossy again. His bird-bright eye blinks up at me. Lin says it's adoration, the way he looks at me, and maybe she's right. I've never been good at reading the salamanders. No better than I was at reading their master. If Jou ever looked at me with adoration, I missed it.

I let Wizard jump down to the floor.

———

Lin knows better than to walk in on me when I'm calling lightning. So, I'm surprised to see the door to my hearth room crack open while I still have my hands stretched to the sky and energy crackling whitely around my fingertips.

Lin closes the door behind her and leans against my worktable. She watches me as I lower my hands and pick up the paddle to give the magic milk a final stir.

"What's up?" I ask her.

"What the hell happened to your arms?"

The question takes me so off-guard that I actually check my forearms before I realize what she's seen. Then I tug my sleeves down to my wrists to cover the webwork of burn scars that crisscross my forearms. "Nothing. It happened when I split up with Jou. You know."

She doesn't know. Not the full details. Not that he'd bound me with his will and my desire so deeply, that when I broke the binding, the backlash gave me third-degree burns. Not that he was a demon and wanted to make me one, too. Not that I sent him back to Hell and have been dying inside ever since. I haven't shared any of that with her, even though she's my best friend and the one person who might understand.

All Lin knows is that Jou and I broke up. I've told her that he went back home, which is a bit of the truth. And that we split up because I didn't want to go with him, which is a larger bit of the truth. But nothing's close to the whole truth. And nothing I can tell her ever will be.

"I don't remember you mentioning anything about *that*. What's all over your hands?"

"Residue from a healing spell I did last night on Wizard's brother. I'm hoping it will fade. What's up?"

She shifts against my workbench, and I can tell she's not going to buy the brush-off about my arms for long. "I came to see if we could go early. My five o'clock has cancelled."

"Yeah, sure." It might not make the vampires happy, but getting Wen's move out of the way will help me concentrate on finding Toby's killer.

"Now tell me what really happened to your arms." She sounds a little belligerent. She sounds that way a lot lately.

I sigh.

"Aww, Lin." I put a little whine into it. She hates whining and sometimes that alone will put her off.

She grimaces but crosses her arms over her chest. Nope, not going to be put off by whining today. I try another tact. Brushing my foot through the shimmering line of light behind me, I break my casting circle. The potion's finished, so breaking the circle won't hurt anything. Pre-demon, I would have retraced the circle widdershins to take back the power I expended by casting it. But my magic didn't just come back, it came back with a vengeance. So much that most days I do minor castings to bleed off the excess before I brew. I don't want any more of my clients having quintuplets. Like poor Mrs. McNulty.

As he always is as soon as Lin's in the vicinity, Wizard's waiting by the edge of the circle to streak over for a petting. Once the circle's broken, salamander and human react exactly the way I expect. Wizard streaks. Lin pets. One awkward question avoided.

"Wen's feeding us pizza, right?"

Lin, preoccupied with the salamander, who has flipped over in her arms to present his tummy for scratching, nods absently.

"Good," I say to myself, and begin ladling the potion into pint containers.

# CHAPTER 3

'm careful to change my shirt before Lin comes to get me. Something with long, tight sleeves. I don't need any more questions about Jou. Particularly not in front of Lin's brother, Wen-Long, who knows way more than he should about the demon, and who isn't always good about keeping what he knows to himself.

I rummage through the small closet in my office where I keep a few spare clothes. There's nothing that really fits the bill except a short, swingy dress. When I take it off the hanger to look at it, I realize why I didn't immediately recognize it. The demon gave it to me. I wore it out to dinner one night. The night he seduced a college student in my guest bedroom. I put it back on its hangar and shove it to the back of the closet. Memories I don't need.

I stare into the closet in frustration, then picture my closet at home very clearly, building a mental picture of the shirt I want and exactly where it is. When I've got that image diamond-sharp in my mind, I kneel and shove my hand through the floor. A moment later, I pull my hand out, clutching the shirt I want. I carry it over to the trash can and brush it off carefully. Reaching through the Earth is just as messy as Earth-Walking, but this is going to be the first of many trips through the Earth tonight, if all goes to plan, so surely Lin and Wen won't care if I'm dusty.

I slip the blouse on, pull the tight sleeves down over my wrists and button them. It's an embroidered green peasant blouse my Dala made for me. I haven't worn it since her death, and I don't think it really suits me. Particularly not when paired with the faded cargo pants I'm wearing. Jou wouldn't be impressed. But it serves a purpose.

With my burns safely covered, I go to find Lin.

Everyone experiences Earth-Walking differently. Or so I'm told. To me it feels like coming home after a long journey. I come out of my Element so relaxed I feel boneless. And as grubby as if I'd just stepped off a trans-Atlantic flight.

Wen-Long came out of the ground screaming, after his single, involuntary Earth-Walk. Since it was the first time that I'd Earth-Walked anyone, I was glad he came out at all. But I haven't told him that. Nor do I tell his sister that it's only the third time I've Earth-Walked someone else as I take her hand and *reach* into my Element.

She comes out calmly, stepping forward like she's walking through a door. She shakes a little dust from her ponytail and sneezes, and then looks like she always looks. Pretty, put-together, a little inscrutable. She's admitted to me that she works on looking inscrutable, and she's good at it. I'm probably her best friend and I can't see through it most of the time.

Wen looks up from stacking books in a brown cardboard box. He doesn't look surprised at our appearance. Maybe his living room floor opens and spits out people all the time. He's a necromancer, so his life is just as filled with weirdness as mine. I think I'd raise an eyebrow if two people climbed out of my living room floor, but I suppose it depends on how bad a day I'd had. Some days, people climbing out of my living room floor would be the least weird part of my day.

I shake off those thoughts and head toward the open doorway. I know from visiting Wen at Thanksgiving that his kitchen is through the doorway, but even if I didn't know, the mouth-watering smell of pizza would lead me in the right direction.

"Pizza break," Wen says cheerily. "I've been packing all day."

"Aww, poor you," Lin scoffs as she follows me. "Like you haven't had your ghosts do it all for you."

"They went on strike after the bedroom. Now, where'd I pack the plates?"

A pair of misty hands appears before me as I move into the small kitchen. The hands open a packing box, and three plates float out to settle on the counter next to a stack of pizza boxes.

"Yeah, they really look like they're on strike," I snort.

"Show-off," Wen grumbles. "How're you doin', Tsara?"

I help myself to a slice of pizza before answering. Ham and pineapple. Mmm-mmm.

"I'm okay," I say. "It still feels a little unreal." Wen knows about Toby's death. He's the second call I made after Ana called me.

"Oh, God." Lin puts her hand over her mouth. "The wake was last night, wasn't it? You must think I'm a psycho, insensitive bitch. I didn't even ask."

I absolve her with a shake of my head. "It's strange, you know. I don't feel any sense of closure. I keep expecting him to drop by. Usurp my X-Box."

Lin touches my shoulder gently. "Oh, Zee."

Wen busies himself with flipping through the pizza boxes, and I know he's afraid I'm going to ask him to summon Toby's shade.

"I'll get over it," I say, to put him at ease. Nod when he glances at me. He has his own version of his sister's inscrutable face, but I see relief lighten his eyes.

I could summon Toby's shade myself if I wanted to, although Wen probably doesn't know that, since I've kept my Air powers to myself. But I wouldn't for the same reason he doesn't want to do it. It's disrespectful to summon a spirit that's at rest. The unquiet dead will speak to anyone who opens the pathways, or anytime to necromancers like Wen, who are born with them open. But the quiet dead should be left in peace.

Toby hasn't tried to speak with me since his death, which means that, no matter how violent his passing, he's at peace now. And I'm going to leave him there.

It's the living who are unquiet. I think of the loss in Ana's eyes as I take another bite of pizza.

"I told Toby's foster mother I'd try to help," I say after a moment. "Try to find out who did it."

Lin frowns at me. "Shouldn't that be left to the police?"

"Sis," Wen groans. "Get real."

"No, I'm serious. You don't have any business going after a murderer, Zee. Who do you think you are, Dirty Harry?"

"Dusty Mary, more like," I say, shaking a little from my sleeve. "C'mon, Linnie. If I can figure out who did it, I'll tell the shapeshifters. That's it. They can deal with it their own way. I've got no intention of doing anything dangerous. I know my limitations."

That's a complete lie. Every time I think I'm beginning to understand the limits of my magic, I discover some new ability. Like what's staining my palms. Or flashing in my eyes. But I do know that getting physically involved with supernatural nasties usually turns out worse for me than for them. Witness the scars that I'm hiding from Lin. And the mental scars she can't see but are harder to hide.

"Promise me you'll be careful."

"Yes, Ma," I say at the same moment Wen pipes up.

"I'll help you."

"Wen!"

I'm not sure what's more upsetting to poor Lin, the possible danger or her brother offering to help me so quickly when it's taken months of guilt-trips to get him to move to Boston to help her with their dementia-stricken mother.

"What? C'mon, Mom doesn't need me every minute of every day. 'Sides, I owe Tsara one." He winks at me and several of the faces tattooed on his neck follow suit.

I nearly choke on my pizza. Swallow quickly. It's disconcerting enough to have his tattoos wink at me, but more indigestion-inducing is the possibility that the conversation is veering toward demon-territory. "You bought the pizza. We're even." He begins to protest, and I wave a hand at him. "Seriously, if I need help, I'll call you, but I have no idea where to start, so I'm not even sure what I'm going to be able to do."

Lin's shoulders lower a little. "You just told Ana that to be nice."

"No, I meant it. I just don't know what I'm going to be able to do."

Lin chews her pizza with a sour expression. "Do you remember the last time someone asked for your help in finding something?"

Only too well. "If you're referring to—"

"I am. You looked like you'd been hit by a truck after you tangled with that ghost."

It wasn't a ghost that did that to me. It was my old college pal, and the freaking demon she summoned. "It's not going to be like that. But thank you for reminding me. Manny Goldberg owes me, and he has contacts in the police department. Maybe they know something."

"Zee—"

"I'm just asking the question! If they know something, I'll tell the shifters. If they don't know anything, then they don't. At least I've asked. I owe Ana that much."

"I thought she owed you."

I shrug that aside. "It's not about obligation. It's about giving Ana peace. You should have seen her at the wake, Linnie. She's a mess."

"Finding Toby's killer won't bring him back."

"No, but shifters are all about honor and retribution. Finding the thing that killed Toby will help Ana move on."

"The *thing*?" Wen asks.

I lean against the dusty counter and take another piece of pizza. "Toby was young, but he was strong. He survived being savaged by a Naga a couple of months ago. Whatever killed him had to be hellaciously strong and fast. And you know what lycanthropes are like. Once they engage, they never back down. I wouldn't lay odds on anything I know of around here . . . well, around Boston anyway, going up against Toby and surviving. A ghoul pack, maybe, but this wasn't a ghoul attack."

Lin makes a choking sound, pounds herself on the sternum and says, "And you know that how?"

"I just know," I say into my pizza. Avoid meeting her eyes. Sometimes gathering the herbs I need for the magic milk and other potions I make takes me into graveyards. Sometimes worse places. Ghouls aren't the scariest things I've come across in those places—they take a dim and distant place behind the barghast pack that hunted me through the Estabrook Woods one night, for example—but Lin doesn't need to know any of that.

"What does that leave?" Wen asks.

I shrug. "There isn't much else. There was a barghast pack, but it was destroyed." By a faerie Knight protecting me, but neither of them needs to know about that, either. "The Hobomock's strong enough, I guess, but he's slow, and he hasn't killed anything in centuries."

Wen lifts an eyebrow and several of the tattoos around his neck goggle at me.

"He also hasn't left his ledge in centuries. In Cohasset. Toby died near the Charles."

"Near the river? Something in the water?"

I chew thoughtfully for a moment. "There are some fae living in the Basin. And there's something up at the Watertown Dam that might be a kelpie. I'm not sure. I keep meaning to go and look, but, you know, other things keep coming up."

"Like demons," Wen mutters. I glare at him, and he has the grace to look a little sheepish. Some of his tattoos roll their eyes.

"Anyway, water fae drown their victims. Toby wasn't drowned, he was eaten."

"A maneater," Lin muses.

Wen gets there a second before I do. "What about a shark?"

"There used to be sharks in the Charles," I say, remembering an article in the *Globe* about it over the summer after a couple of Great Whites were spotted off the Cape. "Sharks can't come up into the river anymore because there are gates or nets or something." I chew as an idea takes shape. "What if it's not a natural shark? What if it doesn't have to stay in the water all the time? It could have walked right over the Craigie Bridge."

Lin shivers. "That's an image I don't need."

"A wereshark," Wen says. "Cool."

I bet Toby didn't think so, but I don't say anything to avoid embarrassing Wen.

"Are there weresharks?" Lin asks.

"I knew you'd get into this, sis," Wen says with a smirk. "Of course, there are weresharks. Don't you remember *Scooby Do*?"

She gives him a repressive glare.

"There are definitely weresharks," I say, recalling my Bevvy classes on shapeshifters. "Hawaiian mythology is full of them. I think there's a Japanese shark-shifter, too. *Samehada*, or something like that."

Lin shudders. "And I thought snake-shifters were icky."

"Don't diss the forefathers," Wen says.

"None of our ancestors were snakes!" Lin hisses, sounding rather snake-like. "Dragons and Naga are wholly unrelated."

I'm not sure about that, but I let Wen and Lin argue while I make some serious headway into another slice of pizza.

When the argument about the interrelatedness of *huanglong* and Naga finally dies down, Lin asks, "Why would a wereshark attack Toby?"

Since the question seems directed at me, I put down my pizza and answer, "Shifters are territorial. Especially with other shifters. I've seen them ignore fae incursions deep into their territory but go on the warpath when they scent another shifter near their borders. If a wereshark has claimed the Charles River Basin and Toby got too close? It wouldn't have stopped until it killed him." I rub the bridge of my nose with my thumb and forefinger, feel pizza grease smear my skin and hastily wipe it off with my knuckles. "Poor Toby. He could just have been in the wrong place at the wrong time."

"Poor Ana," Lin says. "If you're right, the wereshark didn't really do anything wrong. It was just defending its territory. Will she take revenge for that?"

"I don't know." Although I suspect the answer is 'yes.' "Wen, you got anything to drink?"

Whether it's the Earth-Walking or the dust from packing or thoughts of Toby, my throat feels tight.

A spectral hand floats a glass out of another box over to the sink. Its partner turns on the tap and when the glass is full, the pair of hands float it over to me.

"That's kinda creepy," I say. "But thank you very much." I salute the hands with the glass before taking a sip.

"What are you going to do?" Lin asks. "You're not going to try to trap the wereshark, are you?"

I snort into my water. "Hell, no."

"Really, Zee?"

"Really," I reassure her. "The only water you'll ever find me in is the clear, highly chlorinated kind. I'm not getting anywhere near the Charles." The depth of my own aversion surprises me, since I'm not a bad swimmer, and I wonder if the demon imparted his fear of running water, along with the other "gifts" he's given me. "My investigation's strictly theoretical. End of."

"Then how do you prove the wereshark theory?"

"I'm not proving anything. I'm just telling the shifters what I think." We've all finished our pizza and Wen is glancing anxiously towards the living room. "Anyway, I'll think about it while we pack."

But I've already started thinking about it, and as I help Wen stack books into boxes and then begin transporting the boxes, first one at a time and then as my confidence grows, in twos and threes, through the Earth to Wen's new apartment in Medford, my conviction grows. What I need isn't a shark-trap.

It's a water-witch.

———

What is it about moving that always requires superhuman effort? And where does all the dust come from? I visited Wen before Christmas and was actually impressed at how clean his apartment was, particularly for a guy's place. But after five hours of packing and moving, I'm so covered with grit that I feel like I've been playing in a sandbox. Earth-Walking all over the world wouldn't leave me this dirty.

I stand beside my bed, contemplating whether I need a shower. I should. But I'm too fatigued and there's no one to complain that I'm gritty. I'll shower in the morning and use a cantrip on the sheets.

Wearily, I climb into bed. A glance at my bedside clock shows that it's after two a.m. and now that I'm no longer moving around, I'm cold. I lie between the chilly sheets and shiver, feeling my sticky skin goosebump. I don't get any warmer; I'm never going to get to sleep while I'm shivering. Finally, I climb out of bed, cross to my dresser and pull out a nightgown, soft leggings and fuzzy socks.

I work on not thinking about Jou's warmth, the way he held me, the perfect fit of our bodies, as I get back into bed. It's useless. I lie, cold and alone, and wail for my demon-lover. But my cries are silent, and my eyes are dry. I cried all my tears for Jou long ago.

# CHAPTER 4

'm dreaming.

I know I'm dreaming because I can feel Jou's hot mouth on mine, his hands moving over my skin, the wonderful weight of his body. Sensations I can't feel again anywhere but my dreams.

*Hey, sweetness. Miss me?*

Because it's just a dream, I answer unreservedly. *God, yes.*

His wicked chuckle. A sound I've missed so much that hearing it makes my bones ache. My unconscious is really working overtime tonight.

*Good,* he thinks. *Step sideways with me.*

Stepping sideways is the way the demon stops time, creating a loop time has to follow. Within the loop, many things can take place. I've created my own version: a stitch-in-time, but it only lasts a few minutes. The demon can blow out the loop into hours.

*We've never had to step sideways before in my dreams,* I think at him.

*Who said this was a dream?* he replies.

We don't really step sideways. It's more of a metaphysical shift, into a different place where normal time blurs into ribbons of color and sound. Because we're in my bed in my dream, all that really blurs is my bedside clock, and the blue rose that sits beside the clock, still as fresh and perfect as the day Jou gave it to me three months ago. They blur into blue and white streamers that wave gently across the bedcovers. I watch them until Jou distracts me by running his fingertips down my cheek.

He tucks my bangs behind my ear. *You cut your hair.*

*After that night when you tied me to the bed with it.*

And fucked me to death.

*Did I?* He sighs. *Yeah, I guess I did. Feels like a long time ago.*

I nod. The pillow scrunches under my head. Feels like a long time ago to me, too.

He brushes his fingertips across my mouth. *You're different, sweetness.*

*It's been a crappy couple of months.*

The understatement of the millennium, given how many times during those months I've contemplated trying one of the darker concoctions in my herbarium.

*Yeah?* He strokes my jaw and moves a little closer to me. *That why you called me?*

Did I call him? I wasn't trying to. I was just missing him so much tonight. I miss him most nights, most days, too, but tonight it felt as sharp and fresh as those terrible black nights right after he stopped speaking into my head. Maybe that's why I'm dreaming about him again.

*Don't you know? C'mon, sweetness, you can't be that clueless.*

I shake my head. Feel embarrassment heat my cheeks. Then it becomes something much sharper, clawing up my throat, filling my eyes with hot tears.

"Don't do that," he says aloud. Softly, in his baritone whisper, the brush of black fur across my nerves. He slides his arms around me, draws me close so I'm enveloped in the heat of his body. "I'm here. You called an' I came."

I choke on tears and irony. "This is just a dream."

"Your whole world's a dream."

"Jou—" I choke. There hasn't been this much conversation in my dreams before. Usually, he just fucks me. Hard and vengefully.

"Do I?" he asks softly. He's reading my mind again. Even without his blood inside me, or the bindings that I broke. "Sorry, sweetness. It's all tangled up in my head. Too long on that fuckin' tree."

"What tree?"

"Not tonight. Ask me another time." He brushes his mouth across mine. "Tell me what you were thinking about when you called me. I can still taste it in your mind." He licks his lips. Then flicks the tip of his tongue over mine. He tastes like cinnamon, liquor, and smoke. "Mmm. Were you dreamin' about us fuckin'?"

Probably. I usually do.

"Tell me."

I don't remember what I was dreaming, if I was dreaming. Instead, I tell him the fantasy I've had for the last month. The fantasy that has helped me through some of the worst nights, like the night I spent by myself on my couch, watching "New Year's Rockin' Eve," with all the people in Times Square celebrating with their families and friends. I almost rang in the New Year with a glass of belladonna.

"We can do that," Jou says, when I finish describing it. He slides away from me; pulls me up the bed with him. He sits with his back to the headboard and guides me onto his lap. "Mmm, don't think we ever tried this."

I know we didn't, because I've been over every time we were together so many times in my head that each position, each kiss, each thrust, is inscribed indelibly into my memory.

I relax back into him, into that broad, warm chest that pillows me perfectly. Into the hard-muscled arms he closes around me, exactly the way I want to be held. He can see inside my head; he knows what I want, and he gives it to me. Just the way he did before that terrible night when he killed Timmi and her cabal, and I sent him back to Hell.

"Jou—"

"Yeah, sweetness?" He cups my breasts through my nightgown. Why am I not naked? I'm naked in my dreams often enough when I don't want to be. Can't I be naked now when I do?

When my nightclothes don't disappear the way they should, I wriggle in his lap until I can pull my nightgown off and push my leggings and socks down over my feet. When I sit back, the silken heat of his skin envelops me. It's like sinking into a hot bath. Soothing and stimulating. I feel blood rush to the surface of my skin, sensitizing it to his touch as he feathers his hands from my shoulders all the way down to my thighs. I reach back and grasp the thick column of his neck. Turn my head so I can breathe the scent of him deep into my lungs. I rub my cheek against his throat. Take breath after breath, each faster than the last as he strokes my thighs, playing with the small curls between my legs as they grow damp. Each inhalation fills me with the hot ginger and cinnamon scent of him. Each exhalation blows out the despair of the last three months.

He lifts his knees, spreading my legs. I know what comes next; I arch my hips against his. Jou takes the invitation. He shifts under me and when he draws me back down against him, pushes himself slowly into me.

"Jou, Jou, oh." I jerk in his arms. I expected his penetration. I wanted it. But it always takes me by surprise, that thick, hot cleavage of my body. The invasion of closed spaces. I open to him, in ways I'm not ready for. I'm never ready for what he does to me. But I want it. I crave it.

I begin rocking on him, keening with pleasure as he burrows deeper and deeper into me. He's not really thrusting. Not yet. He's just seating himself inside me. Wedging himself in. Heat blooms in my belly. Rushes in a burning pulse all the way to my fingertips. I shudder and Jou groans, clutching me tight to him.

"Forgot how soft you are," he murmurs against my temple. He pulses his hips and that hot length shifts within me. I clench down on him, so hard my toes curl, digging into the rumpled sheets. I grasp at him, with my hands, with my inner muscles, as he pulls back then plunges deep, over and over, finding his rhythm.

He takes my hands and guides them up to his horns. Polished bone under my palms and fingers as I grip them. He closes his arms tight around me, holds me to him and fucks me, his pace accelerating with each thrust until he's pounding into me and I'm writhing, holding onto his horns for dear life, whimpering with the exquisite pleasure of being held and taken like this. The heat blooming inside me expands until my skin can no longer contain it. It ripples outward, a ring of white light that flares neon blue when it hits his aura. He reaches down and closes his hand over my mons, holding me still as he pumps inside me. I explode: my magic, my heart, my soul, everything I am flinging open, flinging wide, as he takes me. I feel him drawing me down, into that fathomless well of darkness inside him, devouring what I offer him, as I collapse back against him. He fills me with a cold fire like starlight. It quenches the burning inside me, refuels me.

Jou groans, deep and low. "Fuck, sweetness."

"Jou. Dear God, Jou," I pant. "Are you okay? Do you . . . do you know who I am?"

He chuckles. "Not likely to forget."

He gets amnesia after he climaxes. The most scary, awful amnesia. "Jou, can you look at the wall behind my bed? It's important."

He wrote a memory charm or something on the wall behind my bed. In his spit. I hope it hasn't worn off or gotten scoured off by one of the extra-strength cantrips I've been casting since my magic came back.

"Huh?" I feel him twist and I release his horns. My hands and arms cramp, protesting how long and how tightly I've been holding on to him. "Yeah, I remember that," he says.

"You do? I mean, do you know who you are? Is everything okay?"

"Mmm."

He rolls his hips under me, reminding me that he's still inside me. This is the part I really hate. The part where I just want to cuddle and bask in the afterglow. Instead, I have to cope with a terrifying, demonic stranger.

I put my hands flat on the bed and begin to push myself off him.

"Where're you goin', sweetness? I like you where you are." He tugs me back against him.

He never uses that nickname right after sex. Because he doesn't remember it.

"Jou." I twist so I can look at him. He's resting against the headboard, face slack, head back, eyes closed. Like any man relaxing after good sex. But he's not a man. Not at all. Not even in my dreams. "Jou, are you okay? Do you remember?"

"I'm fine." He rearranges me so I'm resting against his chest again. "Just enjoying feelin' so full."

He feeds during sex, and I felt him draw hard on me that time, so he probably is feeling glutted. But if he remembers who he is, and who I am, that means he didn't climax, and that's a major issue for me. "Jou, did you come? It felt like you did, but if you remember everything—"

He grunts. "You know what I don't remember? You bein' this twitchy. Settle, sweetness, everything's fine now."

"Are you sure?" I try to twist around again to see his face, but he holds me in place.

"Settle. Or gimme a minute and we can go again but stop twisting around. That's my dick you're usin' as a pivot."

"Oh." I sit back and stop moving.

Jou's quiet for several long minutes, except for a purring hum he makes on each exhale, and I begin to relax. It's nice to sit here in his arms. His skin's warm and it blankets me against the cool night air. The blue and white streamers of his stitch-in-time are still waving across the bed; they're hypnotic. Jou pets me, stroking his fingertips up and down my arms. The hum and gentle motion cradle me. There's a wonderful hot fullness in my belly—a reminder that Jou's still deep inside me—that adds an edge of excitement. But it's not too much. Just something I can enjoy as I bask in the afterglow.

And then I realize that Jou's done it again. Somehow, he's given me exactly what I wanted, despite my best efforts to fuck it up.

"I'm so sorry, Jou," I whisper.

He grunts. "For what, sweetness?"

"Everything. Absolutely everything. I am so, so sorry."

He takes a deep breath, his chest expanding against my back.

"It's okay," he says slowly. His warm hand slides up my arm, skims my shoulder and throat, then settles in my hair and begins stroking. "Everything's gonna be okay now."

No, it's not. Because I'm going to wake up and none of this will have happened. He won't have come back. We won't have had soul-exploding sex. He won't have told me it's okay. And I'll still be missing him so much that it feels like my heart has turned into a super-massive black hole.

Jou growls, a sudden, scary sound in the darkness.

I start. "What?"

He lifts me off him and sets me on the bed. Then he slides down, stretching across the mattress, and pulls me down next to him. Once he pulls the covers over us, he rolls me under him. I gasp a little when his weight settles onto me. He supports himself on his forearms so he's not crushing me and looks down at me. His eyes are as dark as a cloudy night.

"Say it," he says.

"Say what?"

"What you wouldn't say when you banished me. Say it."

"What? No. Jou—" I twist under him, but his weight keeps me pinned down.

"You missed me. Not a little. Not just 'causa the sex. You missed me. You missed me the way humans miss their mates. You missed me 'cause I'm part of you. You couldn't say it then. Say it now."

Oh, fine. I've said it once before and thought it a million times. "I missed you."

"And?"

Damn. It's just a dream anyway. "I love you, Jou."

His grin lights up my dark bedroom. "That's better. Say it again."

"No. Jou, you've been gone for three months, and yes, I have been totally miserable without you, but missing you and loving you and wishing I could be with you doesn't *change* anything. You are what you are, and I am what I am—"

"An' never the twain shall meet?" He shakes his head in a rustle of dreadlocks. "Sweetness, I don't know what I am anymore except tired. I'm so fucking tired. I'm tired of fightin' and tired of hurtin' and tired of not being with you. I've had enough. I'm gonna rest and heal and when you're ready, summon me. For real. See what sending me away did to me, and see how fucking much I need you. Do it 'cause you can finally admit that you need me. Do it 'cause I have paid the fucking price of being with you."

"What does that mean?"

"Nothin'." He raises himself up on his arms and looks down between us. I have an urge to grab the sheets and cover myself, but he's looking at his own body, not mine. "I wish," he grunts. "Do it 'cause I'm in pieces without you. You feel like you got a black hole in your heart? I'm caught in the fucking singularity. Do it 'cause you know how much I hate feelin' trapped, and 'cause whatever you're sorry for, I forgave you a long time ago."

"Jou—" My breath catches, and his face blurs in my vision. "Do you really forgive me?"

He shifts to my side, no longer pinning me down. I roll so I can look up into his eyes. He brushes back my bangs and cups my face in one huge, warm palm. "What's done is done. I can't take it back. Neither can you. But if you miss me like that, then we don't need to be apart. We can heal together."

"Really?"

"Yeah." He brushes his lips over my eyelids. "Go back to sleep, sweetness. I'm too tired for this. So're you. Here, gimme a cuddle."

He's never too tired for more, so I don't believe that, but if he wants to cuddle, I'm not going to argue. He opens his arms, and I throw myself against him. I want to believe him so badly. Lying tucked tight to his chest, his hard arms around me, his cinnamon and smoke scent filling my lungs, his warm skin insulating me from any chill, I almost can.

----

I wake shivering. I'm lying across the head of my bed, curled around a pillow. No covers. No nightgown. No demon.

Dammit, I *knew* it was just a dream.

I throw myself out of bed. Dress in black to match my mood and swear to call lightning down on the first thing that irritates me today.

Breakfast is another bowl of granola, which tastes like sawdust this morning. Maybe because my mouth is still full of dust from Wen's. Maybe because the memory of Jou's amazing breakfasts makes everything else pale to ash.

I throw my empty bowl into the sink with a clatter. What is *wrong* with me? So I dreamed about him again. So it felt real. So fucking what? It doesn't *mean* anything. Every one of my dreams about him has felt real. It doesn't mean he's thinking about me. Doesn't mean he cares about me. It doesn't mean he really could forgive me. It's all just wish-projection, as my ex-therapist would say. Unhealthy, self-destructive, wish projection.

I give myself a hard shake. I'm not letting myself spiral back down into the darkness that consumed me after I banished Jou. Dust days, Lin called them. I'm done with dust days. No more grey days without magic. No more black nights spent crying over a lover who doesn't come, or worse, crying after he does.

I brew a pot of coffee. Coffee makes everything better. So does magic, and after a moment's contemplation, I hold out my hands and *call*. Thunder rumbles in the distance. Lightning leaps from my eyes to my hands. I let the energy play around my fingertips for a moment, then wrap it into a bright ball that sits, humming, in my palms. I *reach* with my mind and begin sculpting the energy. Pushing, pulling. Shaping the energy into the image twisting in my mind's eye. A serpentine, scaled shape I've seen on the scrolls decorating Lin's office. A *huanglong*.

When I'm finished, a small dragon sits on my palms. It's about Izzy's size: a little over a foot long. Electricity crackles beneath the frosted surface, like a plasma lamp. I close my fingers around it. The surface is cool, glassy. I run my thumbs over the ridges of the dragon's scales. Watch the light stain my skin pink. Caged lightning.

As housewarming presents go, it's . . . kind of useless, like most housewarming presents, I guess. Decorative at best. At least I can be sure Wen won't get anything else like it.

I set it on my kitchen table while I make some phone calls. Look at it while I speak first to Lin, then to Wen, then to Manny. I've never made anything like it before. I have no idea why I did it, except that I needed to do *something* to avoid spiraling back into grief and despair.

When I finish my calls, I hunt for a brown paper bag to wrap up the dragon. I used up all my wrapping paper over Christmas, so I hope Wen isn't picky.

As I'm scrabbling through the bags stuffed under my sink, the doorbell rings.

I lift my head warily. I'm not expecting anyone. I have a brunch appointment at one, but I'm meeting her in Porter Square. I don't think she even has my home address. So, it's not this long-lost cousin or whatever she is. And unexpected visitors have not turned out well for me in the last year.

I extend my will, feeling my way through the familiar confines of my house, across the steely shimmer of my house's threshold, to the porch.

The power of the fae standing at my front door slaps me like a spray of icy water.

Róisín.

I climb to my feet, cross through the house, and open the door.

She's standing a respectful step back. Pale and perfect. She's dressed less formally today, more like the first time I met her: jeans and an emerald silk blouse, topped with a black leather jacket.

She holds out my dress shoes.

I accept them a little ruefully, and after a moment's hesitation, invite her across the threshold. "No vampires," I say.

"I am alone. Bone is too young to be active during the day," she says. "And the older vampirii will not bother you. Leid's wishes on this point have been made extremely clear."

"I guess I should be reassured."

She gives me her sad, beautiful smile. "He would be gratified if you were."

Not my highest priority, gratifying the scary vampire. "Do you drink coffee?"

Róisín nods. "It smells delicious."

If she likes coffee, she can't be all bad. "Come on in, then." I drop my shoes on the bottom riser of the staircase and lead Róisín into my kitchen. She sits down at the kitchen table while I take down another mug from the cabinet for her. When the coffee's ready, I take the pot, the mugs and milk over to the table and sit down across from her.

She's examining Wen's housewarming present. When I pour a cup of coffee and offer it to her, she puts down the ornament and smiles. "This is very beautiful."

"Thank you," I say.

She picks up her cup and holds it close to her face. I think she's smelling it at first, and hope she likes Gingerbread Spice, but then her eyes close and her lips move. I wonder if she's enchanting the coffee or checking for poison. She opens her eyes after only a moment and takes a sip, which makes it the shortest spell known to man or fae, or something else. Her beatific smile convinces me. She was praying.

"The Goddess?" I ask.

The fae I've met don't talk about their religion, but I was taught at college that they worship the Mother.

"Yes. Do you follow Her?"

I shrug. "I don't really follow anyone."

"Because you are undecided? Or because you do not believe?"

"The latter, I think."

She nods, but doesn't pursue it, which makes her unique amongst the devoutly faithful I've met. "I would like to apologize to you," she says.

That's a surprise. "For what?"

"Our insistence in the car after the therian's wake. I see now that it was insensitive."

I chuckle into my coffee. "I bet Bone doesn't agree. Is that why you came during the day?"

The corners of her mouth twitch. "And to set you at ease."

"I'm guessing that if Leid or the older vampires want to move around during the day, they don't have too much trouble."

"They are extremely photosensitive, even after centuries."

"Really? I assumed that was a myth. Like crucifixes." Which, after the wake, I'm very sure is a myth, since a number of people, including me, were wearing them and the vampires didn't seem affected in the slightest.

"They're undead, not damned." Her dark eyes hold mine for longer than the moment calls for.

I tilt my head to the side and hold up my left wrist, around which dangle several silver bracelets, gifts from my Dala. Crosses tinkle amongst the other silver charms.

"Ah," she says. Her eyes drop to her coffee. "We were misinformed."

"Someone told you I'm damned?"

She shrugs. "We were told a lord of Hell made you his familiar."

"He's not a lord of Hell." At least, not that he ever told me. "And I'm no one's familiar."

"So I see. May I ask a personal question?"

"Ask whatever you want." Whether I answer her is a different question.

She nods. "If you do not believe in the Son of Man, or the Lady, then why refuse the dark gift?"

"Dark gift?" I wasn't aware the vampires were recruiting.

"The Hellion's favor. He has marked you." She nods at my arms. Damn, she must be able to sense the burns. Unless she has fae x-ray vision, since I've been wearing long sleeves every time we've met. "Yet you are here, now, alone. Wearing the Son of Man's sigil. Rumor claims that you banished the Hellion. If you do not believe in damnation, why refuse him?"

I sigh. "It's complicated."

Really, really complicated. Particularly this morning.

"Forgive me," Róisín says. "I do not wish to pry."

"It's over."

If it's over, why did I dream about him again last night?

"Is it?" Róisín asks. I glance at her sharply. "Hellions rarely give up. They have long memories. And the luxury of time."

Jou said something similar once. Is that why I've started dreaming about him again? Because he's remembered me? I shiver and push that idea aside. I'll make myself crazy – again – thinking those sorts of thoughts. Jou's gone; he's not coming back and last night was just the pathetic yearning of someone who can't pick her ass up and move on.

But it seemed so *real*.

"May I ask how you came to the Hellion's attention? The *Tylwyth Teg* have long shielded you. Even the vampirii were unaware of you until the boy's unfortunate death, and Leid knows most creatures of power in his domain."

The fae have been shielding me? That's news to me. "It was an accident. I freed him without realizing what he was. I actually thought he was a vampire."

Róisín's mouth doesn't smile, but her eyes do. "It is heartening that you freed him believing he was a vampire. Leid will be pleased."

That's the second time she's mentioned Leid in two breaths. It catches at me this time. "Are, uh, you and Leid?"

She lifts one dark eyebrow. "Are we a couple? Older vampirii don't have those needs, and fae blood is not palatable to them. I offer companionship for the sanctuary Leid has granted me. He seems to think that a fair exchange."

"Right." Sounds kind of dry and hollow to me, but then the vampires themselves seem kind of dry and hollow. Maybe that's why they drink blood. Ick.

"And after you freed the demon you believed to be a vampire?"

I shrug. "I sent him back to Hell when I figured out how." There was a lot between freeing him and sending him back – but absolutely no one needs to know anything about that.

Róisín turns her coffee cup around in her hands. "I am in no position to judge you."

"I didn't—"

She holds up a pale hand. "You sounded extremely defensive. You have no reason to be with me. Humans have long regarded my kind as demons."

And from everything I've read, cyhraeth do feed on certain types of human emotion—specifically misery and grief—which makes Róisín more like Jou and his kindred than she'd probably like to be. But there are some big differences. Some of which are burned into my forearms.

"Sorry, it's been a rough couple of months."

"Because you freed him? Or because you banished him?"

"Both," I say honestly, but that's as much as she's getting out of me. "Anyway, you didn't come here to talk about my sordid past."

Róisín gives me a small smile. "No, but I admit that I've been very curious since Leid tasked me with finding out about you. No one knows much about you. I have to think that is by design." When I don't respond, and she realizes I'm not going to, she says, "Thank you for indulging my curiosity."

I nod. It's been sort of a painful indulgence for me, given last night's dream. I refill my coffee cup and take a sip. "Demons aside, I've been giving some thought to Toby's death."

"That will please Leid greatly."

I constrain an eye roll. Maybe vampires don't have those needs, but the fae do and Róisín sounds like a lady with a serious case of *want*. "Then he'll be doubly pleased to know that I don't think it's a vampire. Or any of the undead."

Róisín leans forward over her coffee cup. "This is what I believe. How did you discover this?"

"It wasn't really a discovery. More of a deduction. Toby was killed on the Charles River Bike Path, next to the river. The undead shun running water." Something which has just occurred to me but should have days ago. "A vampire wouldn't get that close to open water, would they?"

Róisín shakes her head. "Even the oldest and most powerful would not dare."

"Neither would demons." Not even old and powerful ones like Jou. "That leaves other shifters."

Róisín leans back in a self-satisfied way that reminds me of Leid and irritates me the same way. "You will tell the therians this?"

"I will."

She shakes her head. "They swear it was not one of them."

"I agree, it wasn't one of them."

A tiny frown beetles her pale brow. "But you said it was a shapeshifter."

"Yes, but not one of the clans. This is something that hunts alone. It doesn't have a clan and doesn't want one. It probably doesn't even live among humans."

"There is no such thing. All of us—therian, vampirii, fae—we all live amongst your kind."

"This doesn't."

"There is no such creature."

See? This is what bugs me about supernatural creatures. They live a few centuries and develop egos the size of a second-term senator. "There's no such creature *here*. But there are plenty such creatures in other cultures. The Japanese call it *samehada*. It's a shark-shifter. A shapeshifting shark."

"A what?" Róisín breathes, but that breath vibrates weirdly in her throat, in my ears, and I'm reminded of what she is and what she can do.

"A wereshark. They're common in the mythology of the Pacific Rim. Hold on." I leave her at my kitchen table, walk through into my dining room where I keep a bookcase of books that are definitely not for public consumption. Selecting one of my Bevvy textbooks, I scan down the index, flip it open to the page I want and carry it back through to the kitchen. I place it on the table in front of her, holding it open with two fingers.

She leans over and scans the page, then looks up at me. "Forgive me, I do not read your language very well."

"Oh." It didn't occur to me that a modern fae wouldn't read English. "Sorry. This is Nanaue, the shark-man of Waipio Valley. That's in Hawaii. He was the son of a human and the king of sharks. Nanaue could turn into a shark in the water, but on land he was a man. But he always had a shark's jaws on his back, even in human form, which is how he was eventually identified." I trace my finger down the page to an illustration of a prolapsed maw on a well-muscled back. "It would be nice if our wereshark were as easy to spot."

"Do you think he will not be?"

I shrug. "No idea. Something like that seems hard to hide, so I'd guess that weresharks have evolved a little more protective coloration over the years. But I really have no idea."

"Then how will you catch him?"

I snort. "Who says I'm catching anything? I said I'd try to figure out what killed Toby. I've got a theory, which is what I'll tell the therians. If they want to try to catch it, that's up to them, but games I'm not playing include hunt the wereshark." I tap the toothy illustration for emphasis.

A tiny beetling of that pale, perfect brow is probably Róisín's version of a scowl. "You must prove your theory. What if the clans don't believe you? The whole point of this is to end the war."

"Wrong." I give her my version of a scowl right back, which involves a lot more facial muscle. "The point of this is to give Ana some closure. *Therian*-vampire relations are not my problem. Call the United Nations."

"The what?"

"Never mind." She's probably never heard of the U.N. The fae are pretty insular. Vampires probably are, too. "Listen, I'm not doing this for Leid or you or any of your pointy-toothed buddies. Ana was Toby's mother in every sense that matters. She needs to know what killed her son. *That's* why I'm doing this. If it ends a war between the therians and the vampires, hey, that's gravy, but it's not why I'm doing it."

Róisín shakes her head. "Leid will not be pleased if this is left unfinished."

I start to say that Leid can bite me but think better of it. "Well, there's an easy way to prove my theory. There are fae in the Charles. Why don't you go have a chat with the Watertown Kelpie? Ask it if there's a maneater in the Basin."

"Sassthen and I aren't on speaking terms."

Well, well, well, so there *is* a kelpie lairing in the Watertown Dam. I tuck its name away for future reference. "Are you on speaking terms with any of the water fae? I mean, aren't you one of them yourself?"

"I was." Róisín sighs. "But no longer. None but the *Fir Darrig* will speak with me, and they will find a way not to tell me the truth. What of your contacts among the fae? Could you not ask one of them?"

"What part of, *this isn't my problem*, was unclear? I'm not getting indebted to the fae over this." I already owe them enough. "If Leid wants to end the war, he can figure out a way to prove my theory."

Róisín's mouth sets in a tight line and the pale flesh of her throat quivers. If she's thinking of unleashing her wail in my kitchen, she has another thing coming.

I lift my left hand, splay my fingers, and release the lightning striking in my pupils. Electricity arcs between my fingertips like a miniature Van De Graaff generator and the smell of ozone fills my kitchen.

Róisín clears her throat and looks down at the table. "We were so very misinformed."

Meaning the undead didn't know I could call lightning. Surprise, you creepy bastards. "I told you, I've had a rough couple of months." Made all the rougher by last night. "Pushing me is a bad idea. I push back really fucking hard. So, if you're done." I nod at her empty cup.

"You'll excuse me. I've got kind of a full day. Thank you for bringing back my shoes."

She silently hands me the coffee cup. Glides up off my kitchen chair. She stands next to the table that looks like it's been trendily charred and polished but is really just another casualty of my time with the demon. She stands there with her head down, brushing her fingertips over the polished tabletop, like she's brushing away crumbs. I don't think she is. Between my frequent visits from the Squire, who will only come into my house if it is skinlessly clean, and the excess power I've been bleeding off into the housekeeping cantrips, I'd be surprised if there's so much as a water-ring on the table.

"I will tell Leid what you have said. I know . . . I have no right to ask, but he will try to prove your theory. Ending this war is very important to him. But running water is anathema to the undead. If he seeks this thing in the river, it could kill him. Would you . . . if he asks, would you help him? It would put the Five Houses in your debt. That is no small thing."

I set the coffee cups in the sink. Lean against it while I chew on my lower lip. I know that a lot of supernatural creatures work on a system of honor and obligation. I respect that, and I've done things before for the purpose of creating such a debt. That's how I ended up with the Squire's protection, and probably why the fae have been hiding me. But not with the undead, who totally, completely creep me out. I push my lower lip out when I taste blood and shape a word on the motion. "Fine."

Róisín looks up and smiles—a real, pleased smile—for the very first time.

# CHAPTER 5

Wen and Lin are sitting at the island in his kitchen, eating donuts out of a Dunkin box, when I emerge from the Earth. I doubt Wen got a basement apartment so I could Earth-Walk into it, but it sure makes life easier. Wen pushes the kitchen trash bin towards me with his foot and I hand Wizard to Lin before I dust myself off.

"How's the unpacking going?" I ask.

Lin snorts as she bends over my wriggling salamander.

"That good, huh?"

"My place in Philly was bigger," Wen grumbles as he offers me a donut. I shake my head. Still not Jou's breakfasts. "Half of my stuff's going to have to go into storage."

"My attic is hardly 'storage,'" Lin snaps.

I take a step backwards, withdrawing physically and emotionally from their argument. I know Wen took this apartment because it's close to the nursing home Lin's put their mother in, and because it was what he could afford. I also know he doesn't like it as much as his apartment off U. Penn.'s campus. And I know the sibling sniping is really about him feeling that Lin forced him to move.

"Your phone's already working," I say, to divert the conversation. "It took like two weeks to get my line set up when I moved."

"Helps to know the dead mother of your customer service rep," Wen says. "You've got my cell anyway. Why did you need my landline?"

Because cell phones only work about half the time around me. And because Manny Goldberg has a thing about call charges, so he'll only use a landline. "I really don't want to miss this guy's call, and he won't talk to voicemail."

"Old school, huh?" Wen asks.

"Very." I hold out the paper bag, a little nervously. What if he hates it? Worse, what if he drops it? I should have put a warning label on it.

Wen takes the bag from me and unwraps the little dragon. "Wow." He holds it up, and the tattooed faces on his neck and arms crowd around to where they can see it, too. Even Lin looks up from petting Wizard.

"That's—" she begins.

"Unique?" I swallow hard.

"Wicked," Wen says. "A lightning lizard of my own."

He's referring to my familiar, who is a lightning salamander, and is currently trying to nose his way up onto the counter in search of donuts. I give the salamander a warning tap on the tail. Donuts give salamanders gas, and salamander gas can burn down whole city blocks.

Wen gives me a broad grin. "Gets pride of place." He hops off his stool and moves through the open doorway of the kitchen into his parlor, where there's a fake fireplace. He sets it on the mantelpiece.

It does look amazing there, casting a flickering glow onto the freshly painted white walls. I smile. When Wen returns to the kitchen, backing through the doorway so he can continue to admire his present, he gives me a one-armed hug. I hug him back. "Welcome to Beantown, Wen."

He turns his head and whispers into my ear. "Thanks, I'm feelin' better about being here."

Understanding his conflict perfectly this morning, I nod and pat his back.

When he releases me, I look around the kitchen, which is still stacked with unopened boxes. "So, you want me to start in here?"

"Yeah, thanks." Wen moves away and starts opening cupboards in the cramped kitchen. "Put stuff wherever it fits."

I chuckle to myself. Just like a guy to not care where his things go.

———

I'm unpacking glasses when Manny returns my call.

"Okay, kid," he says. "I've got something for you. You owe me, you know."

I let that go. If Manny knew what getting that thrice-cursed ring for him cost me, he'd be in my debt for eternity. But he doesn't know and I'm not telling. "Next coffee's on me."

Manny grunts. He's got ulcers and doesn't drink anything stronger than Pepto Bismol. "Here you go. My friend in the C.L.U. said they didn't get much chance to process the scene before the feds moved in." That would be the shifters arriving to take care of their own, but I keep that thought to myself. "But they did a basic examination and collected some trace, which I'll get back to in a minute. The basics are that your boy was killed between eleven p.m. on Sunday and one a.m. on Monday morning. There was something wrong with the core temperature reading, which is why they couldn't narrow down the time of death further."

Toby was a shifter, and they tend to run a little hot, even in human form, so that doesn't surprise me. I don't comment, though, and let Manny continue.

"He was found on the Charles River Bike Path at about four a.m. by a jogger. There were no reports of screams, but a couple of the guests at one of the hotels facing the bike path complained to the night manager about noise around midnight. Possibly related. Your vic. was found on concrete and there was significant spatter . . . sorry, there was a lot of blood at the scene. The C.L.U. took samples, but the feds got those, so they're not sure if it was all the kid's blood or not."

"Was the concrete wet?" I ask.

"Uh, no, I don't see anything about that. It hadn't rained."

He's right. It hasn't rained all week. Or snowed. Or sleeted. Or hailed. Or done anything normal for Boston in January. "Okay, go on."

"Right, let's get to the trace evidence, which was what really interested my friend. She collected a good amount of it at the scene and said it was animal fur. It was all turned over to the feds, so C.L.U. didn't type it, but my friend said she was sure it was dog fur and would have said this was a feral dog attack except for one thing."

He pauses, and I'm not sure if it's for dramatic effect or because he's reading.

"What is it?"

"The bite marks. Do you want me to go into the technical detail? It's not very nice."

I swallow. "Yes, please."

"Well, my friend said your boy was defleshed. That means partially eaten. Particularly his stomach and thighs. The skin was distorted around the wounds, which she says means that whatever ate him was tearing away the flesh . . . I said this wasn't very nice."

"It's okay, Manny, go on."

"Okay, she couldn't get clear impressions or measurements because of the tearing, but she said the bites themselves were huge. Eight inches across, at least. There's no dog with a jaw that big. She said there are some bears with an eight-inch jaw, but not in this area. She was going to call in an animal attack expert before the feds hijacked her show."

Something with a huge mouth that eats flesh. Wereshark.

"Manny, was there any sign of infection?"

"Around the wounds? He died within minutes, kid."

"Does it say? Do you have the report in front of you?"

"No, just copies of my friend's notes. But I can ask her if you want."

"Please. It's important, Manny."

"Okay, kid. I'll ask."

"Thanks."

He doesn't ask why I need to know. Or anything else, for which I'm grateful. And he calls me back within five minutes.

"Kid, I gotta run, grandkids are on the way, but my friend says no, the wounds were clean. No sign of infection."

"Thanks, Manny, I really appreciate it."

Which rules out ghouls. And puts me squarely back in wereshark territory.

———

After asking Wen if it's okay to use his phone, I call Ana. Her machine picks up, so I leave what I hope is a suitably vague message, since breaking the news about her foster-son's killer by voicemail seems like an asshole thing to do. Lin comes into the kitchen while I'm leaving the message. Wizard winds himself around her ankles like a tiny, cream and lemon tiger-cat. She picks him up absently and pets him while she leans a hip against the kitchen island and listens to me.

"What's next?" she asks after I hang up.

"Establish whether there's a wereshark in the Charles."

"How?" There's no belligerence in her tone, but there's plenty of edge.

"Well, the easiest thing would be a water-witch, I guess, but I only know one and she's in Atlanta. Also, she's not big on shapeshifters, so I'm not sure she'd be willing to help."

Wen comes through the archway with a box clearly labeled 'kitchen.' Which has somehow ended up not-in-the-kitchen. Oops. "That bitch."

"Language," Lin objects.

Huh. Lin swears plenty, although evidently not around her younger brother. And Merida really wasn't nice to Wen at Christmas. "That's a question for Ana. She can decide where to take it next." As I said to Wen, shifters are extremely territorial, and Ana may feel I'm stepping on her toes if I take things any further on my own.

I glance at the clock I've put up on the wall over Wen's sink. "Look, I'm really sorry about this, but I've got that thing with my cousin at one, and I desperately need a shower, so I'm going to have to motor—"

Wen nods, a shade too eagerly. Am I in the way or something? I thought I was helping.

"Before you go, Wen and I want to talk to you about something," Lin says. Now she sounds belligerent. I steel myself. Wen puts the box he's carrying down on the kitchen island and leans against it. He doesn't look happy. No wonder he was anxious for me to leave. He must have known this was coming.

"Fire away," I say warily.

Lin nods at the empty stool next to Wen and I climb up onto it. Rest one hand on the countertop and rub my fingertips in the light coating of dust.

Lin puts her hand on my shoulder. Here it comes.

"We want to talk with you about Jou."

I feel a finger of cold run down my spine. Why now? Other than the burns on my arms, I haven't mentioned Jou to Lin in weeks. Why is she bringing him up now?

I glance at Wen. If he decided to break the news that Jou's a demon to Lin while we've been moving, I'm going to kill him.

Wen holds up his tattooed hands.

I'm not sure if that gesture is supposed to say, "I'm innocent," or "she weaseled it out of me." I pursue my mouth sourly at him before I turn my attention back to this sister.

"Look, Lin—" I begin.

"Hear us out."

No way. There's no good place for this conversation to go. And I don't need Lin and Wen psychoanalyzing my mistakes with the demon, particularly not right on the heels of that damned dream.

"There's really nothing more to say, Linnie."

"You know that's not true. Why don't you just call him and see if you can meet up for coffee or something?"

Fuck no. Is this a conspiracy? Jou asked me to summon him, something he hasn't done, even in my dreams, since the very first day after I banished him. Now Lin's suggesting I call him? How would I even do that? Since he's stopped speaking into my mind, I don't have any way to contact him. Unless there's cell cover in Hell. Which, hey, there could be. There's a tower two blocks from my house in Somerville. They're all over the place now.

"Lin," I whine.

"Stop trying to put me off," she says.

Damn, she's figured that one out. "Look, Jou and I are really—"

"Complicated?" She puts it in air-quotes. I guess I've said that too often. "I see you drawing into yourself again, Zee. Not talking to anyone. Coming in late and disappearing for hours during the day."

I start to object. Either I've been out late gathering herbs for the magic milk, or I've been at the Museum working with the Diary. I haven't been hiding out in bed the way I did during the Dust Days. Lin continues over my objection, "And now Wen says you're spending time in the wild lands—"

Wen rolls his eyes. "I said she *smelled* like the wild lands."

Okay, that I am guilty of. "I've been dancing with the fae," I admit.

When Wen smacks his palm against his forehead, making several of his tattoos wince, and Lin gives me an incredulous stare, I protest. "Hey, I know what I'm doing. I've dealt with the fae for years. I know the rules."

Don't eat, drink, fall asleep or let anyone kiss you inside a fairy ring. Pretty simple, actually.

There should be a corollary for dealing with demons. Don't eat or drink anything a demon feeds you, or have kinky, orgasmic sex with him. Because it will fuck you up forever.

I rub my hand over my face and try to focus on the confrontation, intervention, whatever it is that Lin thinks she's doing. I know she's doing it because she's my friend. I know she loves me. But it's still annoying she feels the need to do it. "Are we done?" I ask. "Because I really do need to get going."

Lin gives her brother the stink-eye, like he's done something to derail her. Which is unfair, but, hey, better him than me.

"I still think you should call him," Lin says.

"Okay." I lean over and give her a cheek-peck, so she knows I appreciate what she's trying to do. Or, more accurately, that I know she cares, since I don't actually appreciate what she's trying to do. "I'll see you on Tuesday, huh?"

I've taken Monday off work. It's my Dala's birthday, and she prefers that I visit her grave on her birthday rather than the anniversary of her death. Or so her ghost has told me.

She nods. "Just think about it."

"I will." I promise. And I will. I just don't know *what* I think about it.

———

After another Earth-Walk, I really do need a shower. Putting my gritty clothes back on afterwards has no appeal, and I should make an effort, since I'm meeting family for the first time. I find a pair of black slacks that I don't think I've ever worn before, but I must have bought pre-demon, because I have to loop my macramé belt around the waist to keep them from falling off my hips, and a fitted red shirt.

Red for fire. Aggression. Passion. Funny, Jou never wore red . . . damn, why can't I stop thinking about him today?

No, not red.

I dress again. White polo and a long gray waistcoat that I think I made in a Home Ec. class at Wydlins. Scary that I can wear it in public again.

I look at myself in the mirror. Fluff my bangs. Black. White. Gray. Black.

I look like a black-and-white photograph. Of a Holocaust survivor. Have I really lost that much weight?

I dress again. A chunky sweater my Dala knitted for me in heathered shades of blue and green. Baggy jeans I roll up at the cuffs. Better. Blue and green are nice, soothing colors. The thick knit fills me out a little. The cowl hides how skinny my neck looks without any hair to frame it. The long sleeves cover my scars. The day's so warm that with the sweater, I won't even need a jacket.

I sit on the edge of my bed. Look at the clock. I've still got a half-hour before I should even think about setting off.

I head downstairs. Pick up my bag and shove my feet into high-tops. I can't sit around the house watching the clock. Or change clothes again. Or spend any more time trying not to think about Jou. I don't know what's wrong with me. I'm edgy. Why? I've got nothing to prove to this woman. She looked *me* up. If I can't stand her, if we have nothing in common beyond a couple of genes, then I just politely eat my brunch and leave. Nothing wasted beyond a couple of hours and a little indigestion.

The walk to Porter Square doesn't even take five minutes. I should stroll. The weather is sunny and crisp. Perfect for walking. Late October or early April maybe, but can this really be January in Boston? I turn my face up into the sun and enjoy the feathery kiss of the wind as it sweeps my bangs off my cheeks. I pass hedges of forsythia bushes, which are flowering, as I told Dead. Daffodils poke up out of the muddy ground, the buds lopped over and swollen gold. Bizarre weather.

I should pass through it all at a leisurely pace. Admire each new clump of blossoms. Listen to the songs of the sparrows in the hedges. Let my feet follow the Twisting Path and see where it leads me. Instead, I stride briskly down Somerville Avenue and find myself at Porter Square Arcade with forty minutes to spare.

Crap.

The shops are open, at least. I poke around the Arcade. The Japanese gift shop, *Tokai*, sucks me down the way it always does, and before I escape, I spend money I shouldn't on a beautiful, lacquered bento box. As I take the box to the counter, I steer my eyes away from the kimonos displayed on the walls. No, not another kimono. No-no-no.

Ooo, they have a new one. Beige and black with a flight of swallows. Beautiful. I could just peek at the price tag . . . ouch, no, *definitely* not. I put the bento box down on the counter and when the girl behind the counter asks me if there's anything else, I shake my head firmly. The last time Tokai sucked me down, I almost didn't have enough left at the end of the month to pay the mortgage.

I run my thumbs over the golden carp painted on the top of the box as the girl rings it up. I kept smelling the ocean when I spoke to Shirri on the phone. Scenting magic isn't my best thing—Timmi was teaching me to do it, before Jou killed her—and I could use a lot more practice before I can do it reliably. But maybe it means something. Maybe Shirri will like the bento box. If not, I can always give it to Wen as another house-warming present. It's more useful than the last one, at any rate.

Carrying the Tokai bag, with its stylized cranes and bamboo on the outside that are almost as pretty as the gift within, I wander through the Arcade. Past Hair Company, the hair salon. I've never bothered to have my hair professionally cut. My Dala always said, "why waste money on something you can do yourself?" She cut my hair until I went to college. Ro helped me cut my hair when we were roomies. She always made a huge production out of it, and we ended up giggling so hard she couldn't cut straight. I wore layers all through Bevvy because of her giggle fits.

God, I miss her.

Ugh, don't think of that. The hair salon is advertising bikini waxes for spring. If the demon's going to start making regular appearances in my dreams again, maybe I should get a Brazilian.

No, don't think of that either.

Trying to leave thoughts of both my dead best friend and the demon she summoned behind, I escape the Arcade and make my way up the street towards Mudflat. It's Saturday, Mel won't be working, but I can kill fifteen minutes admiring the new stuff they've got in and leave a message for Mel to see if she wants to do dinner during the week. She was talking about seeing the new Leon Lewis movie. If she hasn't already, we could do an eat-and-drool.

I linger outside the front window for several minutes, looking at the beautiful selection of glazed Japanese tea bowls in the window. When I look up, my reflection has gained a Stetson.

Mel waves merrily through the window. Her boobs jiggle under her tight tee as she waves. A teenage boy crossing the pavement behind me stumbles into the gutter.

I hurry into the shop before Miss El Paso can wreak any more havoc on the youth of Somerville.

Mel and her co-worker Steph are giggling at the poor teen's plight when I push through the front door. Mel gives me a hug and turns away from the window with a flip of the tiny skirt she's barely wearing and a flash of long, tanned legs above cherry red cowboy boots.

"That outfit's straight out of the Combat Zone," I tell her. "Poor kid nearly broke an ankle."

Mel laughs. She has a lovely warm laugh, and she laughs a lot, which is one of the reasons I like her so much. "Did you come to drag me outta here? Steph," she calls over her shoulder. "I might have to rescue a friend in dire need of retail therapy."

I shake my head. "I have lunch today with that cousin of mine."

"Poop. You mean I gotta stay here an' work? Horse poop."

I elbow her and glance meaningfully at a man who is poking around a rack of hand-woven scarves. He has two kids in tow. The little one can't be more than five and is looking at Mel with very round eyes.

"Whaaat?" she whispers. "I'm bein' good."

I elbow her again. "You are never good." Which is true. Mel looks human, her aura's human, she smells human, but she must be part fae, because she's one of the most mischievous people I've ever met. Another reason I like her so much. "Could you really cut out this afternoon?"

Mel nods. "I'm only coverin' until two. You got somethin' in mind?"

I don't, but Mel could rescue me from brunch if it becomes interminable, or indigestion-inducing. "Such a pretty day, we could go for a walk."

Mel rocks back and forth on the heels of her boots. "How 'bout you borrow Click's bike an' we head on out to Arlington?" In her west Texas drawl, 'borrow' comes out 'barra,' but I know what she means. I don't own a bike, so when Mel and I go bike-riding together, I need to borrow a bike. Mel likes to bike ride. Probably because it gives her a chance to show off her legs. Mel also likes to volunteer her boyfriend's bike, probably because of the amusement she gets out of watching me try to manage the bar.

"Doesn't Click need his bike?" Click works as a bike-messenger, so it's not that far-fetched a question.

Mel shakes her head, dark-brown curls bouncing under the Stetson. "He was inkin' last night."

Which means he'll be sleeping all day. No wonder Mel was willing to cover for her co-worker; her boyfriend will be comatose for hours. The tattoos Click creates are both art and magic, and they take a toll. Unless he sleeps for the better part of a day after each session, the intense concentration of his work, and the transfer of his living magic into the tattoo, ages Click. He's younger than me and Mel, but he looks ten years older.

"Deal. I'll just be over at Elliott's. Come rescue me after you get off?"

"Will do." Mel gives me cheek kisses and waves me out, causing another commotion on the sidewalk, where two young men are in the middle of lighting cigarettes. One nearly burns his long emo bangs off with his lighter. Mel really is a public menace.

I cross the square to Elliott's, turning my face up into the wind. The breeze carries a faint salt tang. It makes me think of open water, and toothy aquatic predators, and what lengths I want to go to prove my theory. I don't want to get further indebted to the fae. Nor do I want to ask Merida for help, given how she feels about shifters, although it might quash the irritating parental interest.

I don't have any answers, and I'm glad for the excuse to push the questions aside when a couple cuddling in front of the doorway to Elliott's break off their cinch and the woman turns to wave at me.

Shirri.

She knows what I look like from my profile on the clinic's website, but I don't have any pictures of her. I don't need any. I know immediately who she is. I know it in my blood, my bones. She's family. My mother's kith and kin. The briny smell of the ocean intensifies the closer I get to her, and I know I was right about the bento box.

When I'm a few steps away, Shirri spreads her arms. She reaches out to me, and after a second's hesitation, I let her grasp my shoulders and pull me close for air kisses. I don't like strangers touching me, but she is family, after all.

As she embraces me, I feel sand under my feet. Hear the roll of waves. Both Bo and Dead have said they could feel my magic at ten paces. Is this what it's like? I've never been able to sense someone else's power so strongly before.

When she lets me go, I take a step back and offer her the Tokai bag. She takes it with a huge grin and signals the man standing behind her with two fingers.

"Hello, Tsara," he says.

He has a deep, slow voice. Like molasses. Or the brush of dark fur over skin. Just like Jou's.

I force a smile and hold my hand out to him.

He shakes it, enclosing my hand gingerly in his, the way big men shake if they're afraid of crushing a woman's hand. He is a big guy, over six feet and probably over two hundred pounds, with the beginnings of a chubby hubby tummy. Nothing like the demon's washboard, so I can stop thinking about that any time. Behind round Harry Potter glasses, his brown eyes are keen. I catch a whiff of wet fur. His palm is slightly rough against mine. And I know what he is.

A bear shifter.

Manny's police friend said there are some bears with eight-inch jaws.

My thoughts must show on my face, because he drops my hand, lowers his head, and awkwardly holds out a little pink gift bag that bears the logo of one of Harvard Square's jewelry shops.

I take it and fumble for something to say.

Shirri glances between myself and the therian. "Tsara, this is my husband, Will."

"Nice to meet you, Will," I offer.

He nods, still not looking at me. Reaches out and pulls Shirri to his side. He kisses her temple. "I'll leave you girls to do your thing. See you later."

He releases her and ambles off down the sidewalk towards Harvard Square. Shirri runs her hand down his arm as he moves away, stands looking after him with her hand raised. Then she drops it to her side and turns to look at me. Her blue gaze has gone hard, and I shiver.

"I'm sorry," I say.

"I won't ask how you knew," she says. "Because my aunt says your father had the Sight, too. But he suffers enough from his curse, you know?"

I nod. I know shapeshifting is not an easy "gift" to bear. "I'm so sorry. It just took me by surprise. I didn't mean to embarrass him. And thank you so much for this." I lift the pink bag.

"Oh, it's nothing. Aunt P. said you might like it. It's not—what's in there isn't from that store, well, the frame is—oh, you'll see. Should we go and sit down before I make a complete ass of myself, and you run away?"

I laugh a little to break the tension. "I'm not going to run away." Although I am really counting on Mel to rescue me now. "But I am ready to eat."

Shirri's smile returns, and she holds open the restaurant door for me. Inside, it's darker than I remember; they've redecorated with a vaguely Mexican theme since the last time I ate here. Terra-cotta tiles on the floor, massive cacti in pots and booths around the edges of the room with red and beige patterned seat-covers. There's an open kitchen at the back of the restaurant with a wood-burning oven. The rich scent of smoke underlies the stronger tang of fried onion. A waitress in the same classic black and white outfit that I remember from my previous visit shows us to one of the booths. I bet she's glad the redecoration hasn't extended to the staff uniform.

I sit and take a minute to swap my sunglasses for my indoor glasses. They're purple and round and don't make me look nearly as cool as John Lennon, but the purple offsets the yellow of the lightning streaking in my pupils.

Shirri sits across from me and pushes the mini-cactus table topper to the side so she can set the Tokai bag between us. She pulls out the bento box with a soft exclamation. "Oh, it's lovely."

"I'm glad you like it."

Once she finishes admiring the bento box, I open the pink jewelry bag. Inside, neatly wrapped in matching pink tissue, there's a small, square silver frame, set with a rainbow of tiny crystals. The gems glimmer in the restaurant's low light, casting reflections across the black and white picture already in the frame. Two laughing adults and a dark-haired, chubby-cheeked toddler, clutching a stuffed bunny, which is now carefully wrapped in tissue paper inside a shoebox in my closet. I look at my own face: wide-eyed, smiling, happy. Blissfully unaware of what was going to happen to my world not so very long after this picture must have been taken.

I look up at Shirri and smile. "This is very precious, thank you. I only have a few pictures of my parents."

"Aunt P. said it was the only one she had other than their wedding. You must already have those."

I nod. A handful from their wedding. One of my mother in a cap and gown, glowing with pride at being the first woman in her family to graduate from college. One of my father when he was younger, trying desperately to grow a mustache that my Dala said never did fill in. Not much to memorialize the fifty years of their combined lives. And none of them with me.

I tuck the picture away before I get teary and pick up the menu.

"The pickled cactus is amazing," Shirri says, without looking at her own menu. I guess she comes here often, although she lives out near Alewife.

"Would you like to share it?" I ask. I've already decided on the *enchilada verde*, and cactus on top of enchilada is feeling like too much food. But I don't want to seem rude by ignoring her recommendation.

"That would be great. I should mention, the portions are huge. I always feel like a pig after eating here." She sighs and toys with her menu. I find it hard to believe she ever feels like a pig. In comparison to her bear of a husband, she's small and neat. Her glossy dark curls are the only vibrant thing about her; everything else is pastel, from her peaches-and-cream complexion to her rose-hued sweater to the French manicure she taps against the menu. I doubt she even bloats.

After the waitress returns to take our order—and concern over portion-size doesn't stop Shirri from ordering Steak *Adobo*, for which I silently applaud her—we spend a few minutes trying to figure out our exact relationship. I sketch a family tree on a napkin. After realizing that the lady she calls 'Aunt P.' is not actually her blood-relative but my great-aunt Paulina, we finally decide that we're fourth cousins, related through our great-great-grandparents, Ewa and Daniel Chmielewski.

"Aunt P. has always told stories about your parents, of course," Shirri says as she examines my branch of the family tree. "Particularly about the wedding. It sounds like a fairy tale."

I nod. I've heard that, too, and the pictures I have bear it out. My mother has that incandescent glow in every shot, and my father can hardly stop laughing even for the formal poses.

"Do you know what caused the split?" Shirri asks.

I shake my head. I don't know for certain, but I suspect that it was how my grandmother dealt with the grief of losing her only child so soon after losing her husband. She retreated into her family, and their traveling traditions, and took me with her.

"Were you never told anything about us?" Shirri persists.

I'm saved from an immediate answer by the arrival of the pickled cactus, which is delicious, although much spicier than anticipated. Shirri washes her spicy cactus down with a margarita, but margaritas hold really bad memories for me, so I have a Corona with lime. And studiously avoid thinking about how the demon liked his beer, his strong, golden throat working as he drank.

"I don't know much about your side of the family," I admit, once we're well into the appetizer. So Shirri tells me some of the family stories. About her great-grandfather Simon, who died on Christmas Eve in the Siege of Bastogne, leaving behind six sons and a legacy of bitter-sweet Christmases. One of his sons, Michal, ran away to New York to be a dancer, and had an affair with the burlesque queen, Gypsy Rose Lee. Then there was great-aunt Basia, whose poppy swirl cake won the grand prize at the 1973 Vermont State Fair, but she guarded the blue-ribbon recipe so jealously that it died with her. As we're finishing our entrees, she comes up to the current generation, and tells me about her twin, Tomas, who didn't walk until he was four, and whom Shirri carried piggy-back everywhere from the time she could toddle.

"Aunt P. says I put him down one night and refused to pick him up the next morning. I guess he got too heavy," Shirri laughs. I laugh with her, even as I feel a pang. I always wanted siblings. "Within a week, he was running around on his own," she continues. "I'm sure he could walk the whole time and just liked being carried around by his big sister."

"Are you still very close?" I ask.

Shirri shrugs. "I'm married now. And Tomas has a girlfriend. But I still see a lot of him. In fact, we're meeting up this afternoon."

I wonder if Tomas has the same instructions as Mel. "How did you meet Will?"

Shirri launches into the story of their courtship, which started inauspiciously when Will backed into her with his car. Her ankle was broken in the accident and Will was so guilt-stricken that he served as her chauffeur for six weeks until she came out of the cast. I refrain from asking whether she could have healed herself sooner. We order coffee while she's explaining that she refused to marry Will for over a year, until he let her see him shift.

"Did you always know?" I ask.

"Oh, yes, just like you did." Her bright smile turns a little brittle. "It's never bothered me."

"Shirri, I should explain—"

She waves her hand as the waitress sets down two Mexican coffees. I'm going to be too tipsy to go biking with Mel.

"I don't blame you," Shirri says. "I was brought up the same way. Told the same stories. That they're monsters. That they can't control the beast within." She stirs a sugar cube into her coffee. "It's all lies. Will's the most gentle, controlled man I've ever met. He'd never hurt me. He'd protect me with his last breath. I'll never find another man like him."

My own breath catches. Jou said the same thing to me once, almost word for word. Like I need that reminder after last night. I bend over my drink and take a deep sniff. Let the wonderful mix of coffee and Kahlua fill my lungs and chase out the demon's phantom. "I actually have nothing against therians. I'm friends with the Boston clans," I say, when I'm able to speak. "I'm guessing Will doesn't have a clan."

Shirri shakes her head. "His family has always stayed apart."

"Do they—" How can I phrase this? "Get along with other therians?"

"Will avoids them."

Including Sunday night between eleven and one a.m.? "A lycanthrope was killed recently. Near the Charles. He was my friend. The police said." I take a sip of coffee to fortify myself. "They said it might have been a bear attack."

"And you met Will and jumped to conclusions," she says.

There's no mistaking the bitterness now.

"I met Will and realized that I had narrowed my list of suspects too quickly."

Shirri lifts a dark eyebrow. "Your list of suspects?"

"I agreed to try to figure out who killed him."

"I thought you were a midwife," Shirri says.

"I am. But I'm also friends with the shifter's foster-mother, and she needs someone to figure out who killed her son."

Shirri stirs her coffee for a long moment, and I let her think. "I wouldn't swear it wasn't Will," she says finally. "If a werewolf attacked him, Will would defend himself."

"Would he kill to defend his territory?"

She stirs her coffee some more. "Maybe. Where did you say the werewolf was killed?"

"Near the Charles. Along the bike path."

Shirri shakes her head. "Not Will's territory. He's strictly west of Alewife."

The Silver Maple Forest is west of Alewife, and I go gathering around Little Pond quite a bit, particularly in summer. I'll keep an eye open for werebears in the future.

"Before I met Will, I had a theory about the killer." I explain my wereshark theory to Shirri, who listens with wide eyes. I guess she didn't take the same comparative mythology classes I took in college. "The problem I have now is proving it. I really don't want to do anything that leads to a confrontation with a wereshark."

"Understandably." Shirri finishes her coffee and sets her empty cup neatly in its saucer. "What about scrying for it?"

"Not my best thing." We haven't talked about magic, hers or mine. But it's been there, an undercurrent, through our entire conversation.

"Nor mine." She squares her slender shoulders. "Look, I'd like to help. Maybe we could scry for this thing together?"

"That would be awesome."

Shirri checks a dainty silver watch that circles her left wrist. "I'm supposed to meet Tomas and his girlfriend now. In fact, I'm going to be late. Then Will and I are driving out to the Berkshires to visit his parents. What's Monday like for you? I'm finished by four thirty."

"Good. Great. I'm free."

"My place or yours?"

"Mine." I want the power and protection of my circles if we're going to scry for something with that many teeth. I grab a fresh napkin and write down my address for Shirri. "I appreciate this," I say as I hand it to her.

She flashes me a smile without any bitterness. "You're welcome, cousin. It'll be nice to use my gift again. I don't get much chance these days."

Somehow, we didn't get around to what Shirri does. And when I hear a flurry near the door and a familiar west Texas accent, I realize we're not going to, at least not today. My rescue party has arrived.

I turn on the bench and wave Mel over to our table. She waves merrily back, breasts bouncing under her tee and jean jacket, before skipping across the restaurant. A goateed young man in the next booth drops his cutlery with a clatter. I drag Mel onto the bench beside me before she starts a riot.

"Mel, this is my fourth cousin, Shirri. Shirri, this is my barely dressed friend, Melanie Jean."

Shirri grins and shakes Mel's hand across the table. "I love your boots."

"Thanks! I'm gonna drag Tsara away for a bike ride to show 'em off." Mel elbows me.

"Uh, about that. I might have had too much to drink." I offer her my nearly finished boozy coffee.

Mel takes a sniff of the cup and shakes her head. "Alkie."

"Shirri's meeting her family down in Harvard Square now. Maybe we could all walk down together to stretch our legs?"

"Any chance to show off mah boots," Mel agrees.

Shirri waves over the waitress and we settle the bill, splitting it evenly, which I love her for. I don't have any fae blood – at least not that I know of – but people paying for me makes me uneasy. Like an obligation's been created.

Once we're out on the street, Mel links arms with me, and when Shirri doesn't object, loops her free arm through Shirri's. We walk arm-in-arm down Mass. Ave. towards Harvard Square. Giggling when Mel does a two-step to show off her boots. And the incredible shortness of her skirt.

"Aren't you chilly?" I ask, glancing pointedly at her bare legs.

Mel leans in and plants a wet kiss on my cheek. "How could I be chilly when I'm between two such hot tickets?"

I wipe my cheek and shake my head at her. "You're such a loon."

"You're gonna treat me to coffee anyway," she says. "That'll warm me right up."

"I am?" I don't really have any objection to another coffee, but I'm pretty sure I didn't offer.

"You are. Are we shoppin'?"

Shopping with Mel is lethal for my wallet. I don't know where Mel gets her money. Surely what she makes working part-time at Mudflat doesn't cover half of her nice apartment in Union Square, living expenses, and the several hundred dollars she drops whenever she gets too near a boutique.

"Sure," I say. "Window shopping."

"I need a new outfit for church tomorrow."

I elbow her. "You don't go to church."

"I need a new outfit *in case* I go to church tomorrow."

On Mel's far side, Shirri snickers. "Any excuse in a storm."

"Ooo, lady, you got my number," Mel says, then launches into an off-key rendition of Tommy Tutone's "8675309." Shirri and I chime in on the chorus. I'm sure anyone watching the three of us sway down the street, arm-in-arm, singing out of tune, will think we've had a very boozy brunch. But that's the way Mel is, with or without alcohol.

Harvard Square is crowded. In addition to the weekend shoppers and tourists, there are clots of students wearing hoodies and baggy shorts—which it's not *quite* warm enough for—on every street corner. Before we reach the madness of the Cambridge Street intersection, Shirri directs us into the Commons. We wind our way across the green, which is already quite green, even though there might be three more months of winter ahead. We weave around students lounging in the grass and a shirts versus skins game of frisbee that I have to literally drag Mel away from. At the Garden Street end of the Commons, Shirri spots Will. We join him in watching a couple playing ball with a slender silver shadow of a dog.

Shirri unlinks from Mel and tucks herself under Will's arm. He gives her a tender kiss that carries the promise of heat, and I feel my cheeks warm, remembering the demon's kisses.

Mel leans into me. "Gimme a smooch, I'm all jealous."

"Get real."

After Shirri comes up for air, she looks around and points at the couple playing with the dog. "That's my brother Tomas and his girl-friend, Holle."

I could have guessed who Tomas was without Shirri telling me. He looks very like his twin: taller, his dark curls cropped to the back of his neck, but recognizably related. I don't *feel* anything from him, though. Definitely not the tsunami that I got off Shirri. Magic runs in families, I was taught at Bevvy, but it doesn't always manifest in every family member. He might be a null.

His girlfriend crosses in front of him and grabs my attention. She's arresting. An inch or two taller than Tomas, even in her canvas flats, she must be six feet tall, and as whipcord slender as the dog she's playing with. Her hair's pulled back into a long, chestnut-brown braid, which glitters in the sunlight like it's been dusted with gold. Cheek-bones and wide, blue eyes that must have been imported directly from Scandinavia. She looks like a model.

As she twists to throw the ball the dog's brought her, the air around her shimmers. A furnace blast of heat, like August sun on asphalt. Her body shreds away and I see the bones beneath, blackened like they've been burned. Her skull grins at me, the fanged jaw unhinging. A torrent of black wings spills out, darkening the sky. They break over me in a wave of nightmares.

"Hey, you okay?" Mel shakes my arm.

I blink. The wings are gone. I've turned away from our small group and thrown my arm over my head. I'm shaking all over and my brunch is an inch away from making a dramatic reappearance.

I lower my arm and take several deep breaths. Push my glasses back up on my nose and hope that everyone's too blinded by the bright day to see the sparks jumping from my fingertips.

"Tsara, are you okay?" Mel's peering at me a little too closely, and there's something in her eyes that I don't like at all. Other than her relationship with Click, Mel is totally normal as far as I know, and I've loved having a "straight" friend who doesn't treat me like a freak.

"Too much sunshine," I say.

Mel wraps her arm around my shoulders. "Makes me sneeze. C'mon, let's get that coffee."

I nod. Turn to Shirri, who hasn't noticed my flinch, and say my goodbyes. Will solemnly offers me his hand and I shake it with as warm a smile as I can manage. I pass on meeting Tomas and his girl-friend, afraid of what else I might see.

As soon as Shirri releases me from her goodbye hug, Mel links arms with me and pulls me away. She pauses to admire another shirt-less guy showing off with a soccer ball, then drags me across Garden Street, around the Old Burial Ground and into the shops on Church Street. The vision of those burned bones, and the black wings, stays with me. Flickering behind my eyes. When Mel selects a sweater off a rack and a storm of black wings swirls out from between the clothes left on the rack, I startle.

I wrap my arms around myself as Mel replaces the sweater. "Wanna tell me about it?" she asks.

"Kinda," I say. "Kinda not. It's going to sound nuts. Much too nuts for a Saturday afternoon."

Mel nods. "Click tells me things, you know. And Ma Campbell didn't raise no dumb babies."

"I never thought you were dumb, Mel. I just—" I shrug. "I liked having a friend who was . . . uncomplicated."

"Uncomplicated? Ain't you been payin' attention? I got layers. Lots and lots of layers. Like an onion."

I snigger. "You are not quoting *Shrek*."

"I am. Donkey's almost as wise as Saint Tammy. I like this one better, don't you? Shows off mah titties." She selects an even tighter, shorter sweater than the first one. "Lemme buy something for you. It'll make you feel better."

I hold out my hands. "I don't need anything."

"It'll make *me* feel better. Something sexy. C'mon, sexy's next door."

I trail along helplessly as Mel buys the tiny sweater and drags me to the next boutique, which carries lingerie. She picks a wine-colored, lace-trimmed cami and tap-pants set that I can't ever see myself wearing, but they are very pretty, and since buying them seems to make Mel feel better, I don't object. I do insist on paying for the coffees, though, when we finally make it across the street to Starbucks.

Mel somehow secures a couch while I'm paying for the drinks. I find her sitting with her legs crossed, swinging one boot to the ubiquitous Shakira song playing on the café's speakers. She's showing so much leg that in another half-inch, I'll be able to tell the color of her panties. If she's wearing any. I set her decaf. skinny latte down on the table in front of her and spread the logo-ed napkin carefully over her knee.

"When you get arrested for solicitation, do not expect me to bail you out."

Mel grins, swings her foot so the napkin slides to the floor, and picks up her drink. I sit down next to her on the couch, close enough that no one else will hear me over the dull roar of conversation and the hiss of the coffee-machines. That's not close enough for Mel, who scoots across the couch until we're hip to hip and the brim of her hat shadows my face.

"Tell me all your dirty little secrets," she says, wiggling her eyebrows over the rim of her cup.

Not a chance. But I will tell her about my vision. "Do you know what precognition is?"

"Mmm-hmm. Seein' the future. Like them palm-reading gypsies at the fair."

Those palm-reading gypsies are probably related to me, but I know Mel doesn't mean anything by it, so I shrug that off. "I don't have much precognition, but I get flashes sometimes. A lot of those come true. I can't control them, and sometimes, they're really scary."

Truthfully, all of my visions have been horrifying. Like the one of Jou with a monster in his penis.

"What'd you see?" Mel asks.

"My cousin's girlfriend, the one playing with the dog? I saw her turn into a skeleton. A burned skeleton. She opened her mouth and creatures poured out. Black phantasms. They bring nightmares." Of which I already have too many. I close my eyes, push up my glasses and rub the bridge of my nose, which is aching along with the rest of my head. I pull the glasses firmly back into place before opening my eyes. "They came for me."

Mel isn't looking freaked out, for which I'm grateful. She's rubbing her chin and looking thoughtful. "No idea what it means?"

I shake my head. "I never do. I'm not a real precognitive. I don't understand what I see. Sometimes . . . a long time later . . . I figure it out. Not soon enough to do anything about it." Years after the Billy-goat's death, I finally figured out why I'd seen him lying in a boiling bath of bleach. The mistress who incited his wife's murderous wrath was a peroxide blonde. "And it could mean nothing. That close to the Old Burial Ground, I could just have been getting an echo."

Mel's eyes widen. "Why? Do you—see dead people?" she asks breathlessly, and I realize from her tone that she's teasing me.

I elbow her. "I'm looking at one right now."

She giggles. "Just don't bury me north of the Mason-Dixon line, darling. My poor Pappi'd be turning over in his grave."

"Your father is alive and well and cruising the Caribbean," I point out, a fact I know for certain because her parents sent me a postcard from St. Croix. The clinic's receptionist took one look at the palm trees and white sand and began lobbying for another vacation, even though she'd just had a week in Florida.

Mel grins and sips her coffee. "See, that wasn't so bad, was it?"

"No." It was surprisingly painless.

"Now tell me what's really bothering you. Couple of blackbirds ain't what's got Ole Stoic flapping."

I shake my head at her. Click nick-named me "Stoic Tsara" after my first tattooing session with him, during which I didn't make a sound even though he worked on me for more than four hours. After the pain of my break-up with Jou, having a needle stuck in me a few thousand times just didn't compare. "It's just been a crap week, with my friend's funeral and everything."

Mel sneezes dramatically. "I call bullshit."

"Wow, Miss Sensitivity."

"Look, I feel bad for your friend's family an' all, but you've known about that poor boy for a week. You weren't this rattled after you first heard about it. So, tell me what's really eatin' you."

Sharing is not my best thing. And the last person I really shared with invaded my house, tried to entrap my demon-lover and stood by while a psychopath carved my chest to ribbons. But that's something I'll never have to worry about with Mel. She'd jump on the psychopath's back and ride him like a bronco while sticking her thumbs in his eyes. Mel's a fierce friend, and I'm so very, very glad she's *my* friend.

"Put your coffee down for a second."

"Why?" she asks warily.

"Because I'm going to hug you and I don't want to ruin what little you're wearing."

"Aww." She sets her coffee down on the table and opens her arms. "Gimme some of that hot sugar."

I hug her briefly and push her away when she tries to pull me on top of her. "Would you stop?"

She winks and picks up her coffee. "Now you gonna tell me?"

"Yes." I tell her what I can. I leave out the part about Jou being a demon. As I have with everyone, even Lin. Because there are some things I can't be forgiven. But I tell her everything else about him, everything she doesn't already know, since she knows I broke up with someone before Samhain. I tell her everything, right up to last night's dream and Lin's well-meaning but totally misguided intervention this morning, which is still galling me like a stone in my shoe. "I mean, I get that I haven't been Miss Mary Sunshine for the last week or two, but does she really feel she needs to intervene like I'm some type of addict?"

"You ain't gonna like this," Mel says slowly.

"What?" I wipe my mouth, which feels a little sticky because I've been talking for so long. Do I have that gross coffee-rime in the corners of my mouth? I hope not.

"I gotta agree with her."

"Oh, come on, Mel. I'm not going to call him. Not after all this time. How pathetic and desperate does that sound?"

"I don't know. How pathetic and desperate does it sound?"

"A lot!"

"Well, you're pathetic and desperate, which we all already knew."

"Thank you so much."

"I mean it, hon. This ain't about him. It's about you. Don't matter if you sound pathetic and desperate. Don't matter if he really has forgotten about you and moved on. What matters is that it ain't over for you yet. You haven't found, what'd you call it? Closure. You need to get you some closure."

Do I? Maybe I do. I've never felt that it was finished. I understood Ana's need for closure after Toby's death, but maybe I never understood my own.

"So, I just call him up and say, 'I had this dream where you forgave me for the way I dumped you, so can we talk 'cause I need a little closure'?"

"Mmm, maybe a little more subtle."

"I'm open to suggestions."

"How 'bout you wear the pretty panties we just bought and invite him over for coffee?"

"How is that subtle?"

"It ain't a bra and suspenders."

"Very subtle."

"Okay, forget subtle. Call him. How d'you know that dream wasn't for real?"

"I don't," I admit. "But I also don't know if the dreams after we broke up weren't for real. He wasn't . . . he wasn't very happy with me in those."

"That was three months ago."

"He was really beyond not happy with me." In fact, most of the dreams ended with him murdering me in some really gruesome way.

"Things change, darlin'. How'd he seem last night?"

Loving. Maybe that's why it's fucked me up so badly. I could cope with him being murderous. I could cope with him cutting off contact. I deserved all of that. I don't deserve to be forgiven. I don't deserve to have him hold me to that wonderful, wide, warm chest and tell me that we can be together—

My train of thought is broken by Mel taking my coffee cup out of my hand and clasping my hands in hers. "Did he use the magic words?"

Yes. All of them.

"Are you sure you're not psychic?" I ask.

"Your face is such an open book. That's how I could tell you were sufferin' worse than a hound dog with fleas."

I squeeze her hands. "Thanks, Mel. I don't usually, you know—"

"Spill the beans? I know, darlin', do ever I know. Safest place for a secret?" She leans forward so the brim of her Stetson brushes my forehead. "Right in this little pea brain here."

"Thank you. I think."

"My pleasure. Now what're you doing tonight?"

"Seeing a movie and eating too much popcorn?"

"Don't think so."

I sigh. "Calling Jou, then."

"That's right. But first we need to do some caffeine-fueled ruination of our credit cards."

# CHAPTER 6

return home without making too much of a dent in my credit line, which is still suffering after the clinic's disastrous last quarter. The maroon lingerie goes in my dresser. I can't see myself wearing it. Ever. Mel talked me into a new pair of jeans, since the ones I'm wearing are, according to Mel, hanging off me "like a church dress after Lent." I avoid looking at the tag when I tug it off. I haven't been a size four since I was seventeen. I flick off the closet light and close the door without looking at the mirror mounted on it.

I should try to *reach* Jou now. Right now. Before I lose my nerve. Instead, I put it off as long as I can. I rake up the leaves in the yard. Spread more mulch under my trees. Clean the whole house by hand, including degreasing the oven. I shower. Make more dinner than I'll ever eat. I put on Suzanne Vega while the chicken's roasting to remind me that love is messy and horrible and can break me. It's broken me before. So obviously the thing to do is invite what broke me the last time back into my life.

He said he forgives me. He said we could heal together.

I need that so much.

When I've finished the dinner that I barely tasted, washed up and brewed a pot of decaf mocha, I settle on the couch. I pull myself into lotus position, ignoring the faint protest of my knees, stiff from the cleaning. I center myself, hold the warm cup in my hands, and inhale its fragrant steam. Finally, when my mind is still, I *call*.

*Jou?*

I don't dare say his full name. His true name. Which he told me after I banished him. Even after I told him I didn't want to know it. He told me anyway and now it sits in my mind like a lead weight. I'm afraid of using it. Afraid of what else's attention I might attract. But I hope he'll hear me anyway.

When he doesn't respond, I exert more of my will, pushing at the boundaries between his mind and mine, between his world and mine. A small shove, and those boundaries rip like tissue paper. Has the distance between our minds always been so small?

I feel him stir inside my head.

I double over as pain spears through me. My coffee cup clatters to the floor. I shiver uncontrollably at the shock of it, the pain spreading in and out until there's nothing left of me but unbearable, unendurable ache. I clutch at my shoulders, where hard burning spikes have driven all the way through my bones.

There's nothing there. I'm not bleeding. It's not my pain.

It's his.

I pull back a little, creating some distance between our minds, and feel his pain recede.

When I can breathe again, I *reach* for him.

*Jou, what happened?*

*Mmm.*

He sounds extremely sleepy inside my head. Then he shifts and a fresh wave of pain rolls through him, through me. And I realize he wasn't sleeping. He was unconscious.

*How bad are you hurt?* I ask.

*I'm okay*, he thinks slowly. So slowly.

*You're* not *okay*. So not okay. I had no idea he could be so hurt. *I can heal you.*

*Yeah, you can.* He's quiet for a long time. Finally, heavily, he thinks. *But I don't want you to.*

*Jou!*

*I can't read you right now, sweetness. I can't tell if you're ready.*

Ready? Ready for what?

*Jou, let me heal you.*

No.

*Please, Jou.* His injury has brought everything into sharp focus. Whatever doubts I'm harboring about whether we could really be together, whatever indecision was tugging at me, feeling him hurt so badly has swept all that away. I never want him to be injured and alone. *Please. I can't leave you so hurt, not when I can heal you. Tell me where you are, and I'll come to you.*

Somehow, although I have no idea how.

*It's too dangerous for you here. I'll come to you. Summon me.* His thought has a megaton weight behind it. The finality of fate. *If you really mean it, summon me.*

I will. I'll do it now.

I feel a thread of brightness snake its way through the red haze of his pain. *Summon me naked.*

I shake my head, although I know he can't see it. *You are such a demon.*

*Yeah, I am,* he thinks wearily. *Remember that before you summon me.*

He closes the connection between our minds. Or lapses back into unconsciousness. I'm not sure. But that thought spurs me as I jump off the couch, ignoring the spilled coffee and run out my back door to my hearth room.

———

My hearth room stands within a circle of four trees. Oak, ash, holly, and rowan. Huge, mature trees. Witch trees. They create a pocket dimension in my backyard, which cradles my hearth room. I didn't even know my hearth room wasn't part of the normal world until I ripped through the planes when I banished Jou. I saw far, far too much when I tore aside the Veil. Things I didn't even register at the time, so involved in my battle of wills with the demon. Images my mind wasn't meant to hold; new ones keep popping up in my nightmares. But the most vivid, the one that comes back to me most often, was the Great

Tree spreading away from my hearth room, connecting it to all the other places and times cradled in Yggdrasil's branches.

Sometimes that image can make my hold on reality a little shaky.

But right now, I'm counting on it, and being able to walk those branches again, so I can reach Jou. He needs me. He's so hurt. He's always seemed indestructible. Ancient and powerful beyond anything I'd encountered before. Feeling him so hurt has shaken me, but also filled me with resolve. I *will* summon him back to me, and I *will* heal him. No matter what the cost.

I cross my hearth room at a run. Beneath my bare feet, my three circles flare as I cross them. The outer circle of dirt. The pentacle of river stones. The inner circle of sand. I leave Earth, Water and Fire swirling behind me as I stop in front of my cauldron.

There's nothing in my cauldron and no fire laid under it. But I don't need recipes or rituals to reach Jou. Just raw power. The core of my Elements. The universe's own lifeblood. I'm afraid to draw on such untamed, uncontrollable magic for anything but this. Jou's always pushed me right to the edge. When it came down to him or me, I opened myself to that vast current and let it pour through me. I know what it is, and what it can do.

And what I can do with it.

I lift my hands, and a whirlwind rises above my cauldron. *Air*. My second Element, and the one with which I'm still not entirely confident, after so many years of thinking of myself as an Earth witch. But it comes more and more easily every time I *call*, and before I even consciously think about it, the whirlwind throws itself outward, into the cluster of Elements I've already called.

My hearth room explodes. A firestorm, a dust devil, a waterspout. Air propels the other Elements into a violent maelstrom: a tornado of flame, magma and burning gas that twists and torques around me as I stand in its eye. Beneath my feet, the ley line—or more properly, the World Tree's branch—that runs under my hearth room, incandesces, shooting white light up into the maelstrom. Lightning crashes from the cloudless black sky. I lift my hands to the elemental power swirling around me, gather it, and pull my hands apart to rend the Veil that separates Jou's plane from mine.

A ring of fire forms in the air in front of me, within the eye of the burning tornado. Circles within circles. Lightning spears through the blackness at the center of the Hellhole. My power reaches deep into his plane, following those fingers of white light. I rake the ether, twisting my hands as I feel along the branches of the Tree that I can see in my mind's eye, blood-red twigs winding like capillaries through Space and Time. My power snags on a familiar solidity. A will that has as much weight as a star, and bends everything around it. I clutch at him, contracting my hands into fists, and pull him to me.

"Jouvart D'Asmodei," I whisper, too quietly to be heard over the roar of the maelstrom, but I don't need to be heard. I've Summoned him.

There's a reverberation like a great bell being struck. The ground shivers, knocking me to my knees, and kneeling, I watch Jou rise from the Hellhole in an envelope of flame.

Huge crimson wings cup his body. Like an angel's wings. Only these wings burn with Hellfire, and as he lifts his head to the lightning-split sky, skyfire, firelight, leylight, all gleam on the massive black horns that curve above his head. Neon blue blasts from his eyes, brighter than the sun, dimming all the other lights filling my hearth room to shadows.

Then he collapses onto the hard-packed ground. The light dies. The tornado whirls once before dissipating into puffs of dust. The Hellhole closes with a snap and the faint whiff of sulfur and then there's nothing but moonlight and the soft slough of the night breeze through my trees.

Jou's back heaves as he tries to lift himself onto his forearms.

There's something very, very wrong.

His body is warping, bubbling, twisting. The crimson wings and his horns have disappeared, the way his demonic attributes do when he takes human form. But I can still see his tail lashing between his legs as he struggles. His forearms are covered with black spines that sink into his skin as I watch, then rise again to gouge the sand of my inner circle. Jou pulls himself forward a few inches before collapsing onto his back.

I gasp, and gag, when I see the ruin of his chest.

His skin is stretched tight over sinew and bone, as though he's been starving for months. Four huge holes puncture the ash-gray flesh. There are two under his shoulders, through the meat of his pectoral muscles. Two more just above his pelvis, where he used to have a carved six-pack. The holes are so big I could stick my fist into each one. They're full of raw flesh and black ichor. More ichor runs from Jou's mouth and eyes.

I slide across the dirt, reach for him, and catch his wrists when he tries to push me away. I can close my fingers around his wrists, he's so wasted. What happened to him?

*Send me back, sweetness,* he groans into my mind. *I can't hold the glove.*

"Shh, shh."

I call Earth's Blood. It's easier the second time. Not because the healing won't be as deep, but because I know what it demands of me now. I force my heart to keep beating as that thick sludge floods through my veins.

I run my hands down Jou's forearms, smoothing the quivering spines under a layer of goo. His spines feel as soft as a baby hedgehog's quills under my palms. I push them gently back into his flesh and focus on helping him shape his human form. The golden skin over thick muscle. I run my hands up over his biceps, feeling dry gashes and ichor-filled lesions close under my palms, smothered under a layer of healing magic. When I spread Earth's Blood over his collar and up his corded neck, he sighs. I smooth it over his bald, burned scalp and feel the bristle of hair under my palm. I rub my thumb along his jaw, where there's a wound so deep I can see exposed, yellow bone. I work goo into the wound and feel it fill under the pad of my thumb.

When I look back into his face, it's no longer contorted with pain. His eyes, dark as the sky above us, hold mine.

*Hey, sweetness,* he says into my mind.

*Stay with me. I've still got some work to do here.*

*Take as long as you need, but would you mind doing my dick next? I kinda miss it.*

I squeeze my eyes closed for a second. Then force myself to look. The huge puncture wounds—which are even more gruesome up close—caught my attention. I didn't notice the blackened stump at his groin. I reach down blindly and close my hand around it. Gently slide my hand up and down the shortened shaft until I feel it lengthen.

*Mmm,* he thinks. *Don't stop.*

*Jou, honestly.*

He chuckles into my head. *Some things don't change.*

Some do, and I'm not going to forget the burning wings that lifted him back into my world. He told me fire demons don't have wings, after I saw him with wings in a very terrible vision. So, either he was lying to me then, which I don't think he was, or he's grown a pair since I last saw him.

But now's not the time to ask. Not when he's so hurt. I can feel him relaxing with each pass of my hands. As I heal his true form and he's able to generate more of the protective guise that helps him withstand the alien environment of my world. But I know I still have to turn to those four terrible punctures. And I know that Earth's Blood might not be enough.

When his penis feels normal—well, normal for Jou—I slip my hand underneath to coat his balls and find something else that's new. A sharp spine that protrudes from the skin between his testes.

"Jou, is this . . . a piercing?" I ask incredulously.

"No," he grunts. "It's a thorn. I still got a couple in me. You mind taking it out? Real careful. They're barbed."

I do gag then and have to slap my gooey hand over my mouth to keep from lurping up that good roast chicken. I swallow hard, until I've got control of my stomach, then feel carefully around his sac until I find the contours of the thorn. It's as long and thick as my pinkie finger. Gritting my teeth, feeling the prickling rush in my eyes, I push the thorn through his scrotum and throw it to the side, before drenching the damage I've done with Earth's Blood.

Jou reaches up and brushes his fingertips across my cheek. *Thanks, sweetness.*

*You're welcome. Where are the others, Jou?*

*In my back. Don't worry about them. I'll push them out myself. You know what you gotta do next.*

I do. I've been avoiding it, distracting myself with lesser injuries, but I know I have to turn back to those four terrible holes.

I take a firmer hold on my courage and turn so I'm kneeling next to him. Then I finally take a close look at the puncture under his left shoulder.

I have a decent amount of experience with wounds. Boston's therians used to come to me before the clans declared Mass. General a safe harbor. I've seen bites that could have been from a saber-tooth tiger, slashes that look like they were made by Wolverine. But I have trouble looking at Jou's wounds. They remind me of the pictures I've seen of landmine injuries. My eyes try to skitter away, and when I force myself to look, my mind refuses to process what I'm seeing. There's so much damage. They're explosions in his flesh. The skin around them is torn, peeling. Black striations weave outward from the wounds, which in a human would be blood poisoning. I don't know if it is in a demon, but it doesn't look good. The holes themselves—so big I could stick my whole fist into them—are filled with raw meat and bits of broken bone. I swallow hard and do my best not to think of hamburger. Black ichor oozes from that awful raw meat. It looks like he's decaying right in front of me. Although the flesh inside the wounds is too swollen for me to see, I have a terrible fear that the wounds go straight through him.

I swallow hard and put my palm flat over the wound below his left shoulder. Even as I begin pouring Earth's Blood into the wound, I know it's not going to be enough. I can feel the wound's deep malice. It pushes back against me, snarling into my mind. Whatever made this wound wasn't steel or iron, tooth or claw. It was something else. Something that hates intensely. Something designed to cause pain beyond imagining, beyond bearing.

Something with barbed thorns.

I see it in my mind's eye. A great tree, twisted, blackened, leafless. Its grasping branches are covered in thorns, some tiny, like the one I pulled from Jou's scrotum, some thicker than Jou's thigh. They curve, clustered and horned, inflicting the maximum amount of pain on anything unfortunate enough to be impaled on them.

In my mind's eye, I see Jou impaled, pinioned through groin and shoulder, writhing, screaming soundlessly because agony has robbed him of his voice.

I rise and stand over Jou, without knowing why or what I'm doing. I just need to protect him. I reach out with my magic and grasp the thorn I tossed aside. It rises from the dirt to my outstretched hand. I close my hand into a fist, letting the thorn bite deep into my own flesh. My blood mingles with the Earth's Blood caking my palm as I grip the thorn. I reach out with my bleeding hand, feeling my way from this little piece back to its source. Pushing my way back through the planes. I don't tear open the Veil this time. I don't need to. Everything's connected, and the thorn leads me straight back to the Tree.

I lift my other hand and *call* lightning.

*Sweetness, what're you doin'?*

I throw my mind wide to him and let him see as I call bolt after bolt of skyfire down on that monstrosity and burn it to ash.

When there's nothing left but embers, I open my hand and drop the thorn. With the last bolt, I incinerate it.

I drop back onto my knees over Jou. He's looking up at me, propped on his elbows. I can see the white edge of a smile peeking through the goo caking his mouth.

"I've said it before, sweetness, but I'll say it again. Remind me not to really piss you off."

I shake my head at him and get back to healing him.

Without the Tree's malice fighting me, the healing is easier. I take it slow, starting from the inside and making sure I reknit every strand of muscle, rejoin every blood vessel, before I close the wound. I'm aware of Jou as I straddle him. As I Work, he rebuilds his human form. Mounds of muscle push up from the bones I've healed. His mottled skin warms to its usual dark gold. A crimson bristle spreads over his scalp. His breathing steadies, and he takes several deep breaths, his chest lifting under me as I lean over him to reach the hole in his right shoulder.

"Mmm, that's better," he murmurs.

I look down at him. There's still strain around his eyes and mouth, but it's so much less. I lean in and brush my lips across his, tasting the gritty, treacle-y sweetness of the Earth's Blood I've smeared all over both of us.

"Mmm, much better." He wraps one arm around me, and I feel the strength in it again. "You know what would really make me feel better?"

"I have no idea," I say, but I know, of course. The same thing he's always wanted from me.

What's new is that I'm fine with it.

I settle a little harder across his thighs. Wriggle, so I grind his erection between us. Jou groans and collapses back onto the dirt. His hands find my hips. He pulls me more firmly down on him and slides his fingertips under the edge of my sweatshirt until he finds skin.

"Take this off, sweetness."

I trail my hands down his chest, to the holes in his lower abdomen, and lean in, pushing Earth's Blood in pulsing beats into the holes in his flesh.

"Burn it," I tell him. They're old sweats that I wear when I'm cleaning the house, and I'll never get the goo out of them. But more than that, I want to feel the lick of his magic across my skin.

"You do, huh?" he asks, taking that thought from my mind.

I do.

I lean over him, so we're nose to nose, and look into his eyes. "I want everything. Everything I was so stupidly afraid of last time. I was so stupid, Jou. I was afraid of all the wrong things. I thought you were here to hurt me, to take my life away. Then I sent you back and my world went dark. I couldn't even find any happiness in Christmas. I thought I'd be safe with you gone, but all I was, was sad and empty and lost."

He blinks up at me. "Sweetness." He reaches up and cups my face. Runs his fingers through the goo-smeared strands of my bangs. "I didn't expect any of that. I guess we got a few things to say to each other."

"A few," I agree. "But not right now."

He pulls me down for a soft, sweet kiss. "No, not right now."

When he lets me up for air, I say, "So for now, could you just burn off my clothes?"

He nods. Heat slips from his hand at my waist, sliding over my skin like the touch of his tongue: warm and moist and tickling. Sparks leap from my skin, following the blue edge of fire spreading up my back, down over my thighs. The scent of our mingled magic, cinnamon and woodsmoke, ginger and mistletoe, rises and swirls around us in the cool night air. I should grow cold, as he bares my skin. Instead, the tickling, tummy-tightening sensation of his magic running all over my body warms me right down to my marrow.

I sigh and arch my back as I feel the ashes of my sweats fall off my wrists and calves. Jou draws me back down for another kiss.

"One thing I want to say now," he murmurs against my lips. "I missed you every second I was gone." He runs his hand down my side, slips it between our bodies, and guides himself up into me. "Missed this."

"More than breathing." I nod, rubbing my forehead up and down. His skin is warm against mine, but not the silky, fireside heat it should have. He still needs healing, and I know exactly how to heal him.

————

Afterwards, a very long time afterwards, I fall asleep lying on top of him.

When I wake, crawling slowly back up to consciousness, there's a snowy pillow under my cheek instead of his shoulder. "Jou?"

"Mmm?" He adjusts me in his arms and rubs his chin in my hair.

"How did we get in my bed?"

"I carried you. Thought you were awake."

I don't remember. I run my hand down his chest. It's smooth, silky, fever hot. I sigh with relief and snuggle closer. "You're warm again. How are you feeling?"

"Yeah. Good. Really good. Gotta hand it to you, sweetness. You heal me like no one else." He stretches against me. "Was that mud you were coverin' me with?"

"Earth's Blood." Where did it all go? I couldn't have slept through him showering it off us. "I only just learned how to call it, when I healed Izzy."

"He get sick? I musta been pullin' too hard on him."

"His scales started peeling off. It was awful."

"Mmm, yeah, that was probably me." Jou slides his arm behind his head. His dreadlocks haven't grown back; he just has a crimson crew cut, but the loss doesn't seem to be bothering him. "I'll have to make it up to him."

"Ice cream," I say. "He's a complete addict. They all are. I can't keep a tub overnight in the freezer anymore."

"Fuckin' Ben and Jerry. Told you they need a franchise down below."

"Actually, Izzy prefers Häagen Dazs."

"Traitor." Jou chuckles. Then he gives a heavy sigh. "You don't got any ice cream? I'd love some ice cream. Feels like I haven't tasted human food in a century."

"They haven't found my secret stash in the basement."

"Sneaky," says Jou.

"*Wiley*," I correct him. "I have to be when I'm living with ice cream-guzzling salamanders."

"Sorry I had to leave them with you, sweetness. Home ain't safe, or it wasn't. Probably fine now if you want me to send 'em back."

Do I?

"Um, no, I've gotten used to them. I'd miss them if you sent them home now."

"Good. I like havin' 'em around, too."

"So, you're, uh, staying?" I ask hesitantly.

Jou grins, his white teeth flashing in the darkness. "Definitely. Unless you banish me again."

"No . . . I wouldn't . . . Jou are you *teasing* me?" I ask disbelievingly. This is such a raw nerve. Isn't it for him?

His chuckle fills the warm darkness, as thick and rich as melted chocolate. "Relax, sweetness. Everything's gonna be okay this time. Especially if you've got ice cream."

# CHAPTER 7

ou does midnight snacks like no one I've ever known. While I'm in the bathroom cleaning up, Jou locates my ice cream stash, pops popcorn, makes chocolate sauce for the ice cream and toffee sauce for the popcorn, and, because Jou can't do anything by halves, he toasts peanuts and cashews, salts them and mixes them with the popcorn.

I stand over the feast, shaking my head in amazement, before I offer Jou a terry-cloth robe and sit down on the couch to dig in.

Jou shrugs the robe over a pair of dark, loose pajama pants. He found his clothes, I see. They're still all in the dresser drawer he appropriated while he was here last time. I should have gotten rid of them, but I couldn't bring myself to.

"You didn't have this before," he says, sitting down next to me and setting two mugs of hot chocolate topped with whipped cream on the table. Where did he get whipped cream?

"The robe? I bought it in the Christmas sales," I tell him.

"Christmas . . . when was that?"

He doesn't have a good sense of human time. I should have remembered. "Almost two weeks ago."

"I musta been gone for a while by then."

"Three months." I shrug. "I'm an idiot."

I certainly felt like an idiot when I hung it on the back of my bathroom door. And watched it hang there, unused.

The corner of his mouth kicks up. "Not an idiot. An optimist. I've always liked that about humans. Not a lot of optimism in Hell."

"There's probably a reason for that," I say, munching down a handful of nutty toffee popcorn while I pour chocolate sauce over two scoops of *Dulce de leche*. I won't be fitting into those size four jeans tomorrow, and I'm totally fine with that.

"Probably," Jou admits. "All the screaming. Makes it hard to look on the bright side of life."

I lift an eyebrow at him. "Are you quoting *Monty Python*?"

He grins before stuffing his own handful of popcorn into his mouth. When he can speak again, he says, "One of the junkies they fed me in New York was a huge fan. He musta seen *Life of Brian* fifty times. Fuckin' hilarious. I took it outta his memories. Kept me laughin' for days while those fuckers danced around, shakin' their beads at me an' chantin'. Really pissed them off."

"This is the coven that entrapped you in New York. The Wolfshook? I read about them." I researched Jou's history during those ugly days when I couldn't do magic. When I could drag myself out of bed. Access to a millennium of eldritch records I'd always understood were lost—records I found carefully preserved on microfiche in the archives of Timmi's Museum—made it easy. Timmi herself made it easy. Bugs weren't the only thing she categorized. She assembled dossiers on all of the demons known to be summoned by Solomon's Seal. Jou's dossier was the first in the pile, and the information she'd amassed about him was impressive.

Including the information that she'd amassed about him and me.

If I felt bad about lying to the Museum staff about my relationship with Timmi, if I felt any guilt about covering up her death and inventing a story about how she asked me to continue her research, all of that evaporated when I opened that dossier and found pictures of me and Jou. Sitting together on a duck boat. Walking together along Boylston Street. Those photos were taken days before I even met

Timmi. They were the first thing I burned when I cleaned out her office.

She lied to me from minute one.

"I couldn't find anything about how you escaped them."

Jou chews before saying, "You won't like the answer, and no, it ain't the same."

I shudder, because that tells me everything I need to know.

"What'd I just say? It's not the same."

"You seduced one of them, right? You told her you loved her and begged her to set you free."

"Him. You know I don't discriminate the way humans do. An' I never even told him I liked him. 'Cause I didn't. He was a hypocritical prick. An' he was doin' all the beggin'. But I did seduce him, that I'll admit."

Because he's a lust demon and that's what he does. "What happened to him?"

"He's still alive. Art dealer in New York. Fancy showroom. Nice car. Nice yacht. Nice family in the Hamptons. Two or three kids. I don't keep track. Couple of well-built boys in New York and Miami he sees when he's not playin' family man. Everythin' his little heart desired."

"And when he dies, you get his soul," I say.

"His and the first-born of his blood for the next six generations." At my gasp, he says, "They had me encircled for *years*, sweetness. Can't tell you how hungry I was. I spared him and a couple others, but they owed me. Big time."

"You-you can't," I wheeze, choking on my popcorn. Jou thumps me on the back to clear my windpipe. "You can't damn an entire bloodline!"

Jou props his feet on the coffee table, away from the food, and crosses his ankles. "Sure I can. They'll get a choice, just like everyone else. But the taint's in their blood. Pretty much guarantees which way they'll choose."

Dear God. Is that what's wrong with me?

"Is my bloodline tainted?"

That would explain so much.

Jou growls. "Choosin' to be with me ain't wrong."

Oops.

I take a long swallow of my hot chocolate before I try to fix my bungle. "I didn't mean it like that. Please, Jou?"

Jou tilts his head to one side. Watches me for a moment. "Don't think so," he says finally. "I'm drawn to you, but I think that's just you."

"One of my great-aunts said she dealt with a demon. She didn't tell me how she banished it. Could she have made a deal that's somehow carried down through the generations?"

"This one of your ghosts?"

I nod before taking another handful of popcorn.

"Naw. I'm not sure what a great-aunt is to you humans, but the bloodline needs to be direct. Father to son. Mother to daughter. Also, if she'd traded her soul, she wouldn't be around to talk to you now. Gotta have a soul left to be a ghost."

I didn't know that. I eat a spoonful of ice cream as I mull it over. "Things without souls can't be ghosts?"

"You ever met any demon ghosts?"

No, but my experience of demons is limited. "I've met a cat ghost. And possibly a raccoon ghost, or it might have just been albino and rabid."

Jou chuckles. "Animals got souls. Funny-tastin', but some lemures can feed off 'em. I couldn't. Always had to go for humans."

"Because only humans can feel lust? Some animals go into heat."

Jou shrugs. "Dunnow. All I know is that tryin' to feed off 'em didn't get me anywhere." He spoons up his own ice cream. "This is better'n I remembered."

It is good. The perfect balance of salty and sweet. But it's more than that. Jou's sitting on my couch. Safe. Healed. Relaxed. We're not throwing razor-edged words at each other. In fact, I'm not sure we've ever been this comfortable together. I reach out, take his toffee-sticky hand and squeeze his fingers.

He squeezes back. "I heard that."

"I didn't say anything," I say, but I feel a silly grin spread across my face.

"You thought it plenty loud. This feels pretty damn good to me, too, sweetness."

When we've eaten as much sugar as we can stomach, we waddle back upstairs and crawl into my bed. I expect Jou to want more sex, but he surprises me. "We got plenty of time for that," he tells me as he lies back in the pillows and holds out his arm. "You got anywhere you need to be in the morning?"

"No," I say, snuggling against his side and feeling the wonderful warmth of his body sink deep into me. Sunday's my day off. I never plan anything beyond which book I'm going to curl up with.

"Then we'll wait until we're both not too full to enjoy it." He catches my hand with his and laces our fingers together. Squeezes. Then he trails his fingertips down my wrist, tracing the crisscrossed scars until he reaches the edge of my nearly finished tattoo. "Tell me 'bout this."

"If you'll tell me what happened to you. In my dream—"

"Wasn't a dream," he insists. "But I know what you're gettin' at. I was whole an' healthy. I think that's 'cause you hadn't summoned me. You saw what you expected to see. I couldn't see your tattoo, although I could see your hair, but that's changed since you sent me back. Once you summoned me, I couldn't just see your tattoo, I could feel it."

"What does it feel like?" I ask, curious.

"Like comin' home. Except it's kinda fuzzy. Your magic's usually more solid."

"It's not quite finished. I need another session. It's a protective charm. When I cross my arms in front of me, it'll close the circle. I'll be protected by nothing more than my skin."

Jou strokes the soft splashes of color that wrap around my forearm. "And it's pretty. I don't go much for humans markin' up their skin. But I like this."

"I'll introduce you to Click. He's the tattoo artist who's been doing it. He's a genius."

"Ink mage, like those scribblers in China. Only he uses skin instead of parchment." Jou rolls me over and examines the tattoo as it crosses my back. I feel his warm breath on my skin before he leans in and licks a line across my ribs. I giggle at the sensation. "Mmm, tasty. He mighta done the work, but this is your magic. I can taste it."

"I've been casting the charms that he seals into my skin."

"I like it. Think you could do one for me? I'd like t'carry the taste of you on my skin."

"Sure, but it's taken Click weeks to do mine."

"I'm not goin' anywhere." He licks the small of my back. "Delicious."

I giggle. "My skin or the charm?"

"Both. Mmm." He rolls me over and settles me against his side. "What made you thinka this?"

I shrug. "Since Thanksgiving I've had a really bad feeling. Like something's watching me. I wanted protection that I could use any time, any place, without having to cast a circle or cut myself."

"Any idea what it is?"

I shake my head against his shoulder. "Just a bad feeling. It could be anything. You know I'm a lousy precognitive."

Jou feathers his fingers through my hair, strokes it off my temple, and winds the long strands of my bangs around his forefinger. "What's it feel like?"

"Nothing specific. A shadow." I remember all the times I've felt it, so Jou can see my memories. Sitting alone in my office at night and feeling like the window behind me had grown eyes. Walking up Somerville Ave with a bag of Christmas shopping and hearing whispering in the shadows between streetlights. Standing on one side of my closed front door and feeling the vibration of claws scraping down the other side. "Nothing tangible. Just a feeling."

"Somethin's stalking you."

"Honestly, I thought it was a demon. I thought that was why all these imps have been targeting me. They were feeling me out for something bigger."

Jou grunts. "If so, they're in for a nasty surprise. I'll eat them for fuckin' breakfast."

I snuggle tighter to him. For all that he's the thing that used to scare me the most, there's a huge amount of comfort in having him back and knowing he's on my side. "Could it be your father, Jou? That's something I've wondered."

"Don't think so," he says.

"He knows who I am, and that I was harboring you—"

And he was really, really pissed off about it.

"He'll leave us alone now. I've done my time. He'll honor that for a while."

"What do you mean?" I rub my hand up Jou's chest, over the healed wounds, which haven't even left a scar.

"I don't want to talk about it, sweetness. Not tonight. I just want to enjoy bein' with you and feelin' this good. Not talk about somethin' that'll give us both nightmares. Tell me about this instead. What's this one mean?" He traces a fingertip over the stylized God's eye circling my elbow.

I let it go and tell him about the protective charms I've had Click ink into a winding, colorful band around my body. But, like the bad feeling that's been haunting me since Thanksgiving, I know we're going to have to talk about what happened to him, sooner or later, and that whatever it was, was bad enough to give a thousand-year-old demon nightmares.

———

"Wake up, sweetness."

Jou's whisper brings me awake. Out of a very strange dream. Fire. Everything was on fire. Blue flame licking charred concrete. Piles of blackened bones. The sky choked with smoke, red with flame. My hair and skin, flaring white gold. Burning all the way down inside me to where my heart pumped liquid flame into my veins.

I blink. Everything's on fire.

"Wake up, Tsara."

Jou's voice pulls me further into consciousness, but everything's still on fire. He leans over me, his horns curving above his head, sheathed in blue flame. Behind him, my bedroom curtains incandesce and crawl with tiny, dancing flames.

My house is on fire.

"Jou—"

"It's okay, sweetness. I'm containin' it. Nothing's burnin'. But I need you to wake up and turn it off."

Turn it off? I don't know what I've turned on. I'm awake now. Why is everything still on fire?

"I dreamed of fire," I whisper.

And the fire goes out. Like a snuffed candle. The curtains ruffle a little, as though they still feel those fingers of flame dancing over their sheer fabric, but now they're illuminated only by the very early morning light. A faint smell of smoke lingers in the air.

I sit up slowly and Jou rolls away from me, onto his back. His horns disappear in a shimmer.

"Jou, was everything really on fire?"

He snorts. "Oh, yeah."

"Why?" I ask.

"Got me. Were you projectin'?"

I shake my head. Fire's not my Element. I shouldn't be able to wield it unconsciously. Or subconsciously. Or whatever I was doing.

"You okay, sweetness?"

"Yes." I slide down in the bed next to him. "Did I wake you?"

"Yeah. S'okay. Better than lettin' your house burn down." He settles back into the pillows and cuddles me tight to his side. "You got another Element, huh? When'd that happen?"

I have no idea. "Jou, I can't call Fire."

"That was all you, sweetness. I was keepin' everything from burnin', but you set it alight."

No, I've never heard of anyone wielding three Elements. Never met anyone who could. Not even among the *Aedis Astrum* and they're the *crème de la crème* of mages, or so Bo keeps telling me.

Jou holds up the hand he doesn't have wrapped around my shoulders. A globe of fire spins out of the air and revolves above his palm. "Try."

"You're sure I won't burn myself?"

"I know with fire there's only one way to learn."

Fair enough. I reach up cautiously. Hold my hand out and *call* to the little globe.

I feel it immediately in my mind. A greedy, burning thing. It wants to consume. That's all it does. Light, heat. Those things are incidental. Appreciated by humans. They're not the essence of fire. Fire is pure hunger.

I open my mind to that hunger, shut my eyes, and when I open them again, the ball of fire is hovering just above my palm. Not burning me. How could it? I *am* hunger. I exist only to consume. To pull everything down into the blackness at the heart of me and burn, burn, burn until there is nothing left. *Feed me,* the fire howls and I do, pouring power into that heart of darkness. The ball of fire expands until it takes up the entire space above the bed and burns as bright as the sun.

"Sweetness, shut it down," Jou says softly.

Like turning off a light, I do. There is more to me than hunger. In fact, I'm pretty well sated at the moment, and my magic has always given more than it takes.

"Well," Jou drawls. "That answers that question."

I cuddle against his shoulder and turn this strange, new power over in my head. "Did you give this to me, Jou? I mean, by binding me to you?"

"No idea, sweetness." He yawns hugely.

He's tired. The healing took something out of me, too. I turn my head and kiss his warm, healed skin. "How are you feeling?"

"Good. Nice to be so full. But it's makin' me sleepy."

A full stomach, and a full heart, make me pretty sleepy, too. I cuddle into his side.

He turns so he's facing me, settles me in his arms and kisses me to sleep.

———

When I wake again, it's to golden light. Nothing's burning. It's mid-morning. Sunday morning. I've had a lot of bad Sundays in the past year. Sundays where I woke up so hung-over, I could barely crawl across the hall to the toilet. Sundays where the first thing I did was slam on sunglasses to shield eyes raw from crying all night. Not this morning. This morning I wake to soft, golden light, a clear head and the wonderful, warm weight of my demon-lover at my back.

I lie still for a few moments, not wanting to wake him. I feel the change in his breathing a moment before he asks, "Whaddo you want for breakfast, sweetness?"

"Whatever you want to make," I say. I missed his breakfasts so much I'd eat boiled cardboard if he made it.

He chuckles. "How d'you feel about kedgeree?"

"I have no idea what that is."

"Smoked fish, rice, parsley." At my snort, he says, "Maybe not. You got any raisins? I could make scones."

I think I have raisins, but even if I don't, I'll run all the way to the corner-store and back for homemade scones. "Yes, please."

"Mmm, you make the coffee, I'll make the scones. You broke my favorite toy while I was away, didn't you?"

"The coffee-machine? It lasted less than a week. I told you I have a complicated relationship with electronics."

"Pretty much everything with you is complicated, ain't it?" He smiles at my wordless protest. "I'll get another one. You gotta admit, espresso from that thing was worth sellin' your soul for."

"Not funny," I say, since he could mean that literally.

He snorts. "Don't be oversensitive, sweetness. Told you, it's all gonna be okay this time."

I take a long breath, let it out. Let it go. I want him here. Back in my life. Back in my bed. Whatever that means. Whatever it takes. We'll figure it out. As long as neither of us is alone and hurting again.

He trails his fingertips down my cheek. "That's right. Now for the really important question. Whaddo you want first, scones or another orgasm?"

Gee, that's a tough choice.

Two orgasms and a shower later, I stand next to Jou at my kitchen counter while he rolls out dough and I grind beans for coffee. There's a circle of salamanders at Jou's feet, who are watching him intently. They've already had half the scone dough, which Jou promises me won't hurt them even though it has raw eggs in it.

"Not much can survive the inferno of a salamander's bowels."

"Izzy's looking better, at least," I say, looking down at the crimson and cream lizard, who is watching Jou with bright eyes and twitching tail.

"He should be. He ate a gallon of Cookies 'n' Cream on his own last night."

"He'll get fat," I object.

Jou shrugs. "Won't hurt him. Won't hurt you, either. You eat anythin' while I was gone?"

It's my turn to shrug. "I really missed your cooking."

Jou cuts the scone dough into half-a-dozen neat triangles and lays them on a baking sheet. "We ain't gonna miss anythin' now," he says, popping the baking sheet into the oven. "We're gonna eat and fuck and sleep and cuddle and heal. 'Til we don't even remember where the scars are."

That sounds good to me. "We're not going to do all those things with the lizards, though, right?" I ask.

Jou chuckles. "Thought you wanted to try everythin'?"

"Maybe not that." I pour us two cups of coffee and carry them to my kitchen table. "Will you tell me about it now? What happened to you?"

Jou follows me to the table, sits on the bench and pats his knee. "Remember the part about cuddlin'?"

"Yup." I climb onto his lap willingly, take my cup, fill my mouth with the wonderful, bitter-rich taste of coffee, and wriggle back against his equally wonderful chest. "Tell me."

"I will, sweetness. But not yet. Let's make some good new memories before I have to remember the bad. What were you gonna do today?"

"Nothing specific." I shrug. "I need to do some grocery shopping."

"I'll take care of that. How 'bout you take me to one of your favorite places, we see what there is to see, and while we're there, I'll tell you what happened."

"Okay," I immediately agree, and immediately know where I'm going to take him. "But we can't have sex there."

He chuckles. "We might have to disagree about that. There's nowhere I can't fuck you."

"Not there. It's important, Jou. Promise."

He grumbles, but eventually agrees. Once he does, I climb out of his lap. "I need to make a call."

He listens to me make the call. While I'm speaking to Nicole's grandmother, he rises from the table, pulls the scones out of the oven, sets four on a plate, breaks them open, slathers them with butter and jam, and garnishes the plate with fresh strawberries. He centers the plate on the table a moment before I put the phone down.

I move to the table to admire the tableaux he's created. It looks like a spread out of *Food & Wine*. "That's too pretty to eat."

"Wrong," he says. He picks up a half-a-scone and stuffs it in his mouth to illustrate.

I shake my head at him as I sit down and take my own scone. He sits next to me for about a second before pulling me onto his lap. He was serious about the cuddling.

"How'd you know this kid?" he asks.

"She saw me banish an imp. In Filene's Basement. On the day after Thanksgiving. The store was packed to the rafters. The imp nearly caused a riot. I stopped it and sent it back to you."

"Greed imp? Yeah, I think I remember that."

"Nicole watched the whole thing. Charms, glamor, nothing works on her. She can See through anything."

"Witch like you?" Jou asks.

"I'm not sure. I've met her family and they're all totally normal, as far as I can tell. Sensing magic's not my best thing, but I don't get anything from her. Maybe you will."

"If she can see my true form, won't she be afraid of me?"

"Depends," I say. "Do you really have monster in your penis?"

Jou chuckles. "You got up close an' personal with it not long ago, you tell me."

Not that I noticed. "Just keep your clothes on," I admonish. "I think she saw a reflection of you when I banished the imp. I want to see if she recognizes you."

"Mmm." He nuzzles my ear. "Barely recognize myself."

"You are kind of different," I say hesitantly, running my hand over his crimson bristle, which is the most obvious difference, although the changes in him run much deeper. I don't want to spark off a fight. Not when we're getting along so well. But he is different, and he's avoiding telling me why.

"Not avoidin'," he says, picking up my thought. "I'm just delayin', sweetness. When you've lived as long as I have, you realize that nothin' has to happen right now. Nothin' except this." He nuzzles me again. "Getting in your pants was always the one thing that wouldn't wait."

"Jou." I bat at him, but my hands are full of warm scone.

He just chuckles.

————

We meet Nicole and her grandmother on Congress Street. I suggested they meet us in two hours, and it's taken us almost the full two hours to get here. Not because of Boston traffic, but because that thing that wouldn't wait, wouldn't wait again. First in my herbarium, because it has a door, after I objected to doing it on the kitchen table in view of the lizards; then, after I got myself a healing potion, over the side of my bed. It's a good thing I don't need long to get ready and that Jou drives like a native, otherwise we'd have been late.

He leans against one of the concrete pillars framing the Museum's entrance while we wait for Nicole. He's dressed in jeans, an open-necked black shirt and a leather jacket, after I told him we might get messy. Other than his crimson crewcut, he fits right in with the stream of hip, thirty-something dads streaming past us into the Museum with their hip, cute-as-a-button kids.

He lifts an eyebrow at me. "In my day, we kept 'em in a pen."

"Thankfully, we've progressed since the Dark Ages," I respond, scanning the crowd.

"Tsara!"

I turn and see Nicole barrel through the crowd. The first time we met, she was scared of me. The second time—a week later, when she saw something that frightened her more than I did—she was shy. Since then, we've become buddies. I've helped her normalize the scary things she *Sees*, and she's helped me remember that there's more to life than darkness and grief.

I kneel down, open my arms, and take the impact as she throws herself at me. She winds her arms around my neck and chokes me with a huge hug.

I squeeze her back. She smells like freshly shampooed kid and fried onions. No scent of magic at all. When she unlocks her arms from around my neck and steps back, I see she's wearing the same baggy jeans with holes in the knees—hand-me-downs from her older cousin, she's told me—that she's worn every time I've seen her. But her pink fleece sweater fits her, and she's got the maroon and gold scarf I gave her for Christmas around her neck. I run my fingers over the embroidered school crest.

"Still Ravenclaw?" I ask her.

She nods solemnly.

"'Claws rule." I offer her my pinkie, which she shakes. She turns away for a moment to wave at her grandmother, who is standing halfway down the block. Mrs. Majewski accompanied Nicole the first time we came to the Museum, and when I took her to the Aquarium, but by the time I suggested we see a *Harry Potter* movie, I had graduated to trustworthy status, so Mrs. Majewski just dropped Nicole off at the cinema and picked her up after we'd had ice cream.

Hopefully, introducing Nicole to Jou won't blow that trust.

I lead Nicole to where Jou's standing. He drops his arms from where he's crossed them over his chest, and after seeing Nicole shrink back against my side, he drops to one knee, so he doesn't tower over her. She still looks at the huge hand he holds out with more than a little trepidation.

"Nikki, this is my friend, Jou."

She glances up at me, eyes wide, then back at Jou. There's a bad moment where I feel her shiver and think she's going to bolt. Then she reaches out and shakes his hand.

"Hi," Jou says gently.

"Hi," Nicole responds. "Are you coming with us to the Museum?"

"If that would be okay."

Nicole considers this. "Are you Tsara's boyfriend?"

Jou's dark eyes slide up to mine.

"Yes," I say firmly.

"Then it's okay," Nicole says. She offers him her hand again, which Jou engulfs in his. Hand-in-hand, we walk through the glass entrance of the Children's Museum and into its bright atrium.

———

Two hours later, Jou flops down beside me on a padded chair. We're in the Kid Stage, where Nicole and two other girls are putting on a play that seems to involve a lot of giggling and swapping around of costumes, but very little actual performance. I'm glad to be able to sit and watch, after getting soaked in the Bubbles exhibit and then climbing and crawling through the Big Dig-inspired Construction Zone.

Jou stretches his arm across my shoulders. His shirt is as damp as mine. After some initial awkwardness and a very bad moment when Nicole grabbed his tail instead of his hand, proving that she can see his true form perfectly well, he's gotten soaked, climbed and crawled right alongside us. Watching him squeeze his big frame through spaces designed for bodies a quarter his size, handle kid-sized tools with his huge hands, and try not to crush the dozens of pipsqueaks swarming over, under and around each exhibit has given me some good laughs.

It's also made my chest strangely tight. I've seen him as a lover, and an adversary. I've never thought of him as playful, or paternal.

"Not exactly *Pirates of Penzance*," he murmurs to me.

"Not even *Pirates of the Caribbean*," I whisper back.

I feel him ruffle through my head. He chuckles as he gets the reference. "They need a monkey. Think Iz would like to play a monkey?"

"I think he'd set the place on fire," I say with a nod at the wooden sets.

"Probably." Jou stretches, crosses his legs at the ankles and pulls me a little closer to his side. "My kind's better at burnin' things down than buildin' them up. More I'm around humans, more I see that."

"Humans are pretty good at destruction, too."

"Yeah, but you take the ash and make somethin' new. Demons don't do that."

"Why not?" I ask, curious.

Jou shrugs. "Not the way we're wired."

"Demons build things. You built your home, and I saw that city." An iron city, its turrets and towers stretching up to grasp at the sky like a gauntlet. Without being told, I know that's where Jou's father, Asmodeus, makes his home.

"When we get older, yeah. Once we start feelin' something other than hunger."

"Is that all young demons feel?"

"Uh-huh. The Endless Ache, we call it. When I was a malebranch, nothin' but an orgy would satisfy it—"

I snort. "Really."

Jou chuckles. "It's gotten easier as I got older."

"Tsara!" Nicole calls from the stage. I glance up and find all three girls wearing lab coats and bowler hats.

I control a shiver. White coats have always been ill omens for my family. From my Dala's death in a *gorgio* hospital to the ever-present threat of being stuck full of wires in some secret lab while men with too many letters after their names study my 'gift,' I have lots of reasons to fear white coats.

Jou tightens his arm around my shoulders. "S'okay, sweetness."

I glance at him. Meet his eyes, which are soft and dark. His gentle stare calms me. Allows me to smile at the girls on stage. "What play are you guys doing?" I call to them.

"Frankenstein!" they chorus.

Jou chuckles.

# CHAPTER 8

The kid performance of *Frankenstein* includes lots of running and screaming, particularly after a surprise appearance by the "monster," when Jou climbs out of his chair, stretches his arms out in front of him and shambles after the girls, groaning theatrically. The addition of the monster increases the screeching to such a pitch that it attracts the attention of other kids, even over the general roar that fills the Museum. By the time Jou's chasing a dozen kids around the stage, I join in, because surely Frankenstein's monster shouldn't have this much fun without his Bride.

Jou and Nicole finally collapse back on the chairs. The other kids drift away to their respective parents. I collect the costumes and props that have been strewn around the stage and pack them back in the storage boxes, while Nicole explains the plot of *Frankenstein* to Jou in great detail. She ends up on his chest, with her small arms around his neck. Jou looks bemused by his little cling-on, but he listens intently to her narration, even though I'm pretty sure he already knows the story. Hell, he might even have known its author. His deep tones counterpoint her high kid voice as he asks her questions.

I settle in a free chair on Jou's far side and check my watch. Mrs. Majewski will be making her return appearance in about ten minutes.

She limits my visits with Nicole pretty strictly to three hours, and I haven't figured out if that's for Nicole's benefit or mine. After we reduce our numbers, we should probably think about dinner, since it's getting on towards that time and I haven't done any grocery shopping.

*How do you feel about Italian?* I think loudly and clearly enough for Jou to hear, even over Nicole's chatter.

*Pretty tasty,* he retorts. *Hot, Latin blood. But Chinatown's closer.*

I elbow him and Nicole cuts off mid-sentence. She worms up Jou's chest to peer into his eyes. "Are you doing magic?"

I lean across Jou to gauge the little girl's expression. She's fascinated rather than frightened. "Why, what do you see, Nikki?" I ask.

"His eyes are bright. Like the big sign at night."

The CITGO sign. I've always thought so, too. "Blue?" I ask.

She nods. "And the good crayon colors."

Jou chuckles. "I was talking to Tsara. Inside her head. Can you hear me in your head?"

There's a moment of intense silence that drowns out even the background roar.

Nicole shakes her head. "I can see your crown, though. It's really shiny."

Jou lifts an eyebrow. "I got a crown?"

Nicole nods. "Between your horns."

Jeez, that's the resilience of kids. When I see Jou's demon-form, the last thing I want to do is snuggle up on his chest and have a chat. My foremost thought is to run away as fast as I can.

Jou glances at me. I shrug. I haven't seen his demon-form since he arrived. I don't remember seeing a crown; I have no idea what a demon-crown means, and with Timmi dead, there's no one I can ask.

We return Nicole to her grandmother after a round of hugs that includes Jou and a promise that we'll do something together next weekend. Jou keeps me tucked against his side as we watch Nicole and her grandmother putter away in Mrs. Majewski's antique Chrysler. Then he leads me across the Fort Point Channel, pointing out each tall building in the Financial District that catches his attention. I regale him with stories of windows falling out the Hancock onto hapless passers-by, which the city fathers like to blame on poor design and thermal stresses, but I'm pretty sure was *gaoithe sidhe*. Despite his hick-tourist awe at the skyscrapers, Jou navigates like he's lived in Boston all his life, steering me up Summer Street towards Chinatown.

After he runs out of skyscrapers to admire, I ask, "So what does it mean that Nicole can see a crown when she looks at you?"

He shrugs. "What's it mean that my eyes look like the good crayons?"

"The good crayons are metallic," I say, which I know because I gave them to her. "Jou, why do you keep dodging my questions?"

He takes a deep breath and squeezes my shoulders. "You know what your world smells like to me, sweetness?"

I shake my head.

"Honey. Liquid gold. So sweet." He takes another deep breath. "Thousand days I smelled nothing but ash. Now my lungs are filled with honey."

"I don't understand."

He kisses my temple. "I missed you."

I hug his waist. Feel the whipcord muscle against my forearms. He was never heavy, just hugely muscled. Now he's muscled like a greyhound. Gaunt and graceful. "I missed you, too. What changed?"

Jou hums deep in his chest. "You want to hear this before or after you've eaten?"

"Is it going to make me sick?"

"Probably. Still makes me fuckin' queasy."

Great. "Um, maybe before?"

"Let's get a drink." He steers me to Kingston Street, where he finds *Shochu*, a bar I didn't even know existed. When he turns his high-wattage smile on the waitress who greets us, we get a table at the window. There's not a ton of competition yet; we're early for dinner but late for the pre-theater crowd. All the tables have little 'reserved' tags on them, though, which the waitress whips off our table when she seats us, so I know Jou's demon-charm has gotten us V.I.P.-treatment again. I look out the bar's floor-to-ceiling windows at the leafless trees and winter sunset, which is bleaching the sky to the soft white of a seashell, while Jou orders some unpronounceable booze.

I expect little cups, like *sake*, but instead get a pretty cocktail glass filled with ice and a fizzy drink that smells like lemons. Gamely, I take a sip and feel the fizz rush up my nose. The alcohol hits a second later, burning through my sinuses and down into my stomach. This is not a mellow warmth. It's rocket fuel.

"Jeez! Jou, what is this?"

He chuckles. "Double-distilled *shochu*. Thirty-five percent. If it don't take the edge off, nothin' will."

"You're driving," I tell him. That one sip's probably put me over the limit.

He lifts an eyebrow at me. "You get your pass back . . . whaddo you humans call it?"

"My license? No, I didn't." Because I have a permanent ban for drunk driving.

"Then I'll be drivin' no matter how much you drink. Suck it back, sweetness. Don't be shy."

"You'll be regretting this in an hour when I'm puking into the gutter," I warn him even as I take another sip. Now that I'm expecting it, the fizz and burn is nice. Edgy. It's a sexy drink, which is so Jou.

He stretches his legs under the table and captures my ankles between his. "Glad you still think so, sweetness."

I press my ankles against his. "Of course, I think so." If the seven times we've done it since he came back doesn't convince him, I don't know what will. "Now would you tell me what you're avoiding?"

Jou lifts his glass to me. I take another sip and he downs his drink in a long swallow. Then he refills his glass from the tall bottle the waitress has left on the table and tops up mine. "Remember when my father blew up your kitchen?"

I nod. No amount of alcohol will ever erase that memory. Jou's father, Asmodeus, appeared in the gas jets of my stove, threatened Jou, and torched my kitchen.

"You remember what he said?" Jou asks.

"No, not really," I say around another swallow. Fizz. Burn. Yum. I could totally fall in love with this drink. "He threatened you. I remember that."

"Yeah, he did. He said he'd impale me on the Barbicon for a thousand days. When you sent me back, that's what he did."

My glass drops out of my nerveless fingers. Jou catches it before it smashes; sets it carefully on the table. He takes my hands in his and rubs his thumb over my knuckles. "Sweetness."

"The tree, the one I burned—?"

He nods. His face is set, impassive, but I can see the neon glimmer in his dark eyes. "Tree of Pain. Favorite torture device of demon princes and Erinyes. Bet they're tearin' their horns out tryin' to figure out what happened to it. Can't say I'm sorry the fucking thing's gone."

"Jou—"

He squeezes my hands between his. "Take it slow, sweetness."

I can't. The vision I had of him impaled on that monstrous, evil *thing* fills my mind. "He crucified you."

"Not exactly. He cut off my arms and legs with that blood sword he's got and threw me up on the thorns—"

I pull my hands out of his and stand, furious and unable to direct my fury at anyone but myself. Sparks rain from my fists and the stink of ozone fills the air.

Jou shakes his head and the restaurant around us blurs into streamers of color. "Get it off your chest, sweetness. Just take it easy on the furniture."

I throw my head back and scream. There's no other way of expressing everything I'm feeling. Guilt and horror and rage. I sent him back to be impaled on that hideous *thing*. I lift my hands and lightning crashes down around me. Power billows off me into a glowing bubble of magic. I feel a tug as Jou siphons off the energy I'm calling. His eyes glow, but otherwise he's calm and quiet as he sits at the table.

I let my hands drop and sink back into my seat.

"How can you be so relaxed?" I whisper.

"I had a long time to come to terms with it."

"How long?" I ask. It obviously didn't happen between the time he came to me and the time I summoned him.

"Thousand days," he says.

"You hung there for *a thousand days*?!" I feel that swell of rage rise again to choke me. I find myself on my feet without knowing how I got there.

"Yeah."

"Jou, I—"

He pushes his chair back from the table and pats his thigh.

I shake my head. I can't be calm enough to cuddle right now.

"Sweetness, I earned very second of this. C'mere."

He did. Of course, he did. A thousand days hanging on that abomination. A thousand days of agony. Agony, I sentenced him to—

"Stop thinkin' like that. C'mere an' let me tell you what happened."

I slouch over to him and slump onto his knee. "It's my fault."

He puts his arms around me and breathes warmly into my ear as he speaks. "Had nothin' to do with you. Old Man was lookin' for a way to get at me. He's been lookin' for a while. You were just an excuse. He wanted a big show: to make an example of me for his court and his other get. He got what he wanted."

"Why?" I whimper. "You weren't challenging him. You told me you weren't."

"No, I wasn't. Old Man never does anythin' for just one reason. Took me a while, but I puzzled it out. It was a test. Old Man wanted me to prove I was loyal. Shut up Queen Bitch and the others who keep whisperin' that I'm plottin' against him—"

I choke. "Surely there was a less extreme way?"

"Sure. Lotsa things he coulda done. Only one thing he could do t'make me stronger."

"Make you stronger! Jou, it nearly killed you."

"Uh-huh." He manifests those crimson wings I saw when he first arrived and folds them around us so we're sitting in a cocoon of flame. "Also gave me these. An' the crown your little friend can see. An' turned my eyes the good crayon colors. Now ask yourself, what does the Old Man gain by makin' me stronger?"

"I have no idea." I touch the wing he's wrapped around me wonderingly. I can feel the firmness of muscle and bone underneath, under a fluff of crimson feathers. They flicker under my fingers, staining my skin pink. Licks of flame. And they're so soft, softer than goose down. How can flame be soft?

"I didn't understand at first, either. You know what finally made it come clear?" When I shake my head, he says, "Those imps you kept sendin' me. I was starvin', hanging there. No way for me to feed. But every time you sent me an imp, I got a little stronger. Not full, exactly, just not as hungry as I was. Old Man can't feed off souls anymore. He gets stronger by growin' his power base. Either increasin' the number of his followers or makin' the followers he already got stronger."

I turn a little on his knee so I can put my arms around his neck. With a rustle, his wings close tight around us. Being enfolded by his wings is like being wrapped in a down comforter. It soothes me in a way I didn't think possible, after hearing about his ordeal. "He did it to make you stronger?"

"Somethin' like that."

"That is the most fucked-up parental love I've ever heard of."

Jou snorts. "I didn't say he loves me. Or any of his get. Don't think the Old Man feels love. He cares about power. He saw a chance to increase his power. Didn't really matter what happened to me. If I died, he'd demonstrated his strength. If I survived, he'd shown his Court his get is loyal, and his power base grows. Once I figured that out, all I had to do was endure."

"Endure?" I wail. "How could you possibly endure that?"

Jou tips his head to the side. "Dreamed a lot. Thought a lot." He chuckles softly. "Cursed a lot."

I bet. "You must have cursed me a lot," I whisper.

"No more'n the Old Man. Or Angien. Or the Zes who never even fuckin' came to visit. 'Least I knew you were thinkin' about me."

"You did?" I grab that hope with both hands. At least he wasn't suffering alone, believing I'd abandoned him to that torment.

"'Course I did. I felt you touch my mind all the time, even after I closed it to you. Every night when you dreamed. Every day when you did your greenwitch thing. I felt it when your magic came back. Stronger'n anything I've felt before. I had to knock myself out coupla times t'keep you from seein' me too clearly. Then there were all those imps. Every time you opened the gates to send me another imp, I was sure you were gonna break down the barriers Cyz an' me put up."

"What barriers?" I ask. "Why would you block me out? I mean, I understand you were furious with me for sending you back, but I thought you forgot about me—"

He chuckles and kisses me. "Couldn't forget you, sweetness. You're my *seggurach*. You're parta me. I closed my mind 'cause I know you. If you'd seen what was happenin', you'd have come for me. Even if you'd had to storm the fucking Gates yourself. You can't leave anythin' that's hurtin'. If you'd freed me early."

He takes a deep breath and looks up at the ceiling above us with its fake oak beams before he continues, "I don't know what the Old Man woulda done. Something even more dramatic. I don't know if I coulda survived it. Or what woulda happened to my clutch. He had his claws at all our throats. When he sets out to make a point, he don't fuck around. I just hadda do my time." His jaw flexes and I can see a flicker of pride in those working muscles. He's proud of protecting his family. "I did an' now we're all safe."

I squeeze my eyes closed and press my face into his neck as I try to process what he's been through. "I can't believe he did that to you. I can't believe you survived it. How could you? How could he? You're his *son*. Doesn't that mean anything? You didn't do anything wrong!"

Jou shrugs. "Blood only means somethin' t'him when it's useful. Right an' wrong have never meant anything." He hugs me tight and nuzzles me until I lift my face and look into those dark eyes. "When I finished bein' useful, he let me go. I felt it. He musta been counting down, same as I was. End of that thousandth day, he let me go. I'd done my time, so he let you heal me enough to escape."

"A thousand days," I whisper, still trying to process his ordeal. It's bad enough that I sentenced him to such suffering, but to endure it for *three years*.

He reaches out of our huddle to pick up his glass and take a long swallow. He offers it to me and I take a sip, feeling a tingle cross my lips that has nothing to do with the alcohol.

"Some days, it was hard to remember a time I hadn't been on that Tree. But." He bumps the knobbed joint of his wing against my shoulder, a little clumsily, and I wonder if he's still learning how to control his wings. "I had these to look forward to. Started dreamin' about them pretty much as soon as he stuck me up there. An' comin' back to you. An' babies. Lots of babies. With little red wings."

"Babies?" I flinch before I can control it.

"Yup. I started dreamin' about them as soon as I saw my wings.

That's that half-*Noctil* part of me. Not good for much, but it gave me some nice dreams on the Tree, so I guess I should be grateful."

Small mercies.

I frame his face with my hands, brushing back his dreadlocks. "Jou, that can't be all you dreamed about. You can be honest with me. I don't want any lies between us. You must have dreamed about revenge."

His mouth quirks. "First of all, I haven't lied to you. Second, yeah, I dreamed some about revenge. On you. On the Old Man. On everyone who looked at me the wrong way over the last thousand years. I had a lotta time to think. That was mostly at the beginning. I got more peaceful the longer I hung there."

Or he learned patience.

He flicks the tip of my nose. "I said *peaceful*. I haven't thought about revenge in a long time."

"Jou, I would understand."

"'Cause you're blamin' yourself. Don't think I can't see that in your head. For the record, sweetness, I understand why you did what you did. I pushed you too hard. I thought seein' my home, feeling how much you could be there, I thought it'd be a lure. And it woulda been to anyone but you. You're just not wired that way. I knew that, but I didn't *understand* it. If I'd thought it through, I'd have shared my memories of bein' entrapped with you, so you understood why those fuckers had to die. If I'd told you about Hoshi-san, how Masaharo used her against me, you'd have understood why I let that mother-fucker cut you before I killed him. But I didn't want you to know how weak I'd been. You didn't get why I reacted the way I did, and seein' me kill 'em scared you to fuckin' death, didn't it?" At my nod, he continues. "One of 'em was your friend, wasn't she?"

I thought she was, but I was as wrong about that as I was about everything else. "Yes."

"If I'd been thinkin' clearly, I'd have stepped sideways with you. Given us both time. But I wasn't, and I didn't. Forcin' myself not to show anything while that fucker cut you, so they thought you didn't mean anything t'me hurt worse than anything the Old Man did to me. Watchin' you bleed for me made me fucking insane. I had to wait until I had a clear shot. When I did, I took it, without askin' you or sparing your friend. You can blame me for that, if you need to point the finger."

I rub my cheek against his. "It hasn't been as long for me as it's been for you, but I've worked through some things, too. I don't blame you, and I'm working hard on not blaming myself. Maybe Timmi's death could have been avoided, but I understand that you were defending yourself—"

"An' you. I know it felt like I threw you to the wolves, but I didn't know what they had, sweetness. If they'd had a binding chain, like your dead friend had, or somethin' worse, and they thought you meant anything to me, they'd have used you as leverage. Once I was bound, you know they wouldn't have let you live."

I nod. I'm under no illusions as to what Denys LeConie and his friend planned to do to me.

"One of the things that bothered me the most while I was on that Tree: knowing you thought I let that entrapping fuck cut you 'cause I didn't care if you lived or died. That ain't true."

It's a little true. Seeing me suffer may have hurt him, but my life, or death, are not big things to him if he already owns my soul.

"It's a big thing," he says roughly. "I can't explain it to you. Not in any way you'll understand now. But I promise you, when you're my seggurach, you'll understand."

"No lies, Jou," I say.

"It's not a lie. Nothin' I've said to you is a lie. Some things are . . . I guess you'd call 'em not true *yet*, but it feels t'me like they will be." He holds up his hand and I press mine against it, palm to palm. I feel the tingle under my skin before blue flame sheathes our hands. "You got no idea how rare this is, sweetness. Seggurach bond don't happen that often, even between demons. Between a demon and a human?" He shakes his head. "There's no instruction manual. No one to tell me how this is supposed to work. I'm feelin' my way along, an' all I can tell you is, once you become my seggurach, you'll feel the things I feel and what I do'll make more sense to you."

I thread my fingers through his and squeeze. "I kind of thought I was your seggurach already. You bound me. And I agreed to it. Is there more?"

Jou nods. "There's a ritual."

Great. More scars. "Uh, when do you want to do this ritual?"

"You rushin' our engagement, sweetness?"

I shrug. "You know me. I'm not good with transition. I like to get where I'm going."

"Thought witches were all about walkin' the Path?" When I shake my head, he sighs. "It's less of a *when* and more of a *where*. We either gotta do it in front of the Old Man, or in front of my mother's people. I'm not in a hurry to see either of them."

Ugh. "Please tell me your mother's people aren't as bad as your father?"

"Well, they ain't friendly," Jou admits. "You've probably heard of 'em. Wrath demons. Erinyes. Big with the Greeks. They guard the Tree. Or they used to. You burnin' it down'll piss them off big time."

"Oh, even better."

Jou chuckles. "I don't care. Even if it means we gotta do it in front of the Old Man. It's worth it. Only thing that's made me feel better than you healin' me? Watchin' you burn that motherfucker to the ground."

I lean in and rub noses with him. "I'm glad I've been able to do some things that make you feel better."

"Lots you do makes me feel better. You had enough to drink?"

I glance back at my glass, which is mostly empty. "Uh-huh."

"Good." Jou rises from the table and pulls me up with him. "Gotta be a dark alley around here we can duck into for a minute."

"Um." I start to ask *why*, then I stop myself. I know why he wants to duck into a dark alley. We've done it in quasi-public places before and it was a huge turn-on. With a glamor or another stitch-in-time, no one will see us. He's my lover and we're together and these are the perks. I should enjoy them to the fullest.

Jou watches me for a long moment, and I can feel him following my thoughts. "Like this new leaf, sweetness," he says, and gives me his full wicked grin for the first time since I summoned him.

We find a dark alley less than a block from the bar.

———

After *dim sum* a few blocks from my new favorite alley, I ask Jou if he minds walking back along the Charles. It's in the opposite direction from where we've left the car, but I can Earth-Walk us back.

That thought reminds me that I haven't shown Jou my new trick, so I Earth-Walk us to Lederman Park. Jou sneezes and shakes out his dreads as we emerge from the Earth. He holds his hands out to me, palms up, and when I place my palms against his, burns off the dust of our transit in a burst of blue flame.

"So much for travelling incognito," I say. There's no one nearby, but anyone on the entire Esplanade with the Sight will have noticed that little display.

"Sorry, sweetness. Who're you hidin' from?"

I shrug. I'm not sure I'm hiding from anyone. There's no reason Toby's killer would know who I am or that I'm looking for them. Still, hiding my magic is second nature. Ingrained from the moment my Dala leathered me for *calling* a sock that had gotten lost under my bed instead of crawling under there and retrieving it with my own hands. And then there are those eyes the shadows have grown since Thanksgiving.

Jou takes my hand and leads me past a stand of forsythia, the yellow flowers washed to gray in the hazy moonlight. "You don't have to hide," he says.

"It's safer," I respond. Then change the subject by tipping my chin towards the river. "We won't get too close."

Jou stops and looks out over the water. There's a shimmer at his back, where I think he's just flexed those huge, invisible wings. I feel him take a deep breath, his chest expanding until his leather jacket creaks. Then he lets it out and smiles. "I don't think that's an issue anymore."

"It's not?"

He shakes his head. "You summoned me this time and your magic's groundin' me. Don't think there's much other'n you that could send me back."

"Running water's not a problem anymore?"

"I'm not plannin' on goin' for a swim, but I don't think bein' immersed would hurt me now."

"Wow, Jou." Running water was his Achilles heel.

He squeezes my hand. "Guess my time on the Tree wasn't all bad."

"Yes, it was." I look out over the water and try to find a still point to focus on, block out that burning rage I feel whenever I think about what his father did to him. "I still can't stand it."

Jou reaches out with his free hand and brushes my bangs back from my face. "I appreciate the sympathy, sweetness. An' I know you're pickin' up what I'm feelin'. But we both gotta keep a handle on it. Might come a time when we can get a little retribution, but it ain't right now. Old Man and Queen Bitch, they'll be watchin'. Others, too. Some'll be able to see what your little friend saw. They'll know what it means—"

"What does it mean?"

"Means I ain't what I was. Old Man got what he wanted but others, his enemies, they might see my evolution as a challenge. So, we stay quiet, heal, learn to use what we got—" A breeze ruffles my hair as he beats his wings. "Wait for the opportunity to vent a little of that rage. But you don't need to hide. Neither do I. An' if anythin' comes along that looks unfriendly, we take it down. You and me. Together."

I look up into those dark eyes, swimming with points of blue light, and nod.

"So," he says, turning back to the path and tugging me alongside him. "Your furry friend bought it here, huh?"

He must be taking Toby's death from my mind. I've been distracted by Jou's return, but so close to the spot where Toby was killed, his death has risen to the front of my thoughts again.

"Further down the bike path, I think," I say. "Jou, most demons wouldn't come this close to running water, would they?"

"Not a fire or earth demon," Jou responds. "Water demon would."

A *water* demon. "I thought it was a shapeshifting shark. The bite marks were huge. Could it have been a water demon?"

"Mmm." He tugs me a little closer and wraps his arms around my shoulders. I tuck into his side; slide my arm around his waist. We fit together, like hand and glove, lock and key. "Could still have been a shark. Water demons can change shape, just like I can."

"But you couldn't turn into a shark. Uh, could you?" Now *that's* a horrifying thought.

He snorts. "No. Dunnow if a water demon could, either. I've never seen that kinda transformation. Most demons take human form. But water demons are pretty fluid—"

Being water demons. "Why would a water demon attack Toby? He was . . . eaten, Jou."

Jou shrugs. "If a demon's hungry enough, it'll take flesh. It won't fill 'em the way strong emotion or magic would, but it'll do in a pinch. Was your friend sick? It's usually illness that draws water demons. Cholera, hepatitis, big faves."

"No way. Ana would have mentioned it. And shifters run too hot for most human diseases. I've never even seen one with a cold."

"Mmm." Jou shrugs. "Disease is what they like best. Not sure what else would draw a water demon. Also, they ain't loners. When they come topside, they do it in numbers."

"Manny only mentioned one bite radius. Eight inches." I shudder.

Jou flexes his jaw and I glance away in case he tries to match that distention. Something I do not want to see. His chuckle draws my eyes back to his face. "Got no interest in breakin' my jaw, sweetness. Just thinkin' that is a really big mouth."

"That's why I thought a shark."

"Yeah, you're probably right." He runs the tips of his fingers up my back, under my jacket and shirt. When I lean my head onto his shoulder, he says, "Kiss me right there."

"Right here?" I turn my head and kiss the warm spot where his neck meets his collar. "Why there?"

"'Cause you haven't kissed me there in a thousand days. Do it again."

I do it again, then blow a raspberry into that spot and smile at his chuckle.

"How're you gonna catch it anyway?" he asks.

"Catch it?" My voice shoots up an octave before I can control it. "I never said anything about catching it. I said I'd *scry* for it, but there's no way I'm getting anywhere near it. Two things I'm allergic to. Big, toothy things, and big, predatory, toothy things."

Jou chuckles. "That's okay. Even how I'm feelin' now, fishin' ain't my thing."

Nor mine.

"So, scrying?" At my nod, Jou grins. "You gonna scry naked?"

"My cousin is coming over and no, we're not scrying naked." When he sighs with disappointment, I elbow him. "You've seen plenty of me naked."

"There's never enough nakedness. Fact, I could do with more nakedness right now."

I elbow him again. "Let me just look at the spot where Toby died, then we can go home and be naked."

"Good. Never too soon for nakedness, either."

I find the spot, still cordoned off with yellow police tape. It's on a fairly narrow part of the perimeter path, with the water lapping the granite bank on one side and a metal fence hemming the path in on the other. There's also a lot of cover with bushes and a stand of silver beech on the far side of the fence. No wonder no one saw anything.

"Good place for an ambush," Jou observes.

I nod. Even my untrained eye can see that.

"It definitely wasn't a vampire," I say, slipping from under Jou's arm and circling the yellow tape cordon. "It's closer to the water than I'd remembered." I peer down the bank, but there's nothing but a scum of algae and dark, lapping water. "It wouldn't be difficult for something to jump out of the water here."

Jou wraps his arm around my middle and backs us both up a step. "You got that right. You don't know what attacked your furry friend or why, but you do know it happened here. Use your brain, sweetness. I like all that nakedness intact."

He has a point. "Sorry, that was dumb."

"You seen what you want to see?"

"Give me a minute." I move out of the circle of his arms and as close to the spot where Toby died as the police tape allows. I stare at it for a moment, trying to *feel* something.

Then I *reach* and open myself completely.

Behind me, Jou swallows, loud enough for me to hear. He moves up behind me. His wings beat the air before cupping me in a wreath of flame. "You are a fuckin' beacon," he breathes into my hair.

I pat his hip before reaching out with all my mystical senses. Strong emotion leaves traces. Some I can See: layers of entwined energies staining the air in streaks of fading color. Some I can *Feel*: a cold breeze over bare skin. Some I can *Smell*. This time, it's odors that I catch: blood and rank, wet fur. I follow that thread, pulling it to me, teasing it out of the tangle of other scents: perfume and sweat and wood and asphalt. There are a thousand overlapping scents. A million lives have crossed and re-crossed here. Lovers have met and parted. People have argued, fought, hated. Children have screamed in play and fear. That's the scent I'm looking for: *fear*. The adrenal reek of the death-fight. The cut-edged acid of unbearable hunger.

But that's not what I find.

As I pull the thread, I find a deeper, slower fear. A cold trickle down the spine. The sweaty flinch when the shadows grow eyes. A spike of surprise. Then an ice-tinged breeze, as fresh and raw as the breath of a glacier.

"Something drove him here," I say slowly, as I pick apart the sensations. "He was being hunted, and he knew it. It killed him fast. It didn't hurt." I feel my shoulders slump as that small truth sinks in. Jou's big, warm hands cup my shoulders; his thumbs stroke the back of my neck. "He wasn't alive for . . . what it did to him."

"Anythin' else?" Jou asks softly.

I *reach*, extending my senses as far as I can, and very, very faintly, over the water, I hear the calling of geese.

I turn; Jou turns with me. But there's nothing other than a red line train clattering over the Longfellow Bridge and the hum of traffic on Storrow Drive. There's no night breeze. No late-night joggers. No sleepy birds squabbling over the best roosting spots.

"No birds," I whisper to Jou. "No noise."

His wings circle us again. "Time to go, sweetness."

I agree.

I reach back and grasp his hips, then drag us both into the ground.

# CHAPTER 9

ou claims that our two trips through the Earth have left us in
need of a bath, and when the bath comes garnished with champagne and fresh strawberries, there's no way I'm going to argue
with him.

I make him wait while I call Ana. I get her answering machine
again and leave a more detailed message, hoping that knowing Toby
died quickly and without any pain will give her some of the relief it's
given me. The machine cuts me off before I finish, and when I call
back, the stupid thing tells me, "Mailbox full."

I frown at the phone and make a mental note to try Ana again in
the morning before I visit my Dala's grave.

Upstairs, I find Jou already in the bath. A beautiful black lacquer
tray I don't own perches on my toilet, holding the promised champagne and strawberries. He must have magicked-up the champagne
and strawberries, too, because I didn't have either in the 'fridge.

"Where are you getting this stuff?" I ask as I strip off my clothes. A
poof of dust rises from them, and I snap a cantrip to scour it away.

"Peapod," Jou responds lazily.

"The grocery delivery service?"

"Uh-huh."

"Jou." I step carefully into the bath, in part because I'm nervous about slipping and landing on my ass, and in part because I don't want to spill my champagne. "You're a thousand-year-old demon. How do you know about Peapod?"

He chuckles and holds up a hand to help me settle onto his lap. "I saw it on your talking box. I put in an order before we went to meet your little friend."

"But we were out when it was delivered."

"Your hob was here. So were the lizards, but I doubt they helped."

"My what?"

"Your house hob. The little gray man. Whatever you call him."

I reach back and put my finger over his lips. "He doesn't like to be acknowledged."

"Huh." Jou gives my finger a soft, hot lick. I shake my head at him as I pull it away.

"I didn't know he took delivery."

"It was all put away by the time we got back, an' like I said, I don't think the lizards leant a claw."

Into my mind, Jou asks, *He got a name?*

*Thurman. He's a* bwg. *He showed up just after Thanksgiving and spent three days eating all my leftover turkey, then he started doing things around the house. He likes to rearrange my shoes and hang up my coat. I hadn't thought to ask him to take deliveries.*

Jou chuckles. *I told them to leave it on the back porch, an' figured with your wards it'd still be there when we got back. It was all put away, nice and neat.*

"He's very tidy," I say aloud. It may not be an effort for Jou to read my mind, but it's an effort for me to talk into his. Way too much effort for a hot bath with champagne.

Jou reaches forward and *tinks* his glass against mine. "*Salute,* sweetness."

"I thought you toasted in Japanese?" He did the last time he was here.

"It's Prosecco."

"*Salute,* then. To your very good health, Jou." I take a sip of the fizzy wine, which is as crisp as a good apple. "You deserve it."

Jou reaches across to the tray, picks up a strawberry and holds it while I take a bite. I feel him chewing as he finishes it off. "Don't get dark on me, sweetness. Plenty of time for that. Just enjoy the moment."

"You can't tell me you live in the moment, Jou—" I pause while he feeds me another strawberry. "I don't believe you."

"Why not?"

"Because you've lived a dozen lifetimes. You can't live that long without making plans, thinking into the future."

"I make plans. An' I think about the future. I've had a lotta time to do both. Know what I've learned?" When I shake my head, he says, "Enjoy the fuckin' moment. For every moment like this, sweetness, there's fifty thousand hangin' on that Tree."

"And I'm the one getting dark?"

He grunts, then eats another strawberry before he says, "Let's forget about dark and talk about somethin' you've been avoidin'."

I crane my head around so I can look at him. He's resting back against the tub wall, but he doesn't have his head back or his eyes closed. He looks like he's steeling himself.

"I'm not aware of anything I've been avoiding. You were avoiding telling me about what happened to you."

"We're past that. Next thing. You keep edgin' around somethin'. Like when you asked me about the groceries. You wanna know how I'm paying for human things."

I've wondered about it. "Sure. I figured you were glamoring shop assistants into giving you things. How that would work with an online grocery service, I don't know."

"I been walkin' your world a long time. Some of the fuckers that summoned me didn't want to trade sex for my labors. Some of 'em paid with the shiny shit humans like: metal and stones. Over the centuries, it built up. There's a lot of it now. Too much to stick in a cave like I used to, and you humans keep pokin' your noses into all the old hidden places anyway. When I destroyed the Wolfshook, I got it all together and left it with one of Reece's soul-slaves. He breaks stocks, or somethin'. He gave me numbers to use when I want to buy human things."

"Numbers?" That doesn't make any sense.

"Yeah. There's a card." Jou holds up his hand and a black credit card appears between his fingers for a moment before disappearing in a *fuff* of blue flame. "It has the numbers on it."

"Please tell me that's not a credit card from the Bank of Hell."

"American Express, actually."

Does American Express even issue a black credit card? I've never heard of one. "Okay, how do you pay it off?"

"Whaddo you mean?"

"You charge something on that card and every month a bill comes, and you have to pay it off. How do you pay it?"

Jou shrugs, making the water around us ripple. "I guess Reece's soul-slave pays it. Dunnow. He told me I could buy anything I wanted with those numbers. I took him at his word. It's a lot easier than havin' to hit one of my stashes an' then find a buyer for fucking *Aureus* and *gulden*. That's a ball-ache, I can tell you."

I giggle. I can't help it. All I can think of are the terrible Universal movies from the 1940s. Picturing Jou in a Technicolor turban as he raids his cave of gold turns my giggle into a full laugh.

Jou distracts me with another strawberry. "Look, sweetness, there's a reason I wanted to talk about this."

"What's that?" I ask, before I chase the berry with fizzy wine.

"I've seen in your head how bad things got for you while I was gone. How you had to give your house to a bank—"

"It's a mortgage, Jou. Most people have them. And I'm fine." That's not entirely true. I'm in serious debt for the first time in my life, and I hate it. But the clinic was in trouble because I couldn't make the magic milk, and Lin already had a mortgage, so I stepped up.

"Don't get defensive, sweetness. I've seen you worryin' about it. I don't want you to. An' I don't want you to feel like you have to help humans make more babies just so you can pay the bank, either. I want you to be able to enjoy the moment with me."

"I am enjoying it."

"Yeah. I want you to enjoy *every* moment with me. Without worryin'. I want to use the numbers to pay your bank. Tomorrow, you can show me how."

I exhale incredulously. "Jou, look, I'm not sure how much you can charge on a black AmEx, but my mortgage is thirty-five thousand dollars. That's a lot of money."

"Is it more than a plane? Zeif bought a plane with the numbers."

A *plane*? "A toy plane, right? One of those glider things." A hang-glider can't cost more than a few thousand.

"Don't think so, but the Zes'll probably come up on it tomorrow or the next day, so you can tell me what it is."

That doesn't sound like a hang-glider. You couldn't possibly charge a *plane* on a credit card, could you?

"Look, sweetness," Jou continues. "I don't want to push you. I know it goes bad when you're pushed. But I don't want you worryin' about human gold anymore. You're my seggurach. You're part of me. You gave me wings an' a crown in the good crayon colors—"

"It was your eyes that Nikki said were the good crayon colors." I bump his jaw with my temple, and he chuckles.

"You said no lies between us, so here's the unvarnished fucking truth. There are gonna be times when you'll think meetin' me was the worst thing that ever happened to you. I know you've felt that way already. I've seen it in your head. An' you haven't even met Soae or Angien or Cyz yet. I don't want you thinkin' the negatives of bein' with me outweigh the positives. I want to make sure that the rest of the time makes up for the bad shit. This is the rest of the time, sweetness. Right now. This is the part where we get to heal and fuck and cuddle. You've taken care of me. This is me takin' care of you. Will you let me do that?"

Everything inside me melts. Not just because of the warm water. How could I ever say *no* when he puts it like that? Even my pride's not that prickly.

"Of course, Jou."

"Good. Now, since you've eaten all the strawberries, how 'bout we move this to your bed?"

I can't argue with that, either.

———

I wake up feeling goofy. Totally, ridiculously goofy. Like I haven't felt since I was fourteen and the first boy I had a crush on asked me out. I'm too old to feel this way. And I can't possibly be infatuated with Jou because we've been lovers for months. And he's a demon. But that doesn't stop me from lying in his arms for the better part of an hour after we wake up, grinning at him like an idiot as I trace charms over his cheeks and chin and throat between kisses. At first, they're just random runes I learned at Wydlins. But slowly a shape comes together in my mind: the Great Tree, and at the end of each branch, an eye, and a hand, and a door.

"I'd like this on my back, sweetness," Jou says lazily, as I draw another branch. "When your ink mage friend scribbles on me."

"Mmm-hmm." I can see the tattoo in my mind. Not as colorful as mine. Black runes stark against his golden skin. As beautiful and bold as his horns. I lean forward and rub noses with him.

He grins. "I like what you're thinkin', sweetness."

I'm thinking he's beautiful, no matter what form he's in. I'm thinking that I'm not worried about anything in this moment. Not about being his *seggurach*, or work, or my mortgage, or my sudden ability to call Fire. I'm just happy. For the first time in as long as I can remember.

"That's it," Jou murmurs. "Just enjoy the moment."

"Are you?" I ask.

"You bet. Anytime I got you naked, I'm enjoyin' the moment."

I giggle and nip his chin before pressing kisses all along his jaw. "I can't stay in this moment all day. It's nice for now, though."

"Yeah, I saw that. You visit the old woman's corpse today, huh?"

Gross. "Her *grave*, Jou."

"Yeah." He pauses for more kisses. "Whaddo you get outta that, sweetness?"

"What do you mean?"

"What's visiting her corpse get you?"

I snort. "A less irritable ghost. But it's also respectful. I visit my parents' graves on their wedding anniversary."

"Why's it respectful?" he asks. "I can see in your head you think it is, but I don't get why goin' to a corpse pit's a show of respect. Dead's dead."

"Well, not so much in my family. My Dala's still around to tell me how disrespectful I'm being if I don't go."

"Still don't make sense to me."

"Would you like to come with me? It might make more sense if you see it first-hand."

"Mmm." Jou stretches under me, captures one of my hands and pulls it over his head so I arc over the bow of his body. He grins up at me, and I grin back at him, loving the way our bodies fit together. "This gonna be another place we can't fuck?"

"Probably. I don't think having sex in a graveyard is very respectful."

Jou grunts. "Not likin' this respect thing."

"I'm guessing it's not something demons do. Do you bury your dead?"

"Nope."

"Do I want to know what you do with them?"

"Probably not. Let's just say, there's not much that's wasted in Hell. Gotta be careful, though. Sometimes it's hard to tell what dead is. Most things, you chop their head off, pretty safe in sayin' they're dead. But you'd be wrong with the Old Man. Settin' in on his corpse would really piss him off."

"Okay, that's just weird." Weird and creepy and probably something that should scare me, but I'm too giddy this morning to be bothered by much of anything.

"I'll make you a deal," Jou says. "I'll come with you an' do your respect-thing, but afterwards we do respect my way."

I'm guessing that respect *his way* involves sex.

"Actually, I was thinkin' of dancin'. Liked that time you an' me went dancing."

I did, too. Until the end, when we bumped into my ex-boyfriend and Jou decided to press home a point about the shallowness of my previous relationships.

"Dancing's a celebration of life, so I'm fine with that. Do you mind if we go somewhere other than Man Ray?"

I do not want to see Saul again, with or without Jou.

"Go anywhere you want."

Good, because tonight is a *noswaith lawen*, a dancing night. I've missed the last two, with Toby's funeral and helping Wen move. I don't want to miss another. I'm not sure how the fae will react to the demon, but there's only one way to find out.

Jou sits up sharply. "No."

"Huh?" I blink up at him from where I've tumbled off onto the mattress.

"We're not doin' anything that involves the airy fairy."

"Who? What are you talking about?"

"One of the things that drove me crazy while I was hangin' on that Tree? Thinkin' about you and the airy fairy getting jiggy while I was out of the picture. We can go dancin' with the Twittering Throng if you want, but he ain't invited."

"The Squire? Seriously? Jou, *nothing* has ever happened between me and the Squire." Because I've read *Tam Lin*. "I know what happens when a mortal gets involved with the fae."

"Maybe nothing's happened yet, but only 'cause I got my foot in the door first. He was fucking *courting* you. Ain't the way a demon would do it, but fairies do everything backwards. You still got that sparkly bowl? Remind me to burn that fucking thing to a cinder after breakfast."

"I don't still have the bowl. It broke, if you'll remember." And nothing I tried to do to fix it worked, so I ground up the shards and used the glittery powder to reinforce the wards around my house. "Yes, the Squire was the one who first invited me to dance, but I actually haven't seen him in a couple of weeks. I guess he's busy."

Jou grunts, then he turns his face away.

I slide up to sit beside him. "You were jealous of the Squire?"

"I wasn't jealous."

Right. "You've got nothing to be jealous of, Jou. I really never thought of him that way. I haven't seen much of him while you've been gone. I can Earth-Walk to find what I need for my potions now, and, honestly, being with him just reminded me of how badly I fucked up with you."

Jou slides his arm along the headboard behind me and when I lean into him, pulls me against his side. "I told you the seggurach bond goes both ways. This is the way it goes for me."

It makes him into a green-eyed devil, demon, whatever. "Good thing it doesn't go that way for me. Thinking about you and your harem would put me in an asylum." It kind of does anyway. I've always known about them. I've met some of them. Seeing him with them is going to be a whole different level of crazy, though.

"I haven't touched any of them since I been with you," Jou says.

"You haven't?" That's almost as hard to process as his ordeal on the Tree.

"Nope. Stopped wanting to."

"You did? When?" The last time he was here, he had sex with other people, but not after we got together. I never knew if that was because my magic kept him sated, or because he recognized my need for monogamy. Either way, I never expected him to be faithful after I banished him. He's a lust demon, after all. With a harem. And I dumped him.

"Dunnow. Probably after I bound you. All I know is, I only want this." He takes my hand and threads his fingers through mine. "Nothin' else tastes good. It's like eating rotten meat. It fills you up, but you gotta choke it down. And you know it's going to fuck you up inside. Almost worse than the hunger."

"Ick, Jou."

He shrugs. "Just the truth, sweetness."

I squeeze his fingers. "Okay, well, that's weirdly flattering, I think. I honestly didn't expect you to give up your harem, Jou."

"S'okay. I've always liked sex with humans better anyway. Sex with other demons is risky."

"Pregnancy risky?" I know he doesn't have any children, despite his long life and promiscuity.

"Mmm, more, are we gonna fuck or are you gonna try to eat me, risky."

Well, that puts unprotected sex in a whole new light.

Jou chuckles. "I know I'm safe with you. I want you to know you're safe with me, too, sweetness. In every way. I'd never hurt my seggurach. I know that's hard for you to believe 'cause you've felt threatened by me—"

When I start to protest, he strokes the tip of my nose until I let him continue uninterrupted. "I thought about this a lot on the Tree. It'll take time for you to accept, but I want you to know it. All the way down in your bones. I want you to know you're safe with me. That I'll always protect you. That kind of trust'll take time. All I'm askin' is that you give me some."

"Time?"

"Uh-huh."

"How much, Jou?"

"'Til you trust me? I'm hopin' it won't take too long—" He trails off. "That ain't what you're askin'." He takes a deep breath and lets it out slowly. "Sweetness, you know I want more than just one short human life with you."

"Yes, I do." I also know this spooked the shit out of me last time. Eternity without the possibility of parole. That's just too long. It's only slightly less disconcerting when I'm feeling so happy.

"But I ain't in a hurry. We got plenty of time to figure things out."

"We do?"

"We do," Jou promises. "Let's start with figurin' out breakfast. Can't go corpse-pickin' on an empty stomach."

I slap his chest in mock-disgust but let him talk me into blueberry pancakes and dark roast before we head to my Dala's grave.

———

I bought a grave for my grandmother in Forest Hills Cemetery so she could be close to my father. I'm still not sure she appreciates it. Unlike my grandmother, my parents are restful dead, so there's no benefit to the proximity, or so she tells me. Told me, when she was speaking to me.

I'm pretty sure she wouldn't appreciate me bringing the demon to her grave, either. But I appreciate it. I appreciate him driving, so I don't have to endure the Orange Line's slow clank down to the Forest Hills station. I appreciate the warmth of the car as the weather has finally remembered it's January and turned decidedly nippy, if not quite seasonably cold. I appreciate him holding my hand as we walk between the manicured boxwoods to my grandmother's plain, square headstone, for no reason other than I love holding hands with him.

I place the flowers that I've brought—a small bouquet of lilies and orchids from the florist in Central Square—into the little metal stand at the base of the headstone and step back beside Jou. I feel him ruffling through my thoughts. I think about what I always think about when I visit her grave. My best memories of her. The night of my high school prom, when she curled my hair with paper and hot tongs and told me for the first and only time that I was beautiful. The yearly Christmas ritual of baking gingerbread in her caravan's tiny kitchen. Her hugs, which comforted me at a level nothing else has ever reached.

Until Jou.

He puts his arm around me. "Yeah?"

I nod and smile up at him.

My grandmother didn't approve of Jou. In fact, the reason she's not speaking to me at the moment is because I tore apart her ghost during a screaming argument over what she called my *lubbenipen* regarding the demon. But if I lived my life as she wanted me to, I'd still be travelling with the family and safely married to one of my cousins. Probably Hanzi, whose body odor used to distress even the Billigoat.

That was never going to be my Path.

"I couldn't be what she wanted me to be," I say slowly.

He strokes my head down onto his shoulder. "Don't think kids ever are. Pretty sure I'm not what the Old Man wants in a son."

"You don't owe him a fucking thing, Jou," I say through gritted teeth. I can't stand what his father did to him, or that he had to endure it in name of being his father's son. When Jou doesn't respond, I moderate my tone. "What does your father want in a son?"

Jou shrugs. "Obedience. He likes to throw Chaid in everyone's faces, and the Red Duke's never had a thought that didn't come outta the Old Man's mouth first. That's probably what he wants in a son."

"You proved you were obedient. You proved it by suffering on that tree for three years," I say. "That's above and beyond what any parent should ask of their child. You don't owe him a goddamn thing, Jou."

"You don't owe the old woman anything, but you're still here."

"It's a little different."

Jou shrugs. "Family's a bitch, sweetness. Yours and mine. Hard to walk away from 'em, though. Chains family puts on you, they don't break. They just go slack for a while."

I rub my cheek against his shoulder. "That's the truth."

"Both of our families have asked for shit we shouldn't have had to give. An' we've done a lotta giving, sweetness. I figure those chains have slackened off enough for us to do our own thing for a while."

I nod. "I don't think either of us should have to conform to our families' expectations. I don't care that they don't approve of me being with you." I shrug uncomfortably, remembering my Dust Days. "Being without you made me more unhappy than I've ever been in my entire life, Jou. I didn't even know I could *be* that unhappy."

He rubs his hand up and down my back.

"I know we both have duties to our families," I continue. "I'm here today because of that. I know there are things you'll have to do because of your duty to your family, although I'll *never* agree that being spitted on that tree for three years was part of any duty you had to your father, but I appreciate your family probably doesn't think very much of you being with a human, do they?"

He sighs heavily. "No. I haven't seen the Zes since before I was last with you, but I can guess what their reaction'll be. As pissed as they are at me for takin' a human as my seggurach and settin' the Old Man on the warpath, though, I've got a few things to say to them about makin' themselves scarce for a thousand fucking days. It ain't gonna be a happy family reunion."

An unhappy demon family reunion. Well, that's something to look forward to. I'm not sure it can be much worse than Sunday dinners with Uncle Walther and all the cousins, though. Particularly during the Gulf War. There were a couple of times I was sure Walther and the Billigoat were going to go at each other with their steak knives.

I slide my arm around his lean waist and squeeze. "We'll weather it. I promise not to let anything my ghosts say about you freak me out, if you'll promise not to kill any of your harem in my house."

Jou chuckles and holds up his hand, pinkie finger extended. I shake it.

"Probably shoulda qualified that," he says. "Whaddo you mean by *kill*?"

"Anything that produces a dead body."

Jou grumbles. "Definitely shoulda qualified that. Some things I could do, they wouldn't *stay* dead."

"No more dead bodies, Jou. Not even temporary ones."

"Ooo-kay. Are we done doin' respect your way, sweetness? I'm beginnin' to resent the lack of nakedness here."

I lean in and nip his jaw. "First of all, you told me respect your way didn't involve sex. And second, we were naked less than two hours ago."

"Respect my way don't *necessarily* involve sex, but even if it don't, we got plenty of time before doin' respect my way to have more sex. An' two hours is much too long."

"All right." I've done my duty, and my visits to my grandmother's grave are never particularly long, with or without a demon. I give Jou's waist another squeeze, which he takes as a signal to start walking back between the boxwoods. "Is showing respect for the dead beginning to make more sense to you?"

"No," he says. "But the scenery's nice." He nods at the rolling lawns, dotted with granite headstones and bare trees, which in spring are masses of pink and white blossoms. "Where's the rest of your family?"

I gesture up the hill to where my parents' graves are. Side by side. Marked with a pair of rose granite headstones that I bought after finding my father's grave marked with just a tiny brass plaque and my mother's grave unmarked. I'm pretty sure my grandmother had something to do with that. "My parents are there."

"Old woman didn't like your dame?" Jou asks, skimming my thoughts.

"No. She never spoke of her. She told me about my father, what he'd been like as a boy, but she never said a word about my mother."

"And you just met this cousin," Jou says, parsing through my thoughts again. "You don't know any others of your dame's family?"

"I remember my Great-Aunt Paulina coming to meet us once. That's when we were still travelling, so it must have been fifteen years ago or more. The rest of my mother's family, no. I didn't even know they lived in Massachusetts. I went to school two hours away. My Dala could have brought me to meet them any time. But she didn't. I don't think she wanted them to know me." I take a deep breath and let it go. This is not the day to speak ill of my grandmother. "We're all stupid for the sake of family, aren't we?"

"You callin' my three years on that tree stupid?"

I look up at him, horrified that he would think I'm trivializing his pain. But he's grinning at me.

"Not funny, Jou."

"C'mon, sweetness, lighten up. It's over and done with."

That is *such* a demon-attitude. A person would be permanently traumatized by his ordeal. But Jou doesn't dwell on the past, as he's told me several times. Although from the sound of the upcoming family reunion, he might hold a bit of a grudge.

"You can really move on that easily?"

He shrugs and rearranges the drape of his arm across my shoulders. "Maybe. Maybe not. We'll see how I feel when I see the Old Man next. But I mean what I've said about enjoyin' the moment. I've told you what happened so you ain't wondering, thinkin' it had something to do with you—"

Which it did.

He pokes me in the ribs with his free hand. "Which it didn't. An' so you'd understand what you're pickin' up on from me. But it's done. I ain't gonna let it bleed over into this time. I deserve this. So do you. We've both been punished enough."

I wrap both of my arms around his waist. "You didn't deserve any punishment."

"Doesn't matter. It's over and done with, like I said. I'm puttin' it behind me. This is my reward."

He deserves a reward. A huge reward, for the penance he's done. "Okay."

"Can we leave the old woman's ghost here, too? She ain't my favorite human."

Probably because she tried to get me to cut off his head when he was transitioning back from Hell through my shower wall.

"Not just that," he says as we reach the car, and he opens the passenger door for me. "When you're not home, she follows me around an' talks trash about my cookin'."

I didn't know that and have to stifle a snort. My grandmother has very definitive ideas about food preparation. "Sorry. I think her ghost is anchored to my house, so we probably can't leave her behind, but she hasn't been able to manifest for a while. Since we had a fight. About you, actually. You might get a break from the trash-talking."

He hands me into the seat and crouches by the car. "'Least your ghosts don't come into the bedroom an' score my performance. Gotta be thankful for that, I guess."

That makes me laugh. The idea of the demon having performance anxiety is too funny. I lean out of the car and give him a big kiss.

"Mmm," he says when we come up for air. "Definitely feelin' the need for more nakedness, sweetness."

I smile at him. I've done my duty to my family, so nakedness sounds fine to me.

We drive back to my house, listening to WZLX on the radio, which obligingly plays The Stones for Jou. Driving forces him to keep his hands on the wheel and stick-shift, mostly, but he makes up for it as soon as we reach my house, sliding his hand under my skirt while I'm still unlocking the front door, working his way between my thighs and driving me wild as I struggle out of the layers I've worn to visit my Dala's grave, leaving a trail of clothes up the stairs and down the hall to my bedroom.

# CHAPTER 10

wake to a tickling sense. Something brushing against me. I snuffle and rub my nose. A tiny bit of red-gold fluff sticks to my fingers.

I hold it out. "Is this yours?"

"Hmm?" Jou murmurs sleepily. I guess he was dozing, too. He didn't sleep this much the last time we were together, but then he wasn't recovering from a three-year ordeal then, either. "Yeah, probably."

I roll over and prop myself on his chest so I can look into his face. Although the feather's gone, I still feel a funny, vague tickling. I wriggle under the covers, but it doesn't go away. Jou rubs his hands up and down my back.

"You okay?" he asks.

"Mmm-hum. It could just be that sense I've had for a while." I try to shrug it off. "So, about these wings."

He lifts a dark eyebrow over very sleepy, very sexy, hooded eyes. "What about 'em?"

"They're gorgeous."

"I like 'em, too." He smiles. "An'?"

"And you told me fire demons don't have wings."

He takes a deep breath, lifting me on his chest, and slides an arm under his head. "We don't."

"You do."

"Now I do. You're changin' me in all sortsa ways."

"Me? How did I have anything to do with you growing wings?"

"You healed me. Wings sprouted outta my back and lifted me off the thorns. That's how I got free. Guess lightning's not the only thing you can call."

I cross my hands over his sternum and rest my chin on them. "You think I gave you those wings?"

"Know you did."

"Did I give you a monster in your penis, too? You know what else I saw through that key." That vision is still really, really bothering me.

Jou lifts the covers and pretends to check. "Can't see one."

"Maybe it's lying in wait. Seriously, Jou, if your form is changing as I gain power, that's a concern."

"Why? You might like it."

I control a shudder. "I really wouldn't."

"I promise you, there's no monster in my dick. I told you, sweetness, there's no instruction manual for this. The seggurach bond." He trails his fingertip down my forehead to the tip of my nose in a line of blue flame. "I think this is just the way it works for us. I've always felt stronger feedin' from you than I should've. It's like, what're those ripples in water that bounce off each other? When they make a bigger wave?"

I've seen that, at the Science Museum, I think. "Coherence or something."

"Yeah, you know what I mean. I get a bigger boost off you than I should, 'cause our magic's in tune. Mine feeds yours and yours feeds mine. We're both more when we're with each other. You kept me alive when I should've starved. You healed me when I should've died. You gave me wings no fire demon's ever had. Maybe I gave you back Fire."

That makes sense. I shift on his chest and feel that tickle again.

"What the fuck is that, sweetness?"

"I don't know. It's like a goddamn rash."

Jou chuckles. "Demons don't get rashes."

"Do you get any diseases?"

"Not human diseases. We got our own forms of malaise. Erinyes can die of sorrow, which I don't fucking understand since most of the time it's them inflictin' sorrow on everyone else, but there you go."

"These are your mother's people?" I ask. When he nods, I ask, "Could you die of sorrow?"

His eyes go very, very dark. "Think I already did."

"You did? When?" Then I realize when and slide up to cup his face in my hands. "Jou—"

His eyes crinkle as he smiles, and although it takes a moment, the smile lights his eyes. "Over and done with, sweetness. Over and done. Just make me a promise. Don't ever shut me outta your head again. I really didn't like that."

"I didn't shut you out on purpose."

"I know. Just happened. Probably only a coupla days for you, but for me, it was over a hundred. I was feelin' pretty sorry for myself by the time I could feel you again. Then your magic came back, so strong I could barely keep you from seein' outta my eyes. I was kickin' myself then for binding you."

"Too much of a good thing," I say, biting my lip. I remember that time. It was longer for me than he thinks. I stopped dreaming about him, and I stopped feeling my Elements at all. It was like my heart stopped beating. I went around in a gray haze. It was after Halloween, and I should have been celebrating Samhain. Instead, I drank myself unconscious every day for the better part of two weeks, to keep myself from drinking something stronger and darker from my herbarium.

He strokes the tip of my nose again. "Over and done," he murmurs.

I nod. "Over and done."

I don't really want to remember that time, either. I wasn't tortured the way he was, but I was still suffering.

That stupid tickle runs through me like a sneeze. It tightens my belly and I feel the beginning of a different kind of suffering.

"Time for the bathroom," I tell Jou.

"Right." He lifts me off him. "Human pee, that I don't do."

I roll off the bed and gather my robe from the back of the bedroom door. "Do you do demon pee?"

If he does, do I want to know?

"Demons don't pee unless we're wearin' a glove and processin' human food. But, no, demon pee ain't my thing, either."

"Good," I toss over my shoulder as I head to the bathroom.

As I'm cleaning up, I feel that tickle again. So strong it's a shudder now. And I finally recognize it: there's something pushing against my wards.

I head down the stairs to check the front door and whatever's testing my wards gives a shove so hard I have to catch the banister to keep from falling over my own feet.

I *reach* and draw my *kama* from the Otherplace.

*Hold up, I'm not allowed to kill anything, but you get to stab the first thing that comes through your door? I'm feeling a basic lack of parity, here, sweetness,* Jou grumbles into my head.

*I have a really bad track record with things coming through my door, Jou.* I fire back.

He grumbles again but doesn't comment. I hear him rise out of the bed and pad to the top of the stairs.

Reassured by the demon at my back, I stand at the door for a moment, stretching my senses, trying to feel what's on the other side. There *is* something, and it's vaguely familiar. Maybe that's why it feels like a tickle rather than something more threatening.

Whatever it is, it's not a shapeshifting shark. I open the door, just as the tall blonde standing on my welcome mat lifts her fist to knock.

"Can I help you?" I ask.

She brushes by me like she owns the place. When she crosses my threshold without exploding, I relax. Rude, but not a threat.

She turns and slaps me full across the face.

I stumble back in shock. Catch myself on the far wall with a thud that will probably rattle the pictures off poor Shah's wall.

I reassess the threat-level and raise my knife.

"Dee's balls, Hairy." Another woman follows the blonde through the door. Where the first one's gorgeous in an accidental, trailer-trash kind of way, the second one looks like a pro. Thigh-high boots, leather shorts so short they must bare her ass-cheeks, a silver-buckled biker jacket open over a gold tube top that leaves a long strip of tanned, taut stomach showing between lamé and leather. In January. "Dast's gonna kill you."

Definitely a demon.

Jou collects me off the wall. With a rustle, his wings circle us, flame brushing my cheeks. He lifts my chin, his fingers gentle on my throbbing cheek, and looks into my eyes. His eyes glow a hard neon blue.

*You okay?*

*Yes. She just caught me by surprise.*

*She's gonna catch something.* He releases me and flicks his wrist. The whip of his will lashes out in a fiery streak and snaps around the blonde's throat. She screams and falls to her knees, clutching at the burning cord.

The hooker-demon shakes her bright pink mohawk and sidles away, into the parlor. Her movement clears the way for a third woman to walk through the door, shutting it behind her. This woman looks like she's just come from a business meeting. Black pencil skirt. White blouse under a sculpted jacket. Black patent leather heels that reflect the firelight of Jou's whip. They must be six inches high. Wow, I'd snap an ankle if I even tried those on for size.

"Don't damage her glove. She has a show on Thursday," the third woman says, stepping disdainfully around the choking demoness on the floor. She strolls a few steps down the hallway and peers into the kitchen. "Bigger than it looks from the outside."

"Don't touch nothin'," Jou growls at her. He takes hold of my wrist and pulls me after him as he stalks through the house, dragging the blonde. He brushes by the other two women, who draw back from him with what looks strangely like deference. Behind him, the blonde screams and twists at the end of the whip. She grabs at the doorframe as we round the corner into the kitchen. Her fingers leave scorching claw tracks in the painted wood. Jou drags her along effortlessly, as though he were carrying out the trash.

The back-door crashes open when he blows at it.

He releases my wrist on the stairs to the back porch, so I don't fall down them, but waits for me at the bottom, with the blonde still twisting at the end of his whip. He takes my hand again to cross the lawn. As we near the trees that demarcate my hearth room, a breeze rises, ruffling my bangs, kissing my cheeks with the crisp promise of snow. I feel it sweep across the stones of my circles, teasing them to life before my presence awakens them fully. Witchlight flares, golden despite the sunlight. The river stones of my pentacle begin singing, snapping tiny sparks towards my cauldron, before Jou even crosses them.

I stop at the circle of sand. How did he cross my circles? He couldn't do that before. I entrapped him in them before I banished him.

He shoves the demoness into the center of the inner ring. She brushes against my cauldron, then flinches away with a hiss of pain.

My cauldron tolerates rudeness even less well than I do.

"Starve," Jou growls at the demoness.

He turns on his heel, catches my hand again, and stalks back into the house, leaving the demoness raging in her prison.

Back in my kitchen, Jou leans against the counter, reels me in, and holds me to his chest. I hug him and we stand together like that for a long moment while, I sense, he draws on me to calm himself.

Finally, he says, "Told you the reunion wasn't gonna go well."

"It could have gone better," I admit. "But no one died. Not even temporarily."

"True," Jou says. "You can put that away now."

I follow his eyes down to my hand, still gripping my *kama*. Ruefully, I slide it into the Other Place.

"Want some coffee, sweetness? I think we're gonna need it." He nods at the open pocket door into my dining room, through which I can see into the parlor. The couture demoness is sitting on my couch while the hooker-demoness stands at the entertainment center, checking out the selection on my iPod.

It's not much of a surprise when she picks Eminem.

"Espresso," I tell Jou.

He chuckles, kisses my forehead, and lets me go.

"I'm going to get some clothes on," I say, retreating towards the hallway. Or possibly body armor. Whatever, I'm tired of being caught half-dressed by invaders in my home.

"Bring me that robe, sweetness. I like it," Jou says, over the sound of running water.

That makes me smile as I head to the stairs. I was in a fairly dark place when I bought the robe. Buying it didn't make me feel much lighter. Nor did watching it hang on the back of the bathroom door, unused, for weeks. That he wants to wear it. That he's here, with me, to wear it, makes me feel a thousand times brighter.

So does the salamander who jumps onto my shoulders from his perch on the banister. I stroke him as I trot up the stairs. "How did you get up there?" I ask my familiar. "That's like me leaping to the top of the Pru."

It's a rhetorical question, since Wizard doesn't talk, not even to me. But he makes his grumbly purr and wraps around my neck: a warm, scaly-soft torc. I pet him as I change into the outfit laid out on my bed. Which I didn't put there and didn't come out of my closet. It's gorgeous, like everything Jou dresses me in. He's making a statement with it, although I'm not totally sure what that statement is. What does patterned, raspberry-colored silk with velvet trim say? When I lift the outfit off the bed, I find separates: a boxy sweatshirt and soft yoga pants. I slide into them and stand in front of my mirror. The velvet makes the silk hang better than I deserve. I actually look like I have a few curves. I brush out my hair, shrug at my reflection, then collect Jou's robe before I head back downstairs.

In the kitchen, Jou's got three cups of coffee made and a fourth on the go. I find the black lacquer tray that held champagne and strawberries last night stored in the tray rack under the sink and set it with milk and sugar.

I look away for a moment when I'm replacing the milk bottle in the 'fridge, and when I look back, the cookie jar is next to the tray with its top off.

"He's fast," Jou observes from the other end of the counter where he's working a very shiny, very fancy coffee machine, which was not there yesterday.

"You both are," I respond, checking the cookie jar, which is filled with biscotti. Whether by hob magic or Peapod, I don't know. "When did you order that?" I nod at the coffee machine.

"Same time I ordered the groceries. An' don't look too hard at my baby. She don't like you."

She won't like it if I have to call power to deal with the two demonesses in my sitting room, that's for sure.

"I could do a permanent circle on the counter," I say. "Or you could just buy stock in Phillips."

I feel Jou skim my thoughts for the reference. As he does, he settles into my mind. Deeper, weightier, and somehow more *there* than he usually is. Given our guests, I don't question him, but I am curious.

"Is it a distraction?" I ask, as I stack biscotti on a plate. When I'm done setting the tray, I move behind him to press against his back.

"You in that outfit's a distraction. Can't wait to get into those little pants."

I rub against him. "Nice to know you still like what you see," I echo his words back to him. "But I meant being so deep in my head. Is it a distraction?"

"Uh-huh. Gotta remember whose lungs to breathe with and whose feet not to trip over. But I want us tight. In case Zef or Zip get any bright ideas."

Ah, the Zes. "Remind me of their names?"

"Zeifyr's dressed like she's got a power lunch. Zippy's in the pink mohawk. Hairy's out back."

I run through their names a couple of times while Jou finishes the last cup of espresso. He places it on the tray, and I feel a pause, like an indrawn breath. Is he waiting for me to take the tray? It is my house, and carrying the tray is a hostess-y thing to do. But things I did not sign on for include being a demon-maid.

Jou chuckles before he picks up the tray. "Pretty much knew when you wouldn't let me hold a door for you, how it was gonna go. 'Sides, I got a housekeeper already. Not what I want from my seggurach."

"At some point it would be good if you tell me what you *do* want from your seggurach."

Jou gives me an absolutely filthy grin over his shoulder, enhanced by him licking his upper lip with the tip of his tongue. "Think you already got some idea."

I roll my eyes at his back as I follow him through the pocket door. "Other than that."

*I want you under me, on top of me, an' at my back for whatever play Zef's about to make. Stay tight and don't let either of 'em touch you 'til I'm sure where things stand.*

That he feels the need to give me such a warning, when he already knows how I feel about his family, gives me the true measure of how tense this reunion could get.

*Okay.*

Jou deposits the tray on the table in front of Zeifyr. The demon in the pink mohawk, I'm still struggling to think of her as *Zippy,* takes a seat on the couch, which limits the seating options to demon-side, or the easy-chair that I almost never sit in because it's not actually that comfortable.

Jou chooses the chair, and I decide to take this whole having-his-back thing literally. I perch on the armrest. He hands me a delicate little demitasse cup of espresso and wraps his arm around my hips.

"How's the huntin'?" Jou asks the demonesses.

Zeifyr takes a sip of her coffee and puts the cup back on the tray before she responds. "Good. Hairy's got one program this week, two next week."

"Sounds like she's doin' all the work."

"Would you like to set me a quota?" Zeifyr asks coolly.

"Sure," Jou says, but his voice drops an octave to a bass rumble. "Whaddo you think's fair? One for every day I was on the Tree?"

Zeifyr's feline, perfectly lined eyes flare. "How many days was that?"

"You weren't countin'? 'Cause I sure was."

Blue sparks rise in those black-on-black eyes. "I tried. Nev tried. Ful tried. We all tried. Father put Nev in the Horns and set Rake on the rest of us. I went to the Hellroarer. I begged. I did everything he demanded, and then he told me there was nothing to be done. Father wouldn't change his mind, wouldn't grant you any reprieve. All our blood and pain, wasted."

"Not wasted. I appreciated it, since it was all I got outta you."

Zeifyr's face changes, thins, her cheekbones going sharp as knives, eyes sinking to burn blue in their sockets. "I gave what I have always given—"

A pink mohawk interrupts the blue glare flaring between Zeifyr and Jou. "Are you two really going to do this? Here? Now? The Hellroarer will call the muster before the human year turns. We should all be hunting."

Jou sits back and tightens his arm around my hips. "I got no need to hunt. You fill your stables. What's the Hellroarer got to say?"

"Father marches on the Gaudermont before the Winter Prince moves Z'kaba at the Turn," Zippy answers.

"He's trying to sever the Nol-Strond again?" Jou's deep voice gravels on the last word.

Zippy's pink mohawk dips. "It's his latest obsession. Even more than Nev. He'll throw a million bodies at it if he has to."

"No, he won't." Jou rubs his chin. "But he wants the Winter Prince to think he will."

"Why do you say that?" Zippy takes a biscotti, dunks it in Zeifyr's coffee cup and munches the wet end. Eating other people's food must be a family trait.

"Somethin' I learned on the Tree. Don't matter, though. The Hellroarer calls, we march. Don't matter where we're goin' or what we're doin'. You need to head back to the Hill? Call up the Zarzaroth?"

Zippy glances at Zeifyr, who is no longer glaring at Jou, but still has very sharp cheekbones. Zeifyr sits back on the couch and crosses her endless legs. She lifts one shoulder. "If you need to go back, go back."

"It could wait a little while," Zippy concedes. "Longer they're gathered, longer we have to feed them."

"True," Jou says. "Now ain't the time to piss off the Hellroarer by not bein' ready, though."

Zeifyr gives a delicate snort. "A thousand days on the Barbicon finally taught you to fear Father's displeasure."

"Thought you weren't countin'—"

"Of course, I was counting!" Zeifyr snaps.

Jou shrugs the arm he has around me. "Anyway, it's the Hellroarer I don't want to piss off, not the Old Man. He's got nothin' on me for now."

"Angien did you no favors while you hung on the Barbicon. None at all."

I feel Jou shrug again. "We'll see. How long we got, Zip?"

She shakes her head. "Red Duke's topside. Won't be before he's back."

"Yeah? Didn't think he could go topside anymore. Where is he?"

"Somewhere hot and sandy." Zippy holds up a black-nailed hand. "Persia? Pakistan? I can't keep track of human borders."

"Th' fuck he doin' there?" Jou asks.

"Something for Father. Toppling an empire. Starting a war. Who cares? It's only meat sacks. More souls for the Red Duke's stables. He's building up. We should be, too."

"Okay," Jou says. "You've seen me. Go build up."

"We've seen something that used to be you," Zeifyr says.

Jou's on his feet before I even feel him move. His wings brush over me as he spreads them. He looms over Zeifyr, horns blazing blue, wings blazing red. "Tell me what I *used t'be*, Zef."

She glares up at him, her own petite horns unfurling from her head, as black as Jou's but with tips as red as his wings. "You used to be Dast. Everything that was my brother. What are you now, *kvarn*?"

Jou returns to his seat in a single movement, horns and wings disappearing like they never were. He pulls me onto his lap, with my legs over the armrest, and tucks me tight to his chest.

"Still your brother. Still the Old Man's son. Still everything I was. Only now I'm more."

Zeifyr gives me a very unfriendly glare. "Are you more because of the meat you cling to?"

I give her that glare right back. "Please call me *meat*. I love it."

Jou snorts.

"Keep out of things that don't concern you, human," Zeifyr snaps. "You have no part in this play."

"Pretty sure I do have a part. Might even be a big part," I tell her, but I don't use the word. Not until Jou uses it and I'm sure he wants them to know what he's named me. "Either way, you're in my house, so you'll at least be polite. Or you can go hang out with your sister. Plenty of space out back."

Jou's laugh bounces me in his lap.

Zeifyr's dark eyes flick from my face to Jou's. "Couldn't you have at least picked a pretty one?"

"Seriously, plenty of space," I tell her.

"Get between me and my brother, human, and you will burn."

I'm not even sure I *can* burn anymore. "Wouldn't be the first time." I twist a little in Jou's lap so I can look into his eyes. "Are we done with the reunion yet?"

"Yep." He lifts me out of his lap and sets me on my feet. He rises from the chair and drapes his arm around my shoulders. "There's room out back, or upstairs, or on the couch, whatever you want, if you're stayin' the night. I expect you'll be gone in the mornin'. We're goin' out later. Don't touch nothin' while we're gone."

"And that's it?" Zeifyr asks acidly. "That's all? After everything?"

"After not seein' you for a thousand days? After bein' left there, armless, legless, dickless, to starve for a thousand days, not seein' you, hearin' you, havin' a sniff of you *for a thousand fucking days*? Yeah, Zef, that's all I've got for you. Gimme some time to forget how you abandoned me, an' maybe I'll have a little more."

Zeifyr leaps up to face him without even wobbling on those six-inch spikes. "I was with you every second!"

"No," Jou growls. He reels me around and positions me in front of him, between him and his sister, with his arms crossed over my chest and his wings unfurling around us. "Tsara was with me every second. Feedin' me. Healin' me. You were nowhere, Zef. *Nowhere.* So, go, build your fucking stable. Maybe it'll protect you. You never marched with me anyway."

"I'm not a soldier!" she shouts at him.

"I am. 'Cause I'm still the Old Man's son. 'Cause I'm still a Hell-roarer. 'Cause nothin's changed, Zef. Except that Tsara was there for me and *you fucking weren't*. That's what's different."

Zeifyr takes a step back and the blades of her cheekbones sink back beneath her skin. Her horns flatten into the shining fall of her hair. "When she is dust and memory, I will still be at your side," she sneers.

"Yeah, well, maybe that'll make up for the thousand days you weren't. Enjoy the coffee. We're goin' back to bed."

Jou turns me around. With his hand in the small of my back, scorching a hole in the gorgeous outfit, he propels me out of the parlor and up the stairs. He slams the bedroom door behind us, and my wards rise like a nuclear blast.

I plop down on the edge of the bed, feeling my bangs and the hems of my pants flutter at the breeze off my rising wards.

"Jeez, Jou."

He stands in the middle of my bedroom and closes his eyes. I see him gather himself. His wings fade to a shimmer. He shakes himself. When he opens his eyes, they're dark and soft. "Glad you were with me, sweetness. Zef can really fuck me up when she tries."

Is that why he kept using me as a shield?

"Yeah," he says, answering my unspoken question. "Compulsion she puts out . . . it's hard to fight. When I'm hungry, I can't. Folds me in half at the dick. Next thing I know, I'm at her feet, beggin' her to let me eat her out an' give her whatever she was hammerin' me for in the first place."

*So* much more than I wanted to know. "Jou, she's—"

"Yeah, I know." He takes a deep breath and slowly lets it out. "But she's also my blood and bone. Hard to ignore."

"You said that you like that I have no agenda. That it's really hard to live for a thousand years with the agendas of others. You were talking about her, weren't you?"

Jou nods. "An' Fulsome. They both push an' pull me in every direction but the one I want to go in."

"I didn't understand half of what you three said, Jou."

He shrugs, then comes to sit beside me on the bed. "We're goin' to war again soon, but that's nothin' new. Old Man's been trying to take out the Winter Prince since this world was new. We gain a little ground, lose a little ground. Nothing we do seems to make much difference. I've come to think that maybe it's the war that's important to the Old Man. Not winning or losing."

"You told me that's how he gains power."

Jou nods. "When his armies are dispersed, like now, he seems, I dunnow, *less* somehow. He's still a scary fuck, but he's not as much as he can be. When he gathers his armies, he's more. He shines so dark when he rides at the head of his Horde, I can't even look at him." He takes my hand and laces his fingers through mine. "Angien's the Old Man's general. When he calls, the troops I lead need to be ready. I can't keep them all fed when we're not fightin', so I leave 'em with the rest of the Horde. They kinda hibernate or find their own food in the Webs. But before they march, I'll need to call them up and raise as much power as I can stuff into 'em. That's what makes them able to fight. It takes some time, although maybe not as long now I've got you. Still, if the Old Man's marchin' this time next year, sweetness, it means that time I thought we were gonna have to fuck and cuddle and heal's gonna be cut short."

I squeeze his fingers with mine. "A year's still a long time, Jou. At least it is to me." Since I've only lived twenty-seven of them. "And this is just another obligation you have to your family. You know I understand those. So, if we need to go to Hell in a couple of months and raise your troops, then that's what we do. I mean, if you want me with you."

"Always, sweetness. An' I know you don't like the idea of *always*, but all I'm talkin' about is now an' tomorrow an' next year. We don't gotta think any further than that yet."

No, we don't. And I'm stupid to have even stressed about it. "Jou, could you be killed in your father's war?"

He shrugs. "Haven't been yet."

"Have you been injured? Badly, I mean?"

He nods without meeting my eyes.

"Worse than on that Tree?"

"No, sweetness. Never been hurt anything like that before. Not even when Essie ripped half my hide off."

"Charming, Jou."

He looks at me and strokes my cheek with his free hand. "You don't got nothin' to be afraid of. I told you, I won't let anything hurt you. You'll stay at the Hill when we march. That close to the Iron City, even if the Old Man lost all the ground he's gained in my lifetime, you'd still be safe."

I catch his hand and hold it in mine. "Excuse me, I'm totally going with you. Maybe I'm not a soldier, but you're stronger with me than you are without me. You've told me so. I'm going, even if I have to stand on the sidelines and just run in with bandages whenever there's a time-out. But you are not leaving me at home while you go to war. No chance, Jou."

He lifts an eyebrow. "Okay."

"Okay?" That was much easier than I expected.

He nods. "Okay. You just helped me face down Zef. I've gone head-to-head with her maybe a hundred times over the years, and more'n half those times I've ended up on my knees with my face in her cunt. Nothin' the ice demons can throw at me's as scary as what Zef can do to me when she tries."

I open my mouth to ask him why he didn't warn me that his sister had so much control over him, but then close it. I know the answer already. It's the same reason he let Denys LeConie cut me: he didn't want me to see him as weak.

"Yeah, that's right," Jou says softly.

"What was she trying to do to you?"

"Push me around. Bend me. Make me forgive her."

"But she's your sister. I mean, they're your sisters. Your harem, right? You'll forgive them, won't you?"

"I'm not feelin' very forgivin'. Not sure I'll know until I get back home how far it went, but I'm pretty sure Zef turned to the Hellroarer while I was gone. She smells like him now. An' he's had his eye on her since we were lemures. I've been waitin' for him to promise her somethin'. Consort. *Leccherouse*. Somethin'. Whatever it is she wants, he hasn't been willin' to give it to her. I thought." He pauses and squeezes my fingers. "I thought maybe she'd lowered her sights while I was on the Tree. She all but admitted—"

"But Jou," I interrupt. "She said she went to him because she was trying to help you."

"Yeah, I heard that. Might be true. Might be an excuse masqueradin' as the truth. It's hard to tell with Zef. She's good at makin' you believe what she wants. Either way, that she's back tells me she didn't get whatever it was she was anglin' for."

I consider that, and the scene downstairs, for a moment. "Without trying to second-guess you, doesn't pushing her away make it more likely that she will go to him? Even if he doesn't offer her exactly what she wants, sometimes second best is better than nothing at all. If you push her away, she might decide to settle."

Jou shakes his head. "I used to be afraid of her leavin'. Without her or Zip or Hairy, I wasn't sure I'd be able to hold the Hill. Now." He shrugs. "Now I don't want her to go just 'cause I don't want her to go. Whatever she does to me, I'll still miss her to fuck if she leaves. If she stays, though, it has to be her choice. I want her to choose to stay. I want her to choose *me*, and I don't think that was the choice she made while I was on the Tree."

"It seems kind of harsh to condemn her for exploring her options."

"Not when leavin' me was one of 'em."

"She's here, now."

"Yeah. But is she here now 'cause she's still mine, or is she here now 'cause she's Angien's, and the Hellroarer ordered her to make sure I'll still do what I'm told after the Old Man fucked me?"

I bow my head and look at our clasped hands. Demon politics are clearly way over my head. "Wow, Jou. I don't know how you could have lived with her for over a thousand years and still be unsure about her loyalty."

"That's my world, sweetness."

I nod. "I get it."

"See why I like your lack-o-agenda so much?"

"I'm beginning to. So, what now? We're not really going back to bed, are we?" I probably shouldn't be squeamish about having sex with Jou with his demonesses in the house, since he's probably done it with and in front of them thousands of times. But I am.

"Yeah. If you don't want to do it with them downstairs, we can just cuddle. I wouldn't mind sleepin' some more. I'm still kinda fucked-up."

Of course, he is. Because he's still healing from what his father did to him. What he endured to protect his family. Without even the comfort of his sisters.

I scoot back in the bed, tugging on his hands to draw him with me. He shrugs out of his robe and stretches out beside me.

"I kind of hate your family, Jou," I say as we wrap around each other. My head on his shoulder. Arms and legs tangling. His skin's wonderfully warm.

"I kind of hate 'em, too."

"You told me you don't miss them like humans miss each other. Do you love them at all?"

"With everythin' I got," he says softly. "Everythin' I done, every day of my life, I've done for them. So I'd have enough power to protect them."

He told me that, and I saw his pride at succeeding. His feelings for his family are complex. How could they be anything else after a thousand years?

"She didn't say *thank you*. None of them did."

One of them attacked his seggurach before she even said *hello*. God, I would be so angry at them if I was him.

"I am," he says quietly.

I cuddle as close as I can. "I want you to know how much I appreciate what you did. What you endured for me, even though I didn't know it at the time. I see it now. I'm grateful, Jou. I'm just so, so sorry you had to go through that."

He grunts and settles a little deeper into the pillows. "S'okay, sweetness. Over and done."

I cuddle tight and blank my mind so he can sleep. It's after he's breathing deep and slow that the thought comes back. It's not over and done. It never will be. Jou will always have to sacrifice himself for his family. And he'll always need me to put him back together after he does.

No wonder he wants forever.

# CHAPTER 11

When the light through my bedroom curtains slants long and golden, I get worried about the time and slide out of bed. I fold up the raspberry outfit, which has a huge scorch mark on the back and is probably ruined. I pull on old jeans and a sweater, since I'm not sure how messy scrying might get, and slip downstairs to get ready for Shirri.

There's no sign of Zippy downstairs, but Zeifyr is sitting at my kitchen table, watched closely by a semi-circle of three lizards. I assumed that since they were Jou's lizards, they'd be his family's pets, too, but seeing how warily they're watching Zeifyr makes me reconsider.

I pass them to turn on the coffee pot—since I have no idea how to operate Jou's fancy machine and no desire to hex it finding out—I'm just going to make myself a normal cup of coffee. Well, Pumpkin Spice, which is as normal as I get. I glance over my shoulder to ask if Zeifyr wants a cup and find her watching me. She smooths her pencil skirt, which is as perfect and unwrinkled as when she arrived several hours ago. I spend ten minutes in a tight skirt, and it gets those accordion puckers all over the place. She's definitely a demon.

Before I speak, she says, "If you're going to offer me a drink, I'd like some tea."

Heathen.

"Darjeeling or herbal?"

"Darjeeling would be fine."

I root around in my cupboard until I find a box of antique tea bags that I think came with the house, since I wouldn't buy tea bags for myself. Zeifyr would have been better off picking herbal, given the variety in my herbarium, but if she wants a drink from a nasty bag of dust, she can have a drink from a nasty bag of dust.

I boil water and pour it over her bag o' dust, then pour myself a cup of Pumpkin Spice—almost the last of the beans, and no more until next Halloween, boo—and stand with my back to the sink, sipping it while she waits for her tea to brew.

"I sense you have something you wish to say to me, human," she says after watching the water in her cup turn an unappealing greyish brown.

"Nope," I answer. "I'd really rather you and your sisters left, and I didn't have to talk to you at all."

"Oh?" She arches a black eyebrow at me. "Do I threaten you so much?"

"You annoy Jou, which means you annoy me. He's been through an unbelievable ordeal, which you and your sisters don't seem to appreciate. He needs to rest and heal, not argue with your ungrateful ass."

She looks up at me and all emotion drains off her face, leaving her looking at me absolutely blankly for a moment. Then, very unexpectedly, she blushes.

"You are a whelp," she says.

Great, more insults.

"So much space out back," I mutter.

"You have walked this plane for a handful of years. You know nothing. You *are* nothing. And yet you see his suffering when I did not."

"I healed him. I got to see it up close and personal." Much too up close and personal. Those wounds are going to figure in my nightmares for a long time to come.

"I'm ashamed that you had to point it out to me, human."

I shrug and take a sip of coffee. Mmm. Better.

"I did not." She pauses and licks crimson lips with a tongue only one shade paler. "I did not see him on the Tree. I know . . . what was done to him. But I did not wish to see him that way. Or have him see me seeing him that way. I thought I was sparing him, but now I understand that I have only hurt him in a way that Father did not."

Where Jou gets his thing for hiding what he perceives as weakness comes into sharp focus. "Yes, you did," I say.

She smiles—just a lot of teeth there—before she takes a sip of dusty-looking water. "Perhaps that is something. To still be able to hurt him."

I slam my hand down on the end of the table and am gratified when she controls a flinch. "You are a sick bitch if that makes you smile. Jou hung on that Tree, in agony, starving, *for three years* to protect you and the rest of your family. He loves you with absolutely every inch of what makes him *him,* and you can only feel some perverted sense of triumph because you can hurt him in a way your equally sick twist of a father can't?"

She puts down her teacup and stares at me, with those blades of bone rising under her skin again. "How dare you presume—"

"I'll presume whatever I want. This is my house. You are my guest. And if you can't show me any courtesy, then at least show your brother some. I'm disgusted by you and your sisters. Storming in here like Jou owes you something. Trying to hurt someone who has done nothing but prove to you with his suffering how much he loves you. You're repulsive, the three of you. I don't see how any human could ever want to give you their soul."

Her eyes swim with neon blue light. "You know *nothing*—"

I pull off my shades and let her see the lightning in my eyes. If she wants to play feral, I can totally go there. "Yeah, you said that already. I know enough to know that you do not deserve what Jou has given you. Not for the last three years. Not for the last thousand."

She pikes to her feet. "I have given Dast everything. Everything! I have followed wherever he led. I have lain with those I had no taste for because he required it. I have risked Father's fury again and again because he promised he would keep us safe. And then I discover that he has thrown it all away, broken every promise, for a short-lived sack of meat!"

"Ladies," Jou growls from the doorway. "Enough."

I back up against the sink, stick my shades back on, and cross my arms over my chest.

Zeifyr sinks back down onto the bench. She glares at Jou in her very chic, put-together way.

Jou ignores the blue-glazed glare aimed at him. He stretches, like a great, golden cat, then shrugs on the robe he's slung over his forearm.

"I'm sorry we woke you," I say.

"S'okay. I'm hungry. You want something to eat?"

We missed lunch and with Shirri on the way, I might not get dinner, so a snack sounds great. I nod and shift so I'm not blocking his path to the refrigerator.

While Jou rummages, Zeifyr sneers, "You still enjoy human food."

"Yeah," he responds without taking his head out of the 'fridge. "You might want to clear out while I'm cookin' if the smell bothers you."

"I'll endure it," she grumbles. "I wish to speak with you."

He backs out of the 'fridge to toss lettuce, tomatoes and a pack of bacon onto the counter. "Zef, I'm really not in the mood."

"I'm not looking for a fight," she says.

Jou shrugs and goes back to rummaging. My refrigerator is extremely full. How much did he order from Peapod?

When he uncovers butter and bread, he assembles everything on the counter, pulls out a pan and starts the bacon frying. I lend a hand by popping the bread into the toaster.

"Your human has pointed out that I've been discourteous and unkind," Zeifyr says to Jou's back as he slices lettuce and tomatoes.

"Yeah, but I didn't expect anything else. I know why you're pissed at me. Ain't gonna change nothing, Zef."

"My feelings mean nothing to you?" she asks.

I shake my head at her. "That's not looking for a fight?"

"It has nothing to do with you, human," she hisses.

Jou sets the knife into my butcher-block and turns around to face the demoness. "Enough, Zef. You know what Tsara is. Stop pretending you don't so you can take cheap shots. I told you, changes nothing."

"The human is bound to you, nothing more."

Jou shakes his head and goes back to cutting up the tomatoes. "You're wastin' my time."

Zeifyr stews for a minute, while Jou turns the bacon over. When the bacon's reached saliva-inducing levels of crispiness, he takes it out of the pan and lays it on a paper towel to drain. I hand him the toasted bread and watch, licking my lips, as he assembles our BLTs.

"I honestly have no wish to fight with you," Zeifyr says finally.

"Gettin' to be too late for that," Jou responds.

"If I apologize, can we start again?"

"Why, you got somethin' to say that I want to hear?"

"Possibly."

"Okay, I'm listenin'." He finishes one B.L.T. and slides it onto the plate I hold out to him. He tips his chin at the kitchen table, but I shake my head. First of all, eating next to Bitchella will give me indigestion. Second, I'm not as rude as his demoness. I'm not eating before he does.

His lips twitch as he starts on the second B.L.T.

"The Fleshwhip has called the *Zeimal*. Will you answer?"

Jou piles lettuce and tomatoes on top of the bacon without responding. When he finishes the sandwich, he cuts it in half and arranges it artistically on the plate, then carries it over to the table and sits across from Zef. I follow him and when he pats his thigh, cuddle up to him. He puts his arm around me as I start in on the BLT. Holy cow, or pig, whatever. Super-crunchy pig fat heaven. With tomatoes.

"Good pig," Jou agrees.

"That smells like overripe Flaming Spider, Jou. How can you put that inside your body?" Zeifyr complains.

He takes another bite with obvious relish.

"When you're finished your puerile attempt to disgust me, would you answer my question?"

"I'm just enjoyin' my pig, Zef. First bacon I've had in more'n a thousand days. But to answer your question, no, I won't. Nothin' to do with me."

"Tem and Angien think it does."

"They're wrong. I just spent a thousand days provin' my loyalty to the Old Man. Why would I fuck that up by throwin' in with the assholes plottin' to kill him?"

I glance at Jou in surprise. *I thought Angien was your father's general?"*

*He is,* Jou responds into my head. *He's also the leader of a conspiracy against the Old Man that's been going on for at least a century. An' just in case you thought we weren't keepin' all the back-stabbin' in the family, the other one Zef's just mentioned? Tem? He's my father's baby brother.*

*Dear God, Jou.*

*Gets better. Pretty sure Tem was also my mother's lover, and the reason Tem keeps tryin' to drag me into this shit's because he believes I'm his son. Welcome to my fucked up little corner of Hell.*

*Jeez, Jou, I'm going to need a chart.*

He chuckles. *Nah, it'll all come clear. Remember, you got plenty of time to learn who's who and who was doin' who.*

I shake my head and go back to my BLT. Pig fat and tomatoes, at least, are uncomplicated.

"If they succeed, and you had a chance to join them and didn't, we'll be exiled from Dis."

"I'm more concerned about what happens when they fail. If they ever even make a move. They've had plenty of chances, Zef. Haven't taken a single one. What makes you think they're gonna now?"

"Father plans to sever the Nol-Strand."

Jou shrugs, his shoulder and side moving against mine. "So? He's been plannin' that since we were lemures. Hasn't gotten any further than the Broken Bridge."

"This time, the Skin-Shredder fights at his side," Zef says.

Great, another demon I don't know. And such a friendly sounding one at that.

"Trecial joined him for the Battle of Blede Mill and summoned the Legion of Air when the Old Man took the Arlech. Each time he gained a little ground before declarin' truce and fallin' back. I'm tellin' you, Zef, I figured it out while I was on the Tree. It ain't about winnin' for him. Not anymore. It's the battle. It's gatherin' his followers, gettin' us to raise power so the Horde can march. It don't matter whether he gains a little ground or loses it. It's the preparation and the fight that make him stronger. That's what he's doin'. And the Hellroarer's goin' against him when he's at the peak of his power? Good fuckin' luck."

"If each battle makes him stronger, then we have to stop him before he marches into another."

Jou goes very still against my side. "We?" he asks slowly.

Zeifyr bows her head. Without her blue-lit stare on me, I feel a weight, a pressure, that I wasn't even aware of, fall away. Is this what Jou feels? This constant, unconscious compulsion?

*Yeah, that's exactly what I feel,* Jou says into my head. *Only I feel it more in my balls than you do.*

*It would be hard for me to feel it there.*

*Why? You got some great big lady balls sometimes.*

I snigger, and Zeifyr raises her head to glare at me. The air thickens. I can feel it shoving at me. Trying to open an inch between my skin and Jou's.

I push my empty plate away, meet her eyes, and nestle more firmly into Jou's side.

*Oh, there they are,* Jou thinks.

That makes me grin.

"You find this amusing, do you, human? All this talk of strategy and battle? The possibility of all of us losing our lives so our father can claim a few more *dechente*?"

I tip my head to look up at Jou. "Is *dechente* like yards or more like miles?"

"Three kilometers." Jou grunts. Shakes his head. "I ate a math teacher in New York, and I can only think in fuckin' metric now."

I chuckle, probably more loudly than is warranted, but I like how it makes Zeifyr's eyes flare.

"What I find amusing," I say to her. "Is how hard you're trying to push Jou around. And me. Kinda puts the lie to 'oh, you've only bound the human,' doesn't it? I also find it amusing that you're trying to win Jou to a side he's already rejected. You've known him for over a thousand years. I've known him for three months. But I already know that's a lost cause. And I find it amusing that after not seeing him for three years, you just keep telling him what's on your mind, rather than finding out what's on his. I don't really get how this harem thing works." I raise a hand. "And I don't really want to. But I'm pretty sure it's not like this."

Her carmine lips pull back from a set of teeth any wereshark would be proud of. "Human—"

I hold up a hand. "Spare me." I glance at my kitchen clock and climb off Jou's lap. "Jou, my cousin's going to show up any minute. Do you mind removing your demoness from my hearth room?"

"Sure. Okay if I stake her to one of your trees?"

Is it? Having tangled with Zeifyr twice, the idea doesn't bother me as much as it should. I definitely don't want all three demonesses in my house. I don't like the idea of being that outnumbered. And speaking of which, where did the pink-mohawk demoness get to?

"Go for it," I tell him.

Jou picks up the uneaten half of his sandwich and takes it with him as he strides out the back door. I pick up the empty plates and my coffee cup and pop them in the sink. I don't offer to take Zeifyr's cup. I'll collect it later, when I do the dishes. I'm bleaching everything she's touched.

"Human," Zeifyr begins behind me.

I raise a hand without turning around to look at her. "Seriously, spare me. You've asked him what you wanted to ask him. He said no. We've got plans for the rest of the day and I think I can speak for Jou in saying that we'd both really love it if you were not here when we got back—"

"I'm *not* leaving him to you," she hisses.

I roll my eyes even though I know she can't see my face. "Okay, whatever. Places to do, things to see."

"Tsara," she says, clearing her throat, proving she knows my name, which I didn't think she did. "I wish . . . I want to talk with you without his interference."

Fuck that. "Sorry, busy."

I hear the rustle of that super-fitted skirt, the click of her heels, as she rises from the table and comes over to stand behind me at the sink. I *feel* her. Her presence has the same kind of weight that Jou's does. Her will is more sinuous, more grasping, than Jou's, but it has the same magnetic draw. I'd know she was his sister, even if no one had ever told me.

She's a lot taller than I am, particularly in those heels, and sometimes I feel intimidated when tall people loom over me. But not right now. I'm perfectly happy to show her how not intimidated I am by backing her up a couple of feet with a bolt of lightning. I turn one of my hands over on the lip of the sink and splay my fingers. Just one little bolt. Surely Jou won't mind as long as I don't do her any permanent damage.

The doorbell rings.

"Saved by the bell," I tell her. I turn from the sink, scoop my familiar off the floor, and go to answer the door.

The lizards make it there before I do—despite their fat, little legs, they can really move when they want to—and poor Shirri is greeted by a horde of salamanders when I open the door. She copes better than I do when faced with overenthusiastic pets. She kneels and pets each of them, including Wizard, when I put him on the floor to participate in the petting.

While she's scratching Izzy's tummy, Jou returns from staking his sister to my tree, or whatever he was doing. I hear him pad up the hallway behind me, even though he usually moves silently. Either he's giving me warning, or I'm more aware of him now. Or he's still too hurt to move like a shadow.

*Little bit of all three,* he says into my mind. *You gonna introduce me?*

"Shirri, this is my boyfriend, Jou. Jou, this is my cousin, Shirri."

Shirri rises, brushing off her hands on her long skirt like she's brushing off dog-fur, and holds her hand out to Jou. The demon engulfs her small hand in his big one carefully and shakes. She smiles up at him, but her eyes track above his head. Is she ogling his dreads, or can she see his horns and wings the way Nikki can?

"Nice to meet you," Jou says, and I wonder if his black-fur voice reminds Shirri of her husband, the way Will's reminded me of Jou. At least I don't have to feel that horrible, sick pang of loss and longing when I hear a man's deep voice anymore.

"And you," Shirri responds. Her smile's warm and genuine, so either she was just admiring his mane, or she has nothing against demons. "I'm usually good with accents, but I can't place yours."

Jou chuckles. "I've been all over the place."

Jeez, *that* is an understatement.

"Is English your second language?" Shirri asks.

"Mmm, tenth or eleventh, I think."

"Wow." Shirri glances at me and widens her eyes. "I thought I'd accomplished something learning four."

"That *is* an accomplishment," I say. "I only speak two, and my family will tell you that my Romani is atrocious."

Shirri grins at me. "That's what Will says about my Latin. I hate conjugations. Really, really hate them."

I return her grin. "You want to come through? I thought we'd scry in the back. I have a permanent circle."

"You have a permanent circle? Wow, you're so lucky . . ." Shirri trails off when first Zippy and then Zeiphyr step into the hallway. "Full house," she murmurs.

"Jou's sisters." I take a deep breath. "Zippy and Zeiphyr."

Shirri doesn't react to their names. Maybe she has even more exotic names in her family. "Hi," she offers, but she tucks her hands behind her back.

I don't blame her for not wanting to shake with either of them. I steer her quickly past the two demonesses. Jou follows behind us, and I feel a stir, in the air, or the aether, as he passes Zeifyr, but when I glance back at him, he's a step behind me, wearing a small smile that could mean anything from him appreciating the view of my butt to him cutting down Zeifyr with that burning sword of his and leaving her in a pile of ash in my hallway. Hard to tell.

He catches my eye and winks at me.

Probably the former, then.

Shirri admires Jou's new toy as we pass through the kitchen, so of course we have to stop for a minute for Jou to show it off. With the promise of coffee later, we head out into the backyard. Jou continues to trail us, and I wonder if that's because he's sticking close to me while his sisters are around, or because he's curious about the scrying, or because he wants to be there to deal with the fall-out of Shirri seeing his demoness staked to a tree in my yard.

*Little bit of the first two*, Jou responds in my head. *Neither of you'll be able to see what I did to Hairy. Not even with your witch-sight.*

*What did you do to her?* I think back, before I catch myself. I probably don't want to know.

*Stuck her on the other side of a Gate. It's in your holly tree, so don't go brushin' up against it. Haulin' you back from where that Gate leads would be a ball-ache.*

Great. Now there's a demon-gate in the middle of my yard. I push that aside for the moment to take Shirri's arm and lead her into the pocket dimension of my hearth room.

Before I even step across the outer circle, I can hear her. A thin whisper that grows and grows until my hearth room is filled with screams. Shirri goes pale as we step across the outer circle.

"What is that?" she whispers.

"Sorry," I say. I turn to the demon behind us. "Jou, we can hear her. There's no way we're going to be able to scry with her screaming like that."

He grunts, steps back out of my hearth room for a second and reaches into the holly tree. The screaming stops abruptly.

"Tsara—" Shirri whispers.

"It's a really long story. I'll tell you over coffee. It has been the weirdest couple of days."

She looks at me, her eyes so big they're almost round. "Why do I have the feeling that your weird and my weird are on wildly different scales?"

"You'd be right." I lead her to my cauldron, which I find filled with shimmering, silvery liquid, even though I haven't called the Elements.

"Oh!" Shirri grins down at the water and stretches her hands out to it before she stops herself. "Is it okay for me to touch?"

"Er—" I'm honestly not sure. My cauldron's never hurt me, but it is a wild magic. It appeared when I built my hearth room. I came out one morning to lay more river stones in the second circle and it was just there, suspended in the air, precisely in the middle of the innermost circle. "Maybe start by touching the rim? See what it does?"

Shirri nods and gently lays her fingertips against the cauldron's iron rim. She's braver than I am; I was hesitant to touch anything in Timmi's Museum, until I was totally sure it was safe. Some magical shit bites back, really hard.

My cauldron chimes softly, and ripples hunch along the surface of the water in geometric patterns. Pretty sure normal water doesn't do that.

Shirri slides her fingers over the lip and into the water.

There's a deep, indrawn breath. At first, I think it's from her and me. Then I feel the pressure expand outward, and I realize my hearth room is breathing. When it blows out, a bubble of water follows it, rising from the cauldron, the surface crackling with blue electricity. It brushes by me, sweeping across my skin with the smell of seawater and ozone. When it hits Jou, sitting cross-legged on the floor between the pentagram and inner circle, watching us, it blasts away his glove and leaves him sitting in all his demon-glory: horns, crown, wings, tail and steaming, dark gold skin. He shakes himself like a dog coming out of water, and I can actually See him spin the glove out again, magic whirling around him, spattering embers across the floor of my hearth room, to spit and sizzle against the river stones.

He grins at me. "That felt good."

I glance at Shirri, who is looking at Jou. Her eyes aren't any wider than they were a minute ago, but she definitely saw his demon-form.

"You okay?" I ask.

She looks at me. "Your boyfriend?"

I nod.

"Wow. I guess it really is a long story."

"Yup."

She slides her hands all the way into the water, up to her wrists, and my cauldron begins to shift. I put my hands on the far rim, feeling the iron warp and stretch under my palms. It widens and flattens, as Shirri and I back up to allow it to grow into a five-foot wide dish. The water firms and Shirri takes her hands out of it, then presses her palms against the hard, mirrored surface.

The cauldron slowly lowers to the ground; Shirri and I follow it and sit facing each other across the mirrored expanse. I put my palms flat on the mirror, echoing her position.

"This isn't my thing," I tell her. "Do we chant, or what?" I was taught how to scry at Bevvy, and the ritual always involved chanting. It also never worked for me.

She shakes her head. "Reach."

Okay, that I know how to do. I close my eyes to help myself focus and *reach*.

*Earth.* My first Element. The one I'm still most comfortable with. I *reach* and feel its gritty warmth fill me. The mirrored surface under my palms warms and when I open my eyes, I see it glowing from within, reddish light spilling upwards, casting rose-lit shadows onto Shirri's face.

*Air.* My second Element. I *reach* and a breeze flutters my bangs, swirls warm, then cool around me. I hear a rustle to my left, where Jou is sitting, and when I glance at him, I see that he's manifested his wings again and has spread them, the crimson tips brushing the holly to the left and the oak trunk to the right. My hearth room is twenty feet across. His wings are massive.

I swallow and *reach* a third time. *Fire.* It comes so easily that I know Jou was right. It is my Element now, and I'm going to have to learn how to control it, because that raging hunger immediately fills me. I push it out, into the mirror, and the surface ripples away from my hands, crackling, blackening, reflective whitecaps forming on the waving surface.

Black water.

"There," Shirri breathes. "Look."

I do. I feel the water's current, swift in the middle, slow by the banks. Man has narrowed the Charles, created ramparts of stone and concrete to hem in the water. The river remembers. It remembers when it used to spread without obstruction, flooding the fens. It chews and chips at the banks, wanting to return to its old paths. I feel its little victories, as a bit of the bank crumbles and falls to the bottom. Past minnows and waving fronds of weed. Down into the muddy darkness.

That's what I want. The deep places. Places a huge predator might lurk. I wriggle along through the mud, seeking. There are larger creatures here. Bass and lunkers. A muskrat wiggles by. No huge, toothy predator. Nothing that causes the smaller animals to dart away in terror. Nothing that disturbs the natural order.

"Shirri, I don't feel it."

"Me, neither."

"Come with me," I say, half a request, half a demand. I drag her upstream, water rushing by us in trails of dark green bubbles.

I feel it the moment we cross into its territory. An icy current. The putrid stink of meat left in water too long. And then a pair of brilliant, blazing green eyes. I pull up short and watch as the kelpie takes shape in the mirror. It shakes a sea-weed mane out of its glowing eyes.

"Sassthen," I say, naming it.

The kelpie pulls half-rotted horse lips back from fangs that don't belong in a horse's mouth and flicks out a tongue, long and black as an eel. "Earthwitch. Airwitch. Firewitch. And a waddahwitch. Two little witches wi'h four little faces. Fuck d'you want?"

The kelpie speaks with a Southie accent. Before I met Jou, that probably would have struck me as strange.

"I have a question. I can pay."

The kelpie makes a hissing noise that also shouldn't come out of a horse's mouth; it might be laughter.

"Think so? Blood and magic? Flesh and bone? What're you offerin' me?"

"Both," Jou says suddenly. He rises and walks over to the scrying mirror. He holds out his left arm and pushes back the sleeve of his robe. "Up to the elbow. That's good payment for a question, water brother."

Is a kelpie a demon? I thought it was fae. Maybe it's both. I'll have to ask Jou later.

"Fire brothah," Sassthen responds. "That's good payment. Ask the question, three faces."

"Is there a maneater in the Charles?"

Sassthen makes that hissing noise again. "Yeah." He bares his extremely sharp teeth again.

Gross. "Other than you?"

"Sounds like anothah question."

I shake my head, not wanting Jou to feel obligated to offer another body part. I know he doesn't feel the same about lopping off pieces of himself; I know he'll regenerate. But it will hurt him to feed the kelpie his arm, or whatever he's going to do, and I don't need to cause him any more pain.

"Then I'll give you the answer to the question you didn't ask, three faces. You're lookin' down when you should be lookin' up. That's all I'm gonna say. Gimme that arm."

Jou nods and plunges his arm into the mirror. I force myself to watch as the kelpie lunges forward. He opens that fanged mouth—more like a piranha than a horse—and snaps down on Jou's arm. He shakes his horse head. The mirror clouds with Jou's black blood. With a grunt, Jou yanks his arm back. Blood spatters across the mirror's surface. I watch it drip from the ragged stump of his forearm.

The B.L.T. I ate like an idiot before doing major magic rises into my throat and I have to swallow hard to keep from yarking it across the mirror.

I pull my hands away from my cauldron and reach out to Jou. At the same time, I *reach* into the Earth and draw that hot, healing grittiness into me. My heart slams in my ears. I close my hands around his torn flesh. Feel him flinch when I brush the heel of my palm against the nub of broken bone. I pour Earth's Blood over his injury. When the Earth's Blood drips onto the mirror, it ignites. The mirror melts and a whirlpool of neon fills my cauldron.

I smooth my hands up and down his forearm, feeling it firm under my hands. By the time I reach his wrist, his fingers grip mine. I massage the Earth's Blood in. It sinks into his warm flesh, leaving just smooth, warm skin behind.

I lift my eyes to his. He winks at me.

"Are you okay?"

"Yeah, sweetness. You get what you want?"

"Well, it's not a wereshark."

"Yeah, I heard. You ready for coffee?"

I smile at him. "Yes, thanks, Jou."

He winks at me again, draws his hand slowly out of mine, and walks back towards the house.

When I glance at Shirri, she's following Jou with her eyes. Not in a creepy, I-want-to-jump-your-boyfriend way, but in a holy shit way.

Which is pretty much how I feel about Jou all the time.

"Could you help me put my cauldron back?" I ask her.

She tears her eyes away from Jou's retreating back and nods.

Without discussion, we place our hands on the iron rim, facing each other over the fading whirlpool. The cauldron responds instantly, lifting and swelling into its normal shape. The whirlpool drains away, leaving a black coating on the inside of my cauldron. I touch my fingertip to it, feel the familiar tingle, and smell Jou's hot ginger scent.

Jou's blood has stained the inside of my cauldron.

I swipe it with my finger, but it's solid and dry: an obsidian coating.

"Um," Shirri begins, watching me.

I shrug. "That's the least weird, least awful thing that's happened today. Let's go have coffee."

She links her arm through mine, giving me the sweet-violet of her perfume and the baby-powder of fabric softener, but no scent of magic at all. But I felt her magic when we were scrying. It was strong and clear, like an ocean current. Now there's nothing.

We walk arm-in-arm out of my hearth room towards the house and I give in to my curiosity. "Shirri, I can't feel anything from you."

"Hmm?"

"Magic? I can't feel your magic. I could in there." I hook my thumb over my shoulder. "But I can't now."

She shuffles her peach suede ankle boots through the withered grass of my lawn. "I didn't tell you what I do, did I? My job?"

"No."

"I'm a primary school teacher. K through three. The littlest kids. The ones who are still sensitive. They can sense it, my magic, so I've gotten really, really good at hiding it. *Cloaking*, Will calls it. Like the Klingon ships in *Star Trek*."

I laugh at the comparison. "You don't have to do it with me."

"Oh, I know. It's automatic now. I don't even think about it."

I feel a wrench in my chest, that she should have to hide her magic so often, so thoroughly, it's become automatic. But Shirri smiles at me.

"Don't feel bad for me. I love teaching. I love my kids. I didn't realize, when I started, that I'd have to hide my gift, but if I had known, I'd have made the same decisions. I wouldn't do anything differently."

"Shirri, still," I object.

She squeezes my arm. "I mean it. I wouldn't change a thing. Come see my class someday. Meet my little terrors. You'll get it."

"I will," I promise as we mount the back steps.

The rich fragrance of dark roast hits us as soon as I open the back door. Jou, standing at his toy, gestures toward the kitchen table, which is already set with milk, sugar and a plate of biscotti.

I scan the kitchen. Izzy is in his usual place on top of the fridge. Wizard is perched on the counter next to Jou, watching what the demon's doing with such interest that you'd think the lizard was about to get fed. No sign of the third lizard, whose name I can never remember, or either demoness. I notice the doors to the hallway and dining room are closed, so Zeifyr and Zippy are probably in the dining room or parlor.

It's too much to hope they've left.

I steer Shirri to my kitchen table. She sits, sets her elbows on the table and props her chin on her folded hands. "So, tell me this long story," she says.

# CHAPTER 12

Over coffee and biscotti, I explain how a demon came to be my lover, how his harem came to be my houseguests, and how I know the name of the Watertown kelpie.

Shirri listens to everything with nothing more than a raised eyebrow, and since she's already proven she's open-minded, I tell her pretty much everything. Even about the demoness currently parked behind a hell-gate in my garden, either screaming into a gag, or lacking the equipment to scream with. I don't want to know which.

Jou sits next to me and interjects occasionally, while drinking his coffee and eating biscotti, adding details designed to make us laugh. I haven't seen him interact much with other humans, but I guess I shouldn't be surprised that he can be charming when he wants to be. He's an incubus, after all.

*I don't need to be charming with most humans*, he says into my head. *They're only too happy to buy what I'm sellin'. This is me. This is what I am when you're not fightin' me tooth and nail.*

I lean into him; he slides his arm around me.

When I'm done, and all the biscotti's gone, I wait, turning my coffee cup around between my hands. I don't think Shirri will judge me, but you never know. Until I met Lin, and then Mel, people were a pretty constant disappointment to me.

Shirri takes another sip of coffee—she's now on her third cup, so she must have no fear of caffeine—before she says, "You win. Your life is officially weirder than mine."

I grin and shake my head. "You're married to a shifter. A *bear* shifter. That's a ten on my weird-o-meter."

"You're dating a prince of Hell," she shoots back, and waves away my protest that Jou isn't a prince. "That's dialing it to eleven, couz."

"Maybe twelve," Jou says. "You've only met the Old Man the once."

I elbow him. "Not helping."

He chuckles.

"I guess I haven't helped much, either." Shirri sighs. "I'm sorry."

She's taking it on herself?

"Don't be sorry. I really enjoyed tonight. I haven't ever *Worked* with a water witch before. It was great. It didn't prove my guess about Toby's killer, but I got something. Sassthen said I should be looking up rather than down. So maybe whatever killed Toby was a creature of Air."

Shirri nods. "I heard that, too. Do you trust the kelpie?"

Jou snorts.

"Was that a, 'no, I shouldn't trust the scary thing that ate your arm'?" I ask him.

"It was a, 'that's a water demon pretendin' to be a fairy. Don't trust it any further than you can throw it.' But it probably wasn't lyin' to you."

"Fae don't lie. Do water demons?" I ask.

"They can. An' don't think the Twitterin' Throng don't lie. They don't lie to humans when they're on this plane 'cause it shreds their connection to the mortal world. But you get them on their home ground, you can guarantee nothin' comin' out of their mouths is the whole truth."

I consider this for a moment, turning my coffee cup around in my hands. I might need more coffee to think this through. "There wasn't anything in the river. That I'm sure of."

Shirri gives an emphatic nod.

"Sassthen's jaws weren't anything like eight inches when he bit your arm off, so that rules him out as Toby's killer," I continue, and it's Jou's turn to nod. He probably got a better look at the kelpie's jaws than I did. "But I don't know any creature of Air that would kill and eat a shapeshifter. Gargoyles aren't meat-eaters. Nethancs are, but their mouths aren't much bigger than ours, and even a pack of them couldn't take down a shapeshifter. I just don't know enough about creatures of the Air, I guess." I take a deep breath and let it out. "Time for more research."

Jou rubs a warm hand up my back, under my sweater. "I'll help."

"Thank you, Jou."

Shirri looks from me to Jou and back, then smiles. She offers me her empty coffee cup. "If you want to scry again, I'm up for it. Any time. I loved that. Even the scary bits."

She was extremely cool during the scary bits, for which I'm grateful. But maybe seeing a fanged, water horse bite off the arm of a winged, fire demon doesn't measure up to the terror a bunch of kindergarteners can lay down. "Thanks, Shirri."

She hangs out with us for another cup of coffee, and she and Jou find common ground when they start talking cooking. She promises to email him her favorite recipes and Jou surprises me by not only knowing what email is, but by rattling off my email address without me even thinking it.

As we wave her goodbye from the front porch, I knock his shoulder with my temple. "How do you know my email address?"

Jou shrugs. "I learned everything I could about you, last time I was here. I guess that stuck. I coulda given her mine, but baronash at dis dot hell mighta scared her off, an' I want those recipes. Particularly that one for lamb goulash. That sounds the fuckin' bomb."

I look up at him. "Da bomb."

"Yeah, that. So, you wanna do this research tonight?"

I would, but I want to go dancing with him more.

He grins. "Works for me, sweetness."

———

Long before we find the faerie ring, I'm wondering what the heck I'm doing trying to bring a demon into the wild lands.

The woods reject him, leading us 'round in circles, even though I know the Estabrook Woods like the back of my hand. The familiar paths have disappeared into browned bracken. The trees have shuffled. Nothing's where it should be, and I know that's because I've brought an infernal creature into woods the fae have claimed as their own.

Finally, more out of perseverance, and me threatening to curse the trees with Dutch Elm disease if they shift again, I walk around a stand of beech and out into the moonlight of the faery ring. The crunch of leaves under my boots deadens as I enter one of the Quiet Places. I push my boots and socks off and step carefully over the border of white mushrooms, unblackened by the winter frosts. Feeling the cold seep into my bare soles, I shiver and open my arms.

The wild fae are already here, all around, but hidden in their way. They send a breeze to test me, which lifts my bangs and fills my ears with the chime of silver bells.

I step back. Jou catches me, folds me against his warm chest.

"He's with me," I say to the breeze.

*Earthwitch . . . queen without a country . . . fae-friend.*

"You know me," I say. "I wouldn't bring an enemy to the dance."

*Hellspawn . . . devourer . . . fae-foe.*

I feel Jou shift behind me, firming up his stance, as the breeze pushes at him.

"No," I say. "He's not an enemy. He's mine. I'm his. If I'm fae-friend, so is he."

The breeze withdraws, leaving a breathless pause behind it. Then the glowing eyes of the wild fae peep out from between the trees on the far side of the circle.

"It's okay," I tell Jou. He releases me, but I don't need to move away. I just crouch in front of him and put my palms to the cold ground. I scrunch my fingers through the dead grass and fallen leaves. The noise reassures me that I've been accepted into the circle. I flatten my hands on the ground and close my eyes for a moment, remembering the music I've memorized for tonight.

The ground pulses. A deep, tympanic swell. The trees around the edge of the circle throb and shudder, bouncing an eerie wail back and forth across the circle.

I lift my hands from the ground. I don't need the contact now. Instead, I take a step and let the rhythm flood away from my bare soles, across the circle, in a burst of sound and color that splashes against the circle of trees, and the wild fae emerging from them.

The fae don't take form at first, still afraid of the demon standing behind me. They're just glowing eyes, a wisp of gossamer fabric, the glint of moonlight on too-pale skin.

I lift my hands and *call*. Lightning crashes down out of the black sky. It hits the circle and illuminates a brilliant dome before grounding out, hissing and sparking, in the ring of mushrooms. The crash and snarl of skyfire completes the music I'm weaving from the pulse of the Earth and the wail of Air. The pounding beat of Darude's "Sandstorm" swells the circle.

The wild fae solidify, swirling out of moonlight, mist and dry leaves. Thorny brown tree nymphs, shimmering moss-haired river nymphs, white-antlered, black-faced *dynion ceirw* and their tiny flitting cousins, their wings tinseled by the moonlight. They're all around me, filling the circle, ready for me to lead them in the dance. I pace forward steadily and unleash my magic.

Several of the wild fae lift their faces to the moonlit sky and howl. More like shifters than fae, but then they are all wild magics, so they're probably related somehow. They follow me as I dance the circle, a swirl of wings and limbs. Their magic adds a thrumming backbeat, and the woods begin to resound; creaking echoes that splash against the dome of skyfire.

On my second circuit, Jou moves, joining the swirling fae. I don't break my rhythm, but I hold my breath. He said he wouldn't join the circle unless he was sure the fae wouldn't reject him. But this is a noswath lawen, the dance of the wild fae, and it's a magic too beautiful, too rare and wonderful, to fuck with.

Jou pulls off his shirt, arches his back and sheds his glove like a snake shedding its skin. He *swells*, growing taller, stronger, more powerful, more beautiful, more terrifying. His black horns unfurl above his head. His crimson wings spread with a rustle. His tail lashes around his leather-clad legs. He spreads his arms and catches fire.

Neon blue flames erupt from between his horns, and I see his crown clearly. It's a blazing, spikey circlet. Fire shoots from it twenty feet into the night sky. I've never seen his power manifest so fully before. He is *awesome* in the true sense of the word. His power calls to mine. Ignites it. Witchlight spills across the circle, gold and red waves of light that crash into his neon blue glow and fracture into a rainbow of interference patterns that fill the dancing circle.

The fae join Jou's thunderous roar: howling and screeching. All ignite to the demon's power. Sparks of burning gossamer fill the circle, calling to the will o' the wisps, which cluster around the edge of the circle like a storm of demented fireflies.

I shift into the second song I've planned for tonight: Tiesto's "Adagio for Strings." It begins with a long fast beat that drums up from the Earth. Then a higher metallic counterpoint that crashes out of the lightning. Some of the fae recognize the tune—I've played it for them before—and cries of "Tiesto!" fill the circle.

I don't know if Jou recognizes the song, or if he just likes Tiesto as much as the fae do; he lifts his clawed hands to the sky, roars loudly enough to shake the marrow within my bones, and joins the line of dancers who are leaping, twisting, pounding their way around the circle.

There's nothing choreographed about the way the wild fae dance. None of the balletic delicacy I expected after seeing all those pre-Raphaelite paintings in my art survey course at Bevvy. The wild fae are wonderfully athletic. Their powerful movements as they leap, twirl, and flip their way around the circle could give any break-dance crew a run for their money. And Jou is just as beautiful, strong and graceful as any of them.

I admire him, and them, and let their magic join and reinforce mine as I play song after song for them.

———

I'm sweat-streaked and drained by the end of an hour's dancing. My magic's still strong, a thrumming pulse just behind my heartbeat, but I wouldn't want to try to use it right now. My cup is full, but my control's shaky.

The wild fae have started to drift away. A few still swirl around the center of the circle to their own music: high silver bells I can barely hear. Jou drops out of the dance when I finish my set and paces over to me. He spins out his glove like a dog shaking off water. His horns, crown, tail and the lightshow disappear. He shrugs like he's putting on a coat and his skin seems to settle around him. Reclaiming his shirt from a tree branch, he shrugs it over his head, and I have to sigh at the disappearance of all those gleaming muscles. Then he gives me an affectionate peck on the forehead and when I lean into him and take a deep breath of his good, warm, male scent, he wraps his arm around my shoulders.

"Worse ways to spend an evening, sweetness."

"Mmm-hmm." I rub my cheek against his warm, firm chest and let my gaze drift into the middle distance.

Three *Tylwyth Teg* stand at the far edge of the circle. The wild fae give them a wide berth, and there's no mistaking them. They stand tall, blindingly fair, amongst the bent and gnarled wild fae. The moonlight glints off their golden armor.

"Shit, Jou," I whisper, nodding at the high fae.

Jou's arm around my shoulder tightens. "Want me to roast 'em?"

"No, no roasting. Not until we know what they want."

"Then roasting."

I grin up at him and shake my head.

"Sweetness, before we say hello to the airy fairies, you want to borrow my shirt?"

"Hmm?" I follow his eyes down to my chest and realize that my shirt has burned off while I've been dancing. I didn't notice; I was so wrapped up in the rhythm and my magic. My jeans are a little charred and sooty, but okay. Still, I probably shouldn't greet the high fae topless. "Crap, yes, please."

Jou shrugs out of his shirt—yay, muscles—and helps me into it. He runs his hands down my sides, and with a ripple of heat, he reshapes his shirt into a leather vest that hugs my breasts, ribs and hips.

"How do you do that?" I ask, leaning into him.

"Trade secret." He winks at me. "Heads up. Incoming."

He turns me around in his arms and I have a moment to prepare, and to appreciate the warmth of the bare chest against my back, before three high fae glide to a halt just inside the ring of mushrooms. One of them holds a silver helmet out to me. I reach forward, through a circle of soft-fire feathers, as Jou manifests his wings and cups them around us and take the helmet.

I turn the helmet around in my hands, look into the empty eye-sockets, and feel the shock of recognition run through me. Then, loss twists its white-hot blade through my heart. There's only one reason the Squire would be without his helmet.

"Where is he?" I ask the *Ellyll*.

"Returned to the Mother," one of the high fae says. Its voice is light and silvery. Could be a female, although I'm not sure how to tell. The *Ellyllon* all look the same, with their long, silver-white hair, ageless, androgynous faces and elaborate armor.

"When?" I ask. "How?"

"Three days ago," the same fae replies. "The how, our lord asks you to determine."

The Oak King wants me to figure out how the Squire died? I control a shiver. "Is this a, um, *formal* request?"

I have a debt to the fae; I want to know if this goes toward settling that debt.

The fae inclines its helmeted head.

"Please tell his Majesty that I'm happy to be of service. Were there any witnesses? Where did it happen? Can I see the body?"

"No, not far from here and Aranan's remains have returned to the Mother," the fae responds. "I can show you where."

Aranan? I didn't know the Squire had a name other than The Squire.

I glance up a Jou. "Do you mind a field trip?"

He's watching the fae with a lazy, hooded stare that could be just, *I got my eye on you,* or could be, *I'm about to burn you down to your bones and eat the marrow.* Hard to say, but it's not a very friendly look.

"Er, Jou?" I ask.

"No, I don't mind. Give 'em back the tin can, though. Smells funny."

I don't smell anything other than spruce and my own sweat. But given how easily his mood could shift towards the burning and eating end of the spectrum, I don't argue. I hand the helmet back.

The one that's spoken takes the helmet, bows, and turns north-west out of the clearing, gliding into the trees. I take Jou's hand and follow.

I feel the road before we reach it. The Old Pilgrim Road, which I would have called a ley line before my vision of three months ago, but now I know it's one of the World Tree's many branches. Animals avoid it, not because they remember when it was tramped by man and horse, but because magic dances just under the leaf-litter. Arcane creatures haunt the old road, drawn to its latent power, and they're not above a little hunting.

The fae carefully doesn't step on the road but stops a few yards short and lifts its pointed chin at the track, left bare by fern and bracken even though it hasn't been used by anyone other than hikers in a century. The demon has no such compunction. He strides forward and stands in the middle, looking around with neon-lit eyes.

I join him. There's a little moonlight filtering down through the branches overhead from where the trees break over the road. It illuminates bare grey dirt. I feel the darkness before I see it. A shadow under stone. A spatter on matted leaves. I take a few steps to where I feel the taint. I kneel in the dirt and feel Jou follow me down, his warm, bare chest at my back, his hands on my hips.

*What is it, sweetness?* Jou asks in my mind.

I pat my fingertips forward until I brush the Squire's dried blood on the leaves. I press the leaves down into the dirt. Into the Earth. I close my eyes and let my Element fill me.

There's a rough brush of metal down my cheek. Under my chin. Behind me, Jou growls, but I *shush* him in my mind. I need to feel the Squire again. I need to know how he died.

He doesn't speak to me. He never spoke to me in life, and he doesn't in death. But I Feel him. That titanium solidity, which I found so un-fae-like. So comforting and reassuring. He protected me, with his presence, with his skills, and with his sword. That was the core of him, and his calling.

A calling he *failed*.

His failure, his loss of purpose, tightens my chest. I pant, trying to draw breath. Jou slides his arms around me and rests his broad hand on my heart. Against that gentle pressure, I take a deep breath, and then another, working through the Squire's failure. Behind that final moment of overwhelming grief, I feel frustration. He was hunting something, tracking it through the woods, but it kept eluding him, and then . . . I feel his fear.

It turned on him. The hunter became the hunted. Then it killed him.

I look up at the night sky. Between the scudding clouds, a perfect *v* of geese fly, heading south. I can hear their faint honking, but nothing else disturbs the quiet night.

The kelpie said I was looking in the wrong direction. What creature of Air could the Squire have been hunting through these woods? What could kill a shield-bearer of the fae and a shapeshifter in his prime?

"Jou?"

"Got me, sweetness," he says in response to my line of thought. "You're the first human who's let me off the leash. I haven't gotten to explore your world much. Don't know what's flappin' around up there."

"Mmm." I settle a little more comfortably onto my knees, shifting when a stone jabs me, and open my mystical senses.

The treacle-sweetness of smokeberry floods my nose, over-whelming the leaf mold and pine trees. These woods are wet, full of springs and little streams that feed the larger ponds. I smell moss and mud, and then the nose-wrinkling scent of vinegar.

Jou's arms tighten around me. "Sweetness."

"It's okay. She's friendly," I say, opening my eyes and looking at the ondine who has appeared in the ferns on the far side of the road. She holds out a webbed, clawed, four-fingered hand to me, revealing a polished river-stone sitting on her palm, which allows her to walk on land and breathe air. I smell the familiar scent of my own magic:

mistletoe and thyme. This is my charm, which means I've summoned this particular ondine to my circle when I've called the Elements.

I rise from my crouch slowly, giving Jou time to rise with me. I'm perfectly happy to stay in the circle of his arms. Feels like a good place to be. I shuffle forward until I can hold my outstretched hand over the ondine's. I take several deep breaths, filling my lungs with the cool night air. As I breathe out, I push Air into the river-stone, re-enchanting it.

When I lower my hand, the ondine bows her head. She doesn't have a face *per se*. More a suggestion of a face: the same way a stingray's gills and ribs look like a human face. But she smiles at me all the same, a smile I can feel rather than see.

She lets the hand holding the enchanted stone fall to her side, then lifts her other hand. When I reach out to her, she drops another river-stone into my palm.

This stone isn't enchanted. It isn't polished. It's a lozenge of granite, worn and pitted from years of tumbling along a riverbed. On the smoothest, flattest part of the stone, there's a shape. Something that wasn't worn or bumped or scraped. I run my fingertips over the stone and feel the deep relief of the shape. It's not a shape I recognize, although my mind's eye immediately spits similar images at me. Two strong vertical lines, three diagonal lines connecting them. It's a rune, although not one I'm familiar with.

*Looks like Futhark,* Jou supplies. *Fucking smelly Northmen. But I haven't seen that rune before.*

That's okay, because I know someone who will have. Someone who spent his eight score years on this plane learning everything he could about mystical symbols in every language he could find.

I bow very low to the ondine, but don't thank her out loud. Old magics don't like to be thanked by young magics. It creates imbalance, obligation. Instead, we've exchanged gifts and can part as equals.

The ondine bows her mossy head in return and steps back until she disappears into the undergrowth.

"What may I tell our lord?" asks the high fae standing off the road behind us.

I close my fingers around the river stone. "You can tell him the

Squire was hunting something through these woods and it killed him. I don't know what it was yet, but I will find out. You have my word."

"Thank you. I will tell him."

I turn in Jou's loose embrace to look at the high fae. "Are there any creatures of the Air that could kill one of the Tylwyth Teg?"

The fae shakes its head without the squeak of helmet or rustle of hair. The fae are just too quiet sometimes. "We are the hunters; we are not the hunted."

They're also just too arrogant sometimes.

"Somethin' thought you were," Jou says.

The fae looks down its long nose at both of us. "When you tell our lord what it was that killed my brother-in-arms, then my kin and I will claim the honor of hunting it down and reminding it that the Tylwyth Teg are not cattle to be fed upon . . ."

"Wait, was the Squire *eaten*?" I interrupt.

The fae glares at me in icy silence.

"Was flesh removed from his stomach and thighs?" I persist. When the fae continues to glare at me, I throw up my hands. "This is important if you want me to find out what killed him."

"Aranan's remains were defiled," the fae says finally.

"Stomach and thighs?"

The fae rubs its hand across its chest.

"And upper chest?" I ask.

"Yes."

Meaty parts of the body. Soft parts with a lot of muscle. Eaten by something with eight-inch jaws. "Thank you," I say to the fae.

"May I take my leave? It is painful for me to remember my brother-in-arms this way."

"I'm sorry," I say, feeling a wash of shame for being so insensitive. "He was my friend. I'll miss him, too."

The fae nods. It gives me a long stare out of its golden eyes, then says slowly, "This place, it is not one of ours. It is one of the *in between* places." The fae sniffs, wrinkling its long nose. "A Tylwyth Teg would not come here by choice."

"The in between places?" I'm not sure what the fae means. I haven't heard the term before. But I Smell it. Just behind the perfume of the evergreens, there's a high actinic scent, like ozone but with an edge of something coppery and sweet.

Lightning in the blood.

"The places the deep ones still walk. Not your world." The fae nods to me. "Nor yours." The fae nods at Jou. "Nor mine. They are the places of doors and mist."

"Gates," Jou says in his deepest tone.

The fae shrugs one shoulder. "I do not know your word."

"If you walked this road, where would it lead you?" Jou asks, his voice so low it's almost a growl.

The fae casts a glance up and down the road. "Not a place me or mine are meant to be. You risk all that you are, Hellspawn, setting foot on that path."

Jou's wings manifest with a *whush* and sweep around us, spattering embers through dirt and fern. I feel the World Tree's power leap in response. "I'm the Lord of Ash and Bone. D'Asmodei. I control the Gates. They don't control me. If the Twitterin' Throng's opened a gate and something nasty's come through, that's on you . . ."

The fae shakes its head decisively. "This is not one of our doors. We are blameless, and our kin a victim of whatever walks this road. We ask for assistance, and you point the finger of accusation—"

"Whoa, whoa," I say, holding out my hands between the supernatural creatures in front and behind me. "There's no need for anyone to point anything. I get it. This place feels strange. All the more reason for us to leave. Right?" I glance over my shoulder at Jou, then at the high fae. They both nod. "Great. Good night. Please give my regards to the King of the Dreaming Court."

The high fae nods and drifts back into the trees.

I reach back and put my hands on Jou's hips, pressing the river stone between flesh and leather. Then I drag us into the Earth.

———

We step back out of the Earth a few feet from my boiler. The smell of heating oil and fabric softener replaces the scent of pine and reminds me that I need to do a load of laundry.

Jou sneezes and shakes dust out of his hair. "Gonna need another bath," he grumbles.

"Sorry," I say, although I'm not. I love Earth-Walking, no matter how dusty I get. "Next time you can fly us home, wingman."

Jou chuckles. "Not sure my wings're up to that yet. I might give 'em a test run tomorrow, though." He puts his palms on the small of his back and stretches. "You want somethin' to eat? I'm hungry."

Again? Wow, he really was starved. I'm not particularly hungry, but I'd never turn down the offer of his food. I nod.

"C'mon." He holds his hand out to me and leads me up into the kitchen. His pink-Mohawked demoness is sitting at my kitchen table, thumbs working as she types on a sleek phone. No sign of Zeifyr.

Jou reaches out as we pass the demoness and ruffles her Mohawk. "S'up, Zip?"

"I have fourteen hundred new followers. Think any of them want a soul-trade?" she replies. The demons exchange grins that contain a lot of teeth and little humor. "Seriously, Dast, you need to get on the humans' interweb."

"Internet," I say. "Or world wide web."

The Mohawked demoness—I'm really struggling to think of her as *Zippy*—glances up at me. "Are you on it?" she asks.

I shake my head. Other than the clinic's website and Google, I don't know the first thing about the Internet. "Why would I want to be?"

She goes back to her technology. "All kinds of possibilities. Oh, and Dast? The Red Duke wants to talk with you."

Jou grunts as he opens the door to my fridge. "At me, more likely."

"Yeah, probably. He's sending something."

"What, an imp?" Jou asks as he pulls strawberries, eggs, and milk out of the fridge.

"No. Some kind of machine. It's coming by courier, *that's* probably an imp. It'll be here tomorrow night."

"Busy," Jou growls, taking a bowl from the cabinet and cracking eggs into it. "Sweetness, find me that waffle iron, would you?"

I don't own a waffle iron. Or I didn't. When I root around under the counter, I discover I do now. I set it on the counter, plug it in, and watch its lights start blinking.

"What are you making?" Zippy asks.

"Waffles," Jou says. "Want some?"

"Waffles with chocolate?"

Jou chuckles. "Could do."

"Yes, please."

Well, at least someone in his harem has manners. I retrieve my chocolate stash and set it on the counter for Jou. He brushes a quick kiss over my temple while he assembles a pan of water and a glass bowl into a double boiler. Once he's turned my stove on, I pour a little milk into the glass bowl and begin breaking the chocolate into pieces.

"Chaid say what he wanted?" Jou asks Zippy as he mixes waffle batter.

"No, but his message was that he requires an interview with Baron Ash."

Jou grunts. "Formal talk, then."

"Is this coming from Father?" Zippy asks, putting down her technology.

"Probably," Jou replies. "You know Chaid ain't had an original thought this millennium. Old Man say anything to you before you three headed topside?"

Zippy shakes her bright head. "I don't think he's spoken to me in a century. Nev's with him, though. She has been pretty much since he put you on the Tree. She's pregnant again, so he'll probably hole her up until she pops."

"Pups his?" Jou asks.

Zippy shrugs. "Court thinks so. The Soae's rumbling around like she's got an ass full of thorns. Nev didn't say anything to me one way or the other. She's been pretty quiet while you've been gone."

"Probably smart, given the Old Man's mood. I'm surprised she let him knock her up again, particularly with the Soae on the warpath. She forgotten what happened to Mother?"

Zippy rests her elbow on the table and props her cheek on her fist. "None of us would forget what happened to Mother. It's just hard to stop him when he wants something." She looks very pensive for a moment, and I wonder what her father forced her to give. "And he's been pressuring her again."

"About becomin' his Consort?" Jou asks.

Zippy nods. "Maybe she let herself get pregnant to divert him."

"Maybe," Jou says, although it sounds like he agrees with her. "Sweetness, you want to open that up?" He nods at the waffle iron.

I open the clamshell for him and then step back to let him pour the creamy batter onto the hot plate. He lets the batter bubble for a moment before closing the clamshell.

"Whaddo you think, Zip?" Jou asks, keeping his dark gaze on the waffle, but there's no question where his attention really lies.

"About what?" she asks. She starts spinning her fancy phone on the table between her palms. I'm pretty sure she knows exactly what Jou is asking.

"Zef's plans."

Zippy lowers her eyes to her phone and shrugs. "She's always had plans."

"Her plans ain't my plans this time, and she ain't gonna push me into them."

Zippy spins her phone faster. "I got that. I think she did, too."

Jou doesn't say anything for a moment, letting the silence stretch. He opens the waffle iron and flips out the waffle onto a plate I hold out to him, with a black talon he extends from his forefinger. Then he pours more batter before he says to the demoness, "If you don't want to get between Zef and me, you might wanna go home."

"Dast," the demoness says softly, watching her brother with the dark eyes Jou and all of his siblings have. "Don't make me choose."

Jou shakes his head. "Not askin' you to. I'm tellin' you to get outta the line of fire."

"You know how she'll take it if I leave. Seriously, would it be so bad just to meet with Tem and the others?"

Jou goes very still. He stops pretending to watch the waffles and turns the full force of his neon-lit glare on Zippy. "She leave you here to soft paw me?"

Zippy holds his eyes and shakes her head.

Jou turns his attention back to the waffles, but I can see a muscle ticking in his jaw. I'm not sure what his question meant, but whatever it was, he didn't like the answer.

He flips another crisply browned waffle onto the plate and nods at my bowl of chocolate. "Put some salt in that and pour it over for her."

When I've decorated the waffles with a crosshatch of melted, salted chocolate that I think will satisfy the demons' culinary aesthetic, I take the plate to the demoness. She nods and gives me a small smile. I retreat to the counter.

Jou's got another waffle on the go, so I take out more plates. "Do you want me to make coffee?" I ask.

He shakes his head. "I got somethin' else to go with these."

I don't ask, because I'm sure whatever he's gotten to go with the waffles will be delicious. I just stir the melted chocolate to keep it from burning.

"Dast," Zippy says around a mouthful of waffle. "Everyone's expecting you to want revenge. What Father did to you—" She shakes her dayglo head. "No one thinks you'll let it lie."

"Then they'll find I'm not that fucking predictable," Jou says, flipping another waffle onto a plate.

"You're just going to let it go?" Zippy asks incredulously.

"I just got done provin' my loyalty to the Old Man, Zip. I'm not doin' anything to fuck that up. You think the Old Man won't mind if I show my face at a meeting of his enemies? You think the Old Man don't got a spy or two in the Zeimal? Think a-fucking-gain."

The demoness shifts her dark eyes to me, gives me a once-over that's distinctly unfriendly, then goes back to her waffles.

"Excuse me," I say, not prepared to take any shit from a demoness who calls herself *Zippy*. "What was that?"

"Before you, Dast would have burned his way through the Iron City if anyone insulted him the way Father has," the demoness responds before stuffing another forkful of waffle into her mouth.

Over Jou's growl, I snap, "What's insulting is that you think your brother was ever that stupid. I barely know any of you, but I've met your father. I've felt his power. He's just proven how ruthlessly he wields it, and what he can do to any of you, whenever he wants. And you're suggesting the smart move is for your brother to retaliate? Or side with a group of people conspiring against your father?"

*Thank you, sweetness,* Jou says warmly into my mind.

*You're welcome,* I think grimly.

"I'm not suggesting anything. I'm *saying* that before you, Dast was a force to be reckoned with."

"Thanks, Zip. Nice to know what a fucking idiot you thought I was," Jou growls.

"Oh, come on!" Zippy holds up her hands, talons painted the same pink as her Mohawk. "You know you wouldn't have let this go."

"Yeah? Lemme remind you what happened th' last time I went up against the Old Man. You remember? He wanted Nev as his Flame. She didn't want it. I tried to stand up to him. Claim her as mine. You remember how long it took Cyz to pull my mind back together after Rake took me apart? I was a droolin' fuckin' blob for the better part of a century. Remember what happened while I was out of it?"

Zippy lowers her gaze. "Stokie," she says softly.

"That's right," Jou growls. "And Nev didn't just become his Flame. He kept her whelping out a pup a Turn the whole time I was out of it. Nearly killed her. You think that wasn't a lesson?"

"We're not malebranch anymore, Dast. You're a lot stronger now," she says, but I can tell that whatever he's reminded her of has squashed her argument. There's no forcefulness left in her voice; the grey cobwebs of grief have gathered around her head and shoulders like a shawl.

"I know Angien and Tem don't believe it, and maybe they've convinced Zef, but lemme tell you, Zip, he's stronger than I will ever be. Than *all* of us will ever be. I felt the force of his will holding me on that Tree. Keepin' Tsara from healin' me. My own seggurach and he kept her from healing me." Zippy looks up at Jou with wide eyes, then at me, then back at her phone. Jou continues, "He hasn't eaten any of us since Dezze 'cause we're useful to him. The second we stop being useful to him and become a threat? He'll make puttin' me on that Tree look like a mild rebuke. I'm not doin' anything to bring that down on our heads."

Zippy folds her lips together. "I didn't realize—"

She trails off without saying exactly what she didn't realize, but I'm pretty sure from that wide-eyed look that it was both that I'm Jou's seggurach and that their Father is powerful enough to keep us apart.

Jou flips a sixth waffle onto a plate and nods at me to pour chocolate over it. He pulls the black lacquer tray from the rack under the counter, sets the plates and utensils on the tray once I garnish the waffles with chocolate, then reaches into the 'fridge and fishes out three blue bottles. "C'mon, sweetness, we're picnicking on your back lawn."

Are we? It'll be kind of cold outside if we're just sitting and eating, but I can always snuggle up to Jou, I guess.

I hold the back door for him. We leave Zippy at my kitchen table, finishing her waffles and watching us go with very dark eyes.

# CHAPTER 13

e walk down my back steps onto the withered lawn. Jou sets the tray down and holds his hands out to me. "Gonna need my shirt back for a moment, sweetness," he says.

His shirt-cum-vest is all that's covering my boobs, and the night air is decidedly chilly, but he's seen them before, and I figure he'll make it up to me.

I shrug out of the vest and hand it to him with a shiver. He takes it between his hands, flaps it, and a huge arc of cloth billows away from his hands. He squats to settle half of the cloth on the ground, lifts the top half, and gestures into the massive sleeping bag he's just turned my vest into.

I climb in and pull one edge around me. The leather's become some soft, waterproof material on the outside, warm silk on the inside. I snuggle into it while smiling up at Jou. He grins back before he joins me in the pocket of cloth, sitting so our knees are touching. He pulls the tray in front of us. With his thumb claw, he flips the top off one of the bottles and offers it to me.

"Blue Moon," I read off the label.

"Belgian white beer. Try it before you judge," he says.

I do, and I like its malty smoothness, but that's nothing compared to what happens in my mouth when I take a bite of chocolate-drizzled waffle.

"Omigod," I mutter around the bitter-sweet, yeasty explosion.

Jou chuckles. "Good, huh?"

"How do you come up with this stuff?"

"Too much time to think on that Tree," he responds, without any bitterness. Surprisingly. "You must have questions, sweetness."

A few thousand, but I'm afraid most of the answers fall into the *I really don't want to know* category. Like every mention of their sister, Nevida. I've met Nevida. Well, I sensed her essence while I was plane walking. Whatever. Of all of Jou's siblings, she was the one who terrified me the least. She's someone I could have liked. To find out she's been her own father's sex-slave for centuries makes me queasy. I know the demons don't view incest—or even rape—the way humans do. It still makes my stomach, and heart, hurt.

"Is there anything your father's done that wouldn't make me want to vomit?" I ask around another bite of waffle.

"Ever?" Jou asks after swallowing his own mouthful.

"Mm-hmm."

"I'd have to think about that some. Nothin' comes immediately to mind."

"I completely understand why you wouldn't want to antagonize him, Jou. I don't understand why your sisters would think it was a good idea. Or even something you'd consider after what you've been through."

Jou scratches his chin with the handle of his fork. "Well, Zip might have a point when she says I've been known to strike first and think later. But never against the Old Man. I've always been smarter than that, even when I was nothin' more than a walkin' gut."

"He's hurt you before. I didn't realize that."

"Yeah, he's made an example of me coupla times. Never like this, though. He just threw me to his pet mind-bender, the way he does anyone who annoys him. This was different. Really fuckin' different. The Zes didn't see what you saw, so maybe they don't get it. But you understand. What you said to Zip was right. He was makin' a point, and I do not need a second lesson."

I shake my head as I take another forkful of waffle and chase it with the beer. Lick my lips as I savor the resulting malt explosion. "Who was the person Zippy mentioned? Stokie? What happened to him?"

"Mmm, he died bad. He pissed off the Winter Prince directly. Ice demons went after him and did what they do best. They shattered him. Crippled him so he couldn't fight."

"Was he part of your clutch?" I ask.

Jou shakes his head. "Earth demon. Hatched out around the same time we did. We were in the Horde together. All of us looked up to Stokie. He was fucking fearless. Nothing stood against him when he led a Horde charge. But after the ice demons broke him." Jou shrugs. "He went looking for true death. In Hell, that's easy to find. Stokie found it in the Fiendyke. By the time I was in a position to do more than drool, it was over. All I could do was avenge him."

"Did you?" I ask.

Jou nods before taking a swig of his beer. "Made the fiend that killed Stokie serve me for a decade."

Wow, when demons hold grudges, they really hold grudges. "Zippy seems like she's still mourning him."

"Yeah. She an' Stokie were real close. We weren't evolved enough back then to bond. But if we had been, Zip and Stokie woulda."

"She would have been his seggurach?" At Jou's nod, I hunker down under the warm silk of the sleeping bag and try not to feel guilty about being a little mean to Zippy. "I didn't realize. I guess, I mean, it's inevitable, isn't it? You've all been alive for over a thousand years. You'll have lost people who were close to you."

"Mm-hmm."

I push the last bite of waffle around on my plate, before deciding it's too good to waste. "Has Zeifyr lost anyone like that?" I ask. I'm not sure I'll be able to muster any sympathy for her, even if she has.

Jou snorts. "Zef seem like she'd ever let anyone get that close to her?"

I quash a sense of relief. "No. When you asked Zippy if she'd been left behind to soft paw you, is that something they do a lot? Play you off against each other? Like good cop, bad cop?"

I feel Jou ruffle through my mind for the reference. He snorts. "Oh, yeah. Exactly like that. Only it's a three-way. Good cop, bad cop, and worst fucking nightmare cop."

I can guess which role Zeifyr plays. "That's unfair."

"According to Zef, she's just evening the playin' field, since it takes the three of them to stand against me."

"Having seen her in action, I find that hard to believe."

"Yeah, you'd be right. Zef can take me on her own, she tries hard enough." Jou finishes his own waffle, takes both plates, and puts them down in the grass. Then he wiggles two fingers at me. "C'mere."

I go to him, licking chocolate off my lips.

He pulls me down beside him and tugs the sleeping bag over both of us. The ground's hard beneath us, so I flatten my hand on it and think loamy thoughts until it softens enough to feel like a mattress.

Jou stretches and pulls me on top of him.

I settle onto his chest, prop myself on my forearms, and look into his face. Smile back at him. He brushes my bangs off my forehead with his forefinger and tucks them behind my ear.

"Hey," he says softly, in the lowest register of his baritone voice.

"Is for horses," I respond, before I realize he's getting serious and sexy. "Sorry. Mel says that. Mel's, um, I made a friend while you were gone. Melanie Jean. I'll have to introduce you. She's crazier than your sisters."

Jou chuckles. "Didn't think that was possible."

I hold up two fingers, barely apart. "I mean, not by much."

Jou runs his fingertips down my bare back, hooking his thumbs in the waistband of my jeans. "I know they can be tough to take. Particularly in big doses. Good news is, once we're at the Hill, you probably won't see 'em that often. They got their own things going on."

"I'll admit, that's a relief."

"We'll have more privacy, too. Nothin' against your digs, sweetness, but we're on top of each other here. Hill's a big place. Easy to avoid the Zes."

I trace the curve of his face, from temple to cheekbone to jaw, with my fingertips. "Is that what you do? Practice selective avoidance?"

"Uh-huh. And go on long walk-abouts. Why d'you think I don't fight bein' summoned too hard? Makes a nice break."

I bet.

"Sweetness." He tugs on the waistband of my jeans. "I'm not complainin', but you got too many clothes on."

Oh.

"Are we, uh, sleeping out here?"

"An' doin' other things."

"Instead of in my nice, warm bed?"

"Don't figure you'll let me fuck you in your nice, warm bed with the Zes in the house."

He's not wrong about that.

"And don't worry. I won't let you get cold."

I grin at him. Being cold isn't something I have to worry about with my fire demon around.

"Like bein' your demon," Jou says, skimming my thoughts.

I push up until I'm straddling him and awkwardly work my jeans off. He doesn't help me and I can tell he's enjoying me wriggling around on top of him by the bulge in his own pants.

Which disappear the moment I lower myself back onto his big body. He reaches down and adjusts himself so the firm, silken heat of him is cupped between my thighs.

He runs his hands up and down my sides and I shiver with the sensation of his hot palms moving over my skin. Then I nearly leap off him when a softer, wetter heat laps up into the juncture of my thighs.

"Jou—"

"Shh, sweetness. I wanna see you in the moonlight."

Oh. That's poetic. And kind of sweet. I settle back onto him and let his nethertongue gently explore.

"Is there moonlight in Hell?"

"Uh-huh. Dis opens to a lot of different places, in a lot of different times," he says, between kisses. "More'n one moon shines through. Sometimes, three moons shine down on the Hill. Opens up places that aren't accessible at other times, like the smoking pools. I'm lookin' forward to showin' you."

Oddly, I'm looking forward to that, too.

The idea of our future—a future of moonlight and magic—holds less terror now. It's not entirely comfortable. I doubt any future with Jou will be entirely comfortable. He's always going to push me in directions I don't expect.

What's changed is that I'm good with that. Because I know the alternative is unbearable.

"Don't want any future you're not part of, sweetness," Jou says softly, following my train of thought, running his hands down my bare back and questing a little deeper with his nethertongue. "I know it feels like I'm askin' you to give up everythin' to be part of that future, but—"

He stops when I shake my head.

"I had no idea how much you've given up until I met your sisters, Jou. I understand now. When you told me you love your family with everything you are . . . I didn't really appreciate what that meant. How much you've had to sacrifice. How much you've endured. You've had to be so strong. I respect that; I respect *you*. I know I'm part of your family now. I know I'm one of those things you protect. I know what you endured most recently, you endured for me, too. Whatever shape your future takes, I want to stand with you."

Jou stares up at me for a moment, his eyes dark and lit with moonlight, his mouth hanging open and damp from our kisses. I nip his lower lip while he's speechless, since that hardly ever happens.

"Sweetness." His arms close hard around me and crush me to his chest.

I wrap my arms around his neck.

"I had no fuckin' idea you felt all that," he murmurs into my hair. "Your mind's usually so full of fury when you thinka my time on the Tree that I didn't see any of that."

"I'm still furious."

"Yeah, I know you are, my fierce bitch. I just didn't know what was behind it."

He tips his head up to rub noses with me, then swamps me in a hot kiss. He lifts his hips and I feel his insistent hardness rub along my core. I slide my hand down over his heavy shoulder, down his side, to grip his ass and give the firm muscle a pinch. He doesn't get to penetrate me right after calling me a bitch, even though I know he meant it as a compliment.

He chuckles into my mouth. "Make it up to you."

I understand what he means when his nethertongue slides between my outer lips and presses insistently against the hood of my clit. My secret flesh swells and pulses against his.

"That's right," Jou growls, his voice dropping. "Lemme worship you."

I nuzzle into his neck, taking deep breaths of smoke and hot spice. "I like the sound of that."

"Yeah." He slides his hot hands over me, warm strokes that bring the blood tingling to the surface of my skin. One hand slides into my hair and fists, lifting my head. He looks up at me and smiles wickedly. "There's my seggurach in the moonlight. Shining in your hair. Kissin' your skin. Lemme see those eyes."

I lift my heavy lids for him.

"Love seein' lightning crash in your eyes. Beautiful. That's the fire spirit in you that calls t'me." Neon sparks flicker through his dark eyes. "I might not have a soul, sweetness, but never think for a second our spirits aren't connected."

I nod. I've felt that, too. I thought it was his bindings, but maybe it's more.

"Definitely more," he whispers before he kisses me again, his hot tongue sliding into my mouth to lap against mine. His nethertongue echoes the motion: sliding hot and sticky and silken around my clit before pushing into my opening. "Lift up, sweetness."

I do, spreading my legs on either side of his. The loamy ground and satiny bag cushion my knees as I slide up onto them.

He reaches between us and positions himself. With his free hand, he grips my hip and lowers me down on him. He hisses out a breath as his tip probes me, pushing inside, spreading me, then slipping back out. He plays with me—worshipping me as he said—penetrating me a little deeper with each stroke, while his nethertongue flicks, flicks, flicks, until my toes curl against his calves.

"That's right," he groans into my mouth as he sinks in half-way. "How soft you are always takes me by surprise."

How big he is always takes me by surprise. His penetration is so slow, so controlled, this time that I can feel every inch of my body opening to him. It's almost as though he's tunneling into me as he penetrates me.

"Like that image, sweetness," he says on a heavy exhale. "Like the idea of openin' you. Want you to be soft and open to me."

I certainly feel like I am as he exerts a little more pressure, slides a little deeper, until his head nudges my cervix.

"Uhn," he groans. "Love this part. That's right, sweetness. Take me in."

I do, wrapping myself around him and letting him notch deep within me. He's still for long, sweet minutes, our bodies pulsing together, before he takes my hips in his hands and begins to move.

"Oh, Jou," I moan as the first of his thrusts pushes white heat up my spine.

Jou makes a deep, satisfied purr in his chest. The kind he usually makes when we're finished. He thrusts deep and holds there, pulsing in time to my body clenching around him. I understand what's prompted his noise. If I could make a similar purr, I would. Our bodies are finally aligned with our spirits. There's a wholeness, a sense of completion, even though neither of us has climaxed, that's as gratifying as when we have.

When he finally begins to move again, his shaft drags against my passage, creating so much friction it's almost suction. I gasp, caught between pleasure and pain. Then his nethertongue flicks up to do its good work, I tip over into pleasure, and grind myself down on him as his hips snap up against mine.

He pinions me against his long, hard body, one hand flattening in the small of my back, the other cupping my nape. He guides me down into each thrust. I pant against his mouth, our hot breaths mingling.

His purr becomes a series of low moans. I love hearing his noises, his pleasure. I give him back mine as sensation coils bright inside me.

"Time t'get crazy," he groans, holding me tight against him as he rolls us over. His weight is immense, suffocating, as he comes down on top of me, and I surrender to it completely, wrapping my arms around his huge shoulders, my thighs around his pumping hips. He holds himself off me just enough to let me breathe, and then takes my breath away with the hard pumping of his body into mine.

His thrusts take me up and up, coiling my body tighter and tighter around his plunging, invading heft. I whimper with the insane pleasure of it. The dance along the white-hot edge. Knowing he could hurt me, tear me, ream me with that hard, driving length. He holds it right on that edge with each thrust. Letting me feel—and for a flickering second fear—his strength, before he draws it back so I only feel the intense, immense pleasure he gives me.

"Jou, Jou, yes."

"Yeah, sweetness. Feel me. Feel how close you bring me. Feel it all."

I throw my head back and let all that sensation rip out of me in a howl. The air pulses. The ground pulses. Lightning crashes down around us. Jou joins the chorus of sound, roaring his release into the night in hard pulses that drive me over the edge, into that dissolution of white light.

I have no idea how long it goes on. How long we lie entwined afterwards, smoke and ozone filling the air that I can barely taste between hot, slow kisses. He stays nestled deep in me, occasionally giving another wet pulse that my body drinks in like the water of life.

Jou finally stretches and shifts so we're lying side by side. His heavy cock slips free and rests, wet and spent, against my thigh. He draws my leg over his, creating welcome pressure against my core, which throbs in time with my heartbeat.

Jou winds a strand of my hair around his fingers, gives it a gentle tug until I look up at him. "Perfect." He smiles lazily. "Just how I wanted you, soft and sated in the moonlight."

I smile back at him. "If this is your version of camping, I'm a convert."

He chuckles. "Generally appreciate four walls around me, but I gotta say I'm a fan of this, too, sweetness." He pulls the upper edge of the sleeping bag around our shoulders. "Haveta find a way to do this at the Hill."

"No camping spots in Hell?"

"Naw. But don't worry, we'll make one, you and me. We'll shape the Hill t'be everything we need. No limits on what we can do together."

"No limits?"

He smiles sleepily and kisses me. "Not a single one."

————

I wake to the smell of pine needles and coffee. Neither smell belongs in my bedroom. But, when I roll over and feel hard earth under my shoulder and hip, I realize I'm not in my bedroom.

Jou, kneeling in the withered grass with the sun rising behind his shoulder, offers me a steaming cup that smells like life itself.

I slide up onto my elbow, prop my head on my hand and take the cup. "I was wrong," I tell him.

"Yeah? 'Bout what?"

"I didn't think I could love you any more than I did last night."

Jou grins, his teeth flashing in the sunrise. "If all I gotta do t'get you to admit how you feel about me is bring you coffee, we're gonna be fine, sweetness."

*We're going to be fine no matter what.*

I think it fiercely. Take it into my heart and seal it with power and promise and caffeine. Jou, watching me, smiles and drinks from his own cup.

We watch the sunrise, drinking our coffee companionably. Steam rises from the grass and my trees as the morning light burns off the rime of frost from the night. Mist swirls through the shafts of golden morning light. I feel it bead on the small hairs of my forearms, exposed as I hold my coffee cup, cling damply to my cheeks and forehead. It makes me shiver, the first chill I've felt since climbing into the demon sleeping bag. I reach down and pat it. "This was great."

Jou nods. "Served its purpose. I'll keep it in case the Zes decide to stay another night."

I make a face around a mouthful of coffee. "Is that a possibility?"

"Anything's possible." Jou lifts one shoulder. "Maybe shootin' Zef down that hard'll send them packin'."

"But maybe not?"

"If she's spyin' for the Hellroarer, she hasn't gotten much yet."

I shake my head. "How can you stand it, Jou? Constantly questioning their loyalty would drive me nuts."

"Ain't the best part of the job," Jou admits.

"What is?"

Jou considers my question while he finishes his coffee.

"Buildin' the Hill wasn't so bad," he says at length.

I lift an eyebrow at him, because I'm aware that he built his home with the stolen life-energy from his million and one sexual partners.

"Wasn't even a thousand," Jou says, but he's grinning. "Naw, this is the best part, sweetness. Right now. Bein' free. No one tellin' me where to go, what to do, who to fuck. This is what I've wanted. Now I've finally got it."

He's certainly paid the price for it, but I don't want to darken his mood, so instead I say, "Camping out on my lawn in the middle of winter?"

He chuckles. "I've slept in worst places. I even got a good night's sleep once the geese shut up."

I nod, remembering hearing geese calling as I was falling asleep, too.

"So, what are we doin' today, sweetness?" he asks.

"I need to go to work—" I begin.

"Yeah, I guess that's okay."

His response isn't. "I wasn't asking permission, Jou."

He looks down at the coffee cup between his hands, not meeting my eyes, and nods.

I've gotten it wrong again. Why can I say the right thing to him?

"Jou, I'm sorry. What's wrong?" I ask softly.

He shrugs. "Kinda afraid you'll disappear an' this'll all turn out t'be another dream. I'll be back hangin' on the Tree."

I freeze. Then I wiggle out of the bag, onto his lap, ignoring the fact I'm now naked, brushing aside both our empty cups, and wrap my arms around his neck. "This is real. It's not a dream. The Tree is gone. I'm not going anywhere."

He rubs noses with me. Closes his fever-hot arms around me. "I know it up top. Just takin' a while to sink in everywhere else."

"Feel it, Jou. I'm right here." I press tightly to him. "You're not alone."

"Wasn't ever alone." He kisses my forehead. "You know, I actually tried to be stoic for a while since the Erinyes were watchin'. Didn't do me any good. Screamin' didn't, either, but it was a distraction."

I stroke his hair. Hug him. There's nothing more I can say. He needs time to process that his ordeal is over and that I won't abandon him, or worse, banish him again.

"I have a new client at one," I say, after holding him for a long, quiet time. "I'll make the magic milk first and be ready to go once I finish the appointment. Say two o'clock. Pick me up?"

"Sure."

"You can hang out with me at work if you want, Jou. I just figured you'd be bored."

He chuckles. "I ain't that needy, sweetness. An' I wouldn't be bored if you'd let me bend you over your cauldron. Didn't get to do that last time."

I'd rather not do it this time, either.

Jou chuckles again.

———

Although Lin doesn't have her brother's gifts, sometimes she has an uncanny sixth sense. She has back-to-back needle appointments all day, but that doesn't stop her from being out at the reception desk when Jou appears at two to pick me up.

She gives him a long look, reaches into her pocket and takes out a coin, then drops it next to the desk.

I bend over to pick it up automatically.

She moves her shoe over it. "I was just checking that gravity's still online."

Jou begins chuckling.

I straighten. "What?"

"You actually took my advice and called him. The world must be ending."

"Ha-ha. Jou, you know my extremely unfunny ex-friend, Lin."

He holds out his broad hand and shakes Lin's. "Dinner's on me this time."

"Tsara says you're a great cook; I'll hold you to that."

Jou grins. How is it that the grin that's completely feral when he gives it to me is just pleasant when he gives it to Lin?

"Say Saturday? You mind if I experiment? I've wanted to try some Ethiopian dishes."

"That would be great," Lin says.

I shake my head at both of them.

Lin strolls away from the desk, which only reinforces my belief that she was there to give me a hard time rather than any legitimate reason.

"Ready, sweetness?"

I nod and take the hand he offers me. His hand is human-warm in mine, but no more. His protective coat is much more solid than it was when he arrived.

*How close to completely healed do you think you are?* I ask into his mind since I wouldn't want anyone or anything to overhear that he's vulnerable.

*Hundred and fifty percent,* he responds. *Ain't about healin' at this point. It's about fittin' into the new shape you've made for me.*

*I'd really like to see your wings again.*

*Want to do that instead of what I had planned?*

*What did you have planned?*

*Picnic and then to that archive to figure out what that symbol is.*

*Archive? You mean the museum?*

*Yeah, that.*

*I'm totally on board with that.*

*Yes, please.*

Jou's double-parked a sleek, silver car around the corner from my office. I don't know where he's gotten the car, although I suppose if he can charge a *plane* on his black AmEx he can rent a car. I also don't know how he's escaped a parking ticket, but lots of things come easy when you're a demon, I guess.

*Makes up for the rest of the shit,* Jou thinks.

"You have a point there." He opens the passenger door for me and holds my hand as I slide in. I wait until he's climbed into the driver's seat before I ask, "Were the Zes still at my house when you left?"

"Yeah." His mouth tightens before his full, demonic grin breaks free. "I had a thought about that. Wanna help me piss Zef off?"

"I thought you were trying to avoid a direct confrontation?"

Jou grunts. "This is an indirect confrontation. Very passive-aggressive. Just Zef's style. I think you need to practice banishing demons, just in case whatever you've felt stalkin' you is one. Wanna practice on Hairy?"

"The demoness in my holly tree?"

Jou nods as he pulls out into traffic. "She's mostly in your cauldron at the moment."

"In my cauldron," I say flatly, not seeing how *anything* good could come out of a demoness in my cauldron.

"I took her out of the tree and gave her an opportunity to apologize. She didn't. I immersed her in your cauldron. She needs some quality time without skin to reconsider."

"Uh, does water do the same thing to her that it used to do to you? The whole glove-stripping thing?"

"She's not as strong as I am, so probably more of a glove-shredding thing."

"Wow, Jou."

"I might have a little unresolved anger at the Zes." Jou shrugs, never taking his hands off the wheel. I can't fault his driving.

"You think?"

Jou laughs and does something in my mind that makes me feel like he's stroked his fingertips down my cheek and tweaked my nipple. I squirm all over the car's heated, leather seat.

Jou's idea of a picnic is just as gourmet as his idea of a midnight snack. He drives us out to Alewife, parks in Acorn Discovery Park, collects a picnic basket and blanket out of the back of the car, and takes my hand. I've spent many nights in the Reservation gathering ingredients for my potions and I know where to go. Swinging our hands, looking like any other couple out for a nature walk on an unseasonably warm winter day, I lead him along the boardwalk to Little River and show him a good spot to spread the blanket.

He won't let me look in the picnic basket. The first thing out is a thermos and two ceramic cups. Jou pours generous measures of what I immediately smell is sake and hands me a cup. When I take a sip, I'm not surprised to find it's the perfect temperature.

The next thing he hands me is a ramekin filled with something that looks like pink foam. Knowing that Jou's never served me anything I didn't like, I take the fork he offers me and dig in. It's a delicate, creamy, shrimp mousse flavored with lemon and chives with just a hint of curried heat. I eat every bite.

"Jou, this is excellent."

He sighs, stretches his legs out on the blanket, and crosses his legs at the ankles. He's wearing heavy leather boots, black leather pants, and a chunky knit sweater in a blend of heathered grays that I'll be stealing as soon as he takes it off. The day's warm enough to go without a coat as long as we're in the sun, but I'm confident Jou wouldn't need a coat anyway. Even from where I'm sitting on the other side of the picnic basket, I can feel the warmth radiating from him.

"Julia. Hard to beat the classics," Jou says. My epicurean demon. "I'll miss human food when we go back."

"So, you don't eat at all when you're in Hell?"

"Naw, I don't need to."

"What about me? What will I eat?"

Jou scratches his chin with the handle of his fork. "Not sure you'll need to eat much of anythin', sweetness. Pretty sure you'll draw off me like I'm drawin' off you now. But if you do need to eat, Ash Hill'll provide. It always does."

"Your . . . home provides?"

Jou nods. "Can't explain it much more clearly than that, but when one of us needs somethin' the Hill shifts to provide it. When Nev was nesting with her first clutch by the Old Man, bunch of caves opened up beneath the Hill so she could hatch them out safely. Cyz moved in afterwards and claimed them as hers, but the Hill didn't make the caves for Cyz. It made them for Nev's babies."

"Adaptive architecture," I quip.

Jou grins. He unpacks the next level of the picnic basket, and hands me a steaming bowl of colorful greens and chicken over rice.

"Tarragon chicken with pak choi and basmati rice," he tells me when I look a question at him.

I take a bite and swoon. The chicken's tender and delicately flavored with the licorice note of tarragon and a light, citrus counterpoint from the greens. The nutty rice provides a base and richness to the dish. I set in like I haven't eaten in years. I don't care if none of my clothes fit me tomorrow.

"Good as it is to see you enjoyin' my food," Jou says in that low rumble of his. "I don't like you not eatin' for months. Somethin' I want to make clear, Tsara—"

I lift my eyebrows at his use of my name.

"We may get separated. You may think I'm dead or whatever. Long as you're alive, I will *always* come back to you."

I blink at him. "How will you know I'm alive?"

"I can feel you. No arms, no legs, no dick, impaled on that fucking Tree, I could feel you. No powers, so depressed you couldn't get outta bed, I could feel you. You *will* take care of yourself from now on. Long as you're alive, I'll know. You don't starve yourself and you don't harm yourself 'cause I *will* be coming back to you."

"As long as you're alive."

He shakes his head. "Pretty sure as long as you're alive, even if somethin' kills me, I'll be able to come back."

"That's, um, not possible."

"Wasn't possible until I spent a thousand days on that tree. Now it is. I'm not sayin' this to spook you. I'm sayin' it so you understand why I do the things I do. I put myself at risk pretty fucking often. I won't put you at risk. You're my damn life insurance policy. Understand, sweetness?"

I rub my forehead. "I guess."

"No, this ain't somethin' you guess at. Yes, or no?"

"Yes, Jou, I understand. I'll take better care of myself. I won't give up."

"Ever. No matter how long it takes. Thousand days on that tree. Shoulda been a blink of an eye to the Zes. Instead, they gave up on me. Swear it to me. On my kingseed that you bear, swear it to me."

Wow, he's serious about this. His harem's abandonment left wounds that didn't heal when I healed his body.

"I swear on your, uh, kingseed that I bear. We need to talk about that, by the way, but I swear, Jou."

He does that in-my-brain stroking thing again and I shiver all over the blanket.

"What the hell is that?"

He laughs. "Somethin' I figured out how to do this mornin'. Can't do it from a distance yet. I need to be able to see you. But I'm likin' the possibilities."

"Can I do it?"

I reach into his mind and imagine stroking my fingers down his cheek.

Blood bursts from his nose and runs in bright streams down his lips and chin.

"Omigod, Jou! I'm so sorry."

I scoot over to him, kneel beside him, and put my hand on his forehead. The damage I've done feels like an open, gasping mouth splitting his skull. *Reaching,* I knit everything back together.

Jou mops his face with a wet wipe and shakes his head at me. "You'll get the hang of it."

"Like I'm ever going to try that again."

"Just takes a lighter touch, sweetness." Jou shifts me onto his lap and gives me a kiss that tastes of copper. "We'll try again the next time we fuck. When you're nice and relaxed."

"I'm not, uh, tense now. Except about the kingseed thing. Can we revisit that?"

Jou traces a fingertip down my nose, between my breasts, and flattens his hand on my stomach. "Can you feel it yet?"

"Can I feel what?"

Jou rubs his fingertips over my belly button.

"Jou, I don't know how to tell you this—"

"You think you're infertile."

"I know I am. It runs in my family. I had a phantom pregnancy in college, and they ran some tests on me. My ovaries are defunct."

He cups my cheek. "I can see you believe that, sweetness, but it ain't so. I gave you my kingseed last time I was here, and you've caught already. I could smell it last night, no question."

"Kingseed, being what exactly?"

"Piece of my essence."

I touch my fingertips to his mouth. "You gave me a piece of your essence?"

He smiles against my fingers. "Course."

"And I've caught it . . . you're saying I'm pregnant? Jou, it's not possible."

"Yeah, it is. I'm a demon, sweetness. You're a witch and my seggurach. Normal rules don't apply to us."

"You're sure I'm going to have your baby?"

"Spawn, yeah."

Spawn. Spawn?

"Um, what does that mean?"

"They'll be demonspawn, sweetness."

"So, like half demon and half human?"

"Demons breed true. They'll have your gifts, but they'll be demons."

His words finally sink in, and a sudden, hot surge of emotion chokes me. "I'm really pregnant?"

Jou smiles indulgently. "Yeah, you are. Thought I felt the spark when you first summoned me, but now, I feel it bright and clear. Won't be long before others can feel it, too. Not many'd try to fuck with a bearer but there's always one, so we'll be extra careful the next few months." He slides his fingers into my sleeves and strokes my unfinished tattoo. "I think that might be the impetus for this. You're nestin'. You'll cast some fuckin' powerful protections over the next few months. Can't wait to feel 'em."

I slide my arms around him and tuck in against his chest. I've started getting used to the idea of forever with Jou, or at least resigned to the fact that I can't live without him. But forever with babies? That's a whole new deal. I wait for the panic to set in, but all I feel is a bright, blooming sense of hope.

"Can we stay here long enough to have the babies?" I ask.

Jou shakes his head. "You need to be in Dis when you bear. In the Hill. It won't be like a human birth. You won't need doctors and there's no danger to you. Anything that happens, I can take care of it. I've delivered hundreds of spawn. I won't fuck up bringin' out my own."

From everything Jou's said, I get the sense that demons don't live bear. They lay soft, leathery eggs that hatch after some gestation period.

I have a brief image of the egg things in the *Alien* movies that I push aside.

Jou chuckles. "Ain't that far off. They're smaller. 'Bout the size of your two fists, one-on-top of the other. Time's different down below, but they hatch out after maybe a month."

"And demonesses don't have any complications with birth? No breech births, no placenta previa?"

"No, demonesses are designed to drop their clutch on a battlefield and keep fightin'. You want a water birth, though, we could do that. Eggs aren't affected by water."

"They're not? Fire demon eggs—?"

Jou shakes his head. "Some fire demons lay their clutches submerged. Keeps those frosty fuckers away. Now, we got all the time you want to talk about demonspawn and clutchin', but these raspberries ain't gonna keep forever. You ready for dessert?"

Ready for his food? Always.

I grin at him.

Jou shifts me slightly but doesn't let me escape his lap as he digs down into the picnic basket and brings out a neatly boxed, raspberry-and-custard tart. He hands me a fresh fork and we eat it out of the box, occasionally entangling tines. Sitting in his lap, with his warmth enfolding me and my tummy comfortably full, feeling the low thrum of his presence in my mind, questing inside myself for the bright spark of life he's sensing, a moment of complete contentment settles over me.

I'm not sure there's ever been a single moment in my life when I've felt so utterly right.

Jou puts the empty box and our utensils aside. He settles his hands on the small of my back and holds me loosely, comfortably. With a flare and a rustle, his wings spread out of his back and fold around us. Closing my eyes, resting my head on his shoulder, I *pull* skein after skein of Air around us, cloaking us so no one will see the winged demon sitting on a picnic blanket in the unseasonably greening grass.

*Can you hold that?* Jou asks into my mind.

I nod contentedly. I can stay here, in this bubble of our shared power, for as long as he wants.

Forever, if he wants.

He shifts under me. With two mighty beats of his wings, we lift off the ground. As his legs drop, he wraps mine around his waist. He hovers ten feet off the ground, ruffling the blanket with the powerful downstrokes of his wings.

*Want to fly with me?*

*Yes.*

He shifts in my arms. I should be like those superhero movie heroines, turning my face into the wind to see where we're going. I'm not, and I don't. I tuck my face into the warm, strong column of his neck and breathe in his cinnamon and smoke scent. I hope our babies will smell like him.

As I *pull* skeins of Air around us, different scents wash over me: licorice, cloves, black cherry, all threaded through with the deep note of woodsmoke. Without asking, I know these are the babies' scents. Three different scents.

*Triplets.*

Jou throws his head back and roars his delight to the sky. I muffle the sound with Air, but the poor people working in Acorn Development Park probably think they're testing supersonic jets at Hanscom again.

Jou circles Little River, wings beating steadily, his strong arms cradling me tightly to his chest. Finally, we return to the hillock where we laid out the blanket. He lands with a little stumble.

"You okay?" He runs his hands up and down my back like the

bump of the landing might have injured me. If he starts treating me like I'm made of glass because I'm pregnant, we're going to have issues.

Jou chuckles as he hears that thought in my mind. "Not like glass, no. But just wait until your feet get swollen. I'll fly you everywhere."

I smack his shoulder lightly. "Don't even offer something like that. I *will* take you up on it."

"Wouldn't say it if I didn't mean it, sweetness." He folds his wings away. "One of the things I like most about bein' with you: I don't have to lie. It's gonna suck going back to the Hill and dealin' with everyone and their fucking agendas."

"I'm sorry, Jou."

He thumbs my lower lip. "Don't be. I got a lot more to look forward to now than I ever have before. That'll soften the sting some. And if they get too far under my skin, I'll just sicc you on 'em."

"I don't think Zef and her sisters are very scared of me."

"Mmm, they may not show it, but they are. Been nearly a thousand years since anyone threatened the status quo as much as you do. Zef's got a damn good poker face, but she's shakin' in her stilettos."

She's definitely not, but the image makes me laugh as we pack up the picnic and head back to the car.

# CHAPTER 14

Jou follows me silently through the staff entrance to the Museum and into the library where my mentor resides. I have no idea what any staff we come across—or Park himself—will make of the fact that I'm escorting a demon into a magical treasure-trove. I should be more worried about it. But that sense of contentment, of rightness and unity, still has me riding high and I just can't muster a single fuck.

We don't come across any staffers, which isn't unusual. I see another person—or whatever they are, because there are definitely some non-humans among the staff—maybe one visit in five. If I stay late, the night guard sometimes pokes his head in, but I gather I freaked him out once when he walked in while I was in a deep trance and levitating. I haven't seen much of him since.

It's getting toward late afternoon when Jou and I settle into green leather chairs on either side of the huge, intricately carved pillar at one end of the library. I immediately feel the ghost fingers of Park's presence ruffle across my mind.

Then I feel Jou gently, but firmly, push him out.

"He can't speak aloud, Jou," I explain. "He needs to be in my head enough to communicate."

"No," Jou says firmly. "Only thing inside you from now on is me. Wait here."

He rises from the chair and stalks off through the library. Where does he think he's going? And shouldn't I be stopping him? Or should I? It's not like Jou can't handle anything he'd come across in here. There's one of the lost fae crowns and a soul chain within five hundred feet of where I'm sitting. Maybe I should be concerned about a demon —lord?—coming in contact with some of the powerful artifacts here. But I'm not. I settle into my chair and relax, crossing my legs and stroking my belly with my thumb meditatively.

Jou's back a few minutes later with an ornately carved crystal skull. He plonks it on the table next to his chair, facing the column.

"There you go, spirit," he says.

I start to protest. The skull still doesn't have working vocal cords, tongue, teeth, or lips. But Park's resonant baritone issues from the skull before I get any words out.

"Son of Asmodei, pass through these halls in peace."

"Nothin' bothers me, I won't bother nothin'," Jou responds.

"There is much here that will not take kindly to your presence," Park says.

"Yeah. I can taste the hostility." Jou licks his incisor, which looks much longer and sharper than usual. "I'm not here for anythin' but information. They leave me alone; I'll leave them alone. I'm not lookin' for a fight."

"Tsara, you brought the demon here. Do you vouch for him?"

Can I vouch for Jou? Can I predict what he'll do?

"He won't burn the place down this time," I say. I'm pretty sure I can promise that. Not a hundred percent sure, but maybe ninety-nine percent.

Jou chuckles.

"Park, I've come to see if you could help us with a symbol. Jou says it looks like Futhark, but he doesn't recognize it. I'm hoping you might."

"Picture the symbol in your mind and I will ponder it while you do today's good Work."

I bow my head. Park always shapes our time together into a lesson.

I'm not adverse to that, since I've always enjoyed magical learning, although I'm not crazy about Park insisting that I call him "master." It's totally different from joking around with Bo. Park means it; he really does think he's my master. I appreciate it's part of the tradition, but I'm not a fan, and I can see Jou blowing a gasket over it.

"What is the subject of today's Work?" I ask.

"Time."

I nod and sit and think. Finally, I begin.

"When I was a kid, eight or nine, I lost my favorite sock. Black with cat faces on it. I couldn't find it anywhere. I stood by my bed in our caravan, and I concentrated so hard on it. Pictured it in my mind. Rubbed my fingers together like I could feel the soft cotton. My hair kept blowing around my face and something in me was tugging and tugging but I didn't stop. I felt like I was getting closer and closer to my sock. Finally, it fluttered up and hit me in the face. It was torn, and I realized it must have been caught on something and by calling it to me so hard, I'd ripped it free. I sat on the floor, holding my sock, and crying. I kept thinking that if I'd just known where it was, I could have freed it, and it wouldn't have gotten ripped. I could see myself doing it in my mind, crawling under my bed, finding the sock, lifting the metal corner so I could pull it out. I pictured it over and over and when I opened my eyes, my sock was in my hand, and it was whole, and the caravan stank like I'd burned dinner. I didn't pay any attention to the smell. I just ran to find my Dala. To show her what I'd done. Do you know what she did?"

"I'm guessin' it wasn't congratulate you for your first successful Time-Walk," Jou says, his voice growly.

"No, she slapped me and taught me the first rule of magic. Do not fuck with Time."

"Time is just another force," Park says. "Like gravity. Taken for granted. Poorly understood. Measured and dismissed. You are a supplicant at the Temple of Knowledge. Here we probe beyond the Veil. Discovering the secrets of Time is just another stage of the Journey."

Until a Time Lord shows up and objects with extreme prejudice.

"My teachers at Bevvy were pretty clear on this, too. Time's the thing nobody wants to mess with."

"You already are messin' with it," Jou says. "That stitch thing you've been doing? Like when you sent me the imps? You're creating a loop in time. Same as I do when we step sideways. There are consequences for shifting Time onto a different path. Small time loops, small consequences. Things you probably didn't even notice. Big time loops? Big consequences."

"How big?" I ask, curious. I had no idea Jou knew so much about Time-magic.

"JFK wasn't assassinated kind of big. Big enough time loop could shift your world onto a completely different timeline."

Wow.

"Is that true on every plane? You said Time runs differently in Hell. Would there be a larger or smaller ripple to messing with Time there?"

Jou shrugs. "Dunnow. Haven't tried it. Want to run some experiments when we go back?"

He grins that wicked grin that's full of too many, too sharp teeth.

I shake my head at him.

"To a Worker, Time is just another tool," Park says. "Before I was abruptly ejected from your mind, Tsara, I saw your grief for the young skin-changer. Unlock the secrets of Time and walk back to see his death for yourself."

That feels like a recipe for big consequences. "And if I'm killed there along with him?"

"Ain't gonna happen," Jou growls.

I guess his grumpiness is understandable, given what he just told me about being his life insurance policy.

"Hmm." How Park makes a humming sound with no working mouth parts is even more of a mystery to me than Time. "I believe I've found your symbol. You are right, demon, it is elder Futhark, as used by the Germanic people of the Elbe. Loosely translated, it means the Furious Host."

"The what?"

"You'd call it the Wild Hunt," Jou answers me. "Huns called them the Furious Host. That's a name I ain't heard in a long time. Makes no sense they'd go after the Airy Fairy, though. They're sorta kin."

"The Wild Hunt has been known to punish transgressors among the fae," Park says. "Generally, the Knights act as enforcers, but the Wild Hunt has been called to do the Oak King's bidding before."

I trade glances with Jou and shake my head. "No way. I felt failure and sorrow, but not guilt. If he'd broken the *weirdlaw* or gone against his King, he'd have felt remorse at least."

Jou shrugs. "Maybe he was hunted for another reason. Too far-fetched for it to be unrelated, though. Particularly the manner of death for both of 'em."

"What was the manner of death?" Park asks.

I guess he didn't see that in my head before Jou punted him. "They were both partially eaten."

"The hounds of the Wild Hunt are hungry," Park says.

"Gross." I rub my fingers over my forehead, feeling a throb of dissonance. "Ugh. I really don't like the idea of reporting this back to the Tylwyth Teg. Or the vampires. They're not going to be happy."

Jou grunts. "They can both go fuck 'emselves. Vampires owe you a favor. You owed the Twitterin' Throng a favor. Give 'em the answer and walk away one up."

That seems like such a demon solution.

*It is,* Jou says into my mind. *And since you're bound to a demon now, time to start embracin' demon solutions.*

*How about you embrace a visit to the Bunker Hill nest and the Ivywhile Court with me?*

Jou shifts in his chair. *How 'bout we just send 'em an email? We got better things to do.*

I don't ask what better things because I know what's on my lust demon's mind. It's already creating an eye-catching bulge in his pants.

*I'm fairly confident the Oak King does not have email.*

*Wanna bet?*

No, I don't, because I'm still trying to get my head around the fact that Jou has an email address *in Hell.*

"Even if I just pass messages to the vampires and the fae, I still owe it to Ana to tell her face-to-face."

Jou holds up his hands. "Ain't gonna argue that one."

"I still don't have any answer for her as to *why* the Wild Hunt would have attacked Toby. Even if it's true that they went after the Squire because he broke the weirdlaw somehow, Toby was a shifter. He's not bound by the same laws."

Jou shifts in his chair. "I got a thought on that, but you ain't gonna like it."

Oh boy.

"Please share with the class," I say.

"Thing they got in common is you."

A cold finger runs up and down my spine. "And the thing that I've felt stalking me?"

"If the Wild Hunt couldn't get to you directly 'cause of the wards you got in place? Maybe they went after your nearest and dearest. You healed anyone since Toby?"

I shake my head. "Just you."

"Been in the Wild Lands with anyone but the Airy Fairy?"

"Just you."

Jou shrugs. "If the Hunt comes after me, we'll know."

"Is that a possibility?"

Jou chuckles. "Anythin's a possibility, sweetness."

"What happens if they do?" I ask warily.

Jou grins, showing waaay too many teeth.

Okay, then.

———

There are three demons sitting on the couch in my parlor when we get home, and they're not the same three demons who were in my house when I left.

The new demon, his glove so ill-fitting that it blurs in my sight as he stands, claws dangling from his spindly arms to scrape across the carpet, creeps forward and bows to Jou. "Sire."

Jou raises an eyebrow. "Who're you?"

"Your brother, the wise and benevolent Red Duke, sent me." The demon points with a shaky claw at a huge monitor sitting on the coffee table. "He offers me as a gift to his beloved kin and asks that you grant him an audience at midnight."

Jou snorts. "Where d'you usually live, the Marches?"

The demon, hairless, gray skin dotted with black spines melting through the appearance of a bland teen, nods.

"You know the Soulfields?" Jou asks.

The gray demon nods a little more enthusiastically.

"My seggurach's gonna send you there. Find Uzal. Tell him I sent you and you're to give him five turns of service carin' for my stable. Then you're free and you can take two from my stable with you."

"Thank you, sire. Generous sire, thank you."

Jou strokes my cheek with those warm, mental fingers. *If I give you an image of where I want him to go, can you open a Gate and push him through?*

*I can try. Not sure how good my interplanar GPS is.*

Jou chuckles into my mind.

Thinking Jou's going to spend time with his sisters, I leave him to it and beckon the little demon after me as I head out into my yard. Jou doesn't just put an image into my mind as I go. He gives me a whole map of Dis, spinning outwards from his home. It's not like any map I've seen before. It's a landscape of feelings: fears, warnings, and odd spots of warmth. The Soulfields, where he wants to me to send the kowtowing demon who won't even meet my eyes, is a hot crevice, a throbbing pleasure-pit. Just brushing my mind over that part of the map makes my body tingle and tighten.

When I enter my hearth room, I discover that there is, in fact, a demoness in my cauldron. Or, partially in my cauldron. Jou's suspended her in a web of sticky black bindings that attach to nothing, hanging in mid-air and holding her bound with her lower body in the cauldron. I see what he means about glove-shredding as flesh sloughs off her in streams to drop into the steaming water. Her head's thrown back; her mouth stretched in a soundless scream.

I stare at her for a long moment, taking in what Jou has done to his sister-lover. It's a good reminder of how ruthless he is. And how strongly he feels about any threat against me.

I breathe out, expelling the toxins of doubt, take the teen-demon's trembling claw, and walk through the first of my circles. It wakes with a blast of wind and a swirl of embers. That's new, but I ignore it as I center myself, *reach*, and open a Gate to the location Jou's put in my mind. I don't need any rituals now. I know the path into his plane as well as I know the path to my own front door. It's seared deep into my mind and magic. There's barely even a Veil to pass through, here in the heart of my power. It's like brushing aside a cobweb. Then I'm feeling my way to that place Jou associates so strongly with the base drives that make him what he is.

There's a moment of seasick disorientation as the swirling, smoking landscape closes around me. Each journey into a plane so alien to my own has a distinct flavor. This time, it feels like a thousand small scabs are being ripped off my skin. Small, sticky tears in the fabric of what makes me, me.

I ignore the sensation and focus on my goal, drawing the teen-demon with me. His glove whisps away as soon as he passes through the Gate. He's a hunched, twisted, gray-skinned thing with spindly arms and legs, a round body and no neck. I'm glad to see the back of him as I push him forward towards the point Jou steered me to. I feel it envelop him and, somewhat disgustingly, feel him convulse in an orgasm before I fully release him.

I start to draw back when a misty hand reaches out of the fleshy pit and grabs mine. There's no hostility to it. It's like a handshake. I wait and a demon takes shape in my mind. He's huge, hulking, red-skinned, spined, with a mane of black hair and beard reaching to his waist. He has the most beautiful, black eyes. The eyes of a child. They meet mine without blinking.

*Dast's seggurach.* His touch in my mind is warmer than Jou's but less weighty. Jou's mind wraps mine like a weighted blanket. This demon's mind brushes mine like feathers.

*Uzal?*

*I've been your mate's friend and ally since we were lemurs. Does he send you to me to protect?*

*No. That demon's a gift to you. I'm just the messenger.*

*Dast has given me many gifts. I owe him my existence many times over. I sense you are threatened. Let me offer you the sanctuary of the Soulfields. I will keep you safe until Dast comes for you.*

Is this a trap? He feels so warm, so friendly. He's not even pushy the way Jou is . . . about everything. But I don't think Jou sent me here intending for me to stay.

*Jou's with me. He's whole and healed. He's keeping me safe.*

Uzal bows his head. *I welcome this news. I shared his pain while he was on the Tree. If he seeks vengeance, I will stand with him as I have always stood with him.*

I don't know if I should speak for Jou. *I'll tell him.*

*If you need refuge at any time, come to me. Tell my brother I look forward to the day I can cross horns with him again.*

Is that a demon greeting? Fighting? Sex? I have no idea, but I thank him, and he fades back into the pleasure-pit.

I blink and the strange, swirling landscape of Hell dissipates back into the comforting contours of my hearth room. I glance at the demoness writhing above my cauldron. I could free her, but I'm fairly sure that would piss Jou off. Instead, I empty my cauldron—which definitely had more than just water in it; the mental touch of it feels like greasy acid—with a flick of my fingers and leave her to regrow her skin.

When I enter my house, I expect to find Jou in the parlor with his sisters. Instead, he's in the kitchen, stirring something on the stove, wearing a plastic Harrods apron with a ring of salamanders at his feet.

"Once the meat's browned, this'll simmer for an hour," Jou tells me without taking his eyes off the pot. "You an' I can have some quality time."

I flinch at him using the same term for our time together that he used for torturing his sister.

Jou moves the pan off the heat. He crosses the short distance to me and folds me into the crinkly plastic apron before I have a chance to twitch.

"That was a bad choice of words," he rumbles into my hair. "An' you're such a soft fuckin' touch." I feel him sifting through my recent memories. "It wasn't a trap. That's what Uzal's like. If he had a soul, he'd have offered it to the Old Man to get me off the Tree. He'd die for you just 'cause you're mine."

"I like him," I say, because I instantly did. "I don't suppose he lives at Ash Hill with you?"

"No." Jou strokes his fingertips up and down my spine before releasing me and returning to the stove. "But he visits a lot. He'll have even more reason to visit now. He liked you, too. I can tell."

"He was very quick to offer me protection. How can he sense that I'm in danger on a minute's acquaintance?"

Jou shrugs, fishes a piece of meat out of one of the pans in front of him, rips it into three pieces with his claws, and tosses the pieces to the circle of waiting salamanders. They're so well-behaved, or his aim is so good, there's no struggle for the meat. They each just snap a piece out of the air.

"You know how I'm half-Noctil? I got that useless touch of fore-knowledge?"

I nod. I remember when he was last here and told me about a book that wasn't published yet. I looked it up. The release was just before Thanksgiving. I should get him to give me lottery numbers.

"Uzal's got more Noctil in him than I do. He always knows when shit's about to go down. That's how he's managed to keep the Soul-fields neutral for so long." He slides a pile of browned meat out of a frying pan and into a bubbling pot, pops the lid on it, and turns toward me, untying his apron. "Upstairs, sweetness."

"Um, what about your sisters?"

"I sent 'em on an errand. They won't be back for hours."

I brighten up at the idea of having the house to ourselves. If he'd ordered me upstairs for nookie while his sisters were in the house, I probably wouldn't have argued too hard with him at this point, but I also would have been very distracted thinking about them listening to us.

I lift my hands to the collar of my shirt. I tease open the three buttons at my throat. "So, you're just ordering me upstairs in their absence?"

Jou's eyes fill with glints of neon. "I am. You goin'?"

"I don't know." I drop my hands to the hem of my shirt and begin to tease it up towards my ribs. "Am I?"

"Thinkin' you are." He takes a prowling step towards me.

I back towards the hallway, wiggling my hips as I walk. "Maybe I'm just going upstairs to shower."

"We can do it in the shower if you want," Jou says, his eyes fixed on my hips as he stalks after me. "And the bed. And the floor. And the wall."

"Promises, promises," I tease.

He growls and his eyes go purely feral.

I shriek in mock fear and flee upstairs, giggling my head off at the pounding of his steps behind me.

# CHAPTER 15

At midnight, Jou and I sit on the couch in my parlor facing the huge screen the teen-demon dropped off.

"Is it on?" I whisper to Jou as the screen remains blank.

"Yeah. Chaid don't give a shit about mortal time."

I nod into my cup of hot chocolate. It's hot chocolate à la Jou, which means its real chocolate beaten into steaming milk—I'm never going back to powdered, either—enriched with cinnamon and nutmeg, and topped with whipped cream and mini chocolate chips. I don't really care what Jou's brother has to say to us because between the many orgasms this afternoon, another of Jou's amazing dinners, a night of watching cop dramas in our pajamas while the Zes are still off on their mysterious errand, and now real hot chocolate, I'm in a really freaking happy place.

The screen blinks without either of us touching it and a white wall appears.

"Ooo, magic," Jou murmurs to me.

I snigger into my cup.

A man in a black-on-black silk suit that I'm fairly sure cost more than my house walks into view and sits down with his back to the wall. "Brother," he says.

Jou's chin wrinkles, then he nods. "Brother."

"I'm pleased to see you've recovered from Father's displeasure."

Jou sits back and crosses his ankle over his knee. He doesn't project at me, but I can feel his puzzlement. "Yeah, I'm good. Haven't known you to come topside since the Crusaders first sacked Jerusalem."

Dang, when was Jerusalem first sacked? Like, a thousand years ago? I should have taken more World History at Bevvy.

The man shrugs, the movement making the fabric of his suit slide over his body like black water. It's kind of mesmerizing, and after a moment, I tear my eyes away. I know Chaid is Jou's much older brother, but I have the sense they're not friends, and getting mesmerized by a very old, very powerful demon who is not Jou's friend *cannot* be a good idea.

"I go where Father needs me. For now, I am needed here. And you, brother, will you go where you are needed?"

Jou wiggles his bare toes. I can feel him thinking. "Father need me t'be somewhere? That the reason you're callin'?"

"Not at present, but the Hellroarer will call the muster before the Turn. Will Ash Hill answer?"

No consideration now. Jou gives a firm nod. "Always."

"That is good to hear. The Marches will also answer. The Fleshmarkets will remain neutral, as they always have. But the Soulfields, what of them?"

Jou leans forward and stares into the screen. "Uzal given you any reason to doubt him?"

Chaid lifts one shoulder elegantly.

"He's never closed his doors to the Old Man." Jou sits back and stretches an arm behind me, drawing me into his side. "You askin' me to make sure where he stands?"

"Asking, no. I need no such favor. But much has changed in your absence. You will find that Uzal has moved the Soulfields. They lie beyond your Hill. At the foot of the Mists. Away from Father's reach. Father has indicated his displeasure, but Uzal claims fealty to none. Friendship to few. If the Soulfields are moved wholly into the Mists before we march, that will weaken many." The demon strokes his close-trimmed beard. "Such course would be *unfortunate*."

Jou gives a little grunt. "Okay. I get it. If I take responsibility for Uzal, what does that get me?"

"Nothing." Chaid spreads his hands, the fiery stones on his pinkie rings glittering. "I have asked no favor."

"Yeah, but if I did, what *would* it get me?"

"I have no power to grant you any boon," Chaid says and, for a moment, I think the discussion's over. Then he says, "*If* I did, what would you wish?"

"Chiobi could stop makin' Nev's life miserable," Jou says.

Chaid crosses his hands over his flat stomach and gives a humorless laugh. "It would take much, much more than the Soulfield's allegiance to cool the crucible of my beloved's ire towards you and your sister. What else do you wish?"

"Nev could come home for good," Jou says, shrugging like it doesn't matter to him one way or the other, although I know it must.

"Father is no fit mood to surrender his Flame, particularly when she is breeding again. What else?"

"Nothin', I guess," Jou says. Then, almost as an afterthought, "He could let me at the Pillar of Fire with Tsara."

The demon's burning gaze flicks to me and I feel the heat of it even through the screen.

"This is your human? She'd not survive."

At least he didn't call me *meat*. He gets more brownie points than Jou's sisters.

I sip my hot chocolate and let him stare.

"Leave that to me," Jou says. "Deal?"

"If I was asking a favor—" Chaid begins.

"Which you're not. I get it. If you were, would Father let me take Tsara to the Pillar?"

Chaid grins, showing a mouthful of terrifyingly pointed teeth. "Yes."

"Fine. Deal. I make sure the Soulfields' doors stay open and I get access to the Pillar with Tsara."

"And the Red Bone Leech."

Jou throws his head back and laughs. "Cyz'd send me to the

Muster in six pieces if I tried to drag her outta her hole. Father wants her there, he's gonna have to do it himself."

"She is beneath his notice," Chaid sneers. "You will carry a message to her."

If she's important enough to warrant a message, that pretty much means she's not beneath their father's notice, but neither Jou nor I point that out.

"Why, 'cause she fed his last three messengers to the Fiends? Sure. I'll carry a message, but that's extra. The cost of a new fucking skin, since she'll rip mine off for carrying Father's word to Skull Cave. It'd take me a Turn to regrow it, so I want Nev home for that long. No bootie calls. And no ultimatums from the Old Man for Cyz. I'll carry an offer, but not a summons. I just got my life back; I'm not throwin' it away."

Jou has mentioned Cyz before. I Felt her, when Jou took me to his home, and we raised power together. Her thoughts were dark, and kind of crawly, but not terrifying. Nothing like some of Jou's other neighbors. But Jou and his brother are talking about Cyz like she's more powerful than either of them, which is new, and not very welcome, news. Particularly since I know that she's been a frequent fuckbuddy of Jou's.

"Agreed," Chaid says, showing his sharp teeth again. "It's good to treat with you, brother."

"Yeah, an' you're easier to talk to without Chiobi or the Old Man around. Anythin' else?"

Chaid strokes his trimmed, black beard and levels a look at Jou that sends goosebumps racing all over me, not just on the outside. I swear I feel them *inside* my spine.

"You intend to breed at last?" Chaid asks.

Jou shrugs. "Depends."

"On the human's ability to survive the Pillar, yes, I glean. If you were to do so, I might suggest a fostering. One of your get to the Marches and a child of my House to the Hill. My Princess will never love your sister, but a fostering might prevent her from venting her wrath quite so often. Then we might talk of your human becoming one of my Princess's attendants. Should she one day become more than she is."

"Lotta 'ifs,' there, but I'll keep it in mind."

Chaid nods and gives Jou another long look. "Ash Hill rises, brother. The Marches have long held Father's favor, while he has ignored your Hill. He does so no longer. Whether he gives you his favor, or determines to finally crush you, depends on where you tread. You have long walked in the shadow of the Hellroarer. That shadow wanes, I warn you. Should you find yourself in need of a new shadow, my umbra is long."

Jou sits forward, letting his hands fall loose between his knees, relaxed but answering Chaid's intensity. "I'll answer when the Hell-roarer calls. I'll go where I'm told, when I'm told, and do what I'm told. But if I was told to camp with the Marches, fight beside the Marches, I'd consider doin' more'n my duty, and bringin' more than just who and what I'm told."

Chaid's face splits into that terrifying grin. "I hear you, brother. Or in the parlance of this time, I feel you."

Jou chuckles. "I feel you, too. Thanks for the warning."

"I gave you no warning," Chaid says, all smiles. "Only an invitation to battle, which you will shortly receive from your leash-holder in any event. Until then, I wish you and your seggurach well, and I look forward to the day when your get graces my hall."

"See you on the field," Jou says, just before the screen freezes and a message pops up that says, "Call ended."

Jou leans back and lets his head thump onto the back of the couch. "Fuck me, sweetness."

He holds his arm out for me, and I slide against his side. After a long minute, he blows out a breath. A sphere of his power expands outward and stops, quavering like a soap-bubble, an inch from the video-screen. The sounds I could hear: the soft scrabble of claws as the salamanders chase each other around the kitchen, the faint hiss of the heating, they fade until all I can hear is our breathing. Jou's is a little slower than mine, which I guess means he's less scared than I am.

"No one can hear us in here. Not even the Old Man. We got a minute to talk, just us. Ask me whatever you want."

"I have no idea where to start."

"Okay, I'll start. My elder brother, who has never taken the time to do anythin' more'n look at me like I'm dirt on his boots, just offered me an alliance. And he offered me access to the Pillar of Fire. *And* he told me Father knows about Angien's little cabal. Fuck, that was more conversation than we've had in a thousand years."

"He said Ash Hill was on the rise."

"Yeah, I get that. I also get the Old Man throwin' a complete fuckin' nutty about Uzal moving the Soulfields. If Uz takes the Soulfields into the Mists, that'd cripple half the Old Man's court. But it'd hurt the Ice Demons, too. Everyone keeps their stable in the Soulfields. And there's no reason Uzal would do that. Unless somethin' threatened him. He didn't give any indication of it when he was talkin' with you, but maybe his offer of protection was really an SOS. Maybe he was tellin' me he needs my help. I might have to go see him, sweetness. Talk face-to-face. Figure out what the fuck's going on."

"Okay," I say, a little warily, because I thought there were good reasons I took the plane-walk alone today: Jou's staying away from Hell for a while. But maybe this is so important it makes the risks worthwhile.

"That can't be all it is, though. Old Man's got other ways to pressure Uzal. He don't need me. And Chaid's never given me a second's thought before. Never, ever called me brother. There's something else going on," Jou says, hugging me tighter. "Sure, he wants me on his side, but this is about somethin' bigger. Notice how he was willin' to give me Nev for a year without an argument, but shut me down when I threw her comin' home for good out there? Old Man's been makin' noises about settin' aside the Soae and makin' Nev his Consort for a long time. I always figured it was just hot air to keep everyone on their toes. If the Old Man wants somethin', he just takes it. Maybe I got it wrong. Maybe he's been waitin', not 'cause he wanted to, but 'cause he needed me to be stronger."

"Stronger, so you can let her go?" I ask, a little fearfully because I can't imagine Jou letting any of his siblings go and being in a war between Jou and his father is not a place anyone wants to be.

"No, stronger so Nev can survive everythin' it means to be the Old

Man's Consort." He brings his hands together in front of us, making a triangle with his fingers and thumbs. "Nev's part of my power base. I draw from her. But power flows both ways." He turns the triangle upside-down. "She draws from me, too. Old Man mighta made me stronger so she can draw enough from me to survive. Whole Court'll be gunnin' for her if he makes her his Consort. She needs to be strong enough to walk their gauntlet. And, fuck me, Chaid's worried about losing his voice in the Old Man's ear if she replaces the Soae. That's why he wants me as his ally."

"Why would Chaid lose his voice with your father if Nev becomes his Consort?"

Finally, a question I can ask.

"Chaid's built up a lotta cred over the centuries. He's not just the Old Man's eldest. He holds the Western Marches, biggest territory in Dis after the Iron City. His Consort's the Soae's eldest daughter, Chiobi. Their fuckin' kids could make their own Horde, there are so many of 'em. For a while I thought he an' the Old Man were havin' some kinda contest, seein' how many they could sire. An' none of 'em are in the Webs. They all hold some little piece of the Marches for Chaid. That's a lotta mouths to feed. If the Old Man kicks the Soae out an' replaces her with Nev, that means Chaid's fuckin' Princess falls from grace, too. Chaid's gotta be worried about his territory if that all goes down, an' how many of his get would come knockin' on his door, expectin' to be fed, if the Old Man takes territory from him an' gives it to Nev's kids."

I blink as I try to process all this. "Would he do that? I mean, take territory off Chaid and give it to Nev's kids? And, wait, Nev has kids?"

I kind of understood that she did. In a metaphorical sense, I guess. But I've never seen any children around Jou or any of his clutch. They sure don't act like parents. Maybe demons don't?

"Yeah, quite a few. Couple hundred with the Old Man."

"A couple *hundred*?!"

"Yeah. Think I mentioned how he kept her whelping out a clutch a year for a century as punishment? Forced to breed like that, she didn't have many in a clutch. Two, three, sometimes just one. They were weak. Most of 'em got eaten before they even made it to the Webs, although Zippy tried to move 'em fast and quiet. Maybe three dozen left, and they're too weak to become anythin' more'n malebranch. Some of her clutches before that are stronger, though. I got my eye on a few of 'em. Old Man probably does, too, but I got first claim."

"Over your father? I mean, not just your father, but the father of her children? I don't quite get that."

"Demon paternity ain't any more certain than human paternity, sweetness. Kids are born into the mother's House. Nev's still part of Ash Hill until the Old Man makes things formal with her. That means I get first dibs on her kids. Old Man could stake a claim, but he'll probably bargain with me instead if there's one or two he really wants. An' it's easier for him if I claim 'em. Feedin' and trainin' 'em are on me, instead of him. He can always tap 'em later. Old Man plays a long game."

I've come to understand that much at least.

"Something else," Jou says. "I might have to go home for this, too. Chaid was talkin' like the Hellroarer's the only ally I got. But he ain't. He ain't even the most important. At least, I didn't think so. Either Chaid don't know about the White Hood, which I can't fucking believe given the last time we marched, Ash Hill marched under her banner, or he's tellin' me something by not mentionin' her. I don't know. Maybe I gotta go see her, too. An' this is somewhere you can't come with me, sweetness. I wish you could. But she'll stick you in her dungeon an' never let you out, I show up with you. She's got a fucking strict policy when it comes to humans."

I swallow hard. Demon dungeons are places I do not want to be. "Can I be in your mind at least?"

"Yeah, no problem with that. In fact, might be best if I go tonight while you're sleepin'. You can dream it with me. Easier to pull from you without you bein' there if you're asleep."

I stroke his cheek. "I'll miss sleeping with you."

"I'll be gone and back before you wake up. You won't even know I'm gone."

Famous last words.

———

I know he's gone even though I'm sleeping, because I wake in a knot of covers from twisting and turning all night. And I know he's still gone when I wake because the bed, the room, heck, my whole house, are cold without him.

I wore pajamas to bed, and I still wake shivering and reaching across the sheets for a body that isn't there.

*I'm here, sweetness. Ain't like before.*

His voice in my mind grounds me, but it doesn't make up for the cold bed.

*Sorry, I just woke up and missed you,* I think to him.

He opens his mind enough that I can sense his surroundings. He's in a bed, too, but his isn't empty. Evidently, demon hospitality, or at least the White Hood's hospitality, involves offering bed partners. I know Jou didn't partake of what was offered, but he still fell asleep in a pile of bodies. I envy him the warmth and comfort of touch, if nothing else.

*My bed's cold and empty without you, too, sweetness.*

Mollified, I slide out of the bed and pad into the bathroom to wash.

I stop in the hall when I hear the patter of the shower.

*Your sisters are back,* I tell Jou grimly.

*Yeah. If it makes you feel any better, they'll definitely clear out tomorrow 'cause Hairy's got a show.*

*It's okay.*

It's not. I'm beginning to really resent the ongoing invasion of demonesses. Particularly when Jou's not here to make me breakfast and I have to settle for cold cereal. I pull on my bathrobe, collect the lizard who is wriggling around in the warm hollow where I slept, and trudge downstairs.

*I promise to make you breakfast tomorrow morning,* Jou says into my mind. *French toast?*

*With homemade brioche bread?*

He chuckles. *Sure, sweetness. I'm gonna sleep some more. I'm still feeling a little stretched.*

I grimace, remembering his rocky transition to Hell.

Where the Gate opened for me with no more effort than opening a screen door, the Gate rejected Jou. He had to battle his way through with a supreme act of will. It left him drained. He doesn't maintain a glove in Hell, but I felt his uncertainty that he could, after that transition.

As I pour myself cereal and start up the coffee machine, which spits spitefully at me, threatening to break even though I haven't cast so much as a cantrip this morning, I rummage through my dreams, which I know weren't dreams so much as Jou feeding me his experiences while I slept.

Demon politics are nearly impenetrable to me, but Uzal did move his territory close to Ash Hill in response to a threat, as Jou's brother intimated. Once Jou found the Soulfields, he communed with Uzal for a long time, horns and hands locked together, as they tried to puzzle out Tem's actions. Jou's uncle has always been a friend and an ally. Even a mentor when the two were much younger. But not anymore. Tem stripped Uzal of the souls he had granted to Uzal over the centuries and warned Uzal to stay out of the Fleshmarkets. I felt Jou's shock. I felt their mutual uncertainty. I don't think they found any answers.

At some early hour of the morning, which was several days later in demon-time, Jou left the Soulfields and traveled through his own lands to a strange, marshy area where every puddle and stunted tree and tuft of grass crackled with white fire. An alabaster tower rose out of the marshes and a scuttling page with a white hood stretched over his blunt features greeted Jou at the tower's gate.

Jou took it as a good sign that the mistress of the tower didn't make him wait. As he walked into Malakaz's court, I understood why I couldn't accompany him. Shackled, naked humans lined the walls, surrounded by small clots of hooded demons feeding off their cries of pain and pleasure. The White Hood herself sat naked on a throne of white bones. She looked human: small and curvy and beautiful, except for the tight white hood covering her head down to her red bow of a mouth and the wide, white horns rising out of the hood's smooth top. She smiled when Jou entered, showing too many teeth to fit in a human mouth. A massive, bestial demon lounged at her feet, his branching horns a playground for the White Hood's fingers as she spun golden threads through the tines.

Neither Malakaz nor her malebranch lover, Gandewara, rose to greet Jou, and from his thoughts, I understood that's not a demon thing. Their greeting rushed across the room and climbed Jou like a tree a moment later: a tiny, brown-skinned, green-haired, silver-eyed woman. Jou hugged her to him and kept her wrapped around him while he greeted Malakaz and Gandewara. She took a deep breath off his neck, reared back in surprise, then put her head down on his shoulder and left it there while she clung to him. If I'd sensed any sexual interest from Jou, although I immediately knew she'd been his lover in the past, I'd have gone into a snit.

But there wasn't even a flicker of interest.

I picked up her name from the hours of conversation that threaded through my dreams: *Ercie.* I'm sure Jou's mentioned her before, but I don't remember when. Despite his lack of interest, I could feel his affection for her, and she was one of the several bodies who joined him for the night.

As I wash out my dish and feed the salamanders from a bowl of something brown and curious Jou's left for them in the fridge, I turn Jou's conversations with Malakaz and Gandewara over in my head. There was no indication that Malakaz abandoned their alliance. She showed Jou her preparations for when the Hellroarer called the muster: her troops of hooded malebranch training in the crackling courtyard. Jou asked her point-blank if she expected Ash Hill to march with the White Marshes and she said yes. I felt him watching her closely, but he never felt she was disingenuous. He was reassured, if still puzzled, when he let Ercie drag him to bed.

*You're thinking too loud,* Jou grumbles sleepily into my mind.

*Sorry, I didn't mean to wake you.*

*Stop worryin' about this for now. You goin' to work?*

*If your demoness ever gets out of my shower.*

Jou chuckles. *It's that lure of indoor plumbin'. Gets 'em every time.*

*Do you want me to come home early so I can help you get back?*

*Naw, this is somethin' I gotta do. Ass of Hell gave me way too hard a time goin' down. It needs to know I ain't gonna put up with that shit.*

*Okay. You'll be home for dinner?*

I can't believe how clingy my own thought sounds; I cringe.

*Don't, sweetness. I miss you, too. And it's nice to be wanted for once.*

Remembering everything I did to push him away the last time he was here, I pour all those clingy, cringey feelings into his mind.

I feel him smile before he rolls over to go back to sleep.

————

Lin's waiting for me at the reception desk, her sixth sense working overtime again. Her mouth is set in a hard line, and I wonder why she's pissed at me this time. I wish I could say I haven't seen a lot of that expression over the past three months.

"We need to talk." She crooks a finger and stalks off into her office.

I give Evonne a wan smile and follow Lin.

As soon as I close her office door behind me, she whirls. "There's a hundred thousand dollars in the clinic's account this morning. Did you take out another mortgage? Without talking to me first?"

Jou. Fuck.

*You're welcome,* he thinks with grim amusement.

*I thought you were asleep?*

*I could feel the little dragon's fury all the way down here. She really don't like charity, does she?*

*Nope, it's her least favorite thing. She hates charity more than she hates her ex.*

*Too bad. Let this be a growin' moment for her.*

"Um, I came into some money. I know I've taken more than I've given the last few months and I just wanted to make it right. So we weren't worrying about money anymore."

Lin scratches behind her ear, looking both annoyed and deflated that she can't yell at me.

"You came into money and didn't mention it to me?"

"You've been busy." I shrug. "I only got notified a few days ago and I had them transfer it straight into our account. I didn't know it would happen so fast."

"Okay." Lin sags against the edge of her desk.

"Hey, this is a good thing, right? We can hire a temp to cover

Evonne's next vacation and even consider asking Ruth back if she hasn't found something else."

"Yeah . . . yes, I mean, it makes things a lot easier. You're going to take some for yourself, right? You could pay off the mortgage you took out."

I nod, even though I'm fairly sure my mortgage is now a thing of the past.

*It is,* Jou thinks with satisfaction.

*You really need more sleep,* I tell him.

*Kinda awake and hungry now. I'm thinkin' waffles with butter and straw-berries. Huh. I've never been interested in human food when I'm home before.*

*Go back to sleep and the weird urges will probably go away.*

Jou chuckles.

"Other than coming into this money, everything's okay with you? You're back together with the red-headed hottie?"

I nod. "Thank you for the advice. I mean it. I called him. We . . . talked it out. We're good now."

"And does he still want to whisk you off to his exotic homeland?"

She would remember that.

"Yeah, but that's long-term stuff. Let's see if we can make it through a month of dating first."

Lin laughs. "You, do commitment?"

"Hey, I'm working on it."

"Work harder." She winks. "We still on for dinner?"

"Definitely."

She smiles and I take that as a win and escape before she asks me anything I can't answer. Like where, exactly, Jou comes from.

I move into my hearth room and *pull* Wizard to me. I'm more than a little surprised when Zippy appears next to him, shakes dust off her leather jacket, and hops up on the long workbench outside my circle. She swings her legs, clad in fishnet stockings and shin-high biker boots.

"Uh—"

"Sorry, I felt you pull on him and thought I'd tag along. I'll stay out of your way." She grins. So many teeth. "You don't mind, do you?"

Kinda? I can make the magic milk in my sleep at this point, but it absorbs my energy and I'm not sure what trepidation will do to the mix.

*She ain't gonna do nothing,* Jou says firmly into my mind. *Tell her I'm watchin'.*

Oookay.

"Jou wants you to know he's watching."

She makes a cross over her heart with two fingers. "My motives are pure, promise. I just want to get to know you. Zef's pissed about you, but I've got nothing against you. And if you really are Dast's seggu-rach, we're going to be seeing a lot of each other. Might as well be on good terms."

I nod and start assembling ingredients. For someone who wants to get to know me, she doesn't ask any questions or make much effort at conversation while I pour and mix. She watches me *call* lightning with wide eyes but says nothing.

As I'm bottling the magic milk, she says, "I like your silence."

"Mmm?"

"Humans fill the quiet places with noise. It's like they can't stand silence. I appreciate you don't."

I nod. I appreciate she's been quiet while I've been brewing.

"Where is Dast?"

"The White Tower," I say.

Zippy's eyebrows shoot towards her mohawk. "Why?"

"I think that's a question better addressed to your brother." I think Jou's finally gone back to sleep while I've been brewing, because his mind is still and silent inside mine.

Zippy swings her legs a little faster. "I probably don't need to ask, do I? I'm not a strategist like Dast and Zef, but even I can see why he'd visit Malakaz. He's checking his alliances are still in place."

"Something like that."

"Did he end up speaking to Chaid last night?"

Jou didn't tell me to keep anything from his sisters, but I know anything I tell Zippy will go straight back to Zeifyr. I wish Jou was awake to help me field these questions. In his absence, I lob it back at her. "What errand were you and Zeifyr running?"

Zippy's purple-painted mouth twists. "A really sucky one. I get that he's punishing us, but that sucked flaming spider ass."

Maybe I don't want to know. Fuck it. Yes, I do. "Uh-huh. What'd he have you do?"

"Immerse ourselves in the big river three times over several hours to see if we were affected by it."

The Charles? They went swimming in the Charles last night? I bet that was chilly. "Given you're here today, doesn't look like you were."

"Ever been flayed?" She lifts an eyebrow at me. When I shake my head, she says, "Take my word for it. It sucks. But he was right. We weren't nearly as affected as we would have been before. The third time, Zef said she barely felt anything. She didn't even lose her glove."

"That's a bonus."

Zippy narrows her eyes at me. "You're not going to forgive us any time soon, are you?"

"Are you talking to me or Jou?"

"Both of you."

"I can't speak for Jou, but I'm having a hard time getting excited over something that's a byproduct of your brother's *three years* of agony. Sorry."

Zippy nods. "You're angry because he is. I get it."

"No, I'm not," I say, slapping jugs down on the workbench for emphasis. "I'm angry because if I'd known what he was going through, if he hadn't *actively prevented* me from knowing, I'd have been fighting whatever fight, making whatever bargain I had to make, to be with him. Even if all I could do was sit with him while he suffered, I would have. You knew where he was. You knew what he was going through. You *abandoned* him. That makes me angry all on my own."

Zippy stares at her knees.

Finally, she says, "I went. I sat in the Bledewood and let the trees drink from me so I could be near him. But I couldn't touch him. His mind was closed to me. I guess, because of you, although I didn't know that at the time. I just thought he was furious at us for not rescuing him. The Erinyes wouldn't let me get near enough that he could see me. But I was there. And, yeah, I was the only one. Zef went to Angien. Ful and Nev went to Father. But I didn't. I sat vigil and paid for it with blood for nearly a thousand days. So, try not to be quite so self-righteous."

An acid bite fills my mouth. I swallow hard to clear the bitterness.

"I'm sorry. I didn't know. Jou certainly doesn't. You should tell him."

"I figure you will. I just wanted you to know that we don't have to be enemies. I love him, too."

I reach out to her. She registers the movement in her peripheral vision, reaches out, and clasps my hand.

"Thank you for telling me." I still can't call her "Zippy." I clear my throat. "I will tell Jou, and I know it will mean a great deal to him."

Zippy nods. "I usually stay out of it. When Dast and Zef go at each other, I just try to stay clear. But I can tell they won't let me this time. They're going to force me to pick a side. I don't expect Dast to take it easy on me. I get that he's angry, and he has a right to be. And Zef is always playing a fucked-up game the rest of us can only half see. I don't know if her endgame is with the Hellroarer. I truly don't. But I won't ever leave Ash Hill. No matter what Angien promises. No matter how pissed off Dast is with me. I will always be at his side. I want Dast to know that."

"I'll make sure he does."

"Thank you. Want to fight with me later?"

I release her hand and step back. "What?"

"Dast probably hasn't mentioned it, but I'm the warrior of the clutch. Dast is good with his whip and his scythe, but no one's better than me in combat. I can tell you don't have much in the way of physical skills. You rely on your magic. I can see your well is deep, but magic can run out."

I nod. My well ran dry when I sent Jou back to Hell. When my magic came back, the well felt deeper, maybe even without bottom, but that's a foolish risk to take.

"I'd like to learn from you, if you're offering to teach me."

"I am. You use any weapons?"

I nod. "A knife. I'm most comfortable with knives."

"Cool. We'll start there. After your last meal, maybe? What do humans call it?"

"Dinner."

"Yeah, after dinner." She pushes off the workbench. "Show me out?"

"You want me to send you back to my house?"

"Naw, I thought I'd take a look around your city. I haven't been to this one in centuries."

While the idea of unleashing the demon who describes herself as the best warrior among Jou's clutch on my unsuspecting city is more than a little terrifying, I escort her to the front door of the clinic. Remembering that Evonne will wonder where the hell Zippy came from, I draw a glamor over both of us. By the time Evonne gets up to close the front door, blown open in a strong gust of Air, I'm half-way back to my office.

Once I get the magic milk distributed, I sit down at my desk and sort through my messages. Three more calls from Peter Buscelli. I'm about to toss those slips in the trash when the last one catches my attention, "Tell Tsara I think I'm in danger."

Fuck.

I pick up the phone and dial his number. It rings seven times before it goes to voicemail.

I don't leave a message. I have no idea what to say to him. *I'm sorry I led you on and then dumped you for a demon? Your last entanglement with me resulted in you losing your memories of the last three years so maybe you should stay away from me?*

Yeah, no.

Giving up on that particular problem, I call the number that Roisin left me. I expect her to answer, but instead a deep voice says, "Master's line."

That's not creepy or anything.

"Um, is Roisin available?"

"No, but I will pass a message to her and to Master when he wakes."

Ugh.

"Um, okay. Please let them know this is Tsara Faa calling, and I have the answer they wanted. It's definitely not a vampire, and I will tell the therians that."

"Just a moment, please."

There's a long silence during which I almost hang up. Finally, a very sleepy, grumpy, deep voice comes on the line.

"What is it, then?"

"Who is this?"

"Bone."

I swallow hard because I don't think he's going to like the answer. "The Wild Hunt."

He swears softly. "Roisin and I will come to your dwelling after dark."

"The hell you will."

"This is not up for negotiation, human. We will come and discuss everything you have learned. We know your demon lord has returned. If he requires that we treat for safe passage, have his envoy call this number after dark and my lord will speak with him."

Envoy? "Buddy, this is my house we're talking about. Any negotiation is with me."

Bone snorts, and that *really* pisses me off.

If he wants to play it that way, fine, I can play. "Have your master call my number after dark and he can discuss it with *me*."

"I will do so."

I'll leave my phone off the hook. Vampires, I swear.

I hang up before he can sour my day any further.

Then I rub my fingers over my forehead. I have another call to make, and it will not brighten my day. I dial Ana's number with trembling fingers.

It goes straight to voicemail and tells me the mailbox is full.

That's not right. Ana would never let her mailbox fill up and not empty it. Maybe a single day, if she got busy, sure. But it's been days since I tried to leave her a message.

I hang up and stare at the phone. A whole handful of cold fingers rake down my spine and my ears ring with the calls of geese.

I shake away the sensations, tidy up my desk, and go to tell my business partner I'm ditching her, again.

Lin makes a face at the news, but she's in the middle of a session, so she can't say much. I escape, knowing I'll hear about my absenteeism when we have dinner, if not before.

I wrap Wizard around my shoulders, settle my bag across my body, and step into the Earth. Ana has two houses: the townhouse where she held Toby's wake, and a sprawling ranch house in Canton where she usually goes on weekends. Call it a twitch of precognition, but I feel like she's in Canton. That's where I direct my mind.

I step out of the Earth between tall pine trees. Ana's house backs onto conservation land and I'm standing at the edge of the forest, looking across a withered lawn at the glassed-in porch at the back of her house. There are no lights on and no movement, but it is the middle of the day.

I hear a high bark, and then a gray shape comes loping around the house. I put my hands out. Either Ana got a dog, or this is a shifter guard, but either way, they'll know by my scent that I'm a friend.

The dog, a tall, skinny, shaggy gray thing that looks like a cross between a greyhound and a Shetland pony, runs toward me with one of those big, doggy grins on its face, tongue lolling out of the side of its mouth. I begin to bend down and reach my hands out for the petting it's obviously coming for.

Between one step and the next, something *shifts*. The dog's stride changes from a lope to a charge. It pulls in its tongue and opens its mouth wider, fangs gleaming wetly in the sunlight.

Wizard stands up on my shoulders and unleashes a vicious hiss.

I stumble, trying to pull back from the sudden threat. My muscles clench. I'm off balance. Too slow. The dog flashes by me. My right arm burns, followed by a wet rush. Damn dog.

I whirl, following the dog's motion. Spread my hands as I turn and *call*.

My hair whips across my cheeks in a sudden gust of wind. The acrid smell of ozone fills the air. Light spills from my hands, casting every pine needle into sharp relief. Tiny spikes of electricity arc from my hands to the ground.

"Hey, pooch," I call. "Bite this."

The dog growls, but it's disappeared between the trees.

I close my eyes and open my Second Sight.

In my Sight, the dog's a buzzing, blurring creature with massive jaws and shoulders and blackened, skeletal hindquarters. Its eyes and mouth drip red flame. Black, winged shapes swirl around its head, peeling off its skin like flakes of ash. I've never seen anything like it before, but that is no dog, and it does not belong here.

Instead of blasting it with lightning, I kneel, put my palms to the ground and tear open the Veil.

I leaf through the planes, feeling them as never before. Branches of the world tree that stretches through the stars in my mind's eye. A bottomless, black river winds through the branches and that's where I sink the hound, deep down into the mirk. I don't know if it will drown or get eaten or thrive there, but that's where it feels like it belongs.

I lift my hands from the ground, breaking my connection with the Earth. A soft wind sighs through the pines. It sounds like a distant bird's cry. Wizard, wrapped in a tight, protective torc around my throat, hisses again.

Ana.

I rise and run toward the house.

No one answers my knock, but when I try the door, it opens. I walk into the silent house.

"Ana? Gallien?" I know he usually doesn't stay here, since the werewolves have a pack house in the Blue Hills where Gallien lives, but I call his name just in case.

Nothing answers. There's a funny smell in the air, like burnt toast.

I find the first feathers in the kitchen. The first spatter of blood. There's no copper smell. Nothing other than the strange burnt-toast scent, but I already know what I'll find.

I follow the blood and feathers down the long hallway that splits the house and turn the corner of the carpeted stairs to the upper floor.

Ana's body lies at the top of the stairs. One hand is still wrapped around a broken banister rung she tried to use to defend herself. Her head is thrown back, her throat torn out, long, red tendons and lumps of white cartilage exposed. Her chest is cracked open, ribs jutting into the air. Her thighs have been gnawed down to the bone.

I sink down onto the stairs, two risers below her body. My knees squish into the carpet and cold wetness seeps through my pants.

*Fuck, sweetness.*

Through my horror, I feel Jou wake, and then his rushing, roaring presence envelops me. His burning wings close around me. There's a ripping sensation, like I've been yanked out of my own skin.

I blink tears out of my eyes and stare at my bathtub instead of Ana's half-eaten body.

"Jou."

"Shh." He strokes my hair back from my face with a clawed hand. His horns brush my bathroom's ceiling and the neon light spilling from him casts strange shadows behind the toilet.

I stand like a statue while he strips my clothes off, runs a bath, and draws me into the tub. It's only when I sink into the hot water that I start shivering uncontrollably. Jou holds me with one arm across my breasts while he sponges bloodstains off my knees.

"How?" I whisper, what feels like a long time later. The water doesn't go cold with a fire demon in the bath, but my skin has gone pruney.

"Your shock woke me like someone took a hammer to my fuckin' head. Ass of Hell didn't even twitch when I tore open a Gate to reach you. Guess it knew better than to try to keep me from my seggurach. I pulled us through another Gate to get here. Sorry, I know that don't feel good to humans."

I shake my head and rest it on his shoulder. He could have literally pulled me out of my skin to get me away from there, and I wouldn't complain.

"I wanna try something with your arm."

My arm? I check my left arm, which is cradled in the curve of his. Looks normal. Then I look at my right arm, propped on the edge of the bathtub.

There are two, long gouges in my forearm. One tear goes right through the muscle, down to the bone. The edges of the wounds are dry. There's barely any blood. They don't even sting until I look at them.

"Oh, shit."

"Lift your arm up."

Not sure of what I'm doing, I lift my arm and let Jou guide it over my head, so my forearm's propped on my crown, in front of his face. It's an awkward position, but that's not what makes me jolt. It's the sensation of a long, wet tongue lapping along the wounds.

"Jou."

*Sh. Let me try this.*

He licks my forearm over and over. I feel the little nudges of power, nipping under my skin, tugging at my bones. The sting fades under the lapping sensation, and when Jou releases my arm and I drop it back to the lip of the tub, the wounds are gone.

So are the scars from where I broke his bindings.

*I thought that might happen. I'll lick away the rest of those tonight, but then I'm binding you again. Don't fight me on this.*

I won't. There are times to stand my ground with him, but this isn't one of them. I want to be bound to him, particularly now that I understand how he uses those bindings.

He's not controlling me; he's protecting us.

He nuzzles my temple. *I am. Thank you for the trust, sweetness.*

"Jou, I have to do something about Ana. I have to report . . ."

What do I report? The Wild Hunt ate my friend?

"No, you tell whoever you need to among the skin-changers. Let them deal with the human authorities."

Ana was always my main contact with the therians. I don't even have the number for the lycanthrope's packhouse, although I know where it is. "I— I'll need a ride out—"

"No, you don't. That seems like a fine errand for the Zes to run. You show me the location in your mind, and I'll put it in theirs."

I do, holding the image of the packhouse, which I've only been to once but remember pretty well, in my mind until he kisses the side of my head.

"Got it."

"Thank you, Jou. I'll have to talk to Gallien soon, but I just—"

"Not now," Jou says, and the gentleness in his voice makes tears well. "Later's soon enough."

"Jou—" My throat chokes tight and the tears that should have been coming for an hour finally burst free.

"Yeah, there it is."

He turns me so I'm lying on my side with my face in the crook of his neck and holds me while I cry.

# CHAPTER 16

lose all sense of time after finding Ana's body.

It could be a few hours or a few days later that I sit in my parlor, wrapped in demon, facing Roisin and Bone. Roisin's perched in the armchair, pale and lovely in a cream pants suit and a fox-fur vest that looks real. I'd be tempted to hiss "fur is murder" at her, except that my mind's still caught in this loop of seeing Ana's gnawed corpse and feeling her blood squish under my knees. Bone keeps pacing around the room and I'm not sure who is going to yell at him first, me or Jou.

"All you have connecting the were's death to the Wild Hunt is a stone given to you by a river spirit," Bone grumbles.

Jou must feel the irritation rise in my mind, because he rubs his palm over my pajama-covered knee. He's conjured another of those silk and velvet lounging outfits, this time in a deep, forest green, and draped me in his bathrobe as well because I couldn't stop shivering after we got out of the bath.

"Tsara owes you nothin'," Jou says. "An' if ancient fucking Futhark don't convince your master, the fact she was attacked by a hellhound this afternoon is pretty good evidence she's on the right track."

Was it a hellhound? I hadn't even put that together. I rub my fingers over my face.

"It could have been the were-hawk's guard dog," Bone says.

I shake my head. I'd thought that at first, too. Until I saw it in my Second Sight.

"If it had been Ana's guard dog, it would have been a therian. That was not a shapeshifter." I shiver. "It was a monster."

Jou's warm hand works up and down my back and chases a little of my internal chill away.

"Tsara," Roisin says gently. "I am very sorry for the loss of your friend."

I nod at her. That's the second time she's given me condolences, and I'm still not sure if its genuine sympathy, if a *bean sidhe* is even capable of genuine sympathy, or if she's softening me up for whatever curveball she's going to pitch next.

"If it is the Wild Hunt," she continues. "You must take word to the Holly King."

I lift my eyebrows at her. "I thought the Holly King fell with the loss of his crown." A crown I know for a fact is sitting in a Cambridge basement. "I thought the Oak King ruled alone?"

"No longer," Roisin says. "A new Holly King has risen. He rules until Ostara."

I shake my head. That makes no sense. The Oak King defeats the Holly King at Yule and rules until midsummer when the Holly King defeats him and starts the inexorable turn of the world towards winter.

"The Courts are shifting," Roisin says, looking at her hands, crossed over her knee. "I find much changed. The Holly King may not welcome this news, but if you are to remain a friend of the fae, you must take this news to him. You and you alone."

"No," Jou says immediately. "If we gotta tell the Holly King face-to-face, we will, but Tsara and I do it together. You got any friends in the Holly King's court?"

Roisin shrugs. "I did."

"By my count, you owe Tsara a favor for pursuin' this for the vamps. Contact your friends and get me an invite to the Holly King's court."

Roisin's face puckers before she smooths it. "If Leid approves, I will do so."

"He got any qualms, have him call me. He's got my number now."

He does? I know Jou disappeared for a while earlier while I was speaking to Sheshdhar, the head of the therian council after Ana's death, but I didn't peek into his mind while I was talking to the Naga, and he didn't mention it afterwards.

Roisin nods. "If this is agreed, it will be on the strict understanding you bring neither hellfire nor true death to the Holly King's court."

Jou plants his hot hands on my shoulders. "Long as nothing threatens Tsara, I'll agree to that."

"The Holly King won't protect you from the Wild Hunt," Bone interjects.

It takes me a minute to follow him. Jou gets there before I do.

"I look like I need protection to you?" he asks the vampire.

Bone bristles. "Everyone needs protection."

"I got plenty."

"I'm offering my sword, demon. The more swords you have protecting her, the less likely your soft human will fall to the teeth and claws of the Hunt."

Jou rubs my shoulders. "What's your price?"

"An end to the war with the weres. The same thing my master has asked from the beginning."

"I got no sway with the skin-slippers," Jou says dismissively.

"You are a *lord* of Hell," Bone responds.

"Like that makes any fuckin' difference." The room fills with harsh shadows, and I don't have to look over my shoulder to know that Jou's manifested his horns and that his eyes are spilling neon light. "You think this crown gives me some kinda sway with anything but my own kind?"

"It gives you sway with my master," Bone responds. "The weres may be beasts of heart as well as of skin, but the word of a lord of Hell carries weight, even with them."

Roisin nods and I wonder if she knows more about therians than she's letting on. "If Leid can call the clans together to treat with him, will you sit at the table and arbitrate?"

I feel Jou stiffen behind me.

*Sweetness?*

I startle, not expecting him to ask my opinion.

He rubs his hands up and down my arms, making me feel warmer than I have since I stumbled up Ana's stairs.

*I don't see any downside to it, Jou. The therians have always been my allies, if not my friends. I've been a neutral party for them before, although not this formally.*

"Okay," Jou says. "If you can get 'em around a table, I'll arbitrate."

Bone bows very formally to Jou, who nods and rests his chin on my shoulder, his cheek brushing mine. His black horns jut in my peripheral vision and I wonder if I'll always know from now on when he's shed his human glove.

"I'll arrange for my travel coffin to be brought here," Bone says.

*You've got to be kidding me.*

Jou chuckles into my mind. *We can stick it out in your yard with Hairy.*

*I thought you said she was leaving?*

*Yeah, that's the thing about house guests. Soon as you get rid of one, another one shows up. Wait until you spend some time at the Hill. Fuckin' revolving door.*

I want to slap my palm against my forehead but restrain myself and Jou wraps his arm around me to assist my self-control.

"Wouldn't hurt to know each other's capabilities," Jou says. "You up for a little sparring?"

Bone's lean face splits into a grin and I look away from the desiccated flesh shredding away from too-long, too-sharp teeth. Vampires, ook.

"I'll retrieve my sword along with my coffin," Bone says.

———

That's how I end up sitting on my back porch steps between Roisin and Zippy at half-past one in the morning, watching a demon and a vampire face off across the grass of my yard. Bone's got his massive sword and a shield that looks way too much like Captain America's except that it's solid black. Jou's manifested his flaming whip and his immense wings, which he's holding up and behind his body, like an angry swan.

Jou strikes first, lashing out with the whip and yanking the shield off Bone's arm and tossing it the length of my yard to tumble against my rowan tree.

Jou nods at the shield. "You weren't ready for that. Let's try it again."

Bone shakes himself. "That has a longer reach than it should."

Jou flicks his wrist and the whip cracks among the rowan tree's bare branches in an explosion of embers. Too fast to see more than a bright blur, Jou coils it between his hands.

"That's not a real whip," Bone observes.

"Nope. Extension of my will. Remember that. Most hellblades ain't physical."

Bone nods as he retrieves his shield and takes up position again.

They circle each other. I expect Bone to quickly gain the upper hand, since he's fighting with two weapons, but I should know better than to underestimate my demon. Jou warms up quickly and once he does, he's a blur of motion, too fast for me to follow, whizzing flame that snaps aside Bone's sword and shield again and again. He holds his wings up and out of the way at first, but once he has Bone spinning, stumbling, trying to defend against blow after blow, he uses his wings to batter at the shield and then to lift himself a few feet in the air so he can rain down cracking, snapping fire from above.

Bone finally falls to his knees, holding his sword and shield above his head. "I yield."

Jou beats his wings a few times as he settles to the ground. Blinking at him, I realize he's barefoot, wearing only a pair of soft, black pajama pants. He went up against that leather-wearing, sword-wielding vampire wearing pajama pants.

Because he deserves it, I clap.

Jou winks at me before he motions Bone to stand. They bow to each other.

"Take a seat," Jou says to Bone before beckoning to me with two fingers.

I walk over to him, feeling cool grass under my bare feet and a night breeze teasing at the edges of my hair.

Jou turns me so I'm facing away from him and tucks me into his chest. His wings flare out to either side of us as he runs his hands down my arms and wraps his fingers around the crisscross burn scars on my forearms.

I feel his power surge within me like never before. Shadows shiver away across the grass, and I know that the light driving those shadows away isn't spilling out of Jou. It's spilling out of me.

*Call Fire, sweetness. I'm right here. I won't let anything burn.*

I gather energy to me. I've never been able to see, hear, taste it so clearly before. It's all around me. My Elements throb with it. The ground under my feet rumbles as power rushes to me through the Earth. A wind harsh enough to scour my cheeks brings the energy of Air to me.

My hands burst into flame.

I lift my hands and watch streamers of Fire run down our joined arms.

"Bigger, sweetness," Jou growls in my ear. "Gimme everything."

I pour out all the power that's come to me. A massive ball of fire grows in front of me, caged by Jou's wings.

It calls to me. Singing. Endless hunger. High and sweet. Lemonade. My fireball's energy tastes like lemonade.

Jou chuckles. "More."

"Any more and I'm going to set fire to the neighborhood."

"I've got it, sweetness. You're not going to burn anything. Show me how much you got."

"Ooo-kay." I lower my head and pull hard on my Elements.

The fireball explodes upward. I tip my head back, onto Jou's broad chest, and watch my power burst into a pillar of fire rising a hundred feet above the rooftop of my house.

"Fuck me," Zippy says from somewhere in the darkness.

"Might make the chilly fuckers think twice, huh?" Jou says, dark amusement lacing his voice. "Now, bring it back, sweetness. Slow. Don't turn it all off at once. Fire don't like that. Pull it in, slow and gentle, like you'd suck my cock down if you were just starting a blow job."

"*That's* the analogy you're using to train me?"

"Whatever works."

I roll my eyes, and ignore how I'd start a blow job, but lessen the pull on my Elements. The fire's hunger strains against my limits, the taste of lemonade in my mouth growing bitter. Then it accepts my control, and the pillar dims. Stars appear again as the pillar reduces, down and down, below the tree-tops, below the roof of my house, until it's a crackling ball between my outstretched hands.

"Instead of takin' it back, let it go."

As soon as he says it, I understand how. I release my control, cut the tie of power connecting me with the Fire. The flames spin madly before flaring out along Jou's wings. He groans like I actually am giving him a blow job. His hips press so hard against my butt that I have to take a step forward for balance. He grunts and drops his face into my neck. His horns appear over my shoulder, burning blackly.

*You are so fuckin' tasty,* he growls into my mind. *Inside. You're not gonna be happy if I fuck you here in front of my girls and the vamp, but I ain't waiting.*

*Aren't we saying goodnight?*

*Sure.*

"Good fuckin' night," Jou growls at the crowd sitting on my porch steps. Zippy moves to make way for us as Jou propels us up the stairs.

"Guess I'll take first watch then," Bone says behind us.

"You do that," Jou tells him as he reaches past me to push the back door open. Evidently frustrated by the distance between my porch and the bedroom, as I pass over the threshold, that ripping sensation tears through me again and when I blink, I'm looking at my bed.

*Jou—*

*In bed now, sweetness.*

*Right now?* I tease.

*Right fucking now.*

———

Jou fucks me into forgetting everything. Ana's death. The Wild Hunt. His sisters down the hallway. The vampire in my parlor amusing himself by watching *True Blood*. None of it matters when Jou's wonderful, warm body is over mine, under mine, inside mine.

But when I wake in the pearly pre-dawn, it all comes back in a rush, particularly the sinking, sickening, visceral memory of finding Ana's body. I sit up, rubbing my knees where I can still feel the wetness of her blood.

Jou sits up beside me, wraps his arms around me, and holds me while I keen out my grief for my friend. He doesn't say anything, not aloud, and not in my mind. He simply holds me and rocks me until I cry myself out, then draws me back down into the bed and tucks me tightly into his side until I drop back to sleep.

When I wake again, the bed's empty, but my mind's full of the demon. He's wrapped himself around my mind like he wraps us in his wings. I feel no grief, no fear, no coldness, only his hot presence.

Understanding what he's doing, I smile up at the ceiling. *Jou, it's okay to let me be sad.*

He eases back a little until I can feel hints of my own emotions.

*Don't like you hurtin', sweetness.*

*I appreciate that. I don't like you hurting, either. Did I blanket your emotions while I was healing you?*

I feel him mentally scratch his chin. *Some. I wasn't as angry as I'd been once you started in on me.*

*Well, I'm not as sad as I was.*

I roll out of bed and find an outfit already set out for me on the dresser. I shake my head in amusement as I draw on the cotton tights, brown leather skirt, white dress shirt, and black blazer. The shirt and blazer swim on me and, when I get a whiff of Jou's cinnamon and woodsmoke scent off the collar, I realize he's dressed me in his clothes.

As I roll up the sleeves, my fingertips brush over the unmarred skin of my forearms. Jou licked away my scars in the night. After he fucked me, he stayed inside me for hours. I slept, rousing occasionally into dozy, toe-curling bliss, then sinking back under the gentle rocking of his body and the warm motion of his tongue.

I rest my fingertips on my skin. The new sigils rise in traceries of green and gold. His name, over and over, circling my wrists like bracelets and trailing down my arms, following the paths of my veins. He carved them into me with his claws and licked them into me with his tongue, healing me even while he came to the taste of my blood. I glance at the bed. There's not even a smear on the sheets; he didn't spill a drop. I trail my fingers up to my palm to watch the sigils flare and glimmer. I feel Jou's satisfaction rise in my mind, thick and rich as cream, over his concern about my grief. He likes me wearing his mark.

*Aren't you worried about anyone with the Sight being able to see your truename?*

*Doubt anyone but your blood or mine will be able to see them. My blood already knows it. Your blood? Nothin' against your family, sweetness, but I ain't afraid of them.*

He has no reason to be. Other than Shirri, there's no one left in my family with true power.

When I go to brush my teeth, I discover three lizards paddling around in the bathtub, looking like crocodiles with their eyes and nostrils poking up out of a steaming bubble bath.

*Why are the lizards in the bath?*

*Yeah, about that. They might have discovered your ice-cream stash.*

I grimace at the three lizards. They suddenly become very interested in the tap at the far end of the tub.

*Is there any left?*

*No, but I put in a grocery order.*

Thank heaven for proactive demons. I shake a finger at Izzy, who I know was the instigator. He blinks at me before he submerges.

I brush my hair out. Jou's been at work again and it's a smooth, red-brown wave to my shoulders with golden streaks framing my face. I sigh and pull it back from my face with a tortoiseshell clip that matches the skirt, so it's not hanging in my face while I brew.

*You're not brewing today, sweetness. C'mon down to breakfast and I'll show you.*

Curious, I jog down the stairs and into the kitchen.

For having three demons in my kitchen, it's very quiet. There are no voices other than Mick Jagger's—Jou has the Stones playing—and no sounds other than the faint sizzle of frying meat.

I walk in warily.

Zippy looks up from her phone and winks at me. Zefyr, sitting at my kitchen table beside her sister, meets my eyes over the rim of her teacup and, unsurprisingly, doesn't wink.

Jou walks between his sister and me, breaking the beginnings of our glare-off, carrying two plates of eggs, sausages, and hash browns. He nods at the table. At first, I think he's indicating that I should sit down.

Then I see the silver and gold holly branch sitting like a centerpiece in the middle of the table.

"Uh—"

"Pretty sure that's an invitation," Jou says.

It certainly is. I slide into the chair next to him, and then onto his lap as he relocates me. After a sip of coffee—and why does the coffee he ekes out of that temperamental little machine taste so much better than what I get out of it?—I pick up with branch and open my mystical senses.

I feel the tug immediately. It's not just an invitation. It's a gate and a key. If I let it, it will pull me straight into faerie.

I put the branch back on the table.

*When we're ready, that will take us to the Kingdom Under the Hills,* I think at Jou.

*Breakfast, then the Twittering Throng.*

I'm not going to argue with him, particularly not with the delicious sausage smell weaving through the equally delicious coffee smell. I eat with far more gusto than I should, given how much Jou's been feeding me, and feel the strain of my belly against the skirt's waistband without regret when I sit back against Jou's chest after clearing my plate.

*Have you met the Holly King before?* I think the question.

*Nope. You?*

I shake my head. *I don't think there's been one as long as I've been alive. I don't understand how there is one without the Crown of the North.*

*Airy Fairy ever poke around in your head?*

*No. So much so that I had to resort to charades with the Squire. Can the fae? That's not a power I've heard of them having.*

*Not with most humans, but we know you're a special case.*

I elbow him.

He chuckles into his coffee.

*Just wouldn't want them finding out where their crown is outta your head.*

*Do you think they'd attack the Museum?*

Jou shrugs against my back. *One way or t'other, once they find out where it is, it won't be there long.*

*From, um, our perspective, would that be a good or bad thing?*

Jou's warm rumble fills my mind.

*Don't give a fuck what the Twittering Throng want. But I like that it's our perspective now.*

I do, too.

I clean up breakfast while Jou goes up to take a shower. He evidently evicts the lizards from the bathtub, because when I turn around from the sink, I find a ring of salamanders behind me. Three sets of black-button eyes watch me unblinkingly.

"Oh, no. You raided my ice cream stash. You do not get breakfast scraps."

But, of course, they do. There are three sausage patties still in the frying pan and I suspect Jou's left them for exactly this purpose, so I distribute them to the lizards who waddle off contentedly while I call in to the clinic and ask Evonne to reschedule my appointments for today.

I'm more than a little surprised when she tells me that Lin's called in, too, and asked her to reschedule her appointments for the rest of the week.

"Is she sick?" I ask.

"No, she didn't say she was sick."

"Okay, thanks Evonne."

"If you're both going to be out today, do you mind if I close up and go home? I'll redirect the phones."

"No, not at all. Enjoy the day off."

After I hang up with Evonne, I dial Lin. She certainly doesn't sound sick when she answers the phone.

"Hey, I called the clinic and Evonne said you were out the rest of the week. Everything okay?"

Lin's silent for a long moment. "Are you mad at me?"

"No, I just want to know you're okay."

"I'm okay. This is going to sound stupid."

"Like I haven't told you a million stupid things."

"That's true." She sighs. "I felt like someone followed me home last night and was watching the house. It was stupid, but I got really scared. Matty came over and the feeling went away. After we talked about it, I realized I might just be stressed. I haven't had a day off since before Halloween."

She starts to sound a little defensive at the end; I immediately make a soothing sound.

"Lin, you absolutely deserve some time off. And it doesn't sound stupid, and—" My heart clenches. "Did you see or hear anything following you?"

"No, I mean, I heard geese. I guess they're starting to migrate early. Global warming."

I rub my hand over my face, remembering the geese we heard that night by the Charles. The geese I heard in my mind when I thought of Ana. "Can you go to Wen's?"

"What? Why?"

"I don't even know how to say this. Ana's dead. I found her body at her house in Canton yesterday. She'd been eaten, just like Toby. I don't have any reason to think they'd go after you, Lin, but, please, could you go to Wen's? His apartment's warded."

My mind drifts to the dragon I enchanted and, somehow, I know that it will keep Lin and her brother safe.

"They? I thought it was a shark-shifter that killed Toby near the water?"

"I don't think it's a shark-shifter. I think it could be the Wild Hunt. Please, Linnie?"

"Okay." She makes a *pffing* noise. "I'll pack up some things and head over. I could use a walk anyway."

I rub the back of my neck. "Would you let me Earth-Walk you?"

"Seriously?"

"Yes."

She blows out a breath into the phone. "Fine. Give me five minutes."

"Okay, see you in five."

I pace for five minutes, bolt in and out of the Earth like my ass is on fire, and grab Lin's hand with a sweaty palm to pull her with me.

When we stand in Wen's living room, Lin pins me with a glare. "You're shaking."

I am. She's right. I walk over to the mantle and put my hands on the glass dragon softly glowing there. I close my eyes and imagine a huge golden bubble of protection growing out of the lightning crashing within it. When I open my eyes, I see the bubble, crawling with the protective sigils Ink has been inscribing into my skin, encasing my hands. I push it outwards, feeling the warmth of it crawl over my skin. When it reaches the threshold, it slaps against Wen's own wards: a cold, slick, gray wall. The two wards merge together and fade from my Sight.

"Holy shit," Lin whispers, rubbing her arms in little puffs of dust.

"Could you feel that?" I ask.

"Feel it? I could *see* it. Better special effects than *The Lord of the Rings*. Well done, Gandalf the White."

I crack a grin.

"What the fuck?"

Wen, dressed in only a David Bowie T-shirt, tighty whities, and his tattoos, stumbles out of his bedroom.

Lin lifts an eyebrow at him. "Aren't you supposed to be in class?"

"Yeah, in four hours." Wen walks over to the front door and puts his hands up, feeling along the double ward. "Damn, girl, that is one serious firewall."

"I think the Wild Hunt may be after people close to me. Ana's dead. She was eaten the same as Toby," I tell him.

"How does that have anything to do with you?" Lin asks.

Shit. I didn't mean to say so much. "Um, a fae that I have—had—a lot of contact with was hunted and killed, too. There's probably something I'm missing but, at the moment, I'm the common denominator."

Lin shakes her head, her lips tight, and I know one of her patented "mom-talks" is coming.

"I'm really sorry," I say to forestall the scolding. "I've got to go. Can you both just stay behind these wards today?"

"Today?" Lin asks archly.

"Or just don't go anywhere alone? Toby, the Squire, and Ana were all killed when they were alone."

Lin sighs. "Okay. I'm meeting Matty for dinner tonight anyway. I'll invite him over to my place afterwards. He's got a couple of days off. He can stay with me until he's back on shift over the weekend."

"Thanks, Linnie. I'm sorry to inconvenience you. I just want you to be safe."

"I know. I'm sorry I'm being bitchy. Here." She holds out her arms. I give her a hug that makes us both sneeze.

When I move back from the hug, I step into the Earth, before she can ask me any more questions I shouldn't answer.

# CHAPTER 17

he Holly King's court is done in shades of green and red, and
that's where anything I expect ends.

I expect it to be empty. The barrow is packed with fae of all shapes, sizes, and descriptions. It's busier than North Station at rush hour. I expected it to be a quiet place. It's filled with music and the babble of voices, from the sibilant bells of the *Ellyllon* to the gravel rumble of *Coblynau*. I expect it to be dark, since it's theoretically underground, but the barrow is filled with gold-green, dappled light, like the noon sun through trees. I expect it to be musty. A thousand fragrances, each blending into the other, none competing, drift across my senses.

The only thing I did expect that holds true is for the fae to react strongly to the presence of the demon.

Without a word or signal, the fae part, making a neat aisle to the Holly King's throne. The green, green grass they clear is unbent, untrodden, a perfect, emerald carpet that smells of the haymow. Tall knights in golden armor stand on each of the three steps up to the massive, wooden throne, composed like a stained-glass window from three intertwined, white trees. A peacock, tail fanned in a brilliant display of green, blue, and purple, stands at each knight's feet.

The Holly King, white of hair and eye but strong and straight and fair in the way of the fae, beckons to us.

Jou takes my hand and walks us to the base of the Throne. He bows and I do my best, slightly fumbling, curtsey.

The knight nearest to me holds out his hand. Unsure, I pass him the silver and gold holly branch that brought us here. He bows, tucks the branch away, and returns to his vigil.

"Jouvart, son of Asmodeus, Baron Ash, Hellroarer, I greet you," the Holly King says.

I wait and watch. I haven't seen Jou show much deference, not even to his father. But now he bows and says, "May I introduce Tsara Elizabeth Faa, my seggurach?"

The word ripples through the barrow.

The Holly King inclines his elaborately crowned head to me. "Miss Faa, you are well-known to the fae. Friend to the great and the small."

I curtsey again. "Sire."

"My defeated brother asked you to pay your debt to us. To find the name of the killer of his Squire, Aranan. Have you found that name?"

"I believe so, Sire." I take out the stone with the Futhark symbol on it and offer it to the knight who took the branch. He bows to me again before taking it, slipping it into the open beak of the peacock at his feet, who struts up the steps to lay it in the Holly King's lap.

He scoops the stone up in one alabaster hand and examines it. As he does, a bright white arc jumps from the stone to me.

It's painless, like when I call lightning, but I jolt backwards into Jou's arms as knowledge fills my mind.

*His name was Aranthann.*

*He was Aranan's older brother.*

*He was a golden-clad knight on the Oak King's stairs until the Squire's death. He found his brother's remains, brought them back to the Oak court, and fought his own king over the king's failure to protect the fae from the encroaching darkness. They dealt each other mortal wounds.*

*Aranthann woke to a being of pure white light bending over him, bathing his face and hands in water so clear, so pure, it was liquid silver. Gaea, he named her in his mind, but she has no name, no title, no form. She IS. She wove a crown of holly and white deer antlers, placed it on his head, and sent him back.*

*He rose from his deathbed the Holly King.*

*His grief for Aranan is still a tearing, howling thing in his chest, undimmed by his resurrection. He cares fiercely for his fading people, but most fiercely of all for his fallen brother.*

I slide out of Jou's arms and onto my knees.

"I'm so sorry," I whisper. "I loved him, too."

And I did, in my own way. Not the way that Jou is jealous of, but as a protector, a symbol of all that is still right in the world. His falling makes the world that little bit darker.

There's an almost-silent swish above me, like one of the peacocks has moved. Then golden-mailed boots drop down the last step and stop in front of me. A warm hand settles on my head.

"He touched many," the Holly King says. "But few, I sense, more than you. I thank you for the friendship you gave him." He's silent for a minute, turning over the rock in his hand with a whisper of skin on stone. "The Wild Hunt does not answer to this court, or any higher power. The Huntsman chooses the prey. I do not understand why he chose my brother, but I fear he may also have chosen you, Tsara Faa. This stone from the river spirit is a warning."

Despite the warmth of his hand on my head, a cold shiver runs down my spine.

"He can try," Jou growls.

The Holly King's hand lifts away. Jou pulls me up off my knees and holds me with my back against his chest, his burning wings cupped around us. Silently, the Holly King retreats to his throne. When he sits, flaring his green velvet robes around him, he places the river stone on the arm of his throne and rests his fingers atop it.

"I wish I could offer you the sanctuary of this hall, Miss Faa," the Holly King says. "But I cannot while you wear a hellion's bindings. Nor am I certain the Huntsman would not follow you here. I cannot risk bringing the Hunt down on my court."

To quiet the growl that I can hear reverberating in the chest pressed against my back, I say, "It's okay. I wouldn't seek sanctuary here. But I appreciate the offer. If I find out why the Hunt went after Aranan, I will get word to you."

The Holly King nods his antlered head and I realize that the holly wreath is a crown, but the antlers aren't. They're part of him.

"I would be in your debt, and although I am newly minted, the favor of faerie's newest king is no small thing."

I feel pressure on my back and realize Jou's bowing, so I drop into a curtsey.

*Jou, should I tell him about the Crown of the North? He seems like a good guy.*

*Not yet. Twittering Throng don't do anything without a reason and the scales still feel unbalanced to me. Hold it back until it can clear your debt to them and put you one up.*

He's right. A few months ago, I would have told the Holly King anyway, but those months have made me wary, and sad, and ready to defer to my demon when it comes to the complicated web of supernatural politics that I barely understand.

"Baron Ash," the Holly King says. "May I ask you a question without incurring a debt or your wrath?"

"Sure," Jou responds. "I'm here 'cause Tsara don't leave my sight. Not because I got any problem with you an' yours."

"Binding Miss Faa ties you to the mortal world. You have a foothold, and she controls a ley line. You must know what that means. Will you seek a kingdom among men?"

I can *hear* Jou grin as well as feel it in my mind. "No. I'm on vacation."

"Vacation?" The Holly King asks, surprise plain in his voice and on his face.

"Got these." Jou flaps his wings before circling them loosely around me again. "Learnin' what I can do with 'em before I head back to the Hellwar. When I go, Tsara's comin' with me. I got no designs on the mortal world."

"And her root of power?"

"It's coming with us, too," I say.

I don't know how I know. Only that I do. When I go with Jou, the trees will wither, no matter how much Miracle Grow they're sprayed with. My hearth room will sink, the World Tree's branch will bend, and be lost to men.

The Holly King rubs his fingers over his mouth pensively. "I am sorry to hear that. If I might, may I keep this as a way to contact you?" He holds up the rune stone between long, pale fingers.

*Any risk?* I think to Jou.

*Always a risk with the Twittering Throng, but I'm not seeing any immediate harm in giving him a way to reach you. None of your energy's in that stone, just the trace of where you've held it. If you'd enchanted it, I'd say no, but this seems safe enough.*

"Yes, of course," I say. "Please be gentle when you use it. I think it's tied more to the ondine than to me."

The Holly King nods. "I would never hurt that kind spirit."

"Thank you."

The Holly King nods again, and I get the sense this audience is over. I've done what I said I was going to do. The scales may not be balanced, as Jou can sense, but the heaviest part of my debt to the fae is paid. The fae can't offer me anything, and I don't really need any information about the Wild Hunt from them. I know from my studies at Bevvy what the Hunt can do. If I was trying to find the Hunt, that would be a different thing.

But I have a feeling that the Hunt is going to find me.

With a final bow, Jou takes my hand and with that sense that he's ripping me out of my skin again, yanks me out of the Holly King's court and back into my bathroom.

"Why my bathroom?" I ask as he starts undressing me.

"'Cause I feel dirty after Gatin'. There's a reason why they call it the Ass of Hell."

Gross. "I don't feel like I've passed through a . . . whatever."

"Don't think you do. Humans walk through the planes differently. You walk along those branches you can see. I don't. We end up in the same place, but our paths are different."

Interesting. "Oookay, but since I walked a different path, I'm not dirty."

"Didn't say you were. I'm takin' a bath an' I want you in the tub with me, dirty or clean, although you might come out dirtier than you went in."

He waggles his eyebrows at me, and I have to laugh.

———

After a bath with Jou, which definitely got me dirtier in spots than I was when I got in the tub, and one of his three course "snacks," I call Lin. I was afraid that time would pass differently for us in faerie and, sure enough, we arrived in my bathroom a day and a night after we accepted the Holly King's invitation. But Lin sounds relaxed, and her calm soothes me. She's embraced taking time off and is having fun with Matty. Neither of them has any sense they're being watched, and I feel a knot of tension in my gut relax. The idea that I might have unwittingly brought the Wild Hunt down on my friend is unbearable.

When I join Jou in the kitchen and find my house free of demonesses, even if not permanently, and the knot loosens even more.

Jou settles on the couch in my parlor with a laptop that's definitely not mine and pats the cushion beside him when I fail to immediately join him. He drapes his arm around my shoulders. I watch while he places another grocery order, since the previous one was eaten by the lizards and my Hob while we were Under Hill.

"I feel you scratching around in all kinda corners. What's eatin' you?"

"Why would the Wild Hunt come after me, Jou?"

"Dunnow. What'd you get up to in my absence? Hellhound hanky-panky?"

I elbow him. "Yeah, sure."

He takes his fingers off the laptop to run them down my forearm, over the new bindings. They flare and dance under his fingers. I smile at the tingling warmth that runs up my arm.

"Hate to think it might be your bindings," he says. "I haven't heard of the Hunt targetin' the demon-touched, but the Hunt maintains the natural order. Hellions? We ain't exactly natural on this plane."

I rest my head on his warm, broad shoulder. "Jou, I'm not . . . doubting you, but the Wild Hunt? Could you really fight them off?"

He rubs my shoulder. "By myself? Dunnow. With you? I'll take those odds."

"I—" I break off at a pounding on my front door. I reach out and feel along my threshold and encounter a familiar presence. "That's my friend, Mel."

Jou grunts. "Want me to answer it?"

"No, I'd rather she didn't run screaming."

Jou snorts. "Ain't me she'd be runnin' from. Let her in. I'm lookin' forward to meetin' her."

I slide off the couch and cast him a stern glance over my shoulder. "Do not terrify my straight friends."

Jou chuckles.

I open the door and admit the hurricane that is Melanie Jean. She wraps her denim-covered arms around my neck. "Where the heck you been?"

"Sorry I disappeared. Were you trying to reach me?"

"I called here and your office 'bout a million times—"

She trails off and, from the warm rush of his presence behind me, I guess Jou's stepped into the hallway.

"I took your advice—" I begin.

Mel pushes past me, stalks up to Jou, and slaps him across the face.

"Holy shit! Mel! Omigod, Jou, I'm so sorry!"

Jou crosses his arms over his chest and chuckles darkly.

"You rat-fuck!" Mel rages, her hands on her lean hips, her nose inches from Jou's as she strains up on the toes of her bright red, cowboy boots. "A week, you told me! A week and she'd break and summon you. You got any idea how hungry I am? How tear-ass angry my master's gonna be? You're takin' the blame for this, ember-dick. I'm layin' it aaall at your door."

"My door's closed to the likes of you, mud-drub," Jou says, but the affection in his tone belies his words.

"You know each other," I say slowly.

Mel turns back to me. "Waaall." Her drawl elongates the word obscenely.

I shake my head. I've already jumped from A to B and gotten C. I lift my eyes to Jou's. "You sent her."

Jou nods. "You think I'd leave my seggurach alone, unprotected?"

"Might you have mentioned it?" I throw my hands up. "I thought you'd forgotten me!"

"Already told you why I had to do that," Jou says, dropping both his arms and his affectionate tone. "Don't get pissy at me for protectin' you. An' you?" He turns his dark gaze to Mel. "Some fuckin' protector you are. She got attacked by a hellhound."

Mel plants her forefinger in Jou's broad, bare chest, exposed where his robe hangs open over black pajama pants. "You were back! I felt the gate open like a sonic boom. Why'm I still protectin' her? Why'm I even still here? Send me back, iron-brain."

Jou shakes his head. "Bigger problems here than back home. You're stayin'."

"You are sooo explaining this to Raud. I'm not losing skin over this, I swear! Where's the tequila?"

"In the kitchen," Jou says before I can say I don't have any. Because, of course, we do. Jou waves at the open door into the parlor. "Have a seat."

Mel flounces past him into the parlor with a flip of her tiny skirt.

I close the front door and follow her. She's inspecting the huge screen left behind after our conversation with Jou's brother that I haven't figured out what to do with. I sit on the couch and watch her.

"Red Duke was here," she says, sniffing at the screen like a basset hound. "I can smell his stink like a fart in Sunday school. What'd he want?"

Not sure what we are and aren't sharing with her, and not sure how I feel about her being a demon, or whatever she is, I shrug.

"He wanted to chat, brother-to-brother," Jou calls from the kitchen.

Mel snorts. "Cause he's so brotherly."

"Yeah." Jou strolls through with a tray of shot glasses, a bowl of salt and cut limes, and a bottle that looks like a black skull. He sets it down on the table, sits beside me, and pours three shots.

Mel plonks herself down in the armchair, licks her knuckles, anoints them in salt, and takes a shot glass. "To the Hill."

She downs the shot and grabs a lime.

"To the General," Jou toasts and downs a shot.

"To knowing what the hell is going on," I say before taking a shot of the silvery alcohol. It should burn going down. Instead, it slips down my throat like hot silk and warms my belly with a fireside glow.

"Dang, you always do have the best stuff," Mel says to Jou.

Jou pours three more shots and immediately downs his, licking his lips. "Ain't bad. I went home after talkin' to brother dearest and saw Ercie. She's at the White Tower. I told her you were still topside babysittin' my seggurach. She'll tell Raud, so stop worryin' about him skinnin' you."

Mel salutes him with her shot glass before tossing it back. "You're still a lemure-humper, but I'll consider forgivin' you. 'Sides." She kicks my slipper-clad foot with the tip of her boot. "Found myself a bestie."

I glower at her. "A bestie you concealed your true nature from for months. You suck."

"Doan be mad at me." She gives me a very contrite face. "I couldn't tell you. He'da skinned me."

She nods at Jou.

He gives me that mental cheek-stroke that makes my brains, and my irritation, leak out my ears.

"I get it, and I get why he did it. But I'm going on the record now. Neither of you hide big shit from me again. I mean it. I won't forgive you a second time."

Jou and Mel trade long glances.

"I'm not my own, uh, person," Mel says. "I belong to General Raud for another hundred mortal years. I can't promise not to hide shit from you. If he orders me not to tell you, I won't be able to tell you."

"Okay, I get that. Who is General Raud?"

I'm sure I've heard the name before, but I can't place it. I really need a chart.

"What Angien is to the Old Man, Raud is to the Great Leech," Jou explains.

"A commander of his armies?"

Jou shrugs. "It's more than that, but it's hard to explain. Right-hand man. Confidante. Rival."

"Definitely rival," Mel echoes. "Raud'd take the Umbrawoods for his own in an instant if the Prince once showed throat."

Jou nods. "He called the muster?"

Mel shakes her head. "I expected a summons before the humans ate their turkeys. Nothin'."

Jou rubs his hand over his chin while reaching his arm out for me. I set my shot glass on the tray and tuck into his warm side.

"Everythin' I'm hearing says the Old Man'll march before the turn of the next mortal year. Hill's gearin' up. You an' your brothers joinin' me?"

I shoot her a glare. "You said you were an only child."

"I am really sorry about that." Mel gives me puppy-dog eyes. I sniff at her, not ready to let her off the hook. "Tellin' you I have three crazy Oiyr brothers, well, I just couldn't find a way to work it into the conversation."

I kick her boot with my slipper, which I'm sure hurts me more than her. "*I'm a demon* would have been a good start."

She becomes very interested in her shot glass, which Jou obligingly refills for her.

"So, I gather you're not the same kind of demon Jou and his family are, but you clearly know each other pretty well. What are you?"

Mel shoots a glance at Jou.

He shrugs. "She's got three now. No reason not to tell her."

*I've got three what?* I ask, and my tone must be sharp enough that he winces before the corner of his mouth kicks up.

*Elements, sweetness. She's an Oiyr, a fire an' earth hybrid. Distant cousin to the White Hood. She's nervous about tellin' you 'cause she knows you're an Earth mage an' she's afraid you might be able to control her.*

*Can I?*

*Dunnow until you try.*

I give Mel a long look while she chews her lip and plays with her shot glass. I'm still a little annoyed with her for deceiving me all these months, but I'm not so annoyed that I want to control her. That's a terrible thing to do to another living being. I don't even like seeing Jou do it to his sisters.

Mel finally finishes whatever internal debate she has going on. "Mah dame was a blood nymph and mah sire's an umbra fiend."

"I don't really know that those are, but I'm guessing—" Ha. "—that you're worried I could control you because of my Elements. I wouldn't do that to a friend, and even though you *suck* for not coming clean with me, I'm not vindictive like that."

Mel's face relaxes. "I know you're mad. I don't blame you, but I 'preciate you not usin' your magic on me."

"Is Mel what you're called? I mean, don't tell me your true name because I definitely don't want that sort of power over you, but is that what Jou would call you if I wasn't here?"

"It wouldn't be the worst idea for Tsara to be able to summon you," Jou says. "Tell her your true name."

Mel shoots Jou a fulminating glare and takes another shot before she says, "Muna Melhanaz."

"Thanks. I won't use it unless it's life or death," I reassure her. "Can I still call you Mel?"

She nods. "It's what Click calls me, too. Speakin' of Click, I need to make a soul bargain with the Stable Master." She levels Jou with a hard look. "You gonna help me? I figure you owe me."

Jou snorts. "Sure. You finally starting a stable?"

Mel glances at me and color stains her cheeks. "Yeah."

"Since I'm really hating everything I don't understand at the moment, can I ask a question?" At Mel's nod, I ask, "Does that mean Click sold you his soul?"

Mel dips her head, hiding her eyes behind the brim of her cherry red cowboy hat. "You know much his magic's agin' him. He's in pain when he don't tattoo and he's exhausted when he does. I can give him peace."

"Peace," I say flatly.

Jou squeezes my shoulder. *Don't be so fast to condemn what you don't understand, sweetness.*

I blow out a breath and try for a more moderate tone. "How will he tattoo in Hell?"

"With Dast's help, I can bring him down now. He'll still have a body. He'll have more clients than ever. Can't think of anyone who'd turn down a chance to have Click's magic under their skin. He won't age, and he won't suffer."

Admittedly, I'm not seeing many downsides. Okay, there's the damnation thing, that's a downside. "How does Click feel about his soul?"

Mel peeps out from under her hat. "He says he's never met it."

That is a Click thing to say. "And immortality? How does he feel about that?"

"He says if some part of him's immortal, he'd rather spend eternity somewhere he can party."

That's also a Click thing to say. It might be glib, but he's not wrong, either. I've started to understand that, like anything, Hell is what you make of it. The souls I've seen writhing in torment either earned it in life or didn't bargain well for what happened to them after their death.

"I get that Christian mythology got a lot wrong . . . I even get that the church has literally demonized your race. But I figure eternity in Hell can't be all wine and roses either," I say.

"You've seen it, sweetness. It's not wine and roses. It's fire and brimstone and things that warp the mortal mind. It ain't your plane and you ain't meant to be there. This soul of Mel's won't be the same in a century. Thing is, nothin' stays the same. Mortality's so fucked. Humans live for the blink of an eye, but while you're livin' you resist change. It's whacked."

"We don't resist *all* change."

Jou snorts. "You don't have enough perspective to predict fuck all, but you cling to the status quo like you're all noctils and know everything around the next bend. I've seen a lot of your world, sweetness, over a long fuckin' time. This little bubble of time you're living in with hot runnin' water and Ben and Jerry's? It's an illusion. Hundred years from now, humans will look back on you and think you were fuckin' savages and congratulate themselves on their evolution. An' they'll still be barely more'n apes. That's assumin' you don't succeed in makin' the whole planet unlivable and killin' yourselves off."

I shift uncomfortably. "That's a perspective I don't have."

We all sit in silence for a moment while the demons do another round of shots.

"If y'all ain't gonna yell at me no more," Mel says. "You wanna tell me why a hellhound attacked you? Sooner we sort this shit, sooner I can go home. Nothing against you and the hot runnin' water an' all, but the mortal world *sucks*. I got permanent tail itch from wearing my damn glove all the time. I'd honestly rather face the Erinyes than spend another minute workin' retail. An' all the country music and cowboy boots in the world don't make up for how fucking hungry I am."

"Why can't you feed?" I ask. "I thought unbound demons could feed off any human emotion."

Mel kicks at Jou, who moves his shin out of the way before she connects.

"Ain't exactly unbound, am I?"

"Jou."

He gives us both a huge grin, filled with teeth. "Take better care of my seggurach and I'll loosen the noose."

Mel throws up her hands. "She's alive."

"Not exactly unscathed, though, is she? You were supposed to make sure she stayed healthy, body and soul."

"Quitcher bitchin'. You're fine, ain't you, Tsara?"

I am now. Not so much before Jou returned, but there's no point dwelling on it.

"I'm not sure why the hellhound attacked me." I rub my eyes as I think back over the attack. "You know," I say slowly. "I have seen something like it before. That day in Harvard Square. Burned bones and black wings."

"You said it was precognition. Did you foresee the hellhound's attack?

I shake my head, feeling my way through memory and my mind's eye. "This was different. Like an echo."

"The premonition in Hahvahd Square or the hellhound's attack?" Mel asks.

"The hellhound. It was like an echo. Or a shadow. It wasn't the thing that's stalking me."

"What's stalkin' you?"

I glance at Jou. He shrugs.

"The Wild Hunt," he tells Mel.

"The fuckin' what? How'd you get from one hellhound to the Huntsman and his whole damn pack?"

Something tugs inside me. A small wrongness, like a note played off-key. I felt it before when Park was talking about the symbol.

"I need to do some research," I say.

*What kind of research?* Jou asks into my mind.

*On the Huntsman. How does he pick his prey? I don't remember any of the legends saying the Hunt goes after the prey's family, so why is he going after people close to me?*

"Okay," Jou says aloud. "I'll help you."

That I did not expect.

*Why? You think I'm too good to crack a book with you? Or d'you think I can't read?*

I never actually considered whether a thousand-year-old demon could read modern English, but Jou's been ordering groceries and navigating Boston somehow.

"Me, too," Mel says.

I lift my eyebrows at her.

"Whaaat?"

"Nothing. Let me grab some books and we'll get reading."

Surprisingly, the demons are helpful as I go through my library of books from Wydlins and Bevvy. Mel grabs a book on urban myths that I pass over. When she hands it to me, I reconsider and nod to her. Many supernatural creatures have made the transition to cities and modern living. No reason the Wild Hunt couldn't.

Once we start reading, Mel, unsurprisingly, proves to have a short attention span. Fortunately, we have a Snack Master. Jou pops in and out of the kitchen, returning with enough finger foods to put us all into a carbohydrate coma. I lost all sense of time in our visit to Faery, but my stomach is letting me know that I didn't eat for thirty-six hours. I join Mel in scarfing down the finger sandwiches, cold cuts, cheese, and sable grapes Jou arranges in the middle of my dining room table where we have the books spread.

We each take a different time-period. Jou takes the oldest books, in part because he reads Latin better than I do, as well as Middle English, which I read not at all. I take everything from Spencer to the eighteen-hundreds, while Mel has the Brothers Grimm to her book on urban legends.

The day outside the windows is overcast, but the gray light is growing long and casting shadows into the corners of my dining room when Jou sets a leather-bound book in front of me and holds it open with a long, black talon.

"Don't like that at all," he says.

I read the entry aloud, "Vulpius calls her Frau Holda, who can change her shape. She rides during the Yule at the head of a crowd of fire-eyed beasts, a furious host, to punish the godless, the sinners who do not observe the fast-days, those women who break the natural order with their spells and incantations, and they are called into the host to serve their penance for a hundred years or fall to the host's hungry mouths."

I lift my eyes from the text and meet Jou's, which are burning dangerously.

"A furious host," I repeat, remembering the Futhark symbol's translation.

"Yeah, that's what caught my attention. I was lookin' for a hunts*man*, but maybe that's the wrong place to look."

"Huntsman, huntswoman, whoever they are, they're hunting me because I'm a witch? There are thousands of witches."

"Yeah, but not many of 'em are bound by a demon. Pretty sure that'd make you godless in the eyes of someone from the late seventeen-hundreds."

"I don't really know who Vulpius is," I admit.

"Goethe's brother-in-law. He worked at the Weimar library and wrote a lotta shit. Some of the historical sources he based his work on were likely forgeries, but where he's relatin' folklore, I'm not sure it matters. Even if he heard it from the old lady down the street, all that matters is enough people believin' it."

"You're saying that if enough people believe in something, their belief can make it happen?"

"I'm sayin' somethin' ate three of your friends and is likely after you. You're a woman who breaks the natural order with spells and incantations, you're bound by a demon, and you're bearin' demon-spawn. Two shifters and a fae been killed. Pretty sure you'd all count as godless. So am I, come to it."

I nod. If any creature could be considered godless, it's a creature without a soul.

"Does it say anything else about Frau Holda? Who she is or what she can do?"

Jou shakes his head. "Not in here, but I'll keep readin'. Now we got a name."

We do, and I comb the indexes of every book I've pulled for references to Frau Holda.

On the fourth book, a dusty monstrosity titled *Gobgoblins and their Kin*, I find an entry that makes such a sharp shiver run down my spine that Jou looks up from his book.

"What'd you find, sweetness?"

I turn the book so he can do the honors this time.

"The early Middle Ages produced the Germanic figure of Perchta, also known as Hulda, Holda, Holle, and Holla. She is the spirit who gathers the souls of children who die as infants. She is both the Dark Grandmother and the White Lady, a being both vengeful and consoling. She rides at the head of an army who travels vast distances through the night to do battle among the clouds, called mirk riders. In some alpine regions in Germany, Austria and northern Switzerland, masked processions are still held at Christmas, celebrating Pertcha and her wild hunt."

"Holle," I repeat. "That's the name of my cousin's girlfriend. She was there on the green when I had that vision. I saw her turn into a black phantasm. She was playing with a dog, Jou."

"Bet it wasn't a fuckin' dog."

"I have to call Shirri."

Jou nods and I bolt from the table into the kitchen where my downstairs phone is.

Shirri's phone rings and rings.

I try to remember if she gave me any other contact numbers. The school where she works—although school should be out, if it's even a school day—I've completely lost track of the days. Did she give me her husband's number? No. I can't think of any other way to reach her. I hang up and call again.

When she doesn't answer after a third call, I turn to Jou. "I need to go to her house."

He stands and dusts off his hands on his thighs. "Okay."

"I can't believe I'm saying this, but if Shirri is in on it somehow, we could be walking right into an ambush."

Jou nods. "I got a way to deal with a water witch. You ain't gonna like it, though."

"Does it involve her soul?"

"Nope, heatin' all the water in her magic to boilin'. Parboiled water witch."

I swallow hard. "She's my cousin."

"She threatens you, she's an enemy, kin or no."

"Okay, let's cross that bridge when we come to it. We'll just . . . be prepared."

Jou nods and holds his hands out to me. When I step close, he runs his hands over me. The silk and velvet pajama set he's dressed me in—royal blue this time—melt into black leather jacket, pants, and boots that would look at home on the back of a Harley.

I hold out my arms. "Leather?"

"There's a reason bikers wear it. Keeps your skin inside. Hellhound might be able to chew through it, but it'll take the fucker a while."

He shakes himself and his robe and pajama bottoms shift into a similar, leather get up.

"Oh look, we match," I quip. "Like the X-Men."

Jou chuckles and takes my hand so I can pull him into the Earth.

# CHAPTER 18

haven't been to Shirri's house before and realize after I step into the Earth that I'm not a hundred percent sure where it is. But Jou seems to have a built-in GPS and guides me unerringly to a small subdivision in Avon Hill. Shirri and Will's house is the smallest on the street, but it's still far bigger and nicer than anything I will ever own.

Except now I might own a fiefdom in Hell, or at least have a vested interest in one.

I shake that thought away as Jou and I walk hand-in-hand toward the front door. The street's quiet and the day's gone cold. I keep a look out for dogs, huntswomen, and blackbirds as we walk up to the porch, but all I see is an older man in an ugly afghan coat walking his similarly suited terrier down the block.

Matching pet coats, really?

I hear classical music coming from inside the house as I ring the buzzer and after a moment, Will answers the door, barefoot, in jeans and a T-shirt that's spotted with what looks like spaghetti sauce.

"Tsara?"

I hold out my hand, which he shakes hesitantly. "Hi, Will. I'm so sorry to just show up like this. I called but no one answered the phone."

"It's out."

He points down the street where I see a yellow repair truck parked beneath a phone pole. Figures.

"Sorry, it's just . . . I'm worried about Shirri. Is she home?"

Will nods. "Worried, 'cause of me?"

"No, no, nothing like that."

He nods his shaggy head, but I can see from his closed expression that he doesn't believe me. Guilt stabs deep. I keep hurting this man without meaning to.

He steps back and gestures for us to come inside. When we're standing awkwardly in the hallway, he calls up the stairs, "Shirri, it's your cousin."

"Just a minute!" Shirri shouts from somewhere upstairs.

Will shifts from foot to foot. Behind his round glasses, his eyes trace the length of the hall runner. I don't have to read minds to know he wants to be anywhere but here.

"Please, don't let us keep you from whatever you were doing," I offer.

His eyes flash up at me. "You don't mind? I was just in the middle of making tomato sauce."

"Not at all. I'm very sorry to show up uninvited like this."

Will waves off my words with a beefy hand. "It's no problem. Shout if you need anything."

He shuffles off down the hall towards the back of the house and disappears through a swinging door.

Shirri patters down the stairs a minute later and immediately throws herself into a warm hug. I pat her back and when she steps back, give her a reassuring smile.

"Well, you two look like you just escaped the Matrix. Have you come to offer me the blue or red pill?"

Her humor lightens the mood a little. I grin at her. "No, but if he offers you anything." I hook my thumb over my shoulder at Jou. "Definitely take the blue one."

Shirri sniggers. She waves at me in a very Morpheus-like "come hither" gesture and leads us into a TV room with comfortable, overstuffed couches and an antique writing desk in one corner.

Shirri nods at the desk. "Aunt P. gave us that for our wedding. It's been in the family since they came over from England. It should probably be yours."

"Oh, no, I wouldn't dream of taking something like that. It's lovely you have a space for it." Once we're seated on the cozy couches, I continue, "Shirri, I don't want to scare you, but I think we found what killed Toby. There have been two other deaths, too. Both, um, individuals who were close to me. I'm worried the killer might be going after my friends."

Shirri chews on her lower lip. "Am I your closest living blood kin?"

I shake my head. My Romany cousins are closer, but I have no way of contacting them. "Toby was the last person I did a major healing on." Before Jou. "The fae that was killed was my protector, and he took me through faerie frequently. You and I did a major casting together. Magic leaves traces and I'm scared the killer might be seeking out those who carry traces of my magic."

Shirri squares her shoulders. "Okay, how can I help?"

I glance at Jou. I expected her to be afraid, or even angry at me for bringing this to her door. I didn't expect her to offer to help. I'm not sure what to say.

Jou spreads his arms across the back of the couch. "Best way you can help is by stayin' safe. Everyone who's been killed was alone. Stay close to your bear-mate. I can't smell any of Tsara's magic on you anymore, but probably wouldn't hurt to purify yourself in water and smoke and then have a good old roll in the hay with your mate. That'll get rid of any traces."

I slap him on his six-pack with the back of my hand. "Jou."

He grins. "I'm not wrong, though."

I shake my head at him. "Shirri, there is one thing. That day we had brunch, I saw something. When your twin and his girlfriend were playing with the dog, I had a vision. I think it might be related. Do you have a way I could get in touch with her? With Holle?"

Shirri nods. "Of course. I've got her number. Oh, and her address. I sent her a Beltane card. Let me get it for you."

She rises and leads us into the kitchen, which is country-eclectic like the rest of the house in shades of robin's egg blue, yellow, and white. Will turns from where he's standing at the stove, frying off meat balls, and lifts his chin at each of us.

"I'm just going to find Tomas's girlfriend's number and address for Tsara," Shirri tells Will, walking over to plant a kiss on the back of his neck. "Then I've got something to tell you that'll make you happy."

The way his neck flushes makes me grin.

Shirri moves to a wooden bookcase with cookbooks, phone books, and what look like photo albums stacked in it. She pulls out a book wrapped in blue calico and flips it open, then writes down numbers and the address on a sticky note to hand to me.

"Thank you so much for this, Shirri."

"I hope you find this thing." She lifts her eyes to Jou, who is standing behind me, one hand on my hip and his body close enough that I can feel his warmth. Although, Jou's hot enough that he could probably stand across the room and I'd feel his heat. "You'll protect her, right?"

"Hey," I say.

Shirri slots the book back in the bookcase and holds up her hands. "Sorry. It's not a sexist thing. I just figure, you know, prince of Hell, he's probably a little better protection than most."

Jou shifts up until he presses against my back. "I'll protect her."

"I'll hold you to that. I only just got my cousin. I'm not ready to lose her."

I shake my head at the two of them. "We should go. I don't want to interrupt your dinner."

Shirri reaches for me. I let her draw me into a hug and hope like hell I'm not shedding any residual magic on her.

Shirri walks us to the door and gives me another hug before turning to Jou. To my surprise, not only does she offer to hug him, but he lets her.

"Call me tomorrow and let me know you're okay, okay?"

"I will," I promise.

"She'll try," Jou says. I glance at him, wondering if he knows something I don't. He shrugs.

"Okay, I'll try. Enjoy your dinner. And your roll in the hay." I wink at her before I take Jou's hand and step into the Earth.

I expect Jou to lead me to the address Shirri's given us the same way he led us to her house. Instead, we step out of the earth in the middle of my yard. I look him a question as I dust myself off.

"Want Mel's ink mage to finish your protections. Right now. If we're gettin' close to the thing that's huntin' you, I want you protected as much as possible."

I don't even think about arguing. "Okay."

"First you go in there." He nods at my hearth room. "Seat of your power. Draw as much to you as you can. I'll help you direct it."

Again, I don't argue, just walk into my hearth room. I haven't purified myself or prepared, but I have a sense that I won't need to. There's not going to be any finesse in this. I'm just going to pull as hard as I can on the wellspring of my magic.

My circles spark to life as I walk across them, without me dancing the circle or *calling* them. Jou follows me, crossing each circle without pause.

"You don't feel anything when you cross the circles?" I ask.

"I feel closer to you."

I reach back and take his hand. Not to pull him through my wards. Just so I feel closer to him, too.

I stop by my cauldron and place my hand on the lip. It's dry and empty but at my touch fills with something black that gives off the copper smell of blood.

"What is that?" I ask Jou.

"Looks like ichor. Demon blood. Your cauldron had a good, long taste of Hairy's. Could be regurgitatin' that."

Charming. I opt not to touch it but hold my hand above the glossy surface. Sparks leap from my fingertips, and I feel the slow crawl of the power the liquid holds. It is power eked from pain and fear, but power, nonetheless.

I turn my other hand in Jou's, so I interlock our fingers, and hold up our joined hands. "Put your other hand over my cauldron. Don't touch the surface."

When he does, I reach deep and *call.*

Magical energy slams into me so hard, so fast, I imagine I light up from inside like one of those cartoon electrocutions. Jou stiffens, his back arching, his glove shredding away. His horns unfurl from his head, the burning crown between them whirling, spitting neon light into the corners of my hearth room. His tail whips out and wraps around my right calf.

I don't move, or fight the power flooding into me, just *call* more and more.

Blood pounds in my ears and runs from my nose. I lick it off my upper lip and *call* more.

When my bones creak and chime with the power hollowing them out, when my hair is standing straight up from my head and each strand is trying to rip out of my scalp, when I'm gritting my teeth against the scream trying to tear out of me, I look at Jou. He's watching me with eyes gone solidly blue. He nods.

I ease back, remembering what he told me about not cutting off my source too fast. Power's murderous grip on my bones loosens and I push it down into a deep place in myself. When Jou reaches out to me with those invisible fingers, I push the excess into him.

He pulls his fingers from mine, lifts his arms toward the sky, and roars.

I watch him. I should feel afraid. He's still a demon. For all that we're in a good place now, he's still going to take me away from every-thing and everyone I've ever known. He's still going to let his home warp my mind into something I'm currently not.

Instead of fear, all I feel is awe when I see his true form.

Jou shakes himself as he lowers his arms and spins his glove back out around himself. As his horns disappear, his dreadlocks flare out around his head, writhing like a carpet of snakes to his shoulders and down his back.

"Nice to see those back," I say. "I like them."

Jou fingers a furry, crimson rope. "Guess I was only ninety-five percent healed. I didn't think these were comin' back." He flips the mass of them over his shoulder. "Feels good. Like I got my sense of smell back after goin' nose-blind."

I reach up and stroke the fuzzy fall, noticing as I move that I've lost my clothes. Again.

As I think it, black smoke spins off the ichor filling my cauldron and wraps around me. At a thought, it smoothes into a black cardigan, sweater-dress, and warm tights. I feel soft boots wrap around my ankles before I look down to see them lace themselves up.

"Huh," I say.

"Huh," Jou echoes. He extends a clawed hand and runs it down the sleeve of my sweater. Blue floral embroidery sparks from his claws and weaves through the black knit.

"Huh," Jou says.

"Huh," I repeat.

"Can you do it without a source? Try makin' a coat without callin' on your cauldron or anythin' else in here."

I can't, as it turns out. When I call on the power stored in my riverstones, a long duster coat lined with creamy shearling wraps around my back. But when I simply imagine clothes spinning out of nothingness, that's exactly what I get: nothingness.

"I need a source."

Jou nods, but I don't sense any disappointment. "Good to know."

"Jou—"

He runs a hand down my cheek, no claws, no spines, human warm. "I need to know our abilities, sweetness, that's all. What I know, I can use."

"What about me?"

"What about you?"

"Shouldn't I know everything you can do?"

Jou strokes my cheek again. "You seen just about everything I know I can do. Can't say I won't be able to do something new tomorrow. Two days ago, I couldn't touch you just by being in your mind." He strokes my cheek with his mind instead of his fingers. "Today, I can. There's one more thing I know I can do, but you ain't gonna like it and I'm not sure I should show it to you."

I firm my chin. "What if it's the thing that ends up standing between me and death?"

Jou sighs. "Yeah. Put your hand on your cauldron. This is gonna hurt like fuck. I'll release you as soon as it's done. Step backwards and imagine yourself back in your body."

"My what?"

"I'm gonna rip your soul outta your skin."

Fuck that.

"I told you, you wouldn't like it. Now you know I can do it. Let's leave it at that."

I breathe long and hard and shake my head. "Do it."

"Sweetness, I really don't like hurtin' you. An' it ain't gonna feel good to me, either. We just sequestered a fuck-ton of power between us. Rippin' your soul out may undo all that. What hurts you, hurts me now." He nods at my wrists. "That's what the bindings mean. Goes both ways. This ain't the time for either of us to be weak."

I see the sense in that.

"Can you do it to demons, too, or just humans?"

"I can rip demons outta their gloves. Lesser demons; it sends them back to Hell. Greater demons, just pisses 'em off."

"What about other entities? Vampires? Fae? Hellhounds?"

"Never tried it with anything but a human or a demon. Doubt it'd work on anything else, but I find my scythe's effective enough."

Having seen the effectiveness of his weapons firsthand, I can't argue with him there.

"Do you have to touch the person to do it?"

Jou nods. "With my claws. Gotta shred my glove enough for them to come out. Leaves me a little vulnerable, but nothin' like it used to."

"You're still trying to get me to see the positives of your father torturing you for three years, aren't you?"

Jou chuckles, wraps his arm around my shoulders, and steers me back into the house. "Sooner or later, you're gonna meet the Old Man face-to-face. I gotta soften you up enough by then that your first reaction ain't to try to kill him."

Not kill. I don't want to kill him. Just give him a little taste of his own medicine.

Jou squeezes me and plants a hot kiss on my temple. "That ain't gonna go down well, either. Thought you were on board with the whole layin' low and bidin' our time thing?"

I am. Mostly. "As long as our time comes."

Jou stops and turns me in his arms, one big, warm hand dropping to my belly. "Our time's here. You an' me. Our babies. The Hill. My clutch. This may be all we get. I'm good with that. Are you?"

I rummage around in my heart for a moment before I slide my arms around his neck, go up on my toes, and kiss him. "Yes," I say between kisses. "But if the chance for payback comes, and it doesn't hurt you or our family, I'm taking it."

Jou chuckles and swings me up in his arms before carrying me inside. "Who knew you'd turn out to be such a vindictive little thing?"

———

My last tattooing session with Click is *nothing* like the ones that have come before. I've been to Click's tiny shop during the day, on my own. Tonight, I Earth-Walk straight into Click's supply room, hand-in-hand with a demon. There's barely enough room to turn around and Jou takes the opportunity to pull me tight to his chest.

"Fair warnin'," he whispers in my ear, breath warm and scented like cinnamon as it tickles across my skin. "I'm fuckin' you while he does it."

"Uh, what?"

"Told you, nothing inside you from now on but me. I get he's got to stick needles in you for the magic to take, but I don't like it. So, I'm gonna be in you while he does it. 'Sides, you didn't really think you'd be doin' your greenwitch thing for hours without me fuckin' you, didja?"

I swat his rock-solid shoulder, but it's without any real heat or force. Sex will help take my mind off the pain, maybe even better than the trance I usually sink into. Besides, Click's going to see far worse things once he goes to Hell.

Jou opens the storeroom door. We step out to surprise Click and Mel, who aren't quite doing what Jou plans to do to me, but aren't far off, either. Mel laughs and climbs off Click, where she was grinding on him. Click fastens up his jeans before he rises out of his tattoo chair to give me a hug.

He stares at Jou for a long moment, then bows.

Jou chuckles. "You don't gotta do that. Cute, though. Uzal'll love it."

Mel smacks Jou's shoulder. "I expected you hours ago."

"So, you got busy while you were waitin'?" Jou laughs when Mel smacks him again. I smile at their easy camaraderie. Hell with Jou won't be so bad, but Hell with Mel might be . . . a good time. "Told you, we might be a while. Pulled a lot of power."

Mel nods. "I can sense it." She glances at me. "You move softly-softly through your Element, though. Nothing like a Gate."

"Great for sneakin' up on people, ain't it?"

"Ember-dick, you're gonna be insufferable."

Jou grins hugely. "C'mon. Let's get this done. I want Tsara and the babies protected sooner than later."

Mel stumbles a step, like she's rolled an ankle in her cowboy boots. *"That's* what I can feel?"

Jou's grin has waaay too many teeth in it. "Triplets."

Mel shakes her head at him. "You always were an overachiever." She elbows me as Click steers me onto the tattoo chair. "You couldn't keep him from knockin' you up?"

Taking off my cardigan and handing it to Click, I snort at her. "You've clearly known him longer than I have. Does anyone keep him from doing anything he wants?"

She lifts an imaginary glass to me. "Point."

I unbutton my sweater dress and fold it down to my waist.

"Might as well take it off, sweetness. Tights, too. Or I can burn 'em off."

His leer tempts me too much.

"Or you could rip them for easy access."

He pops out a claw, flattens me to the chair, and tears out the gusset of my tights while I squirm. His weight comes down on me.

"Can you reach enough of her?" Jou asks Click.

"I'm mostly working on her arms tonight. I'll only need to get to her back for a half-hour or so."

"Lemme know when and I'll shift back," Jou says, pushing my body where he wants me, spreading my legs wide, my knees over the sides of the chair, as he settles over me. I'm about to struggle when the slick heat of his nethertongue strokes me from clit to crack. I collapse face-down into the chair, arms flopping over my head, hands dangling off the top lip of the chair, and let him ravage me. Nothing should feel this good.

Jou's licking completely distracts me from Click setting up, cleaning my skin, shaving off my peach fuzz, and taking the first pass with the needle.

*Lift your hips an' let me in,* Jou says in my mind.

I arch my back and lift my hips like a wanton thing.

*My wanton thing,* Jou thinks with such huge satisfaction that it tolls through me like a *taiko* drum. He fills me slowly, stretching me until I'm gasping. Instead of thrusting, he settles deep in me, brackets my shoulders with his elbows, and props himself up so I'm not bearing his entire weight. Then he starts that mental stroking. This time it is *all* over, starting at the crown of my head and caressing me all the way down to my toes. At first, I shiver at each stroke, but as it goes on and on and his thickness pulses within me and his nethertongue laps over and around where he's sunk deep in me, I sink into warm, drifting peace. The magic I've stuffed into every cell suffuses the air, glittering glyphs swirling through the cloud of magic like snowflakes. I don't need to call or shape this power. It pours out of me. When Click notices, he alters his movements, snatches each sigil out of the air, and drives it into my skin with his needle.

I have no sense of how long it goes on. Hours at least, but it could be days. Jou occasionally shifts to kiss me or adjust himself. Click moves from arm to arm. Magic swirls and surges and settles into my skin.

Finally, Click sits back and turns off his tattoo gun. He looks exhausted, with deep lines carved around his mouth and across his forehead. When he takes off his baseball cap to run his hand through his hair, I see it's gone completely gray.

"Click," I say.

He follows my eyes and shrugs. "It's getting worse. That's why I agreed to the deal."

He tips his head at Mel, who has come and gone several times while he's finished the tattoo and is now sitting in a beanbag chair in the corner with her long legs stretched out in front of her and her cowboy hat pulled down over her eyes.

"Are you really okay with it?"

Jou leans in and nips my ear.

"Ow."

*Don't get in the middle of a soul-trade, sweetness.*

*Don't tell me what to do, Jou. Click's my friend, too. This is a huge decision. I should know.*

He lets out a long sigh into my mind.

Click tidies up the little table where he's set his ink caps and wipes without meeting my eyes. "Yeah. There's nothing for me here but pain. Mel says you've been. You've seen it. What's it like?"

"It's not easy to describe." I twist my neck to look at the demon lounging on my back. "Can we take him?"

"Dunnow. He's got his own magic, but it ain't like yours." Jou lifts his eyes to Click. "You ever walked a Path to any plane but this one?"

Click shakes his head.

"What about doors to *another* place?" Jou asks. "You ever inked a door and felt you could walk through it?"

"Kind of. I have a thing for skulls." He twists his arm so we can see the line of skulls marching up his forearm from wrist to elbow. "I've inked some skulls and felt like their eyes were drawing me in. I thought that if I went, I could step through into somewhere else. But I always figured it was death calling me, so I never went."

"Yeah, coulda been," Jou concurs. "Not sure I'd take that chance, if I were you. Not without being soul-tethered to Mel already an' that kinda defeats the purpose."

*Smooth,* I grouse at Jou mentally.

He strokes me from head to toe again.

After I shudder through what feels more like an earthquake in my soul than an orgasm, I buck against his weight. "Off."

Jou grumbles but withdraws and helps me off the chair.

Click wraps up the fresh tattoo and I pull my clothes back on before giving him a warm hug. "Call me after you've slept, and I'll try to give you an idea of what Hell's like. Maybe I can paint my memory with magic or something, because it's really hard to put into words."

"That's a deal. I'll call you."

Mel, who as far as I could tell was sleeping one second ago, bends her legs and rises smoothly out of the beanbag to give me a hug.

"We're okay, right?" she asks.

"Yeah, we're okay. You owe me coffee for the rest of forever, though."

She grins and hugs me harder.

"You doin' anything life threatenin' tomorrow?" she asks.

I turn in her arms to look at Jou. "Are we?"

"Probably," he grins. "Zes'll be back."

"Great."

"Zip with 'em?" Mel asks.

Jou nods. "She'd love to see you."

"I'll be there for lunch." Mel winks at Jou. "No dairy. I'm cuttin' back."

"Bring your own, then."

She moves away from me enough to elbow him. "An' I want somethin' fried."

"How is this cutting back?" I ask.

"I'm not cuttin' back consistently. Just on shit from cows. Make sure you got plenty of tequila."

Jou starts shaking his head. "I remember what happened the last time you and Zippy drank together."

"What happened?" I ask, steeling myself.

"Great Chicago Fire."

I lift my eyebrow at the two demons.

"Fucking cow," Mel mumbles. "See? Dairy's the devil."

Jou chuckles. "See you tomorrow."

After another round of hugs, Jou takes my hand and I walk us into the Earth.

# CHAPTER 19

My new tattoo is sore in the morning, but I know from experience that I can't heal it without eradicating the tattoo. I brew a rosemary balm that takes the worst of the sting away before setting in on the huge stack of waffles with bacon, peanut butter, and maple syrup that Jou serves me for breakfast. I've never had bacon, peanut butter, and maple syrup together before and it instantly becomes my new favorite thing, even while I can hear my arteries screaming.

"Now that the tattoo's finished, I want to confront Shirri's brother's girlfriend," I tell Jou while I'm drinking coffee and feeding the tiny scraps I've left of my breakfast to the salamanders. "It can't just be a coincidence."

Jou nods. "You want to show up at her place the way we did with your water witch?"

"Yes, but I want to do a little scrying first. I want to call the dead and see what they'll tell me."

"Will havin' me there help or hinder?"

I put down my fork, move around the table, and climb onto his lap. "Thank you for asking."

He gives me a maple-syrup kiss.

"I'd like you there," I say after he lets me up for air. "I'd also like to test the tattoo. It feels strong, but I want to be sure. If I call the dead and instead of protecting myself with my elements, I protect myself with the tattoo-ward, that seems like pretty low-risk."

"An' if it fails?"

"I have you as backup."

Jou nods. "Let's do that this mornin' before the Zes get here."

"Do we have an ETA for them?"

Jou chuckles. "Yeah, once I told Zip Mel was comin', she said she'd make sure they were back for lunch."

"You can speak into Zippy's mind the way you can speak into mine?" As far as I knew, our mental link was unique, but maybe I got that wrong.

"No, sweetness. I called her this mornin' while I was makin' break-fast and you were in the shower. Gotta say how much I'm liking these little phones you humans tote around. I gotta figure out something like that for down below."

"So, you can't telepath with Zippy or whatever?"

Jou shakes his head. "Not while we're wearin' gloves. I can do it down below t'anyone I share blood with."

"That's a lot of people, er, demons, in your head."

"They're not in mine. I'm in theirs."

I snort at him. "Is alpha demon-ness a thing? Because you are there, buddy."

Jou laughs, throwing back his head in a wave of crimson, the strong muscles of his throat working. "Jus' wait until I get you back to the Hill and you start poppin'. You ain't see alpha demon-ness yet."

"Mmm—"

I break off when Jou stiffens. He nods his head at the TV in the corner of my kitchen, which is showing the morning news.

"Someone you know, sweetness," Jou says softly.

I turn in his lap until I can see the screen. Under the earnest face of the morning news presenter a yellow banner scrolls: "Tufts professor brutal slaying."

My breath catches.

I climb off Jou's lap and cross to the television to turn up the sound. I hug my elbows as I listen.

" . . . Professor Peter Buscelli has been found dead in what is apparently an animal attack. Police are asking any witnesses who heard a disturbance in Professor Buscelli's apartment building the night before last to come forward. The shocked neighbor who found the Professor's body had this to say—"

I switch the television off.

"He called me," I say numbly. "He said he was in trouble. I tried to call him back, but he didn't answer."

Jou runs his warm hands up and down my arms. "He was probably dead by then, sweetness."

I turn and let the demon close his warm arms around me and tuck me into his chest.

"I know you're gonna think this was your fault," he rumbles, his breath warm in my hair. "It's not. No way you coulda known the magic you did on that null would call somethin' down on him."

"Jou—"

"No. I need you mad, not sad. I need you focused on findin' what's huntin' you and takin' it down, not mourning someone you couldn't save." He slides a finger under my chin and tips my face up until I meet his eyes. "Yeah?"

I take a deep breath in and let it out slowly. I couldn't save Ana. I couldn't save Peter. But I can save myself. I can save Jou. I can save our babies.

I nod.

"Good." Jou steps back. There's a warm pressure on my forehead, like he's just kissed me.

He's getting better and better at that.

I smile after him as he snaps his fingers at the salamanders, who are watching us both intently, probably in the hopes of more breakfast scraps. They trot after him in a little line as he leads them upstairs to shower.

———

Scrying is a bust. My tattooed ward works much too well. As soon as I cross my arms over my chest, completing the ward, the wind teasing the edges of my hair, the breath of the dead, blows a cold, spiteful gust reeking of the grave across my face and disappears.

Jou, sitting cross-legged on the ground between the first and second circles of my hearth room in all his demon glory with his scythe across his knees, grunts. "Least we know it works."

I run my hand through my hair. "Great."

"Wanna try again?" Jou asks.

I hold my hands out over my cauldron, which is still filled with demon ichor, and *call*. My Elements answer immediately, swirling mistily in the corners of my hearth room. A trio of nethancs. A mossy ondine. No river of the dead.

Then a ghoul uncurls from the gray, grooved bark of my ash tree.

Jou's around me, his wings spread and filling the air with cinders, his scythe held across the front of my body, before I even gasp.

The ghoul grins at us with blackened teeth and slopes over to where Jou was sitting. He—and it is a he, gross—bends over and sniffs at the grass, before coiling himself into the position Jou was sitting in, the bones of his humerus and femurs jutting through sagging, gray skin to gleam in the golden witchlight. He drops his hands with their outsized, black claws to rest in the grass by his thighs and clicks his claws at the wildly hissing nethancs.

I bow to each of the Elementals and release them with a silent apology. I would ordinarily give them gifts as thanks for their help, but I don't dare move out of Jou's embrace with a ghoul sitting less than ten feet away.

As the Elementals fade back into the morning breeze, the ghoul plucks a river stone out of my circle, turns it over in his claws, and tosses it up and down like a person would a quarter.

*That is creepy*, I think, loudly enough for Jou to hear me.

*No fuck. Why ain't he doin' anything?*

*I don't know. But he couldn't have gotten through my wards if he meant me harm.*

*Old Man was able to t'get through your wards and he means you a fuck-load of harm.*

*Right, but Rag and Bone Man over there isn't a Prince of Hell . . . I mean, is he?*

*Fuck.*

Jou clears his throat. "Kartcher?"

"Greetings, Baron Ash," the ghoul says in a voice meant for opera, which couldn't possibly come out of that half-rotted throat.

*Fuck. I do not believe this shit.*

Jou clears his throat again before he says, very, very civilly, "Gray Walker, this is my seggurach, Tsara Elizabeth Faa. Tsara, this is Kartcher, Prince of Ghouls."

It really cannot be good to have the Prince of Ghouls sitting on my lawn.

"Greetings, Baroness Ash," the ghoul prince says. "With three of your elements, you have a call over me and my kin I choose not to ignore. I look forward to seeing what you will do with four."

I've never heard of any mage having four elements. Never. Accepted wisdom at Bevvy was that even three elements would tear the wielder apart due to their conflicting natures.

The ghoul sets down my ward stone in front of his crossed legs, reaches up to his shoulder, and tears away the discolored rags draping his torso, not that they're covering anything effectively.

His sunken chest reminds me of Jou's when I first summoned him: dry, gray skin, pocked with sores and stretched tight over withered muscle and bulging bone. Kartcher's skin is crisscrossed with tiny black veins. As I peer at them, I realize the marks aren't veins. They're writing.

"It's too much to hope you have the history of the Wild Hunt written on your chest," I say.

Kartcher makes a gargling noise that would be more at home in a drainpipe than in a throat. I think he's . . . chuckling. How awful.

"I'm afraid not," he says. "Tsara, may I call you Tsara?"

*Any danger to agreeing?* I think at Jou.

*No more'n having him sittin' right there.*

I realize that for all our ghoul guest looks non-threatening, Jou hasn't relaxed a muscle.

"Yes, please do," I say.

"Tsara, this is my ledger. As your noctil can tell you, I bear another name. I'm called The Debt Collector. You called because you need certain knowledge. I'm willing to provide that knowledge, in exchange for a favor of equal weight. I will inscribe it in my skin if I can find a spare inch." His black, empty eye sockets search his chest and stomach. He pinches a ribbon of skin just above his hip. "Oh, yes, here we go. As I was saying, I'll inscribe it on my skin, and you'll be bound to grant me my favor when I call it in. Do you agree?"

*No.* Jou's thought rings through my mind with unmistakable clarity.

"First of all, I ain't a *noctil*," Jou says. "Second, you're not binding my fuckin' seggurach. You want a favor for the info? Favor'll be from me."

Kartcher spreads his claws. "I'd be delighted to accept a favor from you."

"I fuckin' bet," Jou grumbles.

"And your firstborn," Kartcher says.

"No," Jou and I chorus.

Kartcher chortles. "Joking. Favor's fine. Although," he drawls out the word. "If you're willing to talk babies, I'd wave the favor for being godfather to one of your little ones."

"Godfather," Jou says flatly. "You, Prince of Ghouls, want to be *god*father to my get?"

Kartcher picks his rotting teeth with a black claw. "Has a ring to it, you have to admit. God-daddy Kartcher. I like it. You really want to get in good with me? Offer me a choice of which one." He lifts his noseless face as though he's scenting. "I can smell three. Mmm, definitely know which one I'd pick. I remember that taste. Black cherries. Two thousand years and I still remember what cherries taste like. Funny, huh?"

"Hilarious," Jou says. "Swear to me on blood and bone that you won't hurt my get."

I feel Jou's chest expand as he holds his breath. I do the same and feel my heart thunder in my ears, one beat, two beats, before Kartcher nods.

"Agreed, but your get defines hurt."

"My get? Not you?"

"Not me," Kartcher agrees. "Not you, either. Your get makes up her own mind when the time comes."

"Jou—" I breathe, unable to stomach the idea of bargaining away my daughter's future before she's even born.

*Roll with it, sweetness. Might not seem like it, but he's fucking tripping over himself to ally with us. I've never heard of him offerin' anythin' for free. If he already has his sights set on one of the babies, it's because he's drawn to her. She could be his seggurach. Ain't unheard of for bonds t'form between demons before one of 'em even born an' if he's right, it'd save her a lot of painful searchin'.*

I nod slowly.

"Agreed," Jou says.

"And you, momma? Do you agree?"

"Yes, I agree."

I feel the binding snap into place. Like the gossamer weight of my debt to the fae. It's no more than an awareness, but it's there.

"Good." Kartcher scrubs his claws together, oblivious to the small hail of rotting skin that falls onto his lap. "Want the good news, or the *really* good news?"

"Why do I have the feeling that neither is good news?" I ask.

"Cause you're smarter than the average mortal. Must be all the demon seed in you. The good news is you can't defeat the Wild Hunt. Not with every demon in Hell. The hunt's a primal force. Even if you cut down the Huntsman and every hound, they'll just rise the next night to hunt again."

"Fuck," Jou hisses behind me.

"And the really good news?" I ask.

"Once the Huntsman picks his quarry, he never gives up. He may go after other prey. May let you think he's forgotten you. But he hasn't. He's just biding his time. In the end, the Huntsman always gets his prey."

"Fuuuck," Jou groans.

"Hunts*man*," I say. "We found some legends that say the Wild Hunt's led by a woman."

"Semantics." Kartcher shrugs and his clavicles pop up through his skin. "Huntsman, huntswoman, tomato, tomahto. The Huntsman doesn't have a true gender. It doesn't have a physical form, whatever it might look like. It's the embodiment of every predator who has hunted on this plane from the beginning and every predator who will hunt here until your little world is eaten by the greatest predator of all: your sun."

"What if I take Tsara to Ash Hill now?" Jou asks.

Kartcher lifts his claws. "Mortals have been poking holes in the Veil between this plane and ours for millennia. Don't think it'll keep the Hunt from coming after you."

Jou bows his head, bumping his forehead into the back of my skull, his horns curving around in front of me in a burning, ebony circlet.

"I read that if a sinner offers themselves, they can serve a hundred years with the Hunt to atone and then go free," I say, trying to think my way out of what sounds like certain freaking doom.

"That's true," Kartcher allows. "But you don't want to be separated from your Baron for a hundred years. And I sure don't want to wait a hundred years to meet my goddaughter."

Jou's head lifts. *This is it. This is why he came.*

"The babies would have to ride with me?"

Kartcher nods. "And I don't want to think about what my goddaughter would be like after a century hanging out with hell-hounds. They're such bad influences." He clicks his teeth with a gray, wormy thing that might be a tongue. Or it might be a worm. "So, you've got to be smart, momma. *Think.*"

My mind is utterly blank.

"The Hunt can't be defeated," I say slowly.

"No," Kartcher agrees, leaning forward over his protruding patellas to stare at me with empty sockets lit by the faintest ruby light.

"They can't be bargained with. I can't escape them in Hell."

"No and no."

"And I don't want to spend a hundred years riding with them."

"Definitely not."

"I—" My imagination fails me for a moment.

Kartcher unfolds from the ground and stalks over to us. This close,

I expect him to stink of the grave. Instead, he smells like wildflowers. It's so incongruous I just stare at him, even while Jou growls and stiffens at my back.

Kartcher reaches out across my cauldron and passes a huge, black claw through the air above my wrist. Jou's bindings flare like the sun and fill the air between us with glittering symbols.

"Strong binding," Kartcher grunts, pulling back his claw, which is now running with black ichor.

"Will the binding protect me?" I ask.

"No. But it'll show you the way. Bind the Hunt. Bind it with all four Elements. Bind it in your bones."

"She's still mortal," Jou growls. "It'll kill her."

"You're not and you're bound to her. Help your seggurach."

The scythe Jou was holding across me disappears and his warm arms close around me. "I will."

"Good. 'Cause I'll be really pissed at you if you let her die before I get to meet my goddaughter. God-daddy Kartcher. I love it." He whistles between his teeth. "We're going to have so much fun."

*He's fucking certifiable,* Jou thinks to me.

*In a helpful way.*

"I've never bound anything before," I say. "Jou bound me with, uh, sex. I'm guessing the Huntsman isn't going to jump into bed with me."

Kartcher shrugs. "Probably not. Never say never, but I think you'd do better focusing on your Elements."

I nod. "Four, you said."

"I did say that, didn't I?" He winks an eye socket at me. No idea how.

"So, either I find my fourth Element—"

Or I find a water witch.

———

After Kartcher leaves, by stepping back into my ash tree, which gives me not-good shivers, I call the cavalry.

Dead doesn't even wait for a full explanation. "Luca and I are on the next flight."

"Dead—"

"You don't need to say anything else, chica. I can feel what's going on up there. We're on the way. Don't start the party without us."

"Thank you, Dead."

"Don't thank me yet. You got some 'splaining to do when I get there, girl."

"Gladly."

We say quick goodbyes. Then I call Bo.

He makes me wait through the three rings and leave most of a message on the answering machine before he picks up. "My young apprentice, what have you gotten yourself into?"

"Hell. Kind of literally," I say. "I need you, Bo. You and Merida both. I need a water witch to help me bind the Wild Hunt. Otherwise, I'm dead and my babies die with me."

Bo sputters.

"I need you, Bo," I repeat.

"We'll drive up," he says. "Set off in an hour. Be there by dinnertime."

I glance at Jou, who is sitting across from me at the kitchen table, drinking a cup of coffee.

*Should I Earth-Walk them?*

*No, I want you here behind your wards until we're ready to confront the Hunt.*

Seeing the sense in that, I nod to him.

"Thank you, Bo."

"Stay safe until we get there, my young apprentice."

I smile into the phone before I say, "Yes, Master."

Jou grunts as I say goodbye and hang up.

"What?"

"Don't like you callin' anyone master."

"Jou, seriously? It's mostly a joke and a little bit a form of respect from a younger magus to an older magus."

Jou grunts again and buries his scowl in his coffee cup.

"Okay, I won't do it again," I say. "If it bothers you, I won't do it."

"It bothers me," Jou admits. "Probably shouldn't, but it does."

"Next you'll be wanting me to call *you* master," I tease.

Jou grins before taking another sip of coffee.

"*That* was a joke. I'm never calling you master, Jou."

"Careful, never's a long time," Jou says. "I feel you putting it off. Make the last call."

I am putting it off. Because I don't want to draw the cousin I only just met into danger. With a sigh, I pick up the phone.

Will answers, which makes me cringe even harder. Shirri's at school, which startles me; I really have lost track of days. Will promises that she'll call as soon as she gets home.

"Looks like everyone'll be comin' for dinner," Jou observes.

"Maybe. I don't know how soon Dead will be able to get a flight."

"I'll make extra just in case. While I'm cookin', you do your green-witch thing."

"My greenwitch thing? You want me to brew fertility potion?"

"Naw. You need to make somethin' to bind the Hunt. Magic always works better when it has a focus. Make a focus."

Images begin to swirl through my mind. "Okay, I can do that."

"Before it's finished, gimme a shout. Got somethin' of my own to add to it."

"I will. Don't feel like you need to cook for everyone. I can order takeout."

"It'll keep me busy," Jou says. "Otherwise, I'm likely to distract you while you're doing your thing."

"And by distract me, you mean . . ."

Jou grins wickedly. "It'd definitely add a little sex magic to the binding, sweetness."

I shake my head at him.

After we finish our coffees, and after some kisses that could turn into something more if the Wild Hunt wasn't coming for me, I leave Jou in the kitchen and retire to my herb room. I walk around the small room, pottering between my workbench and drying racks, letting my hands drift over the boxes and baskets of potion ingredients I've collected over the years. I don't pick up anything deliberately. I just let my hands find what they find.

When I finish a third, slow circumambulation, I stop at my workbench and survey the pile of materials. Feathers. Polished stones. Powdered earth from Uluru. A bird skeleton. Shells. I run my fingers through my hair, uncertain of my next step. My fingers catch on a snarl. I work them through, pulling my hand away with a few individual hairs wrapped around my fingers.

I drop them on the workbench atop the pile. Magic shifts, tugs, settles.

I run my hands through my hair, feeling more strands wrap around my fingers. They release from my scalp with barely a tug. I shake my hands out over the pile, then plunge my hands back into my hair.

I feel cool air on my bare scalp long before I register that I've pulled out nearly all my hair. It lies in gleaming, russet hanks over the pile of materials. I rub my hands over my head a final time. I've never felt my bare scalp before. Such a strange sensation.

*What the fuck are you doin', sweetness?*

*It just feels right.*

*I'm lickin' it right back when you're done.*

I chuckle at my fashion-conscious demon and begin braiding the hanks of hair with the feathers, stones, bones, and shells I've assembled. I run out of hair when I have about six feet of thin rope braided. I coil it on my workbench and rub the red earth into the rope, pushing my magic into every fiber. Earth's Blood leaks out of my fingertips, wetting the rope and staining my workbench. Air teases the strands of hair clinging to my scalp. Fire flares and glitters along the focus, drying the Earth's Blood to hard clumps, singing the white shells black, curling the feathers with heat, curing my Work.

"Now that's more like it," Jou says.

I glance in the direction of his voice and find him leaning on one huge shoulder in the doorway, his arms crossed over his chest. When he meets my eyes, he prowls over to me, presses his heat to my back as he licks a long line over my bare nape, and reaches around me to hold his hands above the hair-rope.

Fire pours from his palms. I expect it to render the rope instantly to ash. Instead, fire limns and gilds each hair. When Jou moves his hands away, fire continues to crackle up and down the focus. I touch it hesitantly and watch the flame curl around my fingers but feel nothing more than a pleasant warmth.

Without warning, Jou leans over my shoulder and spits on the rope between my fingers. The flames flare neon blue.

"Good," Jou grunts, running his hands back up my arms. "Havin' been bound more'n once, I can tell you shit like this works best with contact. If you can wrap it around the Huntsman a couple of times, even an arm or a leg, that'll help with the binding."

"Can you show me what you did to bind me?"

"I could, but it ain't gonna help you bind the Huntsman. Think through how you bound those imps you kept sendin' me while I was on the tree."

I think back to the string of imps I banished back to Hell, the most recent just before Christmas, the most memorable a greed imp who almost started a riot in Filene's Basement on Black Friday.

"I had the imp bite me. Then I traced your sigil on its forehead."

"That's a good start. Gimme your finger."

I offer my hand to him over my shoulder and wince when he nicks the pad of my ring finger with his fang. I draw back my bleeding finger.

"Rub the blood into the hair while naming the Huntsman and repeating your name."

I do. With each pass of my finger, the neon blue of the flames flares a blinding, brilliant white. With each chant, I feel my magic lock tighter and tighter.

"This is good Work," I say to Jou, when I'm finished, and a coil of blinding white fire lies crackling quietly under my fingers.

"Yeah, feels strong." Jou rubs his hands up and down my arms. "Once you got it bound, I'm gonna rip it outta its form, whatever shape it's in. I want you to pull the power into you. Bind it in your bones like Kartcher said. I'll be with you. Anythin' you need, you pull on me."

I run my hands over the Work, feelings its power shift and flow, separate and yet part of me. "You told Kartcher you were afraid it would kill me."

Jou rests his lips against my bare scalp, which sends a shiver down my spine, before he starts licking.

*I'm still afraid of that,* he admits into my mind. *But I'm more afraid of losin' you to somethin' I can't beat with all the demons in Hell.*

I nod, bumping slightly against his nose. "Any chance he was lying about that?"

*Not a chance I'm willin' to take. Evidently not a chance he was willin' to take, either. He came a long way t'warn us. Not sure if he's anchored to his realm the way the Old Man's anchored to Dis, but it couldn't have been easy for him. It's important t'him that you and the babies survive.*

"Well, one of the babies. Is being a godparent the same thing to demons as it is to humans?"

Jou licks leisurely up the back of my neck. *Ain't a thing to demons at all.*

"So why would he ask for that?"

*Probably to get us to commit to havin' him be part of our lives. I figure he'll be a frequent visitor to the Hill from now on.* Jou snorts into my mind. *God-daddy Kartcher. Old Man'll have a fucking fit.*

"Your father will care?"

*Oh, yeah, he'll care. Not even the Old Man can interfere with a seggurach bond, though, so if that's what drew Kartcher, Old Man's gonna have to shut up and deal.*

"Is that why your father hasn't struck at me directly? Because I'm your seggurach?"

*Maybe. Maybe, an' don't take this as an insult 'cause it's not, because you're beneath his notice. He barely notices me, and I've been a stone in his shoe for over a thousand years.*

"Bigger fish to fry, huh?" I ask.

*Yup, and we're gonna let him keep right on fryin' 'em, instead of doin' something fucking stupid like joinin' Tem's little cabal and becomin' a big fish.*

I turn in his arms and cup his face in my hands.

"I know I've said I'm sorry, but I'm saying it again. I'm sorry, Jou."

He smiles and pulls me into him, so I rest against his chest. He runs his hands over my head. I feel new hair ripple under his fingers, down to my shoulders. I smile into his shirt.

*I can feel all the things you're sorry for.* He kisses me on the forehead, his lips warm and soft. The gesture sends a frisson through me that's not desire so much as comfort. *I appreciate it, sweetness. I don't need it, an' you don't have to do it, but I appreciate it.*

I circle my arms around his firm waist and rest against him, enjoying his heat and solidity against everything outside the circle of our bodies that means us harm.

# CHAPTER 20

inner, with the assembled mages and demons, is a disaster.
Jou's sisters return in time for lunch—in California—but since they don't need to eat and we already have, it doesn't matter how late they are. They insist on coming to dinner, however. I suspect just to antagonize Bo and Merida.

Although I sit my mentor and his wife down immediately on their arrival and explain everything, leaving out the sexy bits but including the binding so Bo understands what I'm going to attempt, Bo and Merida are seriously unhappy to have five demons in the house. Shirri and Will's arrival in time for dinner doesn't make things much better, since Will keeps growling under his breath at Zeifyr, who returns the favor with a hiss scarier than any Naga.

Bone's arrival in the dining room, after rising from his coffin at sunset, nearly starts a riot.

I try to separate the factions after we finish Jou's amazing poached pears in balsamic reduction. Bone looks undecided, but finally retreats to the kitchen with the demons, while I herd the humans into the parlor with promises of tea and coffee.

By the time I return with a tray of carafes, cups, and fixings, Bo and

Will have declared an uneasy truce, even though they're at opposite ends of the room.

I can't wait to see what happens when Dead and his brothers arrive.

"Bo, I need your guidance on how to orchestrate a mass Work. I've never cast or called with more than one other magus."

Bo runs his hand over his salt and pepper beard while he considers my question. "It's essentially the same, but you're mingling more energies. It's important to come to a mass Work as pure as possible." Bo's dark blue eyes skitter over my wrists, where my bindings have been glowing since he and Merida arrived. I assume all the powerful auras in a small space have kicked them off, but they could be reacting to Jou's stress, since he and Zeifyr have been sniping at each other since she walked through the door.

"What about having a focus point?" I ask, since I'm clearly not going to be able to come to this thing as pure as Bo would like.

"It certainly couldn't hurt," Bo allows.

Once everyone has a cup in hand, I excuse myself to retrieve the binding cord from my herb room.

Bo and Merida carefully uncoil the crackling, white plait. They lay it flat on my living room table and I'm grateful it doesn't actually burn because I really like that table.

They hold their palms above it, sensing its energy through whatever mystical senses they have. It feels like someone's drawing a sharp fingernail up and down my spine. Jou must feel it, too, because he opens the pocket door into the dining room and leans a shoulder on the doorframe, watching the magi.

When I catch his eye, he winks at me. So, I guess whatever they're doing to it doesn't worry Jou. Not that much worries the demon.

Zeifyr comes to stand beside Jou, in another of her impossibly chic and unwrinkled skirt-and-blouse combinations. Instead of watching Bo and Merida, she watches me, which doesn't really raise my comfort-level any. I don't retreat, per se, because fuck if I'm letting Jou's sisters intimidate me, but I definitely shift away from her dark gaze to talk to Shirri and Will.

"Am I crazy?" I ask Shirri in a low tone.

"Definitely," she says. "But having several demons and a vampire in your kitchen is enough to make anyone crazy, so don't sweat it."

That draws a chuckle out of me.

"Have you ever bound anything with magic?" I ask her.

She shakes her head. "Other than giving my water energy to you, I think I'm going to be pretty useless."

"Giving me another element is more than enough. The, uh, demon lord who gave us the information about the Hunt was very specific that I'd need all four elements."

Shirri raises her hands with a tingle of colorful bangles. "The word of a demon lord's good enough for me."

Realizing how that sounds, I rub my hand over my face. "Completely crazy."

Shirri pats my shoulder. "I think it might help to be a little crazy going into this. What was he like, the demon lord?"

"Surprisingly friendly. If he hadn't been sitting there with half of his bones on display, I would have warmed to him pretty fast."

"Are you discriminating against the undead now?" Shirri asks.

"You know, I might just draw the line at ghouls."

She laughs; Will chuckles.

"Tsara," Bo calls me over.

I join him and Merida at the table. Merida reaches out and takes my hand, holding our joined hands over the focus. I stretch out my senses and *feel* her power. It's warm, lapping, soothing, a sun-warmed pond, an underground cave pool, the waters of the womb. There's nothing offensive about it. Shirri's power felt more like an ocean-tide, crashing and salty. Merida's power is the opposite, barely even a current. How can I possibly use it as a weapon?

"Down deep," Merida whispers to me.

I push down into the depths of her power and feel it, a swirling darkness. Even a shallow pond can drown. The underground current can smother and leave you gasping for your last breath in bubbling darkness. The womb can be a tomb.

I nod at her, understanding how to turn her power into a weapon. A little blindly, I reach back for Shirri. She takes my hand and moves to stand beside me over the table. I hold our joined hands over the focus and begin to Work, drawing the fluidity of their magic in and weaving it into mine. Smothering mud. A waterspout. Burning water. I envision each melding, letting them build in my mind, learning how to wield each as a weapon, before pushing them into my focus.

As I'm Working, I feel Jou come to stand behind me, his firm warmth against my back. I pull on him and feel the immediate readiness of the power he's reserved deep in his being. It's so much more accessible in him. There's no *reaching*, no struggle to *call* and shape. He's a creature of magic. It's woven into every cell of his body; it enters and leaves his body with every breath. I've never felt before the sheer resistance of drawing power into a human body but feeling the ease of calling on the reserves in him, I understand a little better why supernatural creatures feel humans are so limited.

My ruminations are broken by a knock on my front door. I don't even need to reach through my wards to feel the exuberance on the other side of my threshold. It's one of those idiosyncrasies I love about Dead: he's the bounciest necromancer I've ever met.

Jou kisses the back of my head and goes to answer the door.

"Ooo, honey!" Dead exclaims. "Aren't you the sexy demon?"

Jou chuckles as he admits the two necromancers into my house.

———

Time doesn't matter much to the assembled demons, vampire, magi, and shifter, but it's nearly midnight when I curl up on the couch in the crook of Jou's arm, with Dead on the other end of the couch and his older brother, Luca, in the armchair. Dead's munching some of Jou's gourmet popcorn while the rest of us are drinking coffee liquor that Jou promises won't keep us up. Dead and his brother have ousted the Zes from my guest room. I don't know where the demonesses have gone for the night, and I don't much care. Shirri and Will left an hour ago with the promise of returning tomorrow for breakfast and Mel left with them. Bo and Merida are staying with a friend in Cambridge for the night. Everyone—well, all the humans—has a bed. And we have the beginnings of a plan.

"We're just gonna show up at this chica's house and bind her ass into your bones, huh?" Dead asks.

Jou chuckles.

"I feel that might be an oversimplification."

"Whatevs," Dead says before taking another handful of popcorn. "And not to be a bitch, but how d'you know binding a primal force in your skinny mortal ass isn't going to kill you?"

"I don't," I admit.

"Seems to me that's a basic flaw in this plan," Dead's brother, Luca, observes.

Like Dead, Luca's ridiculously good-looking, with smooth, café au lait skin, a jawline any model would kill for, and a sweep of hair thicker and darker than raven's feathers. He's lounging on my chair in a T-shirt and board shorts, like he's still in Miami instead of Boston, in January. My house isn't cold, but I'm certainly happy that I have a fire demon sitting next to me. Maybe necromancers don't feel the cold.

"I'm open to suggestions," I tell him.

"I have one," Jou says. "But you ain't gonna like it."

I shoot him a surprised side-eye. He could have told me privately, so the fact that he's airing it in front of the necromancers means something.

"Go ahead," I offer.

"Let me burn the mortality outta your blood. Dead and Luca'll hold your spirit on this side of the Veil while I do it. Once you heal yourself, you'll be a lot harder to kill."

"What does it mean that I won't be mortal anymore?" I ask.

"Means you won't get human diseases. You'll stop aging. Stop decayin'."

"I won't die?"

"You'll die eventually, but not anytime soon. Not of natural causes. You can be killed just like I can, but it won't be easy."

I swallow hard while I consider his offer. I know Jou's very concerned about my mortality. He's told me he wants more than the span of one human life with me. But he also promised me there was no rush.

This feels like we're rushing things.

"It is rushin' things," Jou agrees, which tells me he's shamelessly skimming my thoughts. "I wouldn't be suggestin' it if we weren't going up against a fuckin' demi-god or whatever the Huntsman is." He finds my hand and grips it. "I don't wanna lose you to this thing. Kartcher said it can't be outrun, out-fought, out played. We got one chance to surprise the fuck outta it. I'll do any fucking thing to give us the best chance of success."

I squeeze his hand and rest my head on his shoulder. "I don't want to die, Jou. But giving up my mortality is a big ask."

"I know. Said you weren't gonna like it."

I don't. But I appreciate his dedication to keeping me alive, if not quite mortal.

"Okay," I say quietly.

Jou kisses my temple.

"Okay?" Dead asks. "Okay, you're lettin' hot demon boy here burn your humanity outta your blood and make you, what, unmortal?"

"I said her mortality, not her humanity," Jou growls. "And I haven't been a *boy* since before your savior was born." He nods at the crucifix around Dead's neck.

I tip my head back on his shoulder and wink at him. "Technically, you weren't ever a boy, since lemures are asexual."

Jou snorts.

I look back to Dead. "Yes, I'm letting the hot demon burn away my mortality. If it gives me and the babies the best chance of survival, that's what we're doing."

There's an uncomfortable silence that Dead breaks by throwing a handful of popcorn at me. "So, let's do this."

"Now?" I ask.

"Now," the necromancers and demon chorus.

"Midnight's the best time for necromancy," Luca says.

"May take you a while to heal," Jou says.

"Now," I say, rubbing my hand over my knee nervously. "Anything I need to do to get ready?"

Jou shakes his head.

"Then let's do it."

Famous last words.

———

Another strange procession across the unseasonably green grass to my hearthroom, this time in the company of necromancers.

After the drama my hearthroom has seen recently—between the defleshed demoness in my cauldron and the Prince of Ghouls popping out of my ash tree—I expect it to look a little worse for the wear.

I don't expect a high fae to be sitting cross-legged within my third circle, quietly polishing a blade across their knees.

"Hello," I say warily.

The fae nods its helmeted head. Although the *Ellyllon* all look alike to me, I think this is one of the three who came to my dancing circle. Something about the whorls of its armor, which remind me of the patterns on a blue tiger butterfly, seems familiar.

The fae sheathes the dagger that it's been sharpening and stands, bowing to Jou and then to me.

"You brought us the name of my brother-in-arm's slayer, as you said you would. This is more honor than I've seen from the mortal world in many years. I've come to give you my thanks and offer you my blades. I will hunt with you, if you would have me."

Either me finding the Squire's killer softened up the *Ellyll* or this is a different one, because there's none of the arrogance of last time.

I glance at Jou, who nods.

"Yes, we'd appreciate the help," I say. "You, uh, know what we're hunting?"

The fae inclines its helmeted head. "The witch Pertcha and her pack."

"And you think we can defeat them?"

Hope sparks in my chest. Maybe the fae know a way to defeat the Wild Hunt.

"No, but no battle is certain. Some must be fought nevertheless. Aranan's death was an abomination. His killers must pay, even if I fall seeking vengeance for my brother-at-arms."

I nod grimly. Jou's arm circles my waist, and he draws my back against his chest. *This is gonna work, sweetness.*

I tip my head back to smile up at him, understanding he's trying to give me hope he doesn't completely feel himself. "Let's do it."

The fae tells us their name is Aehelwen—which doesn't clear up my pronoun quandary, but I decide it doesn't matter as long as they're an ally—and I briefly explain what we're doing. The fae withdraws to my third circle and I put the question of how they crossed my circles without setting off my wards aside when Jou takes my hand and helps me climb into my empty cauldron.

*Call the goo you used to heal me, sweetness.*

I reach down into my Element and draw Earth's Blood to me, letting it lap around me as I sink to my knees. The fluid's warm, thick. It buoys and cradles me in a way that has nothing to do with the confines of my cauldron. When I feel like I'm floating in a salt sea, the dark shapes of trees pinpricked by stars overhead, I squeeze Jou's hand.

His fingers tighten on mine and a hot tingle spreads from where we touch.

I breathe slow and deep as the tingle becomes a burn. Heat licks up my arm.

When the burn reaches my heart, it explodes. This isn't a wire in the blood. It's a tsunami of lava roaring through my veins. The pain bows my back, rocking the cauldron around me. I give it voice, a deep roaring that comes from the stones under our feet instead of my throat.

A hideous shimmer takes me, working inwards from the warm liquid around me, down into my marrow. It vibrates me slowly out of my flesh. I grab at corporality, but it slips through my mental fingers like the Elemental fluid buoying me. I scrabble at the remnants of my mortality as they burn away under the demon's power.

Sticky strands catch at my consciousness as it begins to dissolve. There's a honeyed sweetness to the snare that I immediately recognize as Dead's magic. Luca's power binds me a moment later, a treacly depth that wraps my consciousness and hardens like candy, holding me within my frame.

I shake, shattered by the demon's unearthly energies, snarled by the necromancers' hold. The shimmy goes on and on, tearing me from my body, gluing my soul and flesh back together in ways that don't quite fit.

*Hang in there, sweetness. Almost done.*

The demon's sense of time and mine are completely different, because the burning heart attack goes on and on for what must be an eon.

Finally, the deluge ebbs. The shaking ripping me out of my body slows to a rhythmic squeezing, like the pulsing of orgasm or the contractions of birth.

I'm reborn into a body that's not quite mine.

Six hands gently draw me out of the cauldron. Jou pulls me to his chest and carries me into my house.

---

Ringing, strident and persistent, wakes me. I shift and settle a little more firmly into my remade body. Warm, firm bands close around me and the surface I'm lying on rises and falls with a breath like the rush of a Sirocco.

"Not quite as fond of those things now as I was," Jou grumbles. His arm slips from around me, pats around, and returns to press cool plastic against my ear. "Answer it, sweetness. I talk to anyone before I've had some food and I'm liable to steal their soul just for the fuck of it."

I open my eyes and sit up, because I definitely don't want him to do that.

"Tsara?" a small voice on the other end of the line.

"Nikki?"

She breathes out a breath of relief. "You're okay."

"Yeah, I'm okay, honey. Are you okay?"

"I had a nightmare. I saw you with a big thing through your chest. Like a tree branch."

"A tree branch? A spear?"

"No, a tree branch. It was white, with green leaves on it. You were glowing all around it and then you shattered into a million pieces." Nicole finishes on a sob.

Poor baby. Somehow, she felt what the demon did to me.

"I was working deep magic, Nikki. It did feel like I shattered into a million pieces, but I promise I'm okay."

I look around the room. We slept on my couch instead of in the comfortable bed upstairs. I'll have to ask Jou the whys and wherefores of that, because I think I passed out as he was carrying me inside. I didn't shut the curtains last night and the sky outside is pearling towards dawn.

"I think we're going to have breakfast soon," I continue. "Would you like to have breakfast with us?"

"I have school," she responds with a small huff, clearly unhappy about missing breakfast with me and the demon.

I rub my fingers across my forehead. I have literally no idea what day it is.

"I'll make sure she's on time for school," Jou grumbles, stroking his hand up and down my back. My bare back. Why do I always end up naked when we do magic? Demons, I swear.

"Jou says he'll get you to school on time. Do you want us to pick you up for breakfast?"

"Lemme ask Gramma."

After Nicole gets her grandmother's permission, and I finally find some clothes, Jou helps me navigate through the Earth to Nicole's grandmother's small apartment building in Dorchester. We have Nicole back at my house before the sun's risen. She sits at my breakfast table, the lingering clouds of her nightmare clearing from her aura as she tells me all about an Australian mermaid TV program she's been watching. Jou casts her amused glances over his shoulder as he makes enough waffles to feed a small army.

Our army assembles one by one. The two necromancers appear first, probably lured by the smell of browning waffle batter. Zippy's next, gliding through the backdoor from wherever she's been all night in full leathers, her mohawk a brighter orange than the dawn. There's no sign of the other two demonesses and I wonder if this is the day Hairy has whatever show she's doing. They didn't mention it while we were planning last night, and my sense of time is so discombobulated that I don't know if that's come and gone or is sometime in the future.

Will and Shirri arrive as Jou's starting on a second batch of waffles, and they're followed by Bo and Merida. It's no surprise to see Shirri shower attention on Nicole, but what's gratifying is that everyone else does, too. Even Zippy chats to her and lets the little girl feel her stiff mohawk, to Nicole's utter delight.

Nicole's day is made when my bwg, Thurman, makes a rare appearance, slipping out from behind the sugar canister, hopping nimbly off the counter and waddling on his bowed legs over to her. He bows and gesticulates, chattering what sounds like nonsense to me, but Nicole evidently understands him and follows him to the refrigerator, where he produces a packed lunch for her. He hops up on the counter again, pats her on the head, and disappears into the tiled backsplash.

Nicole still has stars in her eyes, and not a single blot on her aura, when Jou and I take her hands and step into the Earth.

When we rejoin our small army, who are still congregated around my dining room table over cups of coffee, there are two more additions: a bean sidhe who is sipping her coffee while keeping one eye on the Ellyll standing sentinel in the corner.

I introduce everyone to Róisín and Aehelwen, who bow stiffly to each other. Bo takes point in explaining the plan of attack to our new arrivals.

"I suggest we wait until midnight," Róisín says, fingering the focus that Bo's laid on my dining room table. "The necromancers will be at the height of their powers and Bone will be free of the sun's influence to join us."

Zippy nods. "Zef and Hairy will be back by then, too."

Jou crosses his arms over my chest with a grunt. "Want to draw them to us. Make 'em fight us here. There starts to be too much collateral damage? We drag 'em through the Gate into Dis. Probably won't make any difference to the Hunt, but we'll be stronger there." He nods to the demonesses. "Magic's more available to Tsara in Hell, too."

I glance at him over my shoulder, both impressed that he'd try to minimize the damage to my world and wary of anything involving a trip to Hell. "I can't control it there as well as I can here."

"That might be an advantage," Jou says. "Unleash a little Hell on the Hunt."

"Merida and Shirri would need to be able to pass through the Veil with you if you're going to use their power to bind the Huntsman," Bo says.

It's not exactly an objection, but I could understand if it was.

"I can pull them with me," Zippy says. "But Hell fucks the mortal mind. They need to be blind and deaf."

"Can you protect four?" Luca asks. "Dead and I have passed through the Veil before. We can shield Merida and Shirri, but we'll need you to shelter our souls."

Zippy glances at Jou, who nods against my shoulder.

"I can do that," she says.

"Bone, Aehelwen, and I will not be much good to you, if you take the battle to Hell," Róisín says.

"Speak for yourself, Washer," Aehelwen responds. "I will chase my quarry to Hell if need be."

"And if you don't come back?" Róisín asks sharply.

"I have made my peace with that."

"I don't want this to be a one-way trip for anyone," I object.

Jou strokes my arms, the light prickle telling me he's extended his talons. "Not askin' that outta any of you. Me an' my clutch'll do our best to make sure anyone who comes through the Veil with us comes back. But understand if you die in Hell, your soul's fair game to anything strong enough to catch it."

*Jou,* I think reproachfully.

*Just tellin' it like it is, sweetness. Lots things stronger'n me in Dis. I can't swear to keep your friends' souls safe if their mortal bodies die there.*

I humph. "I don't want anyone coming if that's the risk."

Shirri clears her throat. "Cousin, not to sound cavalier, but any of us could die any day. I'd rather go fighting for my family than getting hit by a bus."

"A bus doesn't eat your immortal soul," I observe.

*Technically, demons don't eat souls, either,* Jou thinks.

I roll my eyes even though I'm sitting in his lap, facing the table, and he can't see my face. He'll feel it in my mind.

"What about a soul anchor?" Dead asks. "Something that would draw our souls back home if our bodies are killed in Hell?"

Zippy's sunset mohawk bobs. Jou nods into my shoulder.

"Best if a loved one serves as the anchor," Zippy says.

"I can be that for Shirri," Will offers. "Bo can be Merida's anchor. Dead, Luca, if only one of you goes, the other can be the anchor."

"Halves our fightin' force," Jou says. "But it's the smart play."

We break into two groups after that, with the demons, necromancers, Bo, and Will continuing the huddle over my dining table. The rest of us move into the kitchen and, somehow, I end up washing dishes with the fae knight wielding a dishcloth and passing the dried dishes to my hob to put away, which is fairly surreal.

"Shouldn't you have a soul anchor, Aehelwen?" I ask, in part because I'm concerned about the fae knight and in part because I was taught the fae don't have souls, but I've never had a chance to ask a fae's opinion before.

The fae loops the dishtowel over their shoulder in a gesture so human it makes my throat catch. They hook a finger in the neck of their breastplate and draws out a gilded leaf on a silver chain. Half-leaf, I see as the fae spins it with a finger.

"My brother-in-arms Aranthann wears the other half of this leaf. He will anchor my soul should the need arise."

Which tells me the fae—well, at least the *Ellyllon*—believe they have souls.

"Uh, isn't Aranthann the Holly King?" I ask.

"He is. His courage and fortitude elevated him in death as he was not elevated in life. I do not hope for such a blessing from the Great Mother, only the opportunity to avenge my brother-in-arm's ignoble death."

I nod. "I hope you'll get the chance."

"And I hope for your survival. There are many who treat with the courts, but few who do so in the spirit of true friendship. You will be missed, whether you fall to the Hunt or pass outside the mortal realm with your demon lord."

I swallow hard at this summation of my future.

"I suppose the Kingdom Under the Hills isn't really open to visitors from Hell," I say with a weak laugh, trying to make light of what sounds like doom.

"My brother-in-arms Aranthann will open his doors to you whenever you ask. But you would not receive such a welcome from the other lords and ladies of the fae, despite the service you have done the courts in finding Aranan's killer," the fae knight says. "Whether or not they come with ill intent, demons and their kin are regarded as faefoes. Many would try to kill your lord on sight."

My mouth curls down as a measure of sadness settles over me. I've counted the fae among my allies for a long time. Losing the fae on the heels of losing the Squire makes me feel like I'm drifting further and further away from the life I made for myself here.

*I'll make it up to you, sweetness,* the demon promises.

I square my shoulders at his thought. *You already have. I may have had friends and allies here without you, but I wasn't living. I was drifting from gray day to gray day. You've made me feel alive again, Jou.*

He smiles into my mind.

# CHAPTER 21

t's the fae knight who provides the final piece of the puzzle.

It's all well and good to assemble our army, to pick our field of battle, to plan our attack and strategize how to minimize casualties, but it's all for nothing if the enemy doesn't show up.

I had a half-baked notion of confronting Pertcha in her human guise and somehow luring her to my house. That notion is thoroughly squashed when Jou and I Earth-Walk to the address Shirri has for Holle, only to find an abandoned house, the windows boarded-up and cobwebs thick in the corners of the porch and window frames.

When we return to my house and report to our assembled army, Aehelwen lifts their helmeted head from where they're sitting at my dining table, polishing yet another blade. "You need the Horn of Herne to summon the Hunt."

I glance at Jou who shrugs.

"Where might one find the Horn of Herne?" Bo asks, stroking his beard.

"In the court of the Holly King. But Aranthann will not give it to you. Nor will he allow you to sound it in his halls and risk calling the Hunt down on his court."

I glance at Jou again. This time, he nods.

"What if I could give him the Crown of the North?" I ask.

Aehelwen tips their helmet to the side. "You have the lost crown?"

"No, but I know where it is," I say.

"An' I can get it," Jou adds. "Go talk to your king. I'm not riskin' going to his hall again. I'll get the crown. You take it to him. You bring us the horn. No fuckin' around. No airy-fairy double-talk. I want his word in blood."

Aehelwen inclines their head and stares at the shining blade between their gauntlets for a long moment. "Aranthann agrees. I offer my soul as forfeit should Aranthann fail to deliver the horn."

Jou sucks at his teeth for a second before nodding.

"You're in contact with the Holly King?" I ask, stating the obvious but wanting to understand the connection between the king and knight.

"I am." Aehelwen fishes the gilded leaf out from under their breast-plate and shows it to the assembled demons, magi, and shifter. "Aranthann is my king and lord in the same way as you are seggurach to your demon. Aranthann walks freely in my mind. He knows all I know. What you say to me, you say to him."

"And he's willing to risk you in this battle?" I ask.

A smile creeps around the edges of the helmet's crosspiece. "Although Aranthann is my king and lord, there are some things he cannot control. I swore oaths to my brothers-in-arms that are just as binding on my heart as the oaths I gave Aranthann. He would not make me foreswear myself."

*Don't get any ideas,* Jou grumbles into my mind.

I keep from laughing with an effort.

"Let's get a move on, then," Jou says. "I want the horn tonight."

"Aranthann is happy to meet me on the edge of the Hills. I will be back before you know I was gone."

Jou chuckles darkly. "No, this is how you're back before anyone knows you're gone."

He takes my hand, and the room blurs around us as the assembly blurs into streams of color.

"I've never tried Earth-Walking out of a time loop," I tell him.

"First time for everything."

I take a deep breath and hope I'm not walking us into an alternate dimension where the planet's been swallowed by a black hole or something, before I pull us into the Earth.

We step out in a long gallery lit by witchlight that waves in golden and orange streamers, in front of a pedestal holding a plain gold circle. A breeze containing the bite of frost teases my bangs and scours my cheeks.

I look around the familiar gallery. The Museum rarely has many visitors, but there's always a chance a magi will be here studying one of the artifacts. Fortunately, it looks like we're alone today.

Jou puts his hand to the glass surrounding the crown. In a billow of steam, the glass slumps away from his palm and puddles, glowing, on the pedestal. Jou snags the crown with a black talon.

With a hiss, he pulls his hand back. Blood streams down his finger like liquid obsidian.

"Jou—!" I swallow my exclamation before I draw any attention to us. Darting forward, I cover his finger with my palm, *calling* Earth's Blood to heal him.

"Thank you, sweetness. Didn't expect it to bite so hard." He scratches his dreads with his uninjured hand. "Not sure how we're gonna snatch it if I can't pick it up."

I glance from the pedestal to the demon and back. Then I take his hand and put my other palm against the pedestal and step into the Earth.

We step out in my hearth room, since I *really* don't want the Crown of the North in my house.

Two pairs of silvery eyes look up from where a king and a knight are sitting side-by-side, their hands entwined, their backs resting against my cauldron. How do they keep strolling through my circles?

I immediately bow to the Holly King. With the fae's inhuman grace, he rises and walks to us. A faint peal of silvery bells accompanies his movement and I wonder if it's from the crown or whether the fae kings get announced everywhere they go. That would get old, fast.

"I will not ask how or where you obtained this," Aranthann says, eying the pedestal and its golden burden. "Only thank you for returning it to my people."

I glance at Jou, feeling guilty for not telling the fae king about the crown during our first meeting. The demon's mouth twitches, and he drapes his arm over my shoulders.

The fae king takes a small, bone horn out from under his robes and holds it out to Jou. "I know there is much distrust between my court and yours, but I hope that between you and I, there can be understanding, if not yet trust."

Jou accepts the horn and passes it to me, before holding his hand out to the fae. Aranthann shakes, looking undaunted by Jou's talons, before he takes the golden crown. I expect something as the King of the North reclaims his crown. A blast of arctic Air. The horns of Elfland blowing. Something. But there's just the cold, quiet night.

The fae king returns to his knight, who bows low, their silken tabard brushing the grass. When the knight straightens, Aranthann clasps their cuirass with gauntleted fingers.

"Throwing your life away to avenge my brother will anger your king," Aranthann says.

A smile wiggles across Aehelwen's patrician face. "I would never want that, your Majesty."

Aranthann leans in and kisses Aehelwen thoroughly. Aranthann caresses his knight's face. "Come back to me. Your king commands it."

Aehelwen salutes. "As you command, sire."

Aranthann gives Aehelwen one last caress before he walks into my holly tree.

What is it with supernatural creatures using my trees as portals and strolling through my wards? I huff.

Jou chuckles and squeezes my shoulders. "You can lock down the Hill tighter'n a lemure's ass if you want, sweetness. Nothin's walking through the wards you put up last time."

"Good, because that makes me twitchy."

The fae knight shrugs. "He is the Holly King. You must make some allowances for the chosen of Gaia."

I huff again. "Holly King. Prince of Ghouls. They all need to learn how to knock."

The demon and fae rumble with laughter.

———

We assemble our small army on the lawn behind my house. With the various magi and fae, there's plenty of glamor floating around, but I'm glad Jou's arranged for my tenant to be called out of town.

"What'd you do to poor Shah?" I ask as Jou runs his hands over me, recrafting the clothes I created from my cauldron into biker gear again.

"He won a free, long vacation in New York. From a contest he didn't enter. Damndest thing."

"That is a strange thing," I agree.

"Demons distort probability. All kinds of weird shit happens around us." He winds the focus around my neck like a collar.

"No kidding?"

Jou chuckles and kisses the tip of my nose. "You ready?"

"To call the Wild Hunt down on us? Not really."

He strokes my cheek with his knuckles. "No one's ever really ready for battle. It comes whether you're prepared or not. We're better prepared than most, but this could still go sideways. You do whatever you need to do. Take whatever you need. Even if you think it's killin' me."

"Jou," I protest softly.

"Wasn't a request, sweetness."

"Swear to me that as long as I'm alive, you'll come back."

He swipes two fingers in an X over his heart and holds them up. "Scout's promise."

"Ha-ha."

He grins, then swoops in for a kiss. "I promise. Let's do this."

He gives me one last kiss before moving a step away. I glance around at the assembled humans, vampire, fae, and demons. Bo and Will give me firm nods while Dead winks at me.

I lift the horn to my lips and blow.

The horn sounds, but it's no sound I've ever heard before. It sounds in my blood, a thin, clear ringing that sets up echoes in my bones. A hundred dogs in the surrounding neighborhoods take up the horn's call, their barks bugling through the night.

The horn's ringing fades slowly. Each echo softer and more distant than the one before. I tremble with each echo, and with the sound that replaces the horn's call.

The distant calling of geese.

"They're coming," I say to Jou.

I feel his glove shred away from him as much as see it out of the corner of my eye. He's a creature of flame, lighting the night, chasing the shadows into the trees with the light spilling from his eyes, his horns, his crown, his wings, the sword and whip in his hands. I hear a few stifled exclamations among the fae and mortals who haven't seen Jou's true form before.

I smile to myself. Yes, he's terrifying, but my demon lord and lover and the father of my babies is pretty awesome, too.

A deeper, sapphire light laps around the hard, bright blue of Jou's as his sisters take up position on his far side. I'm not surprised that Zeifyr is as chic as a demon as she is in her glove. Her horns are tipped with bright red, like the soles of those ridiculously expensive shoes. Her hair flows in a black wave nearly to her ankles. All three demonesses are naked, their black bodies naturally armored with spines and chiton. Zeifyr and Hairy wield wavy swords longer than my arms, while Zippy carries a double-headed axe that I doubt I could even lift.

Mel's true form comes as a bit of a surprise. She's an eight-foot tall, four-armed, gray-furred goat with white bone antlers that spread three feet on either side of her bearded head. Her eyes burn the same neon blue as Jou's, as do the curved swords she carries in each hand.

"Hi," she says as she takes position to my left.

"You and I are going to have such a talk," I mutter at her.

A yellow-toothed smile cracks the goat's long face.

"My brothers are waiting on the other side of the Gate," she tells Jou.

"Good. Soon as the Hunt arrives, we draw them through," Jou says.

"

Horns nod all along the assembled line of demons.

The Hunt rolls over us like a night breeze. I don't see them until their fangs are sinking into my arms and legs, protected by the leather

Jou made for me. Screams ring all around me as I whirl, closing my eyes and opening my Sight.

We're *surrounded*. Hundreds of the buzzing, blurring hounds descend into my yard from the sky in an endless stream, their huge jaws snapping, skeletal paws churning the ashy air.

"Magi," I yell. "Use your Sight."

I grab the dozen barghasts nearest me with my magic, rip open the Veil, and sink them into the same deep mirk I consigned their kin to.

"Tsara," Jou growls. "Save your magic for the Huntsman."

He's already battling, his burning wings spread, crimson feathers cutting through the hounds as much as his whip and sword. A slick black pool grows at his feet and the stink of oil overpowers the cinnamon and smoke scent of his magic. The *crack* of his whip sounds over the cries of our small army as they rally and fight the shadow hounds. I'm quickly spattered with blood, shattered bone, and gray organs. Even Zeifyr's covered with gore as she beheads hound after hound with her wavy swords. Zippy impales any hound that springs at her on her horns, then shakes them off into the second line, where Will in his bear form tears them apart with his claws.

"Take them down," Jou roars. "Tsara, get ready."

I crouch, flattening my hands on the ichor-soaked grass and digging my fingers into the dirt.

Pertcha appears at the end of the stream of hounds. The beautiful guise she's worn as Tomas's girlfriend shreds in my Sight. I See a head that's a shark's gaping jaws, a lion's roaring fangs, a massive lizard—fuck, is that a T-Rex?—snapping foot-long teeth, over a body that's a man's and a tiger's and a sleek, deadly seal's.

I understand then what Kartcher meant. The Huntsman doesn't wear any form. It IS as much as the spirit that brought the Holly King back into the world IS. These are forces beyond the mortal frame and we've tried to force them into forms our minds can comprehend, but they transcend our limited reckoning.

The Huntsman's flat, deadly eyes meet mine.

*Not you, little witch. The abominations you bear.*

I grab my temple as the Huntsman's voice stabs through my mind.

*Fuck you*, Jou's mental voice pushes the Huntsman's out of my head in a hot flood.

Jou raises his arms to the sky and shakes his claws at the lord of predators. "You got a problem with my get, come for me instead of my seggurach, you fucking coward!"

The howling, honking Hunt wheels, twists in the air, and dives for Jou. His bone scythe appears between his claws and carves a huge arc of blood and skeletal limbs through the stream of hounds.

*Sweetness, open the Gate.* Jou's thought resounds in my mind.

I tear open the Veil between the planes.

In my Sight, Hell unfolds.

My previous visits to Jou's plane help me process what no mortal mind should bear. Instead of the spinning, sickening disorientation, I have a moment where everything heaves, ground, sky, bodies, before it settles. I've drawn us to the place most familiar to me, most comforting to Jou, the rocky plain at the foot of his Hill, where several hundred of his lemure and malebranch troops are currently camped, awaiting muster.

I hear Zippy's call bellow over the encampment before I even climb to my feet. "To Baron Ash! Protect the mortals!"

A hundred throats answer her.

I turn from the cacophony and see the Gate I've opened like a tear in the gray, sunless sky. The Hunt pours through it, seemingly undiminished despite all my army has killed.

Kartcher said we couldn't destroy the Hunt with all the demons in Hell. I think we're about to put that to the test.

I don't watch the clash of hounds and demons because I have Work to do.

Magic is wholly accessible to me in Hell. There's no resistance, no need for ritual or recipe. Hell is pure magical energy, just waiting to be shaped by a will strong enough. I crouch again, sinking my fingers into the rocky ground. This isn't my Earth, but the energy is similar. The wind that rises to my call is not the Air of my plane, but it responds just as readily.

The ground beneath my fingers begins to throb and distort. Lightning crashes around me, spearing through the hounds and sending their burned forms tumbling down to be mired in the shaking soil. Gouts of fire burst up from the heaving ground, silhouetting the demons as they carve a bloody path through the Hunt, blowing hapless hounds back into the sky in pinwheels of flame.

The Huntsman's shifting form weaves toward me, flying without feathers or wings, striding through the air, now on hooves, now on fins, now with a swish of a long, scaly tail.

I hold those death-dealing eyes as I unwind the collar of white fire from around my neck. I push my power outward, touching the magic of the two Water witches protected by Zippy, her malebranch troops, and the two necromancers.

As I begin to draw on Shirri and Merida's power, flares of other energy pull at me. Mel, two of her arms dragging behind her as she fights over the fallen body of one of her brothers. Roisin and Bone, fighting back-to-back against a tide of hounds. Even as they catch my attention, a hound sinks its teeth into Roisin's vibrating throat and tears it out. A final blast of sound levels a swathe of hounds even as the bean sidhe falls.

*Tsara! Stay focused*, Jou roars into my mind.

His thought snaps me back to the eternal predator bearing down on me. The ground beneath me begins to howl.

The Huntsman raises a hand-paw-curled claw. I snap the focus out, drawing on Jou's whip skills and my magic to bridge the fifty feet between me and the Huntsman. The line of white fire wraps around the Huntsman's limb.

For a second, the focus connects us.

Jou bursts off the ground in a hail of embers and crimson feathers. He rams into the Huntsman in mid-air, sending them both tumbling to the ground.

The focus snaps, rebounds, and lashes back at me.

I feel a *pop* against my chest as Jou tears the Huntsman's spirit out of its many forms.

A deep coldness spreads through me. It blinds me with sudden tears as I draw on all four Elements and pull the eternal predator into me.

"Tsara!" I hear Jou's roar, but I'm too occupied with the tumult inside me. The slow curl of giant claws as they sink into my bones. Teeth that burst up through my throat and down through my groin before subsiding back into my flesh. I burn the spirit to cinders with Fire, blast the ash with Air, quench the embers with Water, and bury it with Earth.

Panting, I sag to the trembling ground. Something shifts strangely within my chest, and I look down at myself.

The burning, white focus pierces my chest like a spear. My heart's blood slides red, so red, redder than an apple, redder than Jou's wings, down its twined length.

I look up as Jou lands in front of me.

"Tsara," he chokes.

"I'm so sorry," I whisper, knowing my words will be drowned in the din of the battle.

He falls to his knees in front of me, his taloned hand closing around the focus where it's buried in my chest.

"No," he says. "No."

"Jou."

"No!" He throws back his head and roars to the uncaring, unchanging sky.

Behind him, I see Aehelwen down on their knees, one leg dragging behind them as they continue to fight the tide of hounds who haven't stopped even though the Huntsman is bound within my bones.

When I die, the Huntsman might be freed.

I put one hand over Jou's and flatten the other to the ground. I dimly register the stain of Earth's Blood spreading from my palms up over my forearms as I begin to *call* more power than I've ever summoned before. I thought banishing Jou was the limit of my magic, but that was a cantrip compared to the power available to me in Hell. I call and call, pulling a maelstrom of energy to me. Dimly, I feel Shirri and Merida faint as I siphon off their magic.

Mud explodes upward from the ground all around me. It hangs in the Air, waiting my command.

I blink hazily at it. My thoughts are slow and half-formed, but I know what I need to do.

The last thing I will ever do.

I lift my palm from the ground and stretch it out towards the furious host.

The mud catches fire. Each droplet turns to lava and whizzes toward a hound. Burning earth engulfs them. Magma outlines the barghasts: strange, twisting shapes around gnashing black teeth, for a moment before they burn away.

The fighting stutters to a halt as each opponent turns to ash.

With the last dregs of my magic, I pull all the power back into me and bury the Huntsman, encasing that ancient spirit down, down, down beneath the Hill in a tomb of Earth, Air, Fire, and Water.

I slump into Jou as the trickle of power slips away, leaving me hollow, empty, finished.

His burning, crimson wings close around me. He pulls me gently into his arms, his hand still pressed over my heart.

"I love you," he says softly.

"I love you," I whisper back, each word slurred and slow.

He lifts my bloody, blackened hand from my breast and sets it against his cheek. I stroke him once with clumsy fingers. All my strength is gone. My fingers feel like lumps of wood. He presses them into his skin with his own hand.

"I love you," he says again, turning his face until my palm is pressed over his lips.

I try to form the words back, a rattle rising in my throat, but my lips and tongue won't shape the sound.

"I love you," he repeats as he draws my pinkie into his mouth and crunches it between his sharp teeth.

I blink at him. At the pain, which is a small, tearing pain nearly lost in the very large pain consuming me.

He swallows. With his teeth stained with my blood, he says, "I love you."

He sucks my ring finger into his mouth and bites it off. There's barely any blood now.

I swallow, but it sticks half-way down. A beat. Two.

I close my eyes and let the third beat be the last as Jou bites off my middle finger.

# EPILOGUE

open my eyes. Blink up into Jou's familiar face.

His horns gleam darkly above his crimson dreadlocks. The burning crown sitting between his horns is so bright, it makes me squint. His eyes spill neon blue light over the strong planes of his face, turning his fangs fluorescent. Fangs I feel in my own mouth when I open it to take a deep breath.

"Hi, sweetness. Welcome to the Hill."

**Tsara and her demon will return in Burning Bones.**

# GLOSSARY OF UNUSUAL TERMS

As the magical tradition I was taught is based on Welsh folklore, I thought readers who are more familiar with other traditions might appreciate a glossary of magical terms I've used in this series. I've also included Romani words and words from the demons' language, Dan-Enochian.

*Aedis Astrum*: (magical) the ruling council for wielders of magic in the United States.

*Ash Hill:* (Dan-Enochian) an area of Dis claimed by Jou and his clutch as their home.

*Barbicon*: (Dan-Enochian) the Tree of Pain (not the edifice in London).

*Beng*: (Romani) demon.

*Beti*: (Romani) a term of endearment, often for a child.

*Bez Toma*: (Dan-Enochian) the Mouth of Hell; the Great Gate; a rent in the fabric of Hell that tears through and joins all nine planes.

*Bwg*: (mythological) a small, humanoid fae who lives in human homes and performs housekeeping services in exchange for treats of human food; also known as a brownie or hob.

*Cantrip*: (magical) a simple spell, usually for a single purpose, requiring minimal will or ritual.

*Chavi*: (Romani) a term of endearment, usually for a child.

*Churi*: (Romani) a small knife, usually recycled from an older knife, often passed down through families.

*Coblynau*: (magical) a fae who lives in mines and quarries; similar to Cornish Knockers; also known as gnomes.

*Cyhraeth*: (magical) a fae who feeds on human sorrow and grief; also known as the Washer at the Ford, bean sidhe, ban sith, or banshee.

*Dan-Enochian*: (magical) the language of demons.

*Dearie dubbleskey*: (Romani) an exclamation similar to "goodness."

*Demon*: (magical) a race of Elemental creatures who inhabit planes considered by humans to be "Hell" and feed on the emotional and magical energy of others, usually humans; on Earth, they wear "gloves" of power to protect them from the alien environment that minimize their demonic attributes and help them pass among humans undetected; generally malevolent.

*Dis*: (Dan-Enochian) a layer of Hell; the Burning Hills; largely controlled by Fire Demons and their Prince, Asmodeus.

*Doppelgänger*: (German) a magical double.

*Drabba*: (Romani) medicine practiced by non-Rom.

*Dynion ceirw*: (magical) a wild fae who often appears in stag form or as a humanoid with stag antlers.

*Earth-Walk*: (magical) the ability of a wielder of magic to move from one place to the other via the Element of Earth.

*Ellyllon*: (magical) high fae, courtiers to Gwyn ap Nudd; also known as the Tylwyth Teg.

*Erinyes*: (mythological) wrath demons.

*Fae*: (magical) collective term for several different races of spirits who typically inhabit woodlands; also known as fairies and sidhe.

*Fiendyke*: (Dan-Enochian) a particularly labyrinthine, dangerous area of Dis, lying between Ash Hill and the Iron City.

*Fir Darrig*: (mythological) the little red men; a kind of fae known as practical jokers.

*Gaoithe sidhe*: (mythological) a fairy wind.

*Gargoyle*: (magical) an Elemental spirit of Earth; they frequently inhabit statutes and buildings created by humans; often winged when in these forms; generally benevolent.

*Gavver*: (Romani) police.

*Ghoul*: (magical) a type of undead who feeds on the flesh of the living.

*Glamor*: (magical) an illusion, so often associated with the fae that many witches consider all glamors fae-abilities.

*Gorgio:* (Romani) someone who is not Romani; an outsider.

*Greenwitch*: (magical) a wielder of magic who controls the element of Earth.

*Gwyn ap Nudd*: (mythological) king of the high fae; the Oak King.

*Halya*: (Dan-Enochian) a demon who feeds primarily on human pride and extremism; because they never back down from a conflict, they are often used as battle-fodder in the Hellwars.

*Hearth room*: (magical) a witch's seat of power and safety.

*Hedgewitch*: (magical) a witch of limited power and ability who cannot use Elemental magic.

*Herbarium*: (magical) a room in which herbs are dried and prepared for use.

*Hisaka*: (magical) a shapeshifter who transforms into a giant snake; a Naga.

*Hlore*: (Dan-Enochian) a human who has entered into a soul-trade with a demon.

*Hobomock, The*: (mythological) a vengeful spirit that haunts Cohasset, Massachusetts.

*Horai*: (magical) a shapeshifter who transforms into an avian; also known as werehawks and wereeagles.

*Huanglong:* (mythological) a yellow dragon in Chinese religion and mythology.

*Hydra*: (magical) an Elemental spirit of water; appears as a three-headed, blue-scaled sea serpent; can be malevolent.

*Incubus*: (Dan-Enochian) a type of demon who feeds on the sexual energies of others.

*Inferiarcus*: (magical) an object of power used to bind creatures from Hell to a magi's will.

*Iron City*: (Dan-Enochian) the capital of Dis; seat of Asmodeus and the location of his court.

*Kama*: (Japanese) a hand sickle.

*Káulochírilo*: (Romani) blackbird.

*Kvarn*: (Dan-Enochian) male head of household; less formally, brother.

*Leccherouse*: (Dan-Enochian) a demonic companion who shares the other's wealth and titles and is considered a social equal; offspring born to leccherouse couples or groupings may be claimed by any parent's clan.

*Lemure*: (Dan-Enochian) an early stage of demonic evolution (most demons are born as lemures); mindless consumptive machines who feed off strong emotional and magical energy.

*Lubbenipen*: (Romani) idiocy.

*Lycanthrope*: (magical) a shapeshifter who transforms into a canid; also known as werewolves.

*Mabon*: (magical) the celebration of the autumn equinox; a harvest festival named after the Welsh hero Mabon ap Modron.

*Malebranch*: (Dan-Enochian) an intermediary stage of demonic evolution; most malebranch can shape change but in their trueform have huge horns that give this stage its name.

*Morion*: (from the French) a dark jewel.

*Naga*: (mythological) a half-human, half-cobra Indian mythological race.

*Necromancer*: (magical) a wielder of magic who has a special affinity for the dead; often necromancers control two Elements, Earth and Air.

*Nethanc*: (magical) an Elemental spirit of Air; appears a winged serpent; aerial predator but generally benevolent.

Nethertongue: (Dan-Enochian) an additional appendage some demons can manifest in their nether-regions.

*Noctil*: (Dan-Enochian) a type of demon who can see into other times/places and into the memories of other demons.

*Noswaith lawen*: (magical) a time the wild and high fae gather to dance; connected to the lunar cycles.

*Null*: (magical) a person or entity without any magical conductivity at all.

*Ondine*: (magical) an Elemental spirit of Water; appears as a vaguely human-shaped pile of moss or seaweed; or frequently inhabits small bodies of water like ponds and streams; generally benevolent.

*Other Place*: (magical) a pocket dimension.

*Pillar of Fire*: (Dan-Enochian) the Heart of Hell.

*Pixie*: (mythological) a type of small, winged fae; often used by greater fae as messengers; usually mischievous but not malevolent.

*Pyroclast*: (magical) an Elemental spirit of Earth; appears as a human-shaped pile of magmatic rock; can be malevolent.

*Salamander*: (magical) an Elemental spirit; appears as a small lizard; can be of any Element, but Fire is the most common and Air (lightning) is the least.

*Samehada*: (magical) a shapeshifter who transforms into a shark.

*Scrying*: (magical) a way for a wielder of magic to see things they cannot see with their own senses.

*Seggurach*: (Dan-Enochian) companion; demon mate.

*Smokeberry*: (magical) a berry-bearing shrub with magical properties associated with faery rings.

*Soulfields*: (Dan-Enochian) an area of Hell which spans several planes where human souls are housed.

*Tarocchi:* (Italian) prints of 15th century engravings depicting social classes and abstract ideas; not to be confused with tarot cards.

*Therian*: (magical) the collective clans of shapeshifters.

*Trueform*: (Dan-Enochian) the appearance of a demon without the "glove" that protects it while on the mortal (earthly) plane.

*Tylwyth Teg*: (mythological) high fae; see also Ellyllon.

*Under Hill*: (magical) a term for the dwellings of the fae; also known as mounds and barrows.

*Vampire*: (magical) a type of undead who feeds on the blood of humans; formal plural is vampirii.

*Warlock*: (magical) a wielder of magic who does so with harmful intent.

*Weirdlaw*: (magical) laws regarding dealings with humans that bind non-humans when on the Earthly plane.

*Witch*: (magical) a wielder of magic who does so with benevolent intent; can be male or female but generally human; also known as a magus or sorcerer.

*Wolfshook, The*: (magical) a coven of warlocks in New York known for summoning and entrapping demons.

*Yule*: (magical) the celebration of the winter solstice or mid-winter.

*Zeimal:* (Dan-Enochian) a conclave of the Fire and Earth demons who oppose Asmodeus.

*Zolez*: (Dan-Enochian) a layer of Hell; the Pit of the Winds.

# ABOUT THE AUTHOR

Reader, bunny-wrangler, fire-spinner, and writer of things. I like my science hard and my romance harder.

Constitutionally incapable of settling into a genre, I bounce in and out of contemporary mystery, space opera, and paranormal romance, all with a decidedly kinky twist.

Sign up to The Bevington Arcana for all the news from my paranormal world, including sneak peeks and giveaways: https://dashboard.mail erlite.com/forms/285635/76936365522028390/share

Need more? Get early access and exclusive stories in my Patreon and Ream.

Bring cake.

If you've enjoyed *Blood Yellow*, please consider leaving a review on Amazon, Goodreads, Bookbub, or your platform of choice. Reviews mean everything to independent authors!

facebook.com/emmafrostuk

x.com/ejfrostuk

instagram.com/emmafrostuk

goodreads.com/ejfrost

tiktok.com/@ejfrostuk

patreon.com/ejfrost

bookbub.com/authors/e-j-frost

# ALSO BY E J FROST

If you enjoyed *Blood Yellow*, you may also enjoy *Teddy's Boys*, my magical academy reverse harem romance, set at Bevington College, where Tsara trained as a witch.

*Three boys.*
  *Two murders.*
  *One terrible choice.*

Twelve years ago, my mother climbed into a limo with a fae stranger and left without looking back. Seven years ago, my magic came in, marking me as an Earth-witch, the Element most feared by other mages. One month ago, my father exiled me to college in another country.

I may be a stranger in a strange land, but no one will keep me down.

Charlie, Gabe, and Darwin.
Three boys who are more than my match.

My best friend. My new love. My worst enemy.

Are they also killers?

When a fellow student is murdered, the finger of suspicion points at my boys.

Can I prove their innocence?

Or will I be their next victim?

Meet the Bad Boys of Bevington …

Read *Teddy's Boys* here: **https://books2read.com/u/4NxoEW**.

Need another bad, bad boy? Give my gritty, scifi romance, *Snowburn*, a try.

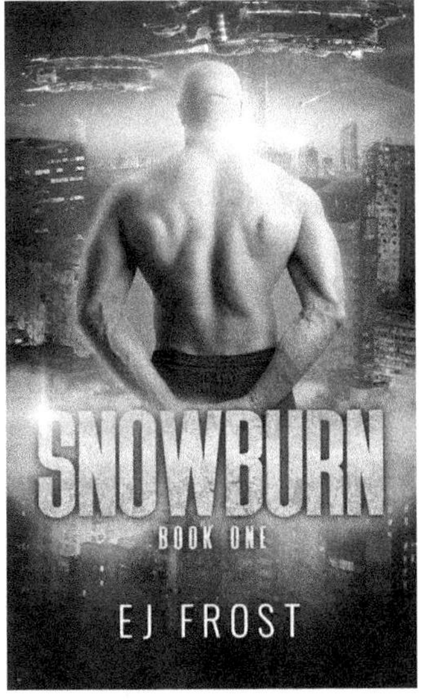

*Unleash the monster. Save the girl.*

Hale Hauser is a Company killer. Perfectly engineered, highly trained, superbly effective. But when ordered to assassinate his own kind, Hale rebels, and the Company buries him in a hole so deep that no one has ever escaped.

After escaping, Hale hides on Kuseros, a backwater Colony on the Deep Frontier. He begins a new life as Sandringham Snow, pilot and smuggler. Hired by Kez, a local runner, to retrieve a box of black-market glands, Hale follows her through the maze of strange loyalties and twisted customs of Kuseros' underground gangs. In payment, he takes the one thing only a woman can give him, and discovers the one thing his new life is missing.

But Kez has a secret, which will threaten them both. To protect her, Hale must unleash the monster. Can he control the killer inside long enough to discover the truth before it destroys them? Or will he lose everything just as he's found it?

Read *Snowburn* here: **https://books2read.com/u/m2Z9ko**.

***Missing Ink***

Standalone Kinky Mystery.
*A thief.*
*A bad tattoo.*
*And a Forever-Dom to the rescue.*

Michael "Mac" McNally is drifting. Finished with the Navy, finished with his marriage, Mac is sleeping on the couch of his good friend, James Logan, while he tries to figure out his retirement.

Brenna "DirtyGurl" Truelove is lost. Floundering after a series of not-relationships, Brenna can't find satisfaction in scenes with one-night Doms or in Missing Ink, the tattoo business she's worked so hard to build.

When the drifter and the lost-girl come together over a bad tattoo, can they build something that lasts among the wreckage of his marriage and her trust in Doms? And can they catch the thief before he destroys Missing Ink?

Read *Missing Ink* here: https://books2read.com/missing-ink

### *The Daddy P.I. Casefiles*
*Kinky Mystery Romance.*

*Death.*
*Pirates.*
*A stalker.*
*A missing collar.*
*And, always, a Daddy-Dom to the rescue!*

Join P.I. James Logan and his little, Emily Martin, on the investigations of their lives in these three collected books.

Start with their first meeting at the Salt City kink expo; explore an exclusive New York City club on their first date; ride the wild waves of the Mexican Sunset cruise as they seek the source of a drug that's killing passengers; return with them to New York as they track down a vicious stalker; and end with their collaring ceremony in a haunted inn in picturesque Niagara Falls.

This box set of the *Daddy P.I. Casefiles* contains Book 0.5 (previously unavailable except via my newsletter), Book 1.0, Book 2.0 and a bonus novella, The Case of the Missing Collar.

Read *Daddy P.I.* here: **https://books2read.com/u/31YOYa**

www.ingramcontent.com/pod-product-compliance
Lightning Source LLC
Chambersburg PA
CBHW071728150726
47998CB00005B/1553